OUT OF CONTROL

Christine closed her eyes. She had to talk Ailin out of this somehow, or he was liable to go around cutting down every man who looked sideways at her! "Please, Ailin—please, just for me. Promise me that you will harm no man who approaches me—not unless I'm really, truly in some kind of danger. Will you promise me this?"

"Does a goddess ever find herself in danger? Can you not defend yourself from true bodily harm? Why would you need me to defend you from such as that?"

Now she was confused. "But I thought—isn't that why you went after Tierney?"

"It was a matter of honor. Of respect for the goddess and those who honor Her."

"But to kill a man for simple rude behavior? You just can't do that! It's not—it's not civilized!"

He stared down at her, and in the darkness she felt rather than saw his blue-grey gaze. "I have not heard this word *civilized* before," he said. "But from what you are saying, I am certain that it is not civilized to allow men like Tierney to abuse the goddess. Nor is it civilized for me to turn my back on her when I should be coming to her defense."

"Of course a goddess can defend herself—but it is up to those who love her to defend her honor."

His face bent over hers, and his long hair fell feather-soft over the skin of her throat as his lips moved hot and gentle over hers....

D0802539

LADY OF FIRE

JANEEN O'KERRY

LOVE SPELL   ◆   NEW YORK CITY

LOVE SPELL®

August 1996

Published by

Dorchester Publishing Co., Inc.
276 Fifth Avenue
New York, NY 10001

If you purchased this book without a cover you should be aware that this book is stolen property. It was reported as ''unsold and destroyed'' to the publisher and neither the author nor the publisher has received any payment for this ''stripped book.''

Copyright © 1996 by Janeen O'Kerry

All rights reserved. No part of this book may be reproduced or transmitted in any form or by any electronic or mechanical means, including photocopying, recording or by any information storage and retrieval system, without the written permission of the Publisher, except where permitted by law.

The name ''Love Spell'' and its logo are trademarks of Dorchester Publishing Co., Inc.

Printed in the United States of America.

Chapter One

Ireland, in a time long past,
some two millenia ago

Beneath the cold clouds of a late winter dawn, accompanied by his father the king and a small army of swordsmen and chariots, Ailin of Eire stood outside the high earthen walls of Dun Orga and faced the woman he had been ordered to marry.

She, too, was surrounded by her family, a grim lot of warriors from the fortress of Dun Fada a few miles away. Theirs was the task of bringing the offered bride to the son of King Donaill and displaying her for approval—all in the hope of winning a much-needed ally for their clan.

She stood with downcast eyes, a small plain figure in a dark gray woolen gown and cloak, lost among the huge warriors. Her cloak was pulled up to cover her head, and Ailin could not see her face; not that he could have anyway, since she kept her gaze fixed firmly on the ground.

A huge red-bearded man clad in black wool trousers and a worn brown leather breastplate pushed his way through the crowd from behind the young

woman. Ailin recognized Flann, the chief of Dun
Fada and a distant cousin of King Donaill.

"Well, here she is," growled Flann. "My oldest
daughter, Mealla." He gave her a little shove, and as
she caught her balance she glanced quickly up at
Ailin before staring down again.

Pity surged through him. She was so young! Just
a girl—a child—and frightened to death. His resolve
hardened.

"She's just turned thirteen," the old chief continued. "She's kept the hearth and her young twin
brothers since their mother died three years ago.
There's no better bread-maker or wool-spinner in all
of Dun Fada than Mealla!"

Ailin tried to smile politely, but his pity for the girl
and his growing anger at the whole situation made
it impossible.

Flann's eyes narrowed. He stared hard at Ailin and
his family. "When next it is Lughnasa, her brothers
will be old enough to be fostered out," he said, his
voice low and grating. "Mealla will be free to marry
at that time—assuming she meets with your expec-
tations." His voice dropped dangerously and he
glared at Ailin, clutching the hilt of the heavy broad-
sword strapped around his ample waist.

Ailin felt the silence of his own family pressing
him into some kind of response. "She is . . . quite
beautiful. I'm sure she will make a very good wife."
For someone else, and many years from now!

The chief apparently took Ailin's words as accep-
tance, for he relaxed his hold on the sword hilt. "Of
that I have no doubt," he said. "She's brought you a
gift to prove it—go on, Mealla, give it to him!"

The pale creature walked forward a few hesitant
steps, just close enough to place a small jug in the
grass at Ailin's feet. Then she hurried back to the
shelter of her kin.

"Mead," said Flann. "The best honey wine you've
ever poured into your cup. Made it herself!" He stood

waiting, the air heavy with expectation.

Ailin knew that they were waiting for his own gift to Mealla. As ordered, he had brought with him a golden ornament that he had made himself, many months ago. It was the most precious of all the fine things he had learned to make at the forge.

Flann cleared his throat and frowned. His grip tightened on his sword.

Ailin's gift was tucked safely into his belt, beneath his red wool cloak where it didn't show. But even as he began to reach for it, he looked at pale, frightened little Mealla—and knew that he simply could not.

He drew his sword from the black leather scabbard at his belt and walked straight over to the other clan, ignoring their sudden tensing. Poor Mealla nearly shrank away to nothing, but he knelt down and presented the sword to her hilt-first.

"Here is a gift for you, lady," he said softly. "May it be to your liking."

The girl peered up just enough to see the shining gold of the sword's hilt. The likeness of a horse's head capped the end. After hesitating for a moment she accepted the heavy sword with shaking hands, tucking it awkwardly beneath her cloak before resuming her study of the ground once again.

Ailin resisted the temptation to pat her on the shoulder, as he might with any upset child, and walked back to his place beside the king.

He could feel his father's anger and disapproval. The tension was a wall between them. Across the expanse of new green grass, Flann and his warriors scowled and glared.

Ailin knew what all of them were thinking. A sword for a bride-gift! What sort of thing was that to give a lady? She should have gold jewelry, fine furs, a team of chariot horses—not a weapon! Did her husband mean to let her do his fighting for him?

But no one spoke. Ailin's sword was no ordinary weapon; it contained enough artistry, and enough gold, to make it a fine and valuable offering. And Flann, who needed this alliance as much as Donaill did, was not about to jeopardize it over an unsuitable gift. Yet the damage had been done.

"The alliance is sealed," the old chief growled. "We will bring her to you at summer's end, at Lughnasa."

King Donaill stepped forward. "Then if you will, bring your chariots into Dun Orga and celebrate the Imbolc feast with us tonight. We will honor both the Mother Goddess and the match between our two children."

A betrothal was always sealed with a feast for both the families, but Flann only turned a cold glare on Donaill. "We will return to Dun Fada at once. It is a long enough journey in this winter dark."

So, insult was to be returned with insult. Ailin saw his father redden at this rude rejection of his hospitality, but before he could say a word Flann's men turned and swung Mealla up into one of the chariots. The entire party lumbered off into the cold morning to return to Dun Fada.

The United States, in the present time,
on a day which might be today

Grabbing her jacket, Bridget Christine Connolly fled her silent apartment and hurried down the frosty sidewalk. In the soft gray light of the January morning, the wind blew sprays of powdery snow down from the old oak trees and redbrick houses. But she had little eye for such beauty now.

Why today? Why would he do this today, of all days?

"Christine!"

Startled, she turned to look behind her. A white compact car pulled into a spot along the curb, and out climbed a short, dark-haired woman with oversize glasses, a huge handbag, and a big smile.

"Hey, where you going?" the woman called, slamming the car door shut and hurrying up the sidewalk. "Jim's home with the kids today, and I've come to take you out for breakfast. Since when do you leave so early? Your class isn't for an hour yet!"

Christine brushed a loose strand of hair from her eyes and then shoved her hands deep into the pockets of her tan suede jacket. Her ragged breath made short plumes of frost in the cold air.

"He's gone, Eliza. He took his things and left this morning. Marco's gone."

Eliza closed her eyes, and then gently touched her friend's arm. "Oh, Christine—I think he's been gone a long time. And I think everybody knew it but you."

"You're probably right," Christine whispered.

"Well, you probably don't feel like going to breakfast right now. Hey—I know! Want to walk? It's a beautiful morning, and it'll take your mind off things. Come on, I'll walk you to class."

Christine managed a small smile. "I was already walking to class. Just to take my mind off . . . things."

"Great idea! I'm glad I thought of it. Come on."

"Wait for me at the gate. I will speak to Ailin alone before we leave for the hunt." King Donaill walked away from his warriors and glared at Ailin, his face pale with anger.

"If you have a reason for insulting Flann and Mealla, I wish to hear it!" he roared as the men and horses moved away. "I wish to hear why you placed a badly needed alliance in jeopardy! You agreed to the marriage—you put your word on it! What were you thinking of, handing that girl a weapon instead of a gift?"

"It was a year ago when I agreed to be married," Ailin answered, "and I did so only for the sake of the alliance. I did not know she was so young!"

"Well, you cannot back out now! This marriage is bringing us the ally that we need! For the last ten years we've lost more than our share of men in the battles—we've become isolated, our army is too small. Dun Fada is larger. Better to have them on our side! The other clans are always restless—even the *gadai* are getting bolder." The king placed his fists on his sword belt. "Besides, it's time you married and began to raise up sons and daughters of your own, as your brothers have done. Dun Orga needs new blood! New warriors!"

"And how do you expect to raise up warriors from one such as her? From a timid child? There's no blood in her veins—only rainwater!"

"You're risking war!"

"War?" Ailin looked closely at his father, amazed at what he was hearing. "I am supposed to fear war? I have been raised all my life to fight and to kill. So has every other man of Dun Orga! How else are we to train if we do not have the occasional war?"

He turned toward the Dun and gave a loud, clear whistle. In answer, a single chariot pulled away from the crowd waiting outside the walls.

"You might not feel that way if you were responsible for all the men yourself . . . if some of them were your own sons. . . ." He glared at Ailin. "You're risking war for all of us, or at the very least a champion's battle for yourself, with an insult like this! You're risking your own life for refusing to take a woman to your bed!"

Ailin turned away in disgust and began to pace. "Oh, I would take her all right—in a few more years, when she is a woman and not a child! I would give her children, if that would help to make amends. I would do anything else for Dun Fada if it will bring us the alliance we need—but I will not be bound in marriage to a timid, simple girl who does not want me either!"

At that moment, a chariot pulled by a snorting team of red-gold horses approached them. Ailin jumped inside and grabbed the reins from Niall, his startled charioteer.

"At Lughnasa," King Donaill said, reaching up and

clamping an iron hand over Ailin's wrist. "The wedding will take place at Lughnasa. Do what you will until then, but be prepared to marry the girl when they bring her—or take the consequences."

Ailin ground his teeth, but said nothing. When his father finally released him he lashed the team into a wild gallop, and Niall grabbed the wicker sides of the chariot as the horses raced away.

Eliza gave Christine a nudge to get her moving, and together the two women walked down the uneven sidewalk that led through the old neighborhood to the university campus.

"So, ah, tell me about, ah, things," Eliza said, hurrying a little to keep up with Christine's long strides. "What happened? Didn't Marco come back from that trip he took up north?"

"He came back, all right," Christine answered, walking steadily. "He came back just long enough to leave a note and his key on the kitchen table." She blinked quickly, raising her chin high, determined not to let the tears begin again.

"He just said that he wanted to see the world and live for a while before being forced—*forced*—to settle down in marriage. He said that going straight from school to work to marriage was no life at all." She took a deep breath. "He didn't even sign his name."

"There was nothing else you could have done," Eliza insisted. "You gave it your best."

"He used to say we had a comfortable relationship. And I'm sure it was—for him. It was convenient, a place to keep his stuff and get his laundry done. But for me—for me . . ." Her voice trembled, and she bowed her head to walk in silence.

Eliza sighed. "Yes, I think you really loved him, though heaven only knows why. Oh, he was easy on the eyes, all right, but there's got to be more to it than that." Her jaw tightened. "He took all you had to give,

13

and gave you nothing in return. I should know. I watched him do it to you for six years."

Bitterness spilled into Christine's voice. "Six years," she said, looking up at the cloudy gray sky. "Six years of English lit and waiting, part-time jobs and hoping, and wasting my life loving a man who turned out to be a stranger."

"Well, honey, I'd hardly call it wasted. You've only got, what, another year, and then you'll have your degree? After that you can look into teaching at a university, just like you've always said you wanted to do."

"And end up like my Aunt Jane? Or like Polly Meade, the woman I work for at the computer center?"

"What's wrong with them?"

"They're not married."

"Huh?"

Christine waved her hand impatiently. "Oh, I know it's stupid of me to feel this way. Nobody has to be married to be happy. It's just that . . . just that . . ."

Eliza patted her arm. "Look, I know it's a modern world and all, but it's not a crime to want to be married. Even to want to be in love." She grinned. "There's still time. You're hardly over the hill yet."

But Christine tensed in frustration and walked even faster. "Jane and Polly devoted themselves one hundred percent to their work. They never spared a moment for anything else. Now they're both in their sixties, and they've got all the success and money anyone could want—and every night they go home to their very expensive, very beautiful, and very empty condominiums in the very best part of town."

"Well, some women are perfectly happy living alone," Eliza said breathlessly as she hurried to keep up. "For heaven's sake, you know what a pain it can be having a snoring, sock-dropping, chili-eating man underfoot! Are you saying Jane and Polly aren't happy the way they are?"

Christine rubbed her bare ring finger against the satin lining of her left jacket pocket. "They seem to be. And I'm sure they are—it's just that I wouldn't be. I'm not. Oh, Eliza—"

She stopped beneath an ancient oak. Its roots had badly buckled the sidewalk in their relentless push for new growth, new life. "I'm so afraid of growing old alone. I'm convinced that people like Polly and Jane end up old and lonely with nothing for company but a fat bankbook. No husband, no children."

Christine raised her chin and looked up, blinking back the stinging tears. "When I turned twenty-one, I made the mistake of announcing to my family that I wanted to be married before I was thirty. And now I know how silly and unrealistic that was. Everyone said that it's not that simple. And they were right. They were right."

"I will not marry her, Niall! I will not! I tell you, I will not!" Ailin shouted above the thundering hooves of the team and the wild rattling of the chariot. The coastline sped past them far below as they raced along only a few feet from the edge of the cliff.

"But what's wrong with her?"

"Nothing—except that she's a child! She should still be running about with the other young girls, not keeping a house and bearing children of her own! I do not take children into my bed and I cannot understand why my father thinks I should!"

"Well, you don't have to take her to your bed right away if you don't want to! You can let her wait a while. She won't always be a child—"

"She will always be timid, pale, and simple!"

Niall said nothing. Finally Ailin slowed the red-gold horses to a jog and then to a brisk walk.

"Old Flann didn't seem too pleased with the gift you gave to Mealla," Niall said. "Even I thought you had something else planned."

"I did." Ailin could feel the circle of gold tucked

15

securely into his belt. "But I have always intended that piece for the woman I love. I do not love Mealla, and even if I were forced to marry her—" His mouth twisted. "I could never give her Brighid's torque."

"Brighid's torque?"

Ailin smiled. "I named it for the goddess, in her gentle aspect. And I will give it to the woman I love or I will give it to no one."

"So who is the woman you love?" asked Niall. "Is it Sorcha? Or maybe Keavy? I've seen you with them, and with plenty of others—I don't remember half the names. They are all in love with you, I think, and would marry you in an instant. There must be one you would accept. If love is so important to you, there must be one who has won your heart."

"I don't know." Ailin shrugged. "So many—maybe none. Not one that I have ever wanted to offer Brighid's torque."

Niall studied him. "I think it is the goddess who truly has your heart. Perhaps she will agree to marry you, since you seem to want no other."

"Now, that's a match I would consider!" The wind began to pick up, cold and damp off the sea. Ailin tightened the reins as the horses shook their heads and moved faster.

"But I can tell you this—even if I was enamored of an unreachable goddess, and would have to take an earthly bride sometime, it would never be Mealla! She is too young and too frightened. She would never come to me unless I forced her, and I have never had cause—or desire—to force a woman into my bed."

Niall sighed. "But why not simply marry the girl, seal the alliance, and leave her to sleep alone until she's ready to come to you? The marriage is just a legal contract; you could still have all the partners any man could wish for. Besides, she'd be in your bed soon enough; they always are. And in the meantime the alliance would be sealed and everyone would be satisfied."

Ailin glared at his charioteer. "Everyone except me—and the goddess! Why can't I make you, or my father, or any of them, understand? I will not stand before the druids and swear a vow of marriage to an unwilling child that I do not love. I would never dishonor the goddess by even considering such a thing. I am not one to live a lie!"

The cold wind blew harder. Ailin welcomed the sting of it across his face. "Old Flann will learn that he cannot buy allies with frightened children as payment. I do not fear a champion's battle—or a war! It's a pitiful day when we need the like of Dun Fada for an ally!"

Abruptly he swung the team around. "I'm going back. Maybe I can still catch up with the hunting party, if this team is fast enough."

"Fast enough! Tintrea and Tirnea are the finest I've ever put to a chariot! Why, they—"

Niall stopped talking and grabbed the sides of the chariot as Ailin shouted to the team. The fiery red-gold horses leaped into a wild gallop for home.

"No wonder this is hurting you so much," Eliza said. "You knew he was going to leave—you knew it was over—but tomorrow's the day you turn thirty."

"And he just didn't want to be around to see it." Christine turned away, gazing down the quiet street. "You're right. It's been over for a long time. But his leaving me this way is like a slap in the face on top of everything else."

"You know age doesn't mean a thing, Christine," Eliza said. "It's nothing but a number. You're young and beautiful and there isn't a man who lives and breathes who wouldn't want you."

"Except Marco."

Eliza snorted. "Well, I always did think he was more like a robot or something instead of a man."

Christine glanced at her, stunned, but Eliza added, "I was just too polite to tell you."

Christine bit her lip. "He wasn't a robot, Eliza."

Eliza looked up at her friend and took a deep breath. "Okay, I'm sorry. Really. You know how I'm always talking before I think."

"He was a toad."

The two women looked at each other. And then both of them burst out giggling as Christine wiped the tears from her eyes.

"That's more like it!" Eliza said. "You always could see the funny side of practically anything. You've got the best sense of the ridiculous of anyone I know."

"Maybe so," Christine said, catching her breath. "In that case, I'll point out that you're a fine one to talk about not needing marriage to be happy. I've never seen any man so devoted to his wife as Jim is to you."

Eliza smiled. "I'm lucky to have him. He's a great guy, and I love him to death. But there's nothing unusual about us."

"Is that a new set of diamond earrings I see?"

"Well—"

"And is he taking you to dinner tonight?"

"Uh, only at the Tea Room—"

"And where are you going on your vacation this spring?"

"Mmm—Monte Carlo?"

Christine sighed, running her hand down the rough bark of the old oak. "He worships the ground you walk on. Don't you know what the rest of us would give to have a taste of that? To be so cherished and adored?"

Chapter Two

Ailin stopped the chariot as soon as he came in sight
of Dun Orga. Just rounding the curve, disappearing
in a little cloud of dust, galloped the teams pulling
the chariots of his father's hunting party.

He stepped down to the windblown grass and
handed the reins to Niall. "Go on—take them in and
see to them. I'll be back after a time."

"Going to speak to your one true love?" Niall
grinned. "Tell Brighid I love her, too. But mind the
storm. The wind—"

"The storm does not frighten me either. Go." Niall
shook his head, but spoke a word to the team and
started them jogging for home.

Standing alone, Ailin looked to the west, toward
the sea, and saw a heavy wall of dark clouds. It was
strange this morning. The sky should be growing
lighter with the day but instead was becoming
darker and closer. A storm was fast approaching, as
Niall had tried to warn him. But Ailin turned away
from the shelter of the Dun and headed up the hill,
toward the cliffs hanging over the restless gray sea.

He paused beneath an ancient oak, one that had
withstood many storms and many years. Its roots

had pushed up through the ground only a few steps from the edge of the cliff. From his belt he pulled the precious shining ornament, the circle of twisted gold that he had so carefully fashioned with his own hands and his own boundless love for the goddess.

Maybe Niall was right. Maybe he had heard the druids' tales so often that he would never find a woman who could live up to his ideal—the shining ideal of Brighid, the poetess, the keeper of the hearth, the beautiful Lady of Fire.

The wind slammed into him. Ailin staggered and braced himself against the creaking oak. Looking up, he pushed his wind-whipped hair out of his eyes and saw the massive wall of black clouds right over him, whirling and roiling in fury. Streaked with purple-white lightning and shaking with thunder, the clouds held power and menace unlike any storm he had ever seen before.

This was no natural storm.

He turned to take the full force of the wind—his lady's caress—against his face. Shielding his eyes with one arm, he stood braced hard against the storm, hearing nothing but the ever-rising wind hissing and creaking in the massive oak trees high on the hill.

"Goddess," he whispered.

He closed his eyes and spread his arms wide. The storm descended down upon him and Ailin welcomed it, embraced it, feeling the power and trembling of it the way he might a woman's body in his embrace. The scream of the wind became a moan of ecstasy; each searing flash of lightning was a sweet stab of pleasure; each roaring roll of thunder was another beat of her heart.

He held up the slender piece of curving gold. Its red jewels gleamed in the dark light of the storm.

"Goddess!" he shouted into the shrieking wind. "Never will I love another as I love you. Never will I take a woman I do not love! Never will I force a child to my bed so that I might avoid a battle! I am a warrior! I am a man! I am your lover, and all the women I love shall be those in whose eyes I see your reflection!"

A blinding flash and a deafening crack were his answer. The force knocked him to the ground. He rolled over and over on the wind-ravaged grass, struggling to stay conscious, fighting to clear his vision and stop the ringing in his ears.

Rounding a corner, Christine thought she saw a faint, distant flash. She looked up at the heavy, rolling gray clouds, and in a moment heard the low rumble of thunder.

"Oh, thundersnow!" said Eliza. "Isn't that good luck or something?"

"I don't know if it's good luck," Christine answered, her boots slipping a little on the icy sidewalk, "but it certainly is unusual."

Then she saw it.

A table stood in the middle of a yard in front of a little brick house. A woman, gray-haired and old, sat behind the table, bundled up in a black jacket. The table was piled high with merchandise, and a fluttering paper sign taped to the edge of it read YARD SALE.

Christine stopped. "Oh, look!"

"What?" Eliza tried to see where her friend was looking. "Look at what?"

"Right there! The yard sale."

Eliza stopped dead in her tracks. "Oh, no. You're not going to another flea market! Are you telling me you want to go to a flea market *now*?"

"Well, you said I needed to get my mind off things, didn't you?" Christine said calmly.

"Flea markets are nothing but somebody else's throwaways," Eliza moaned. "What do you see in those things, anyway?"

Christine smiled. "You never know what kind of

lost treasure might come out of an attic or a basement. I've gotten almost all my antique jewelry at little sales just like this one." She shrugged. "It's better than just walking along feeling sorry for myself."

"But what about your class?"

"This won't take long. It's only the one table." She frowned, puzzled. "Don't you see it? Right there?"

Eliza sighed. "Look, I get the hint. If you want to spend a little time alone, that's okay with me. Just say so."

"Okay." If Eliza was going to pretend that she didn't see the table and the woman right there in front of them, then Christine was not going to push her about it. "I get the hint, too. Why don't you go on home, and I'll call you later? I'm sure you and Jim must have somewhere you can go or something you can do."

"Well—we were talking about taking the kids to that new Amish-style restaurant out in the country for breakfast sometime—you can only go during the week 'cause they're closed on Sundays."

"Go on, Eliza. I'll call you. Don't worry about me."

"All right. But remember, I'll be checking up on you." With a small wave and a broad smile, Eliza turned and began hiking back up the sidewalk.

Christine walked across the frosty grass, stepping over the patches of snow. Browsing at such sales was one of the small pleasures of her life. She was also glad for the distraction, however small. She had never given in to self-pity before, and she knew that she was going to have to get over Marco—get over the whole six years—very soon.

If only she knew how.

"Good morning," she said to the woman at the table, glancing over the inviting display. The table was piled high with bracelets and necklaces, picture frames and silverware, folded lace curtains and old hardback books.

"Mornin', honey," said the woman, bundling a little closer into her coat. "Going to be a pretty day, isn't it?"

Christine smiled at her, fingering a tarnished silver bracelet. "It's still a little cold for me."

"Oh, but I don't mind the cold. Just gives you a reason to cuddle up with your sweetie, now, doesn't it?" The woman chuckled and gave Christine a knowing wink.

Christine forced herself to continue smiling. "Yes, I suppose it does," she murmured. I won't look back, she told herself firmly, and began examining the pieces of jewelry.

Ailin lay unmoving, the twisted gold ornament still clenched tightly in his hand, and then got slowly to his feet. Breathing hard, as though he had just finished battle, he could only stand and stare at the top of the hill.

Flames crept up the branches of the oak he had stood against. It had been split almost in half by the lightning strike. The wind-whipped fire quickly engulfed the ancient tree, crackling and smoking and lighting the late afternoon blackness with brilliant orange-yellow light.

Fire.

Lady of Fire . . .

Ailin walked slowly to the side of the blazing tree. He held out the twisted gold in both hands and raised it high, giving the goddess his answer to her show of power and presence, to the wild storm and devouring flames that were her manifestations in the world he knew.

Shouting above the wind, he cried out, "In my heart, there are none who come before you! This I offer you, Brighid, Lady of Fire, this which I have made with my own hand! I give it now to your sky-kindled flames!"

He took the golden gift and flung it with all his strength directly into the blaze. It flew so fast that he barely had time to shield his eyes from the resulting explosion of flying sparks and glaring light, as the goddess took what he had made and claimed it for herself.

Christine reached into the heaps of jewelry, rummaging for a bright, clear stone set in silver that had caught her eye. As she did her hand closed around something large and heavy.

What's this?

She drew it out, holding it up to study it in the clear pale light of the winter sun.

It was not the silver piece that she had noticed. This was like a circle of dull, heavy gold. It looked as though someone had held a slender, straight bar of gold at each end, twisted it flat like a ribbon, and then curved it into a circle.

Yet the circle was not quite complete. A space a few inches wide had been left open, and at each end was the delicately fashioned head of a woman. The women's faces were young and strong, and masses of long, wavy hair streamed back from each one.

The piece felt warm and heavy in her hand. Even through its thick coating of blackened grime, it reflected the winter sun with a soft glow.

"What is this?" she asked, holding out the piece to the woman behind the table.

The woman half-rose from her chair, frowning as she peered closely at the gold piece in Christine's hand. "Well—now, you know, I just can't say for sure," she said at last. "I don't remember putting that out. Maybe it's something of my husband's. Would you like me to ask him?" She turned toward the house, cupping her hands beside her mouth. "Henry! Henry, come out here a minute!"

"No, no. That's all right," Christine said hastily. "I'll take it."

Even as she said the words Christine was surprised by them. Why was she buying this? She didn't even know what it was! Yes, she loved antique jewelry, and this was certainly an unusual piece—maybe even one of a kind—but it wasn't the sort of thing she normally bought. It was just a curiosity, not something she could wear, like a brooch or a necklace or a pair of earrings.

Yet as the piece rested in her hand, and the sunlight glinted on the long, streaming hair of the women whose faces adorned each end, she knew that she could not walk away from here without it. This strange gold ornament was hers, as if it were somehow meant for her.

"You'll take it! Good, good," said the woman, reaching under her chair for a little black metal box. "That'll be two dollars."

Christine opened her purse and handed over a five-dollar bill. As the woman rummaged in the black box for change, she glanced up at the heavy gold piece in Christine's hand. "Strange-looking thing, isn't it?" she said, holding out three worn dollar bills. "I don't know what you could do with it. Hang it on your wall, maybe?"

"Maybe," Christine answered. She slid the piece and the money into her purse and closed up the zipper.

She wasn't sure just what she would do with the gold curiosity, but the important thing was that she had found it. Out of all the lovely things she might have encountered, this one had come to her, and now it rested safely in her hands.

In the quiet of the classroom Christine sat at her desk, her foot swinging as the professor droned on. She tried to look as though she was concentrating on classical English literature, but it was difficult when all she could think about was the mysterious gold piece closed up in her purse.

She could still see it as clearly as though it rested on the desk before her—the curving, twisting gold, the beauty of the women's faces, and the faint glint of their streaming hair even beneath the layers of dirt and grime.

It was old, very old. Christine was sure of that. Things like that just weren't made anymore.

She sighed. It was not going to be enough simply to take the thing home and hang it on her wall beside the mirror, or let it rest on a shelf above the television set.

She had to know what it was.

Christine walked into the hallway with the rest of the students, and after only a moment's hesitation turned and headed down the hall in the other direction. She rounded a corner and began checking the names on the glass windows of the doors. She soon found the one she was looking for—PROFESSOR JOSEPH VAUGHN, RENAISSANCE HISTORY—and tapped cautiously at the door.

After a moment there was a faint call from behind the door: "Come in," she thought she heard. Christine eased open the creaking door to the small, cluttered office.

"Yes, young lady? Can I help you?" Pen in hand, a gray-haired man sat hunched over his old wooden desk. It was piled high with papers, some of which were sliding down onto the floor. He peered closely at her over his steel-rimmed glasses. "Are you one of my students?"

"Well, yes—ah, I mean, no, sir, not now. I was one of your students last quarter," Christine said. She could feel the blush creeping up her neck as she walked to the desk, and told herself to get a grip on her nervousness. "I was in your Renaissance History class. But if you're busy—I mean, I don't have an appointment or anything—"

"No, no," said Professor Vaughn, laying down his pen. "It's quite all right. I always make time for my students—even last quarter's students. You are . . . ?"

"Christine Connolly, sir."

"Miss Connolly. I must apologize for the untidy state of my office." He pushed the stacks of paper into some kind of order on his desk, and leaned down to pick up the ones that had fallen.

"I've been rather busy shepherding a visiting historian, showing him around the city and the university and such," he said, straightening up once more. "He's leaving tomorrow—going back to his home in Ireland, and I've been quite tied up with—"

He stopped abruptly and lifted yet another stack of papers from the wooden chair beside his desk. "You certainly didn't come here to discuss the university's visitors. Please sit down. What can I do for you?"

Christine sat down in the chair. "Well, sir, I have, ah, a question for you . . . if you don't mind my imposing on you this way. . . ."

She reached for her purse, suddenly embarrassed. What was she doing here, taking up Professor Vaughn's valuable time with a piece of junk she'd picked up at a yard sale? But as she unzipped the purse and brought out the heavy circle of gold, she knew that as silly as it might seem, she simply had to find out exactly what this piece was—and this was as good a place to start as any.

She laid the gold piece on the scratched wooden surface of the desk. "I must apologize for intruding on you with something like this, Professor Vaughn, but—please. I found this at . . . at an antique sale. I've never seen anything like it before. Do you have any idea what it is?"

After adjusting his glasses on his nose, the professor reached for the gold piece and lifted it up. "Well, now . . ." He paused, squinting at it through his glasses, turning it over and studying it closely. "You seem to have found a rather nice example of a torque."

Christine blinked. "A what?"

He laid it gently on the desk and glanced up at her with a kind smile. "A torque," he said. "It's a piece of jewelry, quite fashionable among the best-dressed people of any number of ancient European tribes. Why, in 400 A.D. or so, something like this would have been all the rage."

Christine grinned. "I thought it was just a wall decoration."

"Oh, no. You wear it around your neck; it wasn't meant to hang on the wall." He lifted it up in both hands and showed her the open side. "You can see, here, that the metal is a bit springy—it can be pulled apart slightly, to fit nicely around your neck."

She leaned forward as a surge of excitement ran through her. "Do you mean it's a genuine antique? That it's, what did you say, over fifteen hundred years old?"

He looked closely at the piece again, hefting it in his hand, and frowned. "No, no. I didn't mean to confuse you, Miss Connolly. This couldn't possibly be a real torque. Such a thing would be worth—well, I'm not sure how much. But you wouldn't find one at an antique sale. No, I'm sure it's just a quite nice copy, probably done by a student of art history as a project."

But the professor continued to examine the gold object. He ran his fingers over it, rubbing away some of the grime. "That's strange," he murmured. "It seems to have been damaged . . . it's heavily grimed, and the edges are scarred, as if from heat. Perhaps it went through a fire at some point."

Christine leaned forward to look closer, but the professor only turned over the gold torque once more. "A jeweler, of course, could tell you its intrinsic value, after determining exactly what it's made of. It looks like it might be gold plated, and look—

there's a gemstone of some kind here." Sure enough, as he rubbed at the heavy grime Christine could see the sparkle of a tiny red stone emerge from the gold just behind the streaming hair of one of the women.

"I must admit, Miss Connolly, I'm rather curious about it myself. It couldn't possibly be genuine, of course, but one never knows. . . . I can't recall the last time I saw anyone walking about with a torque."

He handed the torque back to Christine. "If I may, I would like to put the question to our Irish historian before he leaves. He does know quite a lot about Celtic history, certainly more than I do—things like torques were quite popular among the Celtic tribes. Now, if it's anything Italian you want to know about—"

Christine stood up, carefully placing the torque back in her purse. "No, no, Professor Vaughn. I don't want to take any more of your time. Thank you very much for your help."

She hesitated for a moment, and then took a deep breath. "If your visitor does know any more about it—if he would want to call me—I really would like very much to know all I can about this piece."

The professor stood up and walked with Christine to the door. "Of course, Miss Connolly. A gold torque is not the sort of thing one finds every day, is it?"

He smiled at her over the steel-rimmed glasses. "I really didn't mind looking up from grading hundreds of freshman papers to consider a bit of a mystery. Thank you for stopping by."

"Thank you, Professor Vaughn." She reached for the handle of the door. But before she could touch it, the door swung open and a man stood in front of her.

She found herself looking up—and up, and up— at a blond man with blue-gray eyes and a handsome, noble face. "Professor Vaughn," he began, "I—"

Then he saw her.

He stood motionless in the doorway. His shining

eyes widened first with shock, and then with joy, and then with what she would have sworn was recognition. He stared at her with such intensity that she felt powerless to move.

"Christine," he whispered.

Chapter Three

He was long legged and broad shouldered, and even under his conservative wool tweed jacket and crisp white shirt Christine could feel the enormous strength and power in him. The very room was filled with it.

This man was no deskbound academic. He looked to be in his thirties, older and far more sophisticated than the average student. His hair was soft and blond, neatly trimmed just to the edge of his white shirt collar. His eyes shone bright and his fair skin was flushed with excitement.

And at this moment, the full force of his personality was directed at her with the intensity of the sun's focused rays.

"Bridget Christine . . ."

She blinked. He was an incredibly handsome man, and she had no doubt that if she'd ever seen him before she would have remembered him. Yet he seemed to know her. How was that possible?

"My name is Bridget Christine," she said, matching his burning gaze. "Are you looking for someone by that name?"

Some of the light faded from his eyes. He seemed

to draw inward, as if he had lowered a shield over the radiant force emanating from him and carefully placed himself at arm's length from her.

"I am," he said. "I am looking for Bridget Christine, a red-haired lady of great beauty and extraordinary spirit." His voice was gentle and warm, with a soft Irish accent. "But the Bridget Christine I seek already knows me. I am sorry." He looked away, as if it had hurt him to say the words.

"I-I only go by Christine," she said hesitantly, as if that explained everything.

There was a small sound of throat-clearing behind them. "Ah, this is the visiting historian I mentioned," said Professor Vaughn. "May I introduce Mr. Donalson, of County Donegal, Ireland. Mr. Donalson, this is a former student of mine, Miss Christine Connolly—as you already seem to know," he muttered, sitting back down at his desk and shuffling yet another stack of papers.

"I am sorry to have disturbed your meeting with the professor, Chris—Miss Connolly." With great reluctance, the handsome blond man took a step backward and began reaching for the door. "Perhaps I should come back another time."

"Oh, no, no. Here, let me show you." She fumbled in her purse and hastily pulled out the golden torque.

For a long moment, he gazed in silence at the strange object in her hand. His face softened and his eyes shone bright and clear, so bright that it seemed to Christine they were touched with tears. Slowly he raised one hand, reaching out as if to touch the torque, but then he drew it back again.

"Do you recognize it?" she whispered. "Do you know what it is?" When he made no answer, something else occurred to her. "I bought it today at a yard sale on the edge of the campus. Is it yours? Was it lost, or stolen from you?"

He looked up at her and smiled gently. "It is not mine. It belongs to Brighid."

Now she was really confused. "To—who?"

He gestured at the torque, watching it closely as she turned it over in her hands. "Do you see the faces of the women at each end of it? The red stones set into the sides behind their hair? This piece was dedicated to Brighid long ago." He paused and whispered almost to himself, "A very long time ago."

Bridget . . . "Oh, yes," Christine said. "Saint Bridget. The Irish saint. I know. I was born on her day, and named for her."

"So you were," said Mr. Donalson. "But Bridget is an old and beautiful name. Why do you not use it, if I may ask?"

Christine smiled at him. "Well, the other kids used to call me things like Bridget Bardot and Bridget the Midget, so I always insisted on being called Christine. But . . ."

She glanced down at the torque, studying the strong young faces of the women. "This piece looks awfully—well, pagan to me. How could it have been made for Saint Bridget?"

"Oh, it was not made for a saint, Miss Connolly. I am sorry. I did not mean Saint Bridget. Your torque was made for her predecessor, Brighid, a Celtic goddess."

"A goddess?"

"A goddess." Once more he gazed at her, his blue-gray eyes shining right through to her very soul. "In the old Celtic world, Brighid was called the Lady of Fire. She was the keeper of the hearth and the patroness of words."

"Of words?" she whispered.

"Of words. She loved to hear poetry and song, and especially loved to hear it sung on the battlefield by warriors asking her for strength and courage.

"Her festival day was the first day of spring—that was the first of February, back in the ancient world. We still remember it today as St. Bridget's Day, or as Candlemas, or—in your case—as your birthday."

Christine simply gazed at him, held spellbound by his words and by his eyes and by the sheer magic of his presence. Never had she been near a man like this one. He was something completely new to her, a combination of warmth and intelligence and sheer physical power, something that she had never thought existed.

She could have stood for hours, or days, just listening to the sound of his gentle Irish voice.

And then she began to think about what he had said. "Do you mean that you believe the torque is real? That it was actually made hundreds of years ago?"

He cocked his head and studied her, and she found herself mesmerized by the soft fall of his feathery blond hair as he did so. "I cannot say for certain. But there is always that possibility."

Professor Vaughn leaned forward in his chair. "I must say that I agree, Miss Connolly. Notwithstanding what I told you earlier, sometimes these things do turn up in the most unlikely places. People simply don't realize what they have. The most fabulous antiques are thought to be simple novelties, and end up tossed in an attic or lost in someone's basement."

"Yes, I've heard of things like that happening." Christine could barely contain her excitement as she turned back to the blond stranger.

"There is a way for you to know whether it is real," he said softly.

She paused for a moment, curious. "How is that?"

"Wear it."

"Wear it? But what would that tell me?"

He smiled at her. "When it is resting around your neck, you will know. Of that I have no doubt."

Once again she met his eyes, and for a brief moment the sun's rays shone on her again. He was the most extraordinary man she had ever met—magical, beautiful, larger than life.

Slowly she placed the torque back inside her

purse. "I really must be going," she said, making no move to go.

"Miss Connolly—" Mr. Donalson glanced first at the professor, and then back at Christine. "Tonight is my last night in the United States. I must fly back to Ireland at dawn tomorrow. No doubt you already have plans for this evening, but in any case—I should like to extend you an invitation to join the professor and me for dinner."

"Why, yes, yes," said Professor Vaughn. "We'll be at the Village Green tonight at seven-thirty. You would be most welcome to join us."

"Oh," she breathed, looking at the blond man. "I would love to," she said, the words forming before she even had time to think. "I was planning to go out with my friend Eliza tonight, and the Village Green would be lovely."

"Thank you very much, Miss Connolly." He took a step toward her, and Christine felt as if she were floating—the office was so small, and he was so close that she could feel the warmth of him—she could breathe in the sun-scent of his soft blond hair. "You and your friend shall be our guests for dinner, in honor of your birthday."

She opened her mouth to say good-bye, but found that she could not. "Mr. Donalson—I hope you find your Bridget Christine."

He smiled tenderly. "I will find her, Miss Connolly. I will find her."

The flying sparks vanished as the rain began, a rain bright as silver against the night-black clouds. Yet the roaring fire kept its hold on the giant oak tree. The flames grew ever larger and more brilliant, and as Ailin watched, the tree began to give up its ancient life. Layer by layer its wood blackened and curled and turned to smoke, a black cloud of smoke drifting far out over the land where it had grown for so many reasons.

A sudden movement in the distance caught his eye. A man raced up the rain-slick hill, slipping and struggling in the mud and wet grass, and staggered into Ailin's arms.

"Niall!" Ailin grabbed him by the shoulders and helped him to his feet. "What is it? The storm? Is someone hurt?"

"It's not the storm," Niall gasped, beginning to run and pulling Ailin with him, "it's the *gadai*! They're hiding in the woods—I saw them out by the edge of the road, with cattle stolen right out of old Sean's *rath*—and they're coming! Here! Now!"

The driving rain poured down as Ailin raced down the hill, with the terrified Niall close on his heels. They slid to a stop against the high-banked earthen walls of the fort. Ailin pulled the smaller man around to face him.

"Find my father!" Ailin shouted as the water ran down his face and the wind blew cold in his eyes. "Take the team and find the king! Bring him here—bring them all! Hurry!"

Niall nodded, slipping and staggering in the mud as he turned and started off once again through the storm, beneath the clouds of smoke from the fiercely burning oak.

Christine walked home on a cloud, still enveloped in the magic of the ancient gold torque and the mysterious, handsome man to whom it had led her. And she would see him again tonight! There was so much to do this afternoon—she had to call Eliza, she had to do her hair, she had to find just the right thing to wear—

She realized that she was walking past the same house where the yard sale had been this morning. She looked up at it, shielding her eyes from the bright winter sun. Perhaps it would be worth looking there again. After all, she had certainly had good luck the first time.

But the yard was empty. Even the snow was smooth and untracked. It was undoubtedly the very same house, but there was no sign that there had ever been a sale on the front lawn that morning.

A cold feeling crept over her. She made a sudden grab for her purse—yes, the torque was still there, tucked safely away between her wallet and her hairbrush.

Then how could this be? Maybe she didn't quite remember how the table had been set up. Maybe it had actually been on the sidewalk, and not on the snow-covered grass at all.

But she knew that the table had not been on the sidewalk. She specifically remembered stepping through the snowy yard to get to it. . . .

Christine turned away and forced herself to keep walking. Her hands shook. At the sight of the empty yard, the magic faded like smoke on the wind. The world, cold and gray and lonely, came crashing in.

An hour later Christine sat curled up on a corner of the soft blue sofa in her silent apartment, flipping through the pages of a magazine without really seeing them. An untouched cup of chicken soup sat on the small oak table beside her.

The apartment was so quiet that she could hear the slow tick of the wall clock out in the kitchen. Finally she tossed the magazine aside and reached for the cup of soup. It was cold. Christine put it back on the table with a sigh.

Her spirits had been lifted earlier in the day, first by Eliza's visit and then by finding the lovely gold torque at the yard sale. It had been a shock to see the same yard looking untouched on her way home, but perhaps she was just imagining things.

At any rate, she had not imagined Mr. Donalson. Even now, the thought of him sent a thrill racing along her nerves.

She had never before thought of a man as being

Janeen O'Kerry

beautiful. That word seemed reserved for women and flowers. Yet he did have an unmistakable masculine beauty about him, strong and powerful with a fine, noble face and soft feathery hair . . . beautiful the way a stallion is beautiful, or a stag. . . .

Suddenly she slammed the magazine shut and forced the images away. What was she doing? What kind of woman was she? She was practically drooling over a total stranger. How could she forget her six years with Marco at the sight of the first attractive man to come down the road?

She had only to close her eyes and the memories would come flooding back. She could still feel Marco's arms pulling her close, still hear the beat of his heart as she rested her head against his chest.

But his face . . . his face . . .

With a shock, Christine realized that she could scarcely remember Marco's face.

How could that be? It had been only a few days since she had last seen him. It was impossible that she could not see his face. You could never forget the face of someone you loved—could you?

Restless and in pain, she got up off the sofa and paced through the small apartment. Her feet took her first into the kitchen, where the clock ticked so loudly, and then into the bedroom.

She would not let the tears begin again. She caught sight of the gold torque on her dresser, where it rested on a white lace handkerchief, and quickly picked it up.

It was heavy and cold, but somehow alive in her hands. The tears burned behind her eyelids. Holding the metal circle, Christine closed her eyes and tried with all her heart to see Marco's face once more.

But the picture that slowly formed in her mind wasn't Marco at all. She seemed to see someone very different—someone familiar.

He stood before a backdrop of towering flame, a tall blond man, powerful and strong, with long legs and slim hips. His hair was long, very long; it fell down past his shoulders and was bound by a bright gold band across his forehead. He wore a dark red cloak fastened with some kind of large golden brooch. The cloak rippled and moved in the hot drafts from the fire.

He turned as though to look straight at her, and Christine saw his eyes. They were slate blue, piercing and strong, staring like a wild thing. . . .

Suddenly Christine jumped. Her eyes snapped open. Someone was knocking at the front door.

Ailin dashed inside the fort as the cold rain poured and the lighting flashed. He pushed and shoved at the heavy gate of upright logs, working desperately to close it, shouting in fury as the ends of it dragged and caught with maddening slowness in the sodden earth.

The massive gate needed four men to close it. But Ailin braced himself against it, forcing all the strength from his muscles until he thought they would burst. Finally the gate was shut. He lifted the heavy wooden plank by one end, pushed it through the iron braces on the wall beside the gate, and slammed it into place.

He raced across the grounds of the fort, past the barn and the feast hall and the scattered small houses, shouting "Stay inside! Stay inside! It's the *gadai*! Stay inside!" From the corner of his eye he could see the women quickly barring the doors and windows of the houses.

Ailin ran inside his own house to get a sword and spear. The rage in him swelled and grew with each passing moment.

How dare they come here, now, like this, crawling in like sneaking cowardly dogs while the rest of the men were away! *Gadai* was the name for the lowest of the low—the criminals, the fugitives, the outcasts. And that was exactly what they were.

Stealing the cattle, that was one thing. Then there'd be a proper battle among men to get them back and all differences would be resolved in a fair fight among warriors. But this—attacking the king's own fortress home when they thought it would be empty—when they thought they'd find only a few women and children and old serving men inside—this would be a day they would regret.

At the sound of the knocking, the strange thoughts and visions faded away. Still holding the torque, Christine walked to the living room and peered through the tiny glass hole in the door. Smiling, she opened the door.

"Hey, old lady!" Eliza said with a laugh, bustling into the room and setting down her enormous shoulder bag. "I told you I was going to check on you. And since I forgot to tell you earlier—happy birthday!"

Christine's smile faded. "Thanks," she murmured, closing the door. "You really know how to cheer somebody up."

"Oh, come on now. I hit the same three-oh roadblock two years ago, and I'm not in a nursing home yet, am I?"

"Jim would never allow it. Not unless he went in with you."

Eliza sat down on the couch and looked intently at her friend. "Really, I don't want you to stay cooped up in here by yourself for another night. Come on—let's go out. What do you say?"

Christine sighed. The wild emotions of this rollercoaster day were beginning to wear on her. "Eliza, your timing isn't even right. My birthday isn't until tomorrow, remember? And I just don't feel like having a party to celebrate it. I'm sure you understand."

Eliza looked up indignantly. "I didn't think you'd feel like having a big birthday party. That's why I'm here now, because it's not your birthday! And if it's

40

not your birthday, then going out tonight couldn't possibly have anything to do with a birthday—now, could it?"

Christine found her spirits rising just a little, in spite of herself. But she could feel her face begin to grow warm at the thought of having to tell Eliza about her hastily arranged date for this evening. What would her friend think, when just this morning she'd been so devastated? "I guess not. But I'm way ahead of you."

"Way ahead of me? What do you mean?" She frowned, her black brows knitting together in disapproval. "Now don't tell me Mr. Globe-Trotting Marco called—"

"No, no. We—that is, you and I—have ah, been invited out to dinner. By a couple of the history professors."

"History professors?"

"Yes." She slid the torque through her hands. "One of them is from Ireland, and this is his last night here, and—"

"Well, is he less than one hundred years old?"

Christine's heart gave a leap. "Oh, he is. He's—"

"Okay then!" Eliza looked genuinely pleased. "Good for you! And good for us! Even if it is just with a couple of creaky old profs, at least you'll be getting out. Don't worry, I'll be here! I wouldn't miss this for the world! What time and where?"

"Seven-thirty. The Village Green."

"Great!" Eliza stood up, collecting her handbag. "I'll be back at—" She paused, cocking her head as she looked down at Christine's hands. "What is that thing you're playing with?"

Christine stopped. "This?" she said, not moving.

"Yes, this," Eliza said, reaching for the torque. She pulled it out of Christine's fingers and held it up for a better look.

Christine frowned. "Hey, Liza, be careful with that." She reached for the torque, but Eliza turned

41

away and continued to examine it.

"Wow, it's heavy. And dirty!" She laughed. "What is it, anyway?"

"I found it at the yard sale this morning. I went to the history department to ask about it. That's how we happen to be going to dinner with Professor Vaughn and Mr. Donalson tonight. They said it's a torque."

"A what?"

"A torque," Christine said patiently, hovering close as Eliza rubbed her fingers on the edges of the twisted gold. "The ancient tribes in Europe used to wear them."

"Wear them?" Eliza laughed. "I though it was just a wall hanging or something."

"No. It goes around your neck. Hey, wait!"

Christine grabbed the torque away just as Eliza raised it up to her neck. "No! Don't!"

Eliza stared at her. "Christine, what's wrong with you? I just wanted to try it on."

Christine stammered, suddenly embarrassed and a little ashamed. Her strong reaction had startled her as much as it had Eliza. She looked up rather sheepishly at her friend. "I'm sorry. I just— Professor Vaughn said that there's a chance it's a real antique, and I want to be careful."

But even as she spoke, Christine knew that wasn't the reason why she did not want Eliza to put on the torque. The mysterious piece of twisted gold was hers, and hers alone. She had found it, hidden like a secret treasure beneath those heaps of old discarded jewelry, and it was meant only for her.

Most of all, she remembered the look in Mr. Donalson's slate-blue eyes when he had told her to wear it—when he had said that she would know, when she placed it around her neck, whether or not it was real.

No one else must ever think of wearing it.

"Oh, you mean it might be worth some real money!" Eliza said brightly. "Well, in that case I'll let you put it away. Bare skin isn't good for metal, is it? The oils, or something . . ."

"Right," Christine said faintly. "Ah—I'll be right back." She gripped the torque securely in her own hands, feeling the comfort of its heavy weight, and took it back into her bedroom. Gently she laid the circle of gold back down on the white lace handkerchief.

When she returned to the living room, Eliza had slung her bag over her shoulder and was standing by the door. "I'll be back tonight at seven," she said, "so be ready by then. Promise?"

"I promise," Christine said. "Seven o'clock. And—thanks."

Eliza winked at her. "Anytime, kid. See you at seven."

Chapter Four

Christine stepped out of the warmth of the shower, dried off quickly, and pulled on a long white cotton nightgown. Hurrying into the cool air of her bedroom, she glanced at the clock beside her bed.

Two minutes past six. Good. Not as late as I thought. Then she caught sight of the torque where it rested on its white lace handkerchief on her dresser. As she gazed at it, the tiny gleam of one red stone flashed at her.

She frowned. The ancient piece looked so neglected and forlorn, sitting as it was beneath its coat of blackened grime. Why hadn't she realized that before now? Eliza and Professor Vaughn had both been right. It *was* dirty. How long had its beauty been hidden?

Too long, she decided. It just didn't seem right to let such a lovely thing stay in such condition. And though Christine knew she ought to be getting ready for her night out—she still had no idea what she would wear—she found that right now none of that seemed to matter. She carried the torque to the sink, got an old towel and some dishwashing soap, and set to work.

First she got the worst of the blackened dirt and dust to surrender to plain soap and water. It looked better, but now what? She was afraid to put any sort of polish on it, for fear of hurting the metal; she didn't know much about how to clean gold—or whatever it actually was.

She sat down with it at her kitchen table and began rubbing it with the soft towel. As she worked, a glowing luster began to appear beneath her patient fingers. Over and over, around the spirals and over the faces of the women, she polished the ancient surface. Finally, almost mesmerized by the work, she raised it up.

Her discovery was more beautiful than ever, for now it was gleaming and alive with a brilliant gold shine. Two tiny red stones, one on either side behind the streaming hair of the women's heads, shone out from its golden surface.

Christine walked back to her bedroom and placed the torque back on the lace handkerchief. As she did, a strange feeling of excitement and anticipation tingled through her. For a few moments she simply stood in the quiet bedroom, gazing at the torque where it was reflected in the mirror of the dresser. Her fingers caressed the spiraling golden surface and touched the fire-red jewels where they gleamed in the soft light of the late winter evening.

Wear it, he had said.

Ailin ripped off his cloak, rammed his sword into the scabbard at his belt, and grabbed his spear. He raced outside into the darkness of the storm just as three of the skulking, ragged enemy came spilling over the high gates of the fortress, tossed over by their comrades.

They hadn't seen him yet. All three of them were intent on dragging out the heavy plank that barred the gate so they could let in the rest of their band of thieves. Ailin pulled his sword from its scabbard as fury pulsed through his veins, turning his muscles to iron and his skin to a sheet of flame beneath the cold driving rain.

"*Ainmhi!*" he roared. "Animals! Come to me!"

All three of them froze. After a moment of indecision, they let the plank drop to the mud and pulled out their short, battered swords. Then, with what they no doubt thought was a frightening howl, the three of them started running across the fortress grounds toward Ailin.

One of them instantly fell backward, screaming, with Ailin's quivering spear pinning him to the ground. The other two went down before his slashing strokes and lay writhing in the rain-splattered mud as their lives ebbed away.

Just as Ailin pulled his sword free four more of them ran up to him with weapons drawn, howling like crazed dogs. With two hands on his sword Ailin swung and slashed, and dropped yet another of his enemy.

Then came a massive blow to the back of his head. And another. And another.

For an endless moment the world turned black and spinning. Lights flashed and danced before his eyes. And then his sword was ripped from his hands and he fell heavily to the wet ground, pulled down by enormous weights which had somehow gotten hold of his arms.

"Our turn now, *ainmhi,*" said a thick, hissing voice in his ear.

Ailin struggled against the blackness, even as the cold rain on his face helped revive him. He fought to regain his strength and get back on his feet. As though from a great distance, he could hear screams and shouts from the women and children and feel the pounding footsteps of the *gadai* men as they overran the fortress grounds.

His vision began to clear. The gate was standing open. He had to get it shut, had to keep this filthy enemy away from the women and the children—

But the weight on his arms pulled him over backward and held him fast to the rain-soaked grass. The blows to his head had drained his power. Through the downpour he could see a grinning thief standing over him, his short rusted sword held ready for the kill.

Ailin raged against his captors, but the blackness only came flooding back. In desperation he closed his eyes and cried out to the storm, the unnatural storm where the goddess rode and watched.

"Brighid, Queen of War, Lady of Fire! For my family! Give me back my strength! If ever you would hear me, hear me now!"

It was real. This lovely golden antique, resting cool and heavy in her hand, was as real and genuine as the glow that ran through its spiraling surface and flame-bright jewels.

She wondered who had made it. The torque was old, very old; it was not the work of some anonymous art student or modern-day souvenir factory. Some long-ago craftsman, working only with fire and gold and the power in his own strong arms, had wrought this thing of ancient beauty that had now come down to her.

Who owned it before I did? Who had been the first woman to wear it? She was certain that it must have been a woman, not a man. From the slender design of the torque and the women's faces on each end, it was clear to her that the lovely piece had been made especially for a lady.

And what had her life been like, that lady who had lived in such a faraway time and place? Had she been beautiful and brave, wearing her shining gold torque with long flowing gowns and gorgeous fur cloaks, while her man gazed on her with love and pride?

No doubt it had been a man who had given her the torque in the first place, a bold and daring man who had fought to win the woman of his choice . . . a warrior hero bringing a gift, an offering, to the love of his life, a princess, a queen, a goddess. . . .

Christine stood before the mirror and held the torque lightly in her fingers. As she stared into the mirror she saw, once again, a vision of the tall blond warrior. This time she imagined him with a sword in his hand, fighting a fierce battle. She could see herself there in that ancient time looking the way she did now, the way her ancestors must have looked, with their loose flowing hair and long simple gowns.

Only one thing was needed to make the picture complete. Drawing a deep breath, Christine lifted the torque in both hands and slid the cool circle of gold around her neck.

She gazed proudly into the mirror, eager to see the picture she made, but the light suddenly dimmed, as though the sun had gone behind a cloud. The only light in the room seemed to come from the gleaming torque around her neck.

The mirror faded into darkness. She could no longer see herself in it. Trembling now, Christine moved toward the wall to turn on a light, but the air itself wavered and shimmered. Then the walls of her bedroom vanished into the same darkness that had swallowed the mirror.

The blood pounded in her ears. There were distant shouts and screams among the pounding. Christine clapped her hands over her ears and staggered back, completely disoriented, unable to find anything in the blackness that had been her room.

The darkness threatened to swallow her. The shouting and the screaming grew louder, and there were sounds of ringing metal and the heavy crash of thunder.

Her leg hit something low and solid. She stumbled and fell across her bed, clutching the quilts in an effort to regain her balance and not fall off the side of the world. But the spinning blackness closed in, and with à scream of pure terror, Christine felt herself falling, falling, into the absolute dark.

Time passes slowly in a dream, and it seemed to Christine that she had been dreaming for a very long time. She felt herself begin to drift upward through the heavy darkness of sleep, coming to lie on a smooth solid surface.

A dim light filtered in through her closed eyes. She drew a deep breath, preparing to sit up, and immediately began coughing. There was a powerful smell of smoke in the air.

Fire!

She sat up in a panic and rolled to the floor, trying to remember what to do in such an emergency—stay low, check the doorknobs for heat, get outside.

Christine landed on the floor on her hands and knees and immediately recoiled in horror. The floor was covered with some kind of dried weeds! Without thinking she scrambled back up on the bed, looking wildly around at her room—

But it was not her room. She was kneeling on a soft pile of furs on what seemed to be a solid ledge in a small and ancient house. Gathering all her shaky courage, Christine tried to make sense of where she was.

She saw no fire. She saw nothing that she expected to see.

The walls of the little house were made of some sort of smooth clay, and the roof looked like bundles of straw tied together. There was another fur-covered ledge on the opposite wall, and several large, carved wooden chests along the wall near the ledge where she crouched. The entire floor was covered with long dried grasses. A single small doorway was the only way out.

There was an open fireplace, a hearth, in the center of the room. It was the fire on the hearth, smoldering beneath an enormous bronze cauldron, that filled the air with drifting smoke.

Christine's eyes darted left and right, taking it all in. She was too frightened, too startled, and too confused to do more. Where was she? What was this place? How had she gotten here?

With a violent start she realized that she was hearing shouts of rage and screams of panic, punctuated by the vicious clang of metal on metal and the thundering of a violent storm. It sounded like a battle was going on right outside the open door, though she could see little from the ledge.

It might be safer to stay here—but she did not even know where *here* was! She had no idea what this place was or who it belonged to. What would happen if they came back and found her here?

The terrifying sounds grew closer. Christine knew that she had to do something. Her sense of shock and panic would not let her stay another moment in this strange house.

Leaping up from the fur-covered ledge, she ran in her bare feet across the dried grass on the floor and stopped in the open doorway, clutching the thick wooden frame with one hand.

The sky was black with treacherous storm clouds and the rain was pouring down, but Christine barely noticed. Right in front of her was a scene of violence like nothing she had ever witnessed.

His back to her, a tall man with long blond hair fought desperately for his life against four fierce and wild-eyed opponents. The four were shaggy, small, and filthy, and looked for all the world like a pack of mad dogs trying to pull down a noble stag.

The blond man grasped his heavy sword with both hands. He swung it so viciously at the man in front of him that the very air was left cut and whistling. The man dropped to the mud and lay still.

The tall blond warrior pulled his arms back for another swing, but as he did another of his tormentors struck him on the back of the head with a heavy wooden club—struck him again and again. As the tall man staggered from the blows, two others grabbed his arms from behind and all three went crashing down in the slick mud beneath their feet.

The warrior shouted out loud and fought to throw off the two men, who hung on him like snarling hounds worrying their kill. As the three of them struggled, the rough-looking man with the club pulled out a short, thick sword. With a howl he moved to face the blond warrior and raised the sword to run him through.

Christine stared in disbelief. Then she screamed "No!" until she thought her voice would be torn from her throat.

Distracted, the rough man with the sword glanced up at Christine. And as he did, the late-afternoon sun at his back slid down from behind the black clouds. Its sudden brilliance flashed off the gleaming gold torque around Christine's neck.

The rough man, blinded by the reflected light of the sun dancing in his eyes, instinctively threw one arm over his face. The tall blond man roared his rage and rose up to his knees, throwing off the two who hung on his arms. He got hold of his sword and with a shout ran it clear through his blinded opponent, pulling it out again with both hands.

As the rough man wavered and then slowly, slowly toppled to the mud, the blond warrior leaped to his feet and prepared to send the other two to join their companion. But they were already running away, their swords and clubs dropped and trampled into the blood-soaked mud.

Christine's heart pounded in her chest, and her mouth was dry with shock. She could not move from the doorway; her legs simply would not do her bidding. As she stood petrified with horror, trying desperately to make her mind work, the tall blond man turned to look at her.

His face was young and fierce, and his eyes still

glittered with the rage his attackers had provoked. But as he took in the sight of her, his face softened and his eyes grew wide with stunned surprise.

As Christine stared at him, the world began to waver and spin. And just before it faded to black, the man dropped to one knee before her and whispered one soft word:

"Brighid . . ."

Christine burrowed deeper into the warmth of the heavy bedcovers and stretched luxuriously, her eyes still closed. The air was cold and damp and there was a lingering smell of smoke in her apartment—someone must be burning leaves again. They'd get a ticket from the city if they were caught.

What a bizarre dream she had had! It must have been from listening to the handsome Mr. Donalson's talk about the past. She had imagined a gorgeous big blond warrior cutting down his enemies while she looked on, and then he had knelt down before her and called her by name. . . .

She smiled to herself. It was too bad such men didn't exist in the real world. But they were fun to dream about sometimes.

Then she opened her eyes.

Once again Christine saw a high ceiling with heavy beams and a covering of thatch. The smoke that she had smelled upon awakening rose up from beneath a bronze cauldron resting on a central stone hearth.

She was not in her apartment. And no one was burning leaves.

Without moving, Christine glanced down at the place where she lay. It was not a bed; it was a ledge alongside the wall, and the warmth came from the heavy soft furs on which she lay and which covered her from chin to toes. The place was exactly as it had been in her dream, right down to the smooth clay walls of the house and the carved wooden chests in the corners.

She sat up in a sudden panic, throwing off the furs. There were strange people standing near the door—a little crowd of them. And taking a step toward her, slowly, cautiously, his face a picture of awe and reverence, was the warrior of her dream.

Desperately Christine willed herself to wake up. She struggled toward consciousness, trying with all her will to swim up toward the surface from the depths of her sleep.

She was having some sort of recurring nightmare. That must be it. But the nightmare would be over—she closed her eyes tightly—*now!*

She opened her eyes. Nothing had changed.

A cold chill crept over her. She was awake, and she was here. The hard ledge beneath her was real. So were the heavy furs across her legs and the lingering smoke which filled the little house.

Christine kicked off the furs and swung her legs over the side of the ledge, stepping gingerly into the piles of dried grass on the floor. She looked up warily at the little knot of people near the door.

They drew back, looking puzzled and awed, but did not seem angry or upset that she was trespassing in their home. They were wearing strange clothes; the men were in woolen pants and tunics with blanketlike cloaks pinned across their shoulders, and the women wore long simple wool gowns in bright solids and plaids. Even the children looked like miniatures of the adults.

The blond man now wore a bright red cloak over his yellow-gold tunic and brown leather pants. He took another step toward her, but Christine began edging toward the door.

She could not stay here. She had no idea where this place was, or who these strange people were; she wanted only to get out, get away, and try to find some answer to why she was here.

She reached the doorway. The people shrank back slightly but continued to stare at her in silence, with

Janeen O'Kerry

serious faces and an almost dazed expression in their eyes.

The women all had very long hair, she noted, her mind strangely detached. Most all of them were blond or red-blond, and their hair was either braided in long plaits or twisted up high with the back of the hair left long and free. The men had mostly shoulder-to chin-length hair, and many wore mustaches.

Everyone wore jewelry of some type. She saw bracelets and rings and bright, heavy brooches. They were all powerful, strong-looking people, and though they were clearly very curious about her there was not a trace of fear in any of them.

Christine caught hold of the door frame and turned to look outside, squinting in the glare of the setting sun. She was trying to make sense of the surroundings—the rain had stopped and the sky was clearing—when someone touched her arm.

She froze, then spun around. The huge blond warrior stood right in front of her, so near that she could see only the dark red expanse of wool that was his cloak. It was pinned over his left shoulder with a circular golden brooch, which glinted softly in the light from the setting sun. He was so tall that she was obliged to lift her chin to look up at his face.

His skin was flushed and fair, with a delicate trace of red in the cheeks that seemed almost pretty. Yet there was nothing at all girlish about this man. His mouth was firm and set, his nose narrow and straight. Then, swallowing her rising fear, Christine made herself look up into his eyes.

Those eyes were slate blue and shining. He stared down at her as though he had never seen a young woman before. The force of his personality seemed to shine through his eyes, holding Christine suspended in a timeless moment of fear, and curiosity, and—something else.

He was stranger to her, but there was something familiar about him. She had never seen people like

54

these, dressed in this way and living in this place—whatever this place was—yet she felt that somehow she knew this man. Somewhere, she had seen him before; somehow, she should know who he was. And she was convinced that he did not mean to harm her. He wanted to tell her something; he was trying to make her understand. . . .

He raised his hand and reached out for her neck. Ever so gently he touched the golden torque, tracing the faces of the women and moving along the spiral twist. Finally the hard smoothness of his fingers touched her skin and slid upward into the line of her hair.

She closed her eyes, held mesmerized by that touch. There was such strength in it, such raw power—yet his fingers moved featherlight across her sensitive skin.

He was so near that she could feel the heat of his body. Christine felt as though she could stand here forever, forgetting where she was or why she was here, if only she could stay within the presence of this man and feel the gentle touch of his powerful hand.

Suddenly her eyes flew open. Another hand—a strange hand—pressed against her arm. Someone else brushed against her shoulder and her waist and her leg.

The other men and women in the room had crowded around her, curious and unafraid, and were examining this stranger in their midst. They surrounded her and stared at her and jostled her—

It was too much for Christine. Her shattered nerves shot a current of panic through her at those strange touches and she turned and fled outside, desperate to escape the strange house and the silent, staring, crowding people.

Chapter Five

Christine's bare feet skittered over the mud. She stopped just outside the door, looking left and right, trying to take it all in at once.

It was a strange, wild, almost primitive world that surrounded her. There was bright light from the huge gold setting sun, but the sky was still black from the passing storm. The air was heavy with the smell of rain and wet earth.

Christine stood in what appeared to be a tiny village, a small circle of a dozen or so small white buildings. Most of them were like the little house she had just escaped, but the two near the center were long rectangles and were quite a bit larger than the houses.

She blinked. The rainwashed colors were intense and brilliant—the mud brown-black beneath her feet, the scattered grass a deep emerald green, the walls of the small buildings strangely white and shining with thatched roofs turned almost golden by the sun.

There was a sound behind her. The crowd of people had moved into the doorway to watch her. Completely unnerved by the staring strangers, and having no idea where or what this place was, Christine picked up the hem of her long white gown and began to run through the slippery mud and bright green tufts of grass.

She nearly tripped over the body of a man. Horrified, she saw that it was one of the men that the huge blond fighter had struck down. With panic threatening to overwhelm her, she dashed away and looked frantically for a way out.

Rising up behind the houses was what appeared to be a very tall hedge. It was at least twelve feet high, she guessed; or maybe it was a grass-covered rise. It looked like a solid wall of green behind the small white houses.

And it was! Christine looked wildly about her, searching in every direction, but always there was the solid green wall. It formed a complete circle around the houses. This place was not just a village. It was a fortress.

She was trapped! No—no, there was a gate. It was made of wooden poles and looked very high and heavy, but it was a gate nevertheless—and it was partly open. Christine raced toward it.

She would never have been able to open the gate by herself had it been closed and bolted with the enormous plank that slid across it. She squeezed through the small opening that was left and hurried out into the open countryside.

Christine ran beneath the black and brilliant canopy of the sky. Before her rose a hill, crowned with the charred and smoking ruin of a huge old tree near the top of it. The heavy smell of wet and smoldering wood was mixed with another scent on the wind, a scent that was fresh and cold and salt-sweet.

The sea. It could be nothing else. Impossibly, she was somewhere near the sea. If she could just get a look at it—see what sort of beach or boats or resorts or people were at the edge of this sea—maybe she could gain some clue as to where she was.

She raced up the hill, past the black and broken twigs and branches of the ruined tree, some of which still smoldered on the bright green carpet of wet grass. She slipped once, bruising and scraping her bare feet on the rough gray rocks hidden in the lush grass. But finally, gasping for breath, she reached the top of the hill.

Which was not really a hill at all.

The other half of the hill vanished in front of her, dropping hundreds of feet in a sheer cliff to the wild and crashing sea below.

There were no people, or boats, or civilization of any kind to be seen—only barren rocks and a cold gray-green sea. The lowering sun had nearly touched the horizon now, and as Christine watched, it painted the cliffs in eerie shades of dark red.

Bloodred, like the color on the sword of the warrior after he'd run it through the rough-looking man.

Christine fell to her knees in despair, heedless of the cold dampness which soaked through her long white gown. What was this place, where everything was violence and blood, even the stone walls of the cliffs? Was she still caught in some hideous nightmare? Had she died and gone to hell?

Was this what hell was, when you could not wake up from your dreams? Slowly she got to her feet and moved to the very edge of the cliff.

Her fear and confusion began to give way to a kind of giddiness, and her trembling threatened to turn into nervous giggling. This had to be a dream, she thought, for she could never have stood in such a place in real life! It was like looking down from the top of the tallest skyscraper she could imagine, down and down and down, only here there were no familiar streets or cars or pedestrians. There was only the crashing sea and the bloodred broken boulders at the bottom of the cliff.

Perhaps there was one way to wake up. Christine stared down at the sea as the cold fresh wind blew over her. If she fell—if she allowed herself to go over the side of the cliff—then surely that would force her to awaken. And if it did not, if she truly was awake and alive and trapped in this unknown nightmare world, then at least she would be free of it.

She stood motionless, staring out at the line of red and purple where the sea met the black-clouded sky in the glow of the dying sun.

There was a rustling, thudding noise behind her. Startled, she wavered and struggled to catch her balance, her hands reaching out over the waiting sea—

Strong arms caught her around her waist and hauled her away from the edge of the cliff. She was pulled hard into the embrace of some mad giant who threw her to the wet grass and rolled her over and over down the hillside, its wool garments rough against her skin even through her nightgown.

When the rolling finally stopped Christine scrambled madly to her feet, slipping and stumbling on the slick grass and the long gown and struggling to get away from the powerful grip on her waist. "Let me go!" she screamed, desperation making her almost as angry as she was frightened.

The arms released her with a suddenness that made her stumble and almost fall again. She began to run once more, racing along the grass at the edge of the cliffs, knowing she was trapped between the roaring sea and the unseen giant behind her.

Again she was caught and sent rolling in the grass.

Christine squirmed and struggled and fell sprawling, the breath knocked out of her. Finally, her wind-blown hair falling across her eyes, she raised her head to look at her tormentor.

Crouching a few feet away was the blond warrior, his red cloak rippling in the wind from the sea. He watched her closely, one hand open and extended toward her, as if to catch her if she moved again.

Ever so slowly Christine sat up. The man's eyes followed her every move, but he stayed where he was. She studied him, breathing deeply of the reviving sea air, and thought once more about the cliffs just behind her and the waiting sea below.

But she knew, even as she had stood looking out over that fearsome drop, that she could not let herself take the final step over the edge. She was terrified; she might be trapped in a nightmare; she might truly be mad; but she was not one to take her own life.

Not even in a dream.

The man stood up, arms at his sides, and then extended one hand to her in what was clearly an offer to help her to her feet. Christine looked at his blue-gray eyes, staring and solemn, and knew that if there was any help for her in this strange world it did not lie at the bottom of the cliff.

Shaking only a little, she reached out to the powerful warrior. She feared he would haul her roughly to her feet, and then—she was afraid to imagine what might happen after that. But he simply moved close enough for her to close her small white hand over his huge tanned fingers.

There was a feeling of power in him, like nothing she had ever felt from any man she had ever touched before. It was more than the sheer strength of the iron muscles beneath his skin; it was the life force surging through him, like a current of power, that flowed through Christine as she grasped his hand. It made her feel as though she were drawing power from the heat of the sun, or the tides of the sea, or a crackling strike of lightning.

Christine felt strength beginning to return after the shock of suddenly finding herself in this place. The man stood solid as a forest tree while she pulled herself up to stand before him, the sea wind whipping her wet gown about her feet and blowing wide the man's dark red cloak.

"Welcome, Brighid," he said, his voice soft, almost whispering.

She looked up at his face, her mouth open with astonishment. He had spoken to her—spoken in words she could understand! Somehow she had thought she would not be able to understand these people—they were so strange, so foreign to her. But she had understood this man's words.

Even plainer to her was the message in his powerful hands that now slid gently, carefully, beneath her own. She held tight to them, steadying herself, and tried to think of some sort of appropriate response.

"Ah . . . thank you," Christine said. "How—how did you know my name?" One of my names, she thought.

His face softened, and his eyes shone almost like a child's. It was a strange contrast to see that expression on the face of such a huge and powerful warrior.

"I know you well, Brighid," he whispered. "You accepted the gift I offered you. I called on you when the battle turned, and you came. You came to me. I can hardly believe it, but you are here . . . you are here." His fingers gripped her own, and he looked at her with those shining eyes as though she were the answer to a prayer.

With a shock, she remembered where she had seen those eyes before—and that noble face, and that tall, strong body, and that powerful presence.

He was the image of the blond man she had met in Professor Vaughn's office. Standing in front of him was like standing in front of Mr. Donalson. Well, she thought, if I'm going to dream about a man, it may as well be the most exciting one I've ever met! Except, of course, she didn't know if she was dreaming.

"I thought my family would be killed," he went on. "The other men were away, and I alone was there to defend the women and the children. If I had died, they might all have been destroyed."

61

Christine blinked. So he had been defending his home when he had so brutally struck down the rough little man. And yes, there had been women and children in the small house where she had awakened. But why was he looking at her that way, as though she were something much more than just a lost and frightened woman? And why did he talk as if he had somehow been expecting her?

"Tonight begins your festival, Brighid," he said, and she could feel joy and excitement surging through him. "Tonight the fire will be lit. What other time would you choose to walk among men? And because you chose to come to us, to Dun Orga, all our family is alive. We will all be there to celebrate together."

It was all too much. She had no idea what he was talking about. *Your festival*, he had said. Her mind struggled to think. Did he mean her birthday? Yes, tomorrow was her birthday: the first of February. Was that what he was talking about?

But why was this man so transfixed by the idea of her birthday? What did that have to do with why she was here?

Here. Suddenly she had to know. She might not be able to figure out why or how she had gotten here, or what her birthday had to do with it, but she at least wanted to know where *here* was.

The sky was still dark with clouds. The light was fading fast as the sun slid down behind the sea. "Please," she begged, gripping his hands tightly as the cold wind tore at her gown and hair, "where is this place? Where am I?"

"Where, Brighid?" The blond man seemed puzzled, but the ghost of a smile returned. "You have come to Dun Orga, home of the family of King Donaill. And we welcome you."

"Well, of course," Christine murmured, releasing his hands and turning away. "That makes it all perfectly clear." For a hopeless moment she felt the giddiness of despair begin to sweep over her again. "I seem to have met up with the official crazy-lady welcome wagon."

But she refused to give way to helplessness. Drawing a deep breath, Christine sternly told herself that there was nothing to be gained by giving up. Lifting her chin, she turned and looked up into those shining slate-blue eyes. "But where is—what did you say—Dun Orga? What country? Where?"

This time, his mouth opened slightly and his eyes widened. He's afraid he's made a mistake of some kind, Christine thought, wondering why on earth he would be worried about making her angry.

"Eire," he said quickly. "You are in the land of Eire."

It was a word she had never heard before. *Air-eh,* he had said. Eire. The land of Eire.

Eire-land.

Ireland?

Ireland! Quickly she looked around her again. Christine had been to Ireland only once, when she was fifteen, for a brief visit with her very elderly great-grandparents. Could she somehow be in Ireland again?

She tried to remember what she knew about Ireland. It was an island, she knew that much; that would explain the cliffs and the ocean. And she had never seen grass so thick and green at this time of the year. Wasn't Ireland called the Emerald Isle?

But as she looked up at the face of the warrior again, the twilight deepened and the wind grew colder. She began shivering.

How on earth could she have gotten to Ireland? And how would being in Ireland explain these strange, wild people and their primitive little village? Ireland was a modern country now; barbarian tribes hadn't existed there since . . .

What had Mr. Donalson said about the ancient

tribes in Europe? The ones who might have made her torque? 400 A.D.

Christine stared in horror at the man standing next to her. Her mind reeled. It couldn't be. It was impossible.

The last thing she remembered before waking up and finding herself here was putting on the torque. Her hand went up to her neck; yes, the torque was still there, cold and heavy. The blond man had touched it when he had first approached her, back in the little house.

But what had happened after she put on the torque, back in her own apartment? Why could she remember nothing after that? Maybe there had been an accident; maybe she'd slipped and fallen, or fainted, and hit her head; and now she was either dreaming or experiencing a loss of memory.

Christine relaxed slightly. Such things did happen to people, to perfectly sane and normal people. Something had happened to her memory, and if she had no memory that pretty well explained why she couldn't remember what had happened to her memory!

She grinned, and then burst out with a short laugh as relief flooded through her. The huge man looked down at her with amazement, and then he grinned as his own relief and joy lit up his face.

"You are happy now, Brighid," he said. "Happy to be among those who love you, your children in Eire."

She looked at him, not really understanding what he was saying, but certain now that eventually she would. It did not matter where or when she was; it was obviously out of her control. The only thing she had on her side was time.

"Yes, I am happy," Christine said, and shivered again. "And cold, too, I'm afraid."

Quickly he reached up and undid the intricate round gold brooch which held his cloak. He pulled the red expanse of wool from his shoulders, which left him wearing only his simple yellow-gold tunic and dark brown leather pants, and wrapped the warm red wool around her.

It was rectangular in shape, she saw, like a blanket, not long and bell shaped the way she had always pictured medieval cloaks. And so heavy. She'd never thought about the weight of clothes before. Her own suede and nylon jackets kept her warm as toast, but weighed nothing at all. This cloak was thick and heavy around her shoulders and already warm from his body. The heat of it stole through her.

"Thank you," Christine said, and a sudden realization hit her. "I don't even know your name, and you've been very kind. Please—I've told you mine. What is your name?"

He was on one knee before her again, and his eyes were now level with hers. "I am Ailin," he said. "I am Ailin whom you have chosen to walk with here in Eire for a time. I am your servant, and your champion."

Well, yes, thank you, that's very nice, Christine thought, afraid she would burst out laughing again. Just what every lady needs. She knew she had nothing to fear from him; for some reason, this man wanted to help and protect her, and she was certain she was safe with him.

"Ailin," she answered, smiling at him. *Allen.* It seemed funny that such a strange and powerful man would have such an ordinary name.

He stood up again and ever so gently began to draw her down the hill. "Darkness is coming," he said, "and you are shivering. Let me take you to my home. We will care for you as befits a goddess in human form, come to walk the earth."

Yes, she was shivering and cold, even in the heavy cloak. Her bare feet felt like ice on the wet grass. "All right, Ailin," she said. "Please. Take me to your home." Holding on to his strong hand, she began to follow him down the hill to his fortress home.

If anyone had told her that before the day was out she would be walking home with a giant warrior who had killed two men before her eyes, she'd have told them they were crazy. But Christine felt a strange but unmistakable sense of security in Ailin's presence. He knew who she was, even if she didn't, and she certainly had nowhere else to go.

She would go with Ailin to the little walled village and try to stay as calm as possible. Christine could only hope that before too long she would find out what had happened, her mind would begin to heal, and life would get back to normal.

By the time they reached the foot of the hill, the western sky had turned that deep shade of blue that comes just before blackness. A few stars gleamed near the horizon. The heavy gate of the fortress now stood open wide, and the grounds were lit with the flickering, flaring light from dozens of torches.

Christine pressed close to Ailin as they walked through the gate and across the grounds. She drew strength from the warmth and sheer power of his presence, and found that her curiosity about this place was becoming as strong as her fear and uncertainty.

All around them were groups of men and women dressed in bright wool tunics and cloaks, adorned with magnificent golden brooches and headbands and, she noticed for the first time, torques—many of them very like her own. Her hand automatically reached up to touch the heavy gold piece around her neck.

Every head turned to look at her as she passed. But instead of the awed silence of the afternoon, the air was filled with the excited whispers and low conversations of the crowd as they stared at Ailin and the strange new woman who walked beside him.

There was a rattling and pounding behind them. Christine turned just in time to see two chariots sweep through the open gate, drawn by pairs of snorting, galloping ponies. Christine stared at them as the ponies swept past, fascinated by the unexpected sight. She had thought chariots were used only in ancient Rome—but this was most definitely not Rome.

Besides a driver, each of these chariots carried a tall, proud, heavily armed man, standing with one hand clutching the chariot's side. The men's cloaks rippled in the night wind. Each one raised his hand to Ailin in greeting as they passed, and he returned the gesture as the chariots pulled up beside one of the long white buildings.

"Who are they?" Christine asked, as Ailin gently turned her toward the houses. She stepped carefully over the wet and muddy ground, trying to pick her way in the wavering shadows cast by the flaring torchlight.

"They are my uncles, Irial and Lorcan," he said. "They have their own Duns, some distance from here, but because my father is the oldest of them they all come here for the Imbolc feast."

"Oh. Then it's like a family reunion," Christine said. She truly wanted to understand these strange people, and the only way to do that was to try to put things into terms that made sense in her world. "That's what we'd call it back where I come from, anyway. A family reunion, for the holiday."

Ailin smiled down at her. "It could be called a reunion of the family," he said. "Though these are only the ones who live closest to Dun Orga; not many care to travel far in the cold and damp of winter. There are others, farther away, and we will see them in the fair days of summer."

They reached the small house that Christine had escaped just a short time ago. It now had two torches stuck on poles on either side of it. With a chill she remembered the dead man she had seen lying on the grass when she ran out the door. Thankfully there was no sign of him now.

They walked inside the house. This place is becoming pretty familiar, Christine thought. She was almost used to seeing the high-beamed straw ceiling, the fur-covered sleeping ledges, the handsome wooden chests in the corners, and the dirt floor covered with long dried grasses.

She stopped just inside the door and pulled the heavy red cloak from her shoulders. Folding it over, she handed it to Ailin.

"Thank you," she whispered. "I could never have made it without you."

Ailin's eyes shone as his hand tightened over hers, filling her once again with that strange and wonderful feeling of power and warmth. "I will always be here for you, Brighid."

At that moment, Christine had no doubt of that.

Chapter Six

The room was warm from the fire on the central hearth, and there was a wonderful smell of roast meat and fresh-baked bread in the air. A faint wave of dizziness washed over her, forcing Christine to realize how tired and hungry she was. She leaned against Ailin and closed her eyes. The accumulated shocks of the day were beginning to add up.

"Please," Ailin said, and allowed his fingers to lightly touch the thin white cotton of her gown. The heat of his fingertips burned into Christine's shoulder. "Go and rest. We will take care of you."

Gratefully Christine smiled up at him, and as he lifted his fingers she turned away to walk into the house.

She stepped gingerly through the dried grass over to the sleeping ledge where she had awakened. Climbing up on the fur-covered ledge, she sat down with her ice-cold feet tucked up beneath her, trying to work them inside the warm furs, and cupped her hands in front of her mouth to warm her numbed fingers with her breath.

Two women stood across the room, both of them tall and straight and beautiful, dressed in long woolen gowns of bright red. One wore a green cloak over her gown and had her hair in two long red-gold braids; the other had the front of her pale hair pulled up high on the top of her head while the back hung long and free over her cloak of blue.

Christine guessed that they were probably about her own age, though it was hard to tell for certain. Their long hair and smooth, unlined faces made them seem quite young, but both carried an air of wisdom and experience that spoke of greater maturity.

The two women gazed at Christine with the kind of awed respect that, until now, she had seen given only to royalty and movie stars. She offered a timid smile in return, and was rewarded with bright smiles from both of them.

"This is Derval," Ailin said, nodding to the woman with the long braids, "and Slaine." The woman with the flowing hair smiled up at Ailin. "They are my sisters-in-law, the wives of my brothers, Cronan and Finn."

Der-val. Slay-nee. Christine tried hard to fix the unfamiliar names in her mind. "It's very nice to meet you both," she said.

A silence filled the room. They all seemed to be waiting for her to say something. Well, better make a stab at polite conversation, Christine thought. "Ah—do you also live here in—in Dun Orga?" *There—I remembered the name of the place. I think!*

"We both live in Dun Orga," Derval answered.

"With our husbands, in the other houses like this one," added Slaine.

Again Christine marveled that she could understand these people so well and they could understand her. As she sat on the ledge, trying to think of something else wildly clever to say, the drafts from the open doorway began finding their way into the room. An involuntary shiver swept over her and she turned to look at the two women standing near the far wall, uncertain how to ask for what she needed.

Derval and Slaine glanced at each other, and then at Ailin. He took a step toward the door. "I will leave you with my sisters-in-law, Brighid," he said. "You will not find better servants."

"Thanks," Christine said faintly. "I, ah, I guess I'll see you later?" She was suddenly frightened again at the prospect of his leaving—leaving her here, alone, where he was the only thing she knew.

"I will return for you," he said. "If you allow me, I will walk with you to the bonfire."

Relief swept over her. So he would be coming back after all. She almost said "It's a date," but caught herself just in time. They might understand the language, all right, but somehow she just didn't think anyone here would comprehend a "date." So she settled instead for a grateful nod and the best smile she could manage—which wasn't much, under the circumstances. Her teeth were chattering.

Ailin smiled back at her as he left the little house, and Christine felt the warmth of it all the way across the room. But that warmth dissolved as soon as he closed the door behind him, and once again she found herself alone.

The woman with the long braids picked up a soft bundle and approached the ledge where Christine shivered. "Lady, here is a fur-lined cloak," she said softly.

Derval, Christine remembered. This was Derval.

"Perhaps you should . . ." The woman faltered, and then tried again. "If you wish, you could take off the wet gown, and wrap up in this cloak."

"And sit by the fire," Slaine added helpfully, coming over to stand beside Derval.

Christine grinned. "That's the best offer I've had all day," she said, reaching out stiffly for the heavy cloak.

She was beginning to understand now. Apparently it was the custom for the guest to make her needs

71

known, instead of forcing the host to do the offering. Well, she could certainly learn to do the polite thing, if nothing else. It would help her to fit in—she hoped.

"Thank you, Derval," Christine said gratefully. "That sounds wonderful. And don't worry. I'll be sure to ask if I need anything else."

Derval's eyes grew wide, and shone brightly. "The goddess will always make her wishes known to us," she whispered, as Slaine came over to stand silently beside her.

"Yes, I'm sure she—" Christine stopped, looking at the awe and worship in the two staring faces.

They each wore the same reverent expression Ailin had worn when he knelt down before her out on the windy cliffs. The two women gazed at her with luminous, hungry eyes, as though she were a being from another world who had come in answer to their prayers.

The realization finally hit her. When Derval and Slaine—and Ailin—talked about "the goddess," they didn't mean *she*. They meant her. They meant *Christine*.

Christine sat very still. The weight of the fur-lined cloak sank into her lap. She thought back to Ailin's words, hearing once again the things he had said to her out there on the cliffs.

I called on you when the battle turned, and you came.

What other day would you choose to walk among men?

We will care for you as befits a goddess in human form, come to walk the earth. . . .

And more than anything, Christine remembered the look in Ailin's eyes as he had said those things. It had been a look of reverence, and awe, and worship.

These women were convinced she was a goddess. And so was Ailin. Well, she certainly could not let them go on believing such a thing. They might be as confused as she was about why she was here, but the last thing she wanted them to do was think she was some kind of magical deity!

She held up one hand to emphasize her words. "No—no, please. You don't understand," she began.

Derval and Slaine stood together in silence, hanging on her every word. "I am not a goddess. Not even close! I don't know how I got here, and I'm sure you don't either, but I am certain of one thing. I'm just an ordinary, real, live woman, just like you.

"Look at me," Christine pleaded, reaching up to clutch at her thin nightgown as sudden tears burned her eyes. "Would I be sitting here like this, lost and shivering and scared, if I were some kind of goddess? If I were, believe me, I'd just click my heels three times and go straight home to the good old U.S.A.! But I can't make that happen."

She wiped away a tear, and then looked up bravely at them. "I'm sorry to intrude on you like this. Really, I am. But there's nothing I can do about it. Nothing at all."

Derval looked down at her with tenderness and sympathy, and with gentle fingers took hold of Christine's icy hands. "It does not matter, lady," she said softly. "If you are not Brighid herself, you were surely sent by her for Ailin—and for us."

"We saw what happened with our own eyes," added Slaine. "You ran out of Ailin's house just in time to dazzle the enemy. Those thieves would have killed Ailin if you had not been there."

"You were not here before," Derval said. "None of us had ever seen you. But you came at the right time, just as Ailin called on the goddess to help him—and only the goddess could have sent you."

Derval gave Christine's hands a gentle squeeze, and without another word she and Slaine turned back to the tasks they had at hand. Derval stirred something in the great bronze pot hanging over the fire in the center of the room, and Slaine began rummaging through a chest at the foot of the other sleeping ledge. As Christine sat in stunned silence, it was as though she were entirely alone.

Christine looked down at the heavy roll of fur and wool in her lap. She slid her hands beneath it to warm her fingers as the women's words ran through her mind.

Derval and Slaine and Ailin thought she was a goddess. No—not exactly. They thought she'd been *sent* by a goddess.

She closed her eyes and sighed deeply. All right. So they thought a goddess had brought her to this place. Well, what else would they think? This was a primitive, backward civilization compared to the one she was used to. Such thinking was bound to be commonplace here.

A primitive civilization. Though the idea terrified her, Christine forced herself to face the thing she had begun to suspect during those panicked moments when she'd fled the fortress and run out to the cliffs.

Somehow she had come to exist in a world she'd thought to be long past—a world that was dry and dusty history in her own time, but that had suddenly become very real and very much alive for her.

A world that might be the only one she would ever have again.

She considered. If one of these people had suddenly appeared in her own world—her own time— how would modern people have reacted?

By calling the nice men with the white coats and butterfly nets, she thought. She was lucky in that respect; here, at least, they didn't seem to have insane asylums. Ladies who appeared out of nowhere and behaved rather strangely were simply those sent by goddesses.

The people here were explaining her appearance in a way that made sense to them. She could hardly blame them for that. And if anybody was silly enough to believe she really was some kind of goddess, they'd be in for a real disappointment in short order.

The wet and smoldering oak tree glowed in the darkness. Its twisted, blasted limbs ran with lines of flickering flame, and curls of smoke and steam rose up from it into the night.

Ailin ran his fingers over the wounded tree. He brushed away the cracked and broken bark, and leaned down to look deep into the heart of the glowing wood.

There was no sign of the golden torque. He had feared that he would find it somewhere within the tree, ruined by the lightning and the fire. But it was gone without a trace.

Joy surged through him, and a hope and expectation that he hardly dared to feel. His heart was filled with love for his goddess, for she who had finally turned her head to notice him.

"You have heard," he whispered. "You have answered. Can it be true? The goddess come to walk with me at last? All my life has been dedicated to you, Lady Brighid, Lady of Fire. I have always been here for you and you have come to me at last, come only for me, and you are beautiful, so beautiful."

He thought again of the unearthly woman who had appeared so suddenly in front of his house . . . dressed all in white, her eyes bright as she screamed her fury at his enemies . . . and around her neck, shining like the flames that had forged it and sent it on its way, was the torque he had made for her, made with his own hands only for her.

And when she had seen him, and heard him speak her name in recognition, she had allowed herself to fall into his arms so that he might lift her up and care for her—a goddess made mortal, a goddess who knew how he loved her and who had come at last to accept that love for herself.

If he thought he had loved her before, this abstract

goddess, it was nothing compared to the love that filled his heart for the woman form she had chosen, the form that had lain so trustingly in his arms as he carried her into the house—his house.

Tonight was her night, Brighid's night, and he could scarcely wait for the ceremony to begin. He would have the chance to thank her properly for coming to him.

A shadow crossed his mind. Yes, she had chosen to accept his love for a time, as she had accepted his gift of the torque—but how long might she choose to stay?

He closed his eyes, and his fingers dug into the crumbling bark of the oak. He would never lose her; he would never let her go. Love and worship were all that a goddess needed, and he would give her love such as even a goddess had never known. Without it she would fade away and vanish from the world, but that would never happen to the Lady of Fire, his lady. . . .

Christine shivered, and decided she'd been cold long enough. Derval and Slaine continued their work on the other side of the room, and so Christine quickly pulled the thick cloak out of her lap and up around her head and shoulders. Hidden beneath its heavy folds, she began shrugging out of the cold, wet nightgown.

After a few moments of wriggling and pulling, the gown was finally off. She tossed it aside on the ledge and hugged the cloak tightly around her. This one was also made of heavy red wool, like Ailin's cloak, but was lined with the most beautiful creamy tan fur she had ever seen. Christine marveled at the incredible softness of the fur against her cold bare skin.

She had never worn a genuine fur coat. She knew that fake fur was better, of course, since she didn't want any animal to have to sacrifice its own coat for her, but this—this was nothing like the coarse fuzz-

iness of even the best fake fur. This was luxury of a
kind she'd never thought to experience.

The heavy warmth of the fur and wool stole
through her, and Christine was finally able to stop
shivering. Her eyes began to close in relaxation—but
suddenly flew open again.

Slaine stood just a few steps away, holding a stack
of folded fabrics. She waited, standing patiently, as
though she were prepared to wait forever.

Christine smiled up at her. "Ah, Slaine, would it
be possible for me to borrow some clothes? My
nightgown is wet, and it seems to be . . . the only
thing I have with me at the moment."

The blond woman gave her a glowing smile. "Lady,
these clothes are yours, if they are to your liking."
Slaine set down the stack and stepped back a pace,
waiting to see what the verdict was.

"Thank you," Christine said gratefully. "I'm sure
they will be." Slaine's eyes shone, and then she
turned and went back to her tasks on the other side
of the little house.

Alone once again, Christine examined the clothes
Slaine had left for her. Lying on the top of the stack
was a soft belt of dark brown leather; at least, she
thought it was a belt. It was very long, and covered
with curving, interlacing lines that had been delicately carved into the surface of the leather. It must
have taken someone hours and hours to do such
work.

The belt also had a large gold ring at one end instead of a buckle, and she noticed that there were no
holes in it. She'd have to ask someone how to wear
it.

She set the belt aside and lifted up the next piece.
This was a long simple gown of linen, in a color
somewhere between white and cream. It looked like
a long nightgown or a floor-length slip.

The fabric was heavy and a little stiff, very different from her own soft nightgown. A pure linen gown

would have been quite expensive back in her own world—yet here, apparently, everyone wore them every day.

The last piece was a beautiful heavy wool dress in a warm shade of deep golden brown. It had a low, curving neckline and the sleeves were bell shaped; she guessed they would come down just past her elbows. But Christine's attention was drawn to the embroidery that covered the gown's neckline, hem, and cuffs.

Never had she seen such work. Curving, roiling bands of brightly colored embroidery were interlaced and intertwined in a pattern that she found impossible to decipher. And the colors—there seemed to be every color of the rainbow in those intricate bands and lines. Red and yellow were the brightest and boldest, with vibrant blue and green appearing in the borders and outlines.

Christine ran her finger over the incredible work. "Magnificent," she whispered. If the linen gown would have been expensive back in her world, this would have been priceless.

She decided that the longer linen gown must be meant to go underneath the shorter wool one. And even if it wasn't, she'd wear it like that anyway—and start a new fashion if she must. Her own coats and sweaters were not here to keep her warm. With the cold dampness of the night closing in, and the memory of shivering in the wind still fresh in her mind, Christine was determined to put as many layers between herself and the elements as she could.

Slaine and Derval were still working busily, their backs to her, and so she shrugged off the cloak and quickly pulled the linen underdress over her head. Easing to the floor, she stood up and let the dress fall into place.

It was long, too long; the hem of it lay in a heap on the dried grasses around her feet. But there was nothing she could do but wear it, at least for now.

Maybe later Derval or Slaine could loan her a needle and thread and let her take up the hem a few inches.

As she had suspected, the fabric was a little stiff and scratchy, especially since she had no underclothes at all. But she didn't think there were likely to be any pantyhose or nylon slips or camisoles in those carved wooden chests, so she'd just have to make the best of it.

Christine reached for the embroidered woolen gown, and carefully lifted it up and allowed it to slide down over her head. Beautiful as it was, it, too, was heavy and scratchy, and she gave fervent thanks that she was not allergic to wool.

This one fit a little better, falling about halfway between her knees and ankles. She held out the hem to look at the full magnificent display of the hand-worked embroidery. It covered the entire hem, the neckline, and the cuffs of the sleeves. She held up one arm, admiring the splendid winding colors.

She looked up to see Derval waiting for her with yet another bundle in her arms. "This is the most beautiful gown I've ever seen," Christine said, and meant it. "I wouldn't have believed such work was possible if I hadn't seen it."

"Thank you, lady," Derval said with a shy smile. "I began the work over the last Imbolc. It kept me busy for many a night."

"Oh—then this is your gown?" Christine was torn between embarrassment at taking someone else's things and flattery at being given what was clearly the very best. "Really, I don't want to take your things—especially something as fine and special as this."

Derval laid a gentle hand on Christine's arm. "Lady, I never hoped to have it worn by one such as you. I cannot tell you how happy it makes me to be able to offer it to you."

Christine saw the pride and happiness in Derval's expression, and knew that it would hurt the woman terribly if she were to refuse the gown. "Then I am happy to wear it for you."

Derval held out the bundle she carried. "Please try these on, lady," she said. "You will have need of them, too, I think."

Christine accepted the bundle. Like the belt, it was of a dark brown color, and as she took it the bundle fell into two parts. "Oh—boots!"

And beautiful boots they were, made of folded leather so soft that it was almost like suede. They were lined with the same heavenly tan fur that made up her cloak. Christine eased her cold feet into the boots, which came up past her ankles. Derval knelt down in the dried grass and folded the soft brown leather around Christine's ankles, adjusting the boots until the fit was exactly right. Then she fastened the folds with intricate twists of a long leather thong.

Finally Christine was dressed. The linen underdress was a little scratchy, and the wool gown sometimes poked through the linen weave in spots and felt a little prickly, but she was so glad to be warm and dry and decently dressed that she did not mind at all.

Chapter Seven

Christine stood up, the dried grass rustling beneath her soft boots, and smoothed down the woolen gown. Only the belt was left. She lifted it up by the wide gold ring and turned to the two women. "I'm not sure about the right way to wear this, I'm afraid. . . ."

As Derval got up from kneeling on the floor, Slaine stepped forward to help, and Christine caught sight of the belt that the young blond woman wore over her own red wool gown. Her belt was like Christine's, though the carving was not so intricate, with a single ring instead of a buckle. Christine studied it closely and saw how the end of the belt was pulled through the ring, drawn snugly around the waist, and then tied in a single turn around the belt leather behind the ring. The end was left to hang long and free down the front of the gown.

She managed it on the first try. How simple! Her spirits rose a bit at being able to manage the simple task of dressing herself.

The carving on the belt was another work of art, like the embroidery on the gown. Christine supposed that the long belt was worn just for style, since the gowns would have been just as comfortable without it. But then she discovered that here, a belt had a practical use, too.

Derval looked down at Christine's feet. They were hidden by the folds of the too-long linen gown. Both of the women were taller than Christine and she was not surprised that their clothes would be too long for her. But Derval seemed to be trying to tell her something else.

"Lady, is the gown too long for comfort? There is a way to adjust it." She started to reach out toward Christine, hesitated, and finally caught hold of the top of her own linen undergown with the fingertips of both hands. "All you need do, you see, is lift the gown up from the top—just pull it up through the belt, and the belt will hold the gown in place wherever you wish."

Christine did as she suggested, lifting the linen dress up and pulling the wool gown down over it. Sure enough, the long underdress was now just the right length.

"Thank you! I wish I'd thought of that. I guess belts are more than just fashion statements around here."

Slaine beamed at Christine. "We often have the young girls do that when they begin to wear their older sisters' gowns—"

Derval whirled around to stare at Slaine. She stopped, raising a hand to her mouth in horror as she realized what she had said.

Christine giggled. "It's all right, really," she said, feeling both amused and relieved at Slaine's comparison. "I really am just your little sister, in more ways than you can know. And I'll need all the help you can give me as long as I'm—as long as I'm here."

Slaine took a step toward Christine and held out a wooden comb. "We will help you in any way you wish, lady. And now, if you will, I will fix your hair for you."

Christine lifted her hand up to her hair. It was matted and damp and windblown from her desperate race along the cliffs. "I must look like a real mess," she said, a little embarrassed. Here she was supposed to be a goddess, and instead she probably looked more like a little girl who'd been out playing in the rain. "I'd be glad to have you fix my hair, Slaine, if you'd like to."

Christine settled herself on the ledge as Slaine gently, carefully started work on her tangled hair. Now that she was a bit more secure and comfortable, she could begin to think back on the wild events of the day and try to make some sense of them.

"Derval," she said, gazing down at the grasses on the floor as Slaine worked on her hair, "what happened this afternoon? Who were those people who attacked your home? Why did they do it?"

She felt Slaine's fingers tense, and heard the anger and distress in Derval's voice. "They were the *gadai*," she said, her voice low and trembling. "Outcasts. Fugitives. They hide in the bogs, in places not fit for animals to live. They get what they need by stealing."

"Usually they go to small farmsteads under cover of darkness, being too cowardly to fight like men." Slaine tugged slightly at Christine's hair. "They've never tried to come here—never dared get close enough to Dun Orga to touch the refuse in the pits outside the walls!"

"They thought all our men were gone hunting," Derval continued. "Somehow they failed to realize that Ailin was still here." She smiled, her lips tight. "Our brother-in-law is a formidable opponent—especially against thieving bog-trotters like the *gadai*."

"Yet still, he nearly lost his life," Christine murmured. "They ganged up on him—they almost—"

"Yɛ., almost," Derval said. Her gentle smile returned. "But he called on you, and you came to him when he needed you most. He is alive, and so are we all, because of you."

So they all believed the same story. They all believed that she had somehow saved their lives by distracting the enemy long enough for Ailin to regain his feet, kill the rough-looking man, and drive the rest away.

Christine closed her eyes. Whatever she had done, it had been purely an accident. She had simply awakened here, run outside, and screamed at just the right moment to help Ailin. It had not been done deliberately, or by plan.

At least, not by any plan that she herself had made.

"But they will not get away so easily as they think they have," said Slaine, setting down the comb. She lifted Christine's damp hair and began to separate it. "Our warriors will find them. And the *gadai* will regret that the thought of trying to invade Dun Orga ever entered their slow skulls." She began twisting one side of Christine's hair into a braid.

Christine lifted her hand to Slaine's, and the woman froze at her touch. "No, please, Slaine, I—I don't think I want my hair in a braid. Though Derval's is lovely," she added quickly, and so it was. The long red-gold braids fell down past her waist and looked quite elegant on the tall woman, but Christine knew that she would feel about twelve years old if she went about with her own shoulder-length hair in pigtails.

She did not want to look, or feel, twelve years old in front of Ailin.

Slaine's voice trembled. "I'm sorry, lady. Of course, I should have asked you first." She quickly undid the braid she had started. Picking up the wooden comb, she drew it carefully through Christine's long hair, still wavy from the dampness.

Christine sat very still as Slaine worked. She felt sorry that she had hurt the woman's feelings, but was increasingly confident that she had done the right thing.

She would do as much as she could to try to fit in here. She would wear long linen gowns and walk on a grass-covered floor and sleep on a fur-lined ledge and, yes, from time to time put in appearances that saved warriors' lives. But she would not become someone else. And even a little thing like how she wore her hair could make all the difference when it came to maintaining her own familiar identity in a totally unfamiliar world.

A strange and frightening world, she thought, as cold fear crept up on her again. But with a strength of will she'd never known she possessed, Christine pushed those thoughts away.

As much as she wanted to go home, she knew that she would not find the way by giving in to fear and anguish. Christine held on instead to the sight of the two women here with her, trying as best they could to be helpful and friendly.

Keeping her mind calm and open and working properly was certainly the best way to deal with this very strange situation. She had to stay strong. And she would draw strength from wherever she could find it.

Strength. With a rush, that thought filled her mind with the sudden vision of a powerful blond man in a red cloak, his hair bound by a gold coronet.

Ailin. The mere thought of him sent the blood pounding through her veins and filled her with renewed determination. He would be returning soon. And she wanted to be ready.

Derval turned back to the cauldron at the hearth, ladling something into a wooden bowl. The rich scent of the food wafted over to Christine and suddenly she realized that she wasn't just hungry—she was ravenous. Whatever Derval was preparing smelled absolutely wonderful.

Slaine was just putting the final touches on Christine's hair with the wooden comb. "I—ah, Slaine . . ." She paused, still a little embarrassed at having to ask them for everything. But hunger was rapidly trampling such niceties. "I've hardly eaten at all today,"

Christine went on, "and I'm really very hungry. May I please share some of your supper with you?"

"Of course, lady. Look, Derval has already prepared it." As she spoke, Derval came back to the ledge with a large rectangular platter made of polished wood. It was laden with food. Savory steam rose from the platter, drifting enticingly beneath Christine's nostrils as Slaine handed her the platter.

"Oh, thank you, thank you so much," she said, her mouth watering. "It smells wonderful."

I really must find some way to repay them for all this, Christine thought, looking up at their anxious faces. She knew, though, that she'd have to find a way to do it on her own. She'd never be able to just come out and ask them how she could repay them, for she was sure they'd simply refuse any favors she offered to do them. But she'd find a way.

The two women stepped back a pace, their boots rustling in the dried grasses, and waited as Christine looked down at the platter. At the center of it was a wooden bowl filled with a kind of hot stew—chunks of meat and pieces of carrot and onion swam in a thick, steaming brown gravy.

On one side of the bowl were two small, flat, round loaves of bread, still soft and warm. On the other side was a chunk of butter, so pale that it was almost white, and a thick golden puddle of something that could only be honey.

There was no fork or spoon; not even a knife. Christine was so hungry that she was ready to dip her fingers into the hot gravy, but stopped herself. That would be messy and uncomfortable, and quite possibly impolite. Instead she broke off a piece of bread and used that to dip out a bite of the stew.

She chewed cautiously at first, and then faster, savoring the salty gravy, strong, flavorful meat, and sweet, mild carrots and onions. She tore off more of the bread and began devouring the stew. Derval and Slaine looked at each other and smiled.

Christine grinned up at them, feeling better now than she had in quite a while. Here she was in a strange and beautiful land, waited on and worshiped, presented with the finest of handmade clothes to wear and given the most delicious food to eat. Maybe she really had died and gone to heaven.

But just in case she had not, she'd better start finding out more about this place and the people and customs in it.

She wanted to know more about the celebration that was going on tonight. The problem was, she did not know the name of the holiday, and she did not want to embarrass Derval and Slaine—and herself— by admitting it. And she especially did not want them to realize that she knew absolutely nothing about how the holiday was celebrated. That, too, would only embarrass and confuse them.

The bowl was half empty. "Derval," she said, around another large mouthful of bread and stew, "please tell me about the—ah, about the celebration tonight."

There! Not too bad a way to pose the question. She hadn't admitted to being ignorant—she simply wanted to know what they planned to do.

"Oh," said Derval quickly, "we keep the customs as we always have, as we have been instructed."

"Please do not worry," Slaine added. "You will find nothing changed here. We celebrate Imbolc as is proper for those who love and honor the goddess. We think you will be pleased, lady." And with that, Slaine returned to the cauldron and whatever tasks awaited her there.

Imbolc. At least now she had the name of the holiday. But it was going to be difficult to get information about the customs from Derval and Slaine, when they obviously thought she already knew all about it!

But she had to know. She did not want to face

tonight—or Ailin—ignorant and scared of whatever was to happen.

Christine took a last bite of stew and tried to think back on what Ailin had said. He was going to come back for her to take her to the bonfire. Yes, she was certain he had said something about a bonfire.

"Slaine," she said, reaching for the second loaf of bread and breaking off a piece, "is there going to be a bonfire tonight?"

"Indeed there is, lady," Slaine answered, her eyes wide. "On the peak of the highest hill. It will be visible for a great, great distance, over the land and far out at sea."

"Is everyone going?" Christine asked, as if she were just checking.

"Most certainly, lady. Even now, the young men are on their way to the hill, bringing their name-stones for the fire."

Name-stones? For the fire? Christine had no idea what that meant. As she dipped the piece of bread in the butter and the honey, trying to think of some way to find out what Slaine was talking about, there was a rap at the door.

All three women quickly looked at each other, and then Derval walked over to pull open the door.

It was Ailin.

He stood framed in the small wooden doorway, his feet planted wide apart and his fists on his hips, peering into the house with serious, searching eyes. The gold band that held his blond hair glinted and gleamed in the firelight, making the slender band look like a crown studded with brilliant gems. One side of his red wool cloak was thrown back over his right shoulder, exposing his long iron sword in its heavy black leather scabbard.

The bread fell from Christine's fingers. Barely remembering to breathe, she simply sat and stared.

During those first terrifying moments when she had awakened and found herself here, Ailin had raced after her as she fled and then grabbed her out on the cliff. At that time, he—and everyone else here—had been only a source of terror to her. Then, when she'd managed to get hold of herself and try to think her way through this bizarre situation, he had delivered her to the safety of the fortress and the hospitality of this house. He had become a refuge, a protector, a source of desperately needed strength in an unknown and unpredictable world.

But now that her initial fear was past and she could look at him with a calm and rational mind, she found that his mere presence was enough to take her breath away.

"Come in please, Ailin," Derval said calmly. Christine wondered how the woman could be so matter-of-fact when she was standing so close to him. Then she realized that Derval, who was, after all, married to someone else, probably saw Ailin every day and was quite used to him.

Christine did not believe that she would ever get used to Ailin.

He bowed his head and turned slightly to come through the door; his powerful shoulders were so broad that he would scarcely have fit through the opening straight-on. The he looked up again, straight at Christine, and his solemn, blue-gray gaze locked onto hers.

The platter began sliding from her weakened grasp. Slaine quickly moved to catch it before it fell, just as Christine jumped and tried to grab it. Slaine whisked the platter away as Ailin crossed the room and knelt down in the dried grasses, directly in front of Christine.

"I have returned for you, Brighid, as I promised," he said gently. His voice was soft, tinged with the same excitement she had heard in it before. It matched the look in his eyes—his eager, shining eyes.

"I knew you would," she whispered in return, and

meant it. "I knew you would."

He reached for her hand, which she held tensely in her lap, and closed his fingers over it. A glow ran through her like a ray of sunlight at his warm, gentle touch. She sat still and silent on the ledge, caught up in his mesmerizing presence, hardly seeing or hearing anything else.

Ailin lifted his other hand, opening it to show her what was in it. "Oh . . ." Christine gave a sigh of admiration, and of disbelief, when she saw what he held.

It was a bracelet of softly glowing gold, studded with gleaming red gems and beautifully carved with the intricate knotwork patterns that were so common here. She, who loved antique jewelry, had never hoped to own anything like this.

It occurred to her that the gold would have to be real gold, and the gems real gems. No one would be making glass or plastic jewelry in this place—in this time.

Gingerly she reached out for the bracelet and lifted it from Ailin's palm. The lovely piece was heavy and substantial, in a way that made the things she remembered from her own world seem lightweight and flimsy and hardly real at all.

Everything here had a depth of fullness and richness that she had never before experienced. The weather was wilder and more affecting, the furs were thicker and softer, the clothes were heavier, the food was richer.

Even the people were different. They were so vibrant and alive, and Ailin . . . never was there a man so possessed of power and filled with life as Ailin.

"Thank you," whispered Christine, and it seemed so small a thing to say. "It's . . . it's beautiful."

His mouth curved into a smile, and his eyes continued to shine. "I am happy that you like it," he said. "I will bring you all the beautiful things that are mine to give, as many as you wish. There is nothing I would not do for you."

His voice quavered as he stared at her and his face was filled with awe. "Sometimes I simply cannot believe that you are really here."

"It's all right," Christine said, inwardly a bit amused by his incredulous attitude. "I'm not entirely sure I'm really here, either."

A shadow fell across them. It was Derval, holding a wooden cup in each hand. "My lady—Ailin—would you care for water before you go?"

Christine blinked, and then forced herself to look away from Ailin and up at Derval. "Water?" Yes, water did sound good. The stew had been rather salty. "Thank you, yes." She accept the polished wooden cup in both hands—it had no handle—and sipped the sweet, cold water. It was delicious.

Ailin lifted his hand from her fingers to take his own cup, and the heat of his skin still lingered on her hand. She was sure that if she were to look down at it, her hand would be visibly glowing from his touch.

"I must be apologize for using wooden vessels," Derval was saying. "But all the best plates and cups have already been taken to the hall for the feast."

"Feast?" Christine asked. Now that Ailin was no longer touching her, she found that she could turn her mind to practical things again. What else was going to happen tonight besides the bonfire? She wanted very much to know what to expect. "I would like to know about the feast, Ailin, if you would be so kind as to tell me."

Ailin rose quickly to his feet and handed the untouched cup back to Derval. Christine looked up and up at him; from where she sat, he seemed to tower over her. "The feast will be the finest you have ever had placed before you," he said. "We have a great deal to celebrate. And we will try to show you our gratitude by celebrating your presence tonight, though we know that we could never do enough."

Christine held up her hand, halting his eager flow of words. "You have already done more than enough," she said. "You've taken care of me, and made me feel welcome. I wasn't exactly expected, I know."

"You were not expected," Ailin whispered in agreement. "You were called upon in a moment of desperate need. You are here because you were invited—because there was nothing I wanted more at that moment, nothing I will ever want so much again."

He reached down and took the bracelet from her hand. Lifting her fingers, he placed the beautiful golden piece over her hand and slid it halfway up her forearm. It stayed there by itself, its smooth weight pressing gently against her skin.

Christine turned her arm slightly while Ailin still held her fingers, mesmerized by the glints of firelight in the red gems studding the bracelet. Ailin reached up to take her other hand. She held tightly to his hands, drawing comfort from his rocklike presence and something more from his shining gaze—a sweet excitement, a warmth, a strange and joyous feeling that she had never known before.

Something heavy dropped around her shoulders. Startled out of her reverie, Christine let go of Ailin's hands and quickly looked behind her.

Slaine had placed on her the fur-lined red wool cloak she had huddled beneath just a short while ago. "Here is the brooch, lady," she said, holding another flat golden object in her hand. "I will pin the cloak for you. It is always cold on Imbolc night, though it be the first day of spring."

Spring! Now she had it. This was a celebration—a family reunion—for the first day of spring, in the same way that Memorial Day picnics celebrated the beginning of summer.

Slaine fastened the intricate gold brooch over Christine's right shoulder, working so quickly that it was impossible to see how it was done. Finally Christine turned and looked up at Ailin. "I'm ready, kind sir, if you are," she said with a brave smile.

He returned the smile with an almost dreamy look in his eyes. "I am ready, too, Brighid. I have been ready for you all my life."

Chapter Eight

Christine walked close beside Ailin in the darkness. They passed through the gate of the fortress and started down a wide dirt path, one that led away from the sea and into the black silhouettes of the hills. The storm of the afternoon had cleared and they strode together beneath a deep black sky glittering with cold and brilliant stars.

A full moon lit the hills and valleys with a ghostly glow. The shadowed grass rippled like a living thing in the light wind off the sea. Christine held on to Ailin's arm as he moved with grace and power through the night, grateful for his guidance over the unfamiliar path.

The fur of the cloak was warm and soft about her face, and the long gowns were heavy and concealing—but how strange it was to have absolutely no underwear on! Christine had heard about women who liked to go out like that, claiming it added a bit of excitement to an occasion. She reddened at the thought, but then felt a strange, small thrill run through her as she pressed against the hard muscles of Ailin's arm.

After all she had been through, it suddenly struck

her as funny that being out with a man and wearing no panties was the thing that made her feel daring and wild. She grinned, ducking her head so he would not see, and bit her lip to keep from laughing out loud.

Yes, she felt daring and wild, and her emotions were spiced with a dash of fear. Though he had been unfailingly kind and gentle toward her, she knew that this man was as primitive and untamed as the land over which they walked. There was no law here, at least not as she knew it; no policeman who would come to her aid, no other people who followed the same rules as she. Ailin would follow his own rules, here in his own world, and she could never be certain of what those rules might be.

They were alone out here in the darkness. There was nothing between the two of them except her trailing skirts. If he chose, he could lift her up in his powerful arms as though she weighed nothing at all, and carry her off the path into the soft grass behind the rocks . . . no one would see them, no one would hear her cry out. . . .

Ailin stopped and looked down at her. Christine stared up at him, her mouth open, her heart pounding wildly in her chest.

But he only turned her gently, looking back the way they had come, and pointed toward the moonlit hills. "There is Dun Orga," he said. "It has been there since the beginning of time, I think, and it will still be there at the end. My family has lived there for all its generations."

Christine relaxed slightly, and looked where Ailin pointed. Beneath the wide black sky she saw a distant cluster of torchlights sitting atop one of the smaller hills, right beside the long steep hill that led to the cliffs and the sea. In the soft light of the moon and stars she could just make out the circular walls of the ancient fortress.

In another time and place she would only have

thought it cold and primitive, strange and forbidding. But here, now, Dun Orga represented the only safety and security this world had to offer.

It was home.

Ailin stepped in front of Christine and took hold of her hands by the fingers, holding her hands apart so that he could see her. He did not say a word, but simply stood gazing down at her.

His eyes first took in the tips of her soft folded boots, beneath the long linen gown. His gaze moved upward to the long belt with its carved and curving designs and large gold ring, and then studied the golden-brown gown with its wide bands of colorful winding embroidery covering the hem and sleeves and neckline.

He smiled when he saw the gleam of the bracelet on her arm, and became serious once more at the sight of the torque around her neck. The heavy piece of twisted gold was almost hidden by the fluffy tan fur of the red wool cloak. Her red-gold hair rippled with waves made tight by the damp breath of the wind off the sea.

Christine stood motionless, caught in the spell of his searching, studying eyes, barely able to breathe.

"I have often imagined the face of a goddess," he whispered, "wondering how such a one would look. But nothing I ever imagined was near so beautiful as this . . . standing here beneath the stars, shining in the light of the moon . . . robed like a queen and bright with gold."

He gripped her hands tightly, and the strength of him surged into Christine. Her head fell back as she stared into his shining eyes, unable to look away, and her knees felt as though they might give way.

"It is my gold you wear," Ailin said, and with one hand he reached up to trace the spiraling torque at her neck. "I made this with my own hands, hoping I could make something worthy of offering to you."

He followed the line of the torque with his strong,

gentle fingers, and then drew them along the soft skin of her neck. "If it was not worthy before," he whispered, "it is a sacred object now, because you wear it."

Christine's eyes closed. A sweet, warm thrill ran through her body at his touch and at his quiet, fervent words. "I have always belonged to you, Brighid," he whispered. "I always will."

She stood transfixed in the starlit darkness, waiting for more and more of the touch of his exploring fingers . . . but after a moment he withdrew his hand and stepped back a pace from her. Reluctantly Christine opened her eyes.

"All of the clan want very much to see you," he was saying. "They are waiting now at the bonfire, all the people of Dun Orga and all the others of my father's family. I cannot wait to show you to them."

Following his gaze, her eyes shifted to the tallest of the hills, where a line of torches wound its way to the top. She clung to Ailin's hands as a slight trembling began in the muscles of her legs.

"Ailin," she began, trying to keep the trembling from reaching her voice. "Ailin, I hope they won't be disappointed. I mean . . ." Christine paused. This was not going to be easy, but she braced herself and began searching for the right words.

Ailin cocked his head slightly. The gold band around his forehead glinted in the soft moonlight. "How could they be disappointed?" he asked. "You are so beautiful. You are here. You are"—he whispered the final word—"Brighid."

He kept calling her Brighid. Yes, he had called her that before—when she had first seen him inside his house, when she had stood frightened and shivering out on the cliffs, and again when they had left tonight to come out here.

She had not thought to question him about it at those times, but now she matched his gaze with purpose. Lowering her hands, she said, "Ailin, please tell me. How do you know my name?"

He frowned slightly, and confusion flickered in his blue-gray eyes. "I know your name as I know the names of all the gods and goddesses. You are Brighid—the Queen of War, the Poetess, the Daughter of the Dagda; the mistress of feminine arts, the keeper of the hearth, the Lady of Fire. Here among us, at Dun Orga."

Christine let go of his hands. She stepped back from him, her mind running wild with memories as the last pieces of the puzzle fell into place.

Before awakening here, she clearly remembered talking to Mr. Donalson—that handsome, mysterious man who was the image of Ailin in the twentieth century—about Saint Bridget, the saint she was named for, the one whose feast day was the same as her birthday. She'd thought he meant that her torque had been made for the Catholic saint. But he had laughed gently and corrected her—*I did not mean Saint Bridget . . . her predecessor . . . a Celtic goddess.*

A Celtic goddess.

Christine seized Ailin's hands, heedless of the ominous strength in them. She could think only that somehow she had to make him understand!

It was one thing for Derval and Slaine to believe she'd been sent by a goddess. She could accept that, since it made sense in the context of their world, and there was hardly anything else they could think.

But for Ailin to believe that she actually was a goddess herself—that she was some kind of mystic being with supernatural powers—no, she would never allow it! It was not true, and she would never allow any of these people to think it was true!

"Ailin, listen to me!" Her sudden reaction startled him but he stood very still, as solid as a rock implanted in the earth, his gaze riveted down on her.

"I am not Brighid," she went on breathlessly. "I am not a goddess. My name is Bridget Christine Connolly, and I'm from—I'm from . . ."

Her voice faltered. How could she ever explain to him where she was from? Or how she got here? Her world, her people, did not exist in this time. What on earth could she tell him?

Christine took a deep breath. "I'm from a faraway place," she said, hoping that would satisfy him. "And I'm really not sure how I got here. It's just like Derval said—perhaps a goddess did bring me here. I don't know. But I am not a goddess myself!"

His eyes narrowed. "Are you saying that I am wrong about you? That you are simply a woman like any other?"

She sighed with relief. "Yes, yes. That's it. I—"

But he only shook his head gently. "You test my resolve, lady. I know you for a goddess in woman form, and therefore to be treated as a queen. I will give you not only love but protection, for as long as you choose to remain. I swear it."

He released one of her hands and reached up to stroke her hair. "I saw you appear to me today, out of your conjured storm, and save my life. I see you here now, looking so lovely that you cannot possibly be an ordinary woman. You are the goddess Brighid, and none could ever make me believe that you are anything else."

He released one of her hands, giving the other one a gentle squeeze, and then turned and began leading her to the foot of the hill. He never looked back as he started climbing the steep path to the bonfire high at the top. Christine, stunned and speechless, followed like an obedient child.

She did not intend to allow him to worship her. She could not believe that anyone would really want to have a man kneeling at her feet. But as Christine walked close behind Ailin in the darkness, automatically putting one foot in front of the other, thoughts and memories from another time and place filled her mind.

She remembered back, as though it had been a

thousand years before, to Eliza and the intense, loving, almost worshipful way her husband treated her. And Christine remembered how she herself had wished with an empty, longing heart for something of the same.

Loved and worshiped . . . treated like a queen, like a goddess . . .

What was that old saying her mother had been so fond of? *Be careful what you wish for. You might get it.*

Christine's heart hammered and she gasped for breath as she struggled to follow Ailin up the steep hill. They had no torch, and Christine, accustomed to the artificial and ever-present brightness of electric lights, could scarcely see where she was going with only the dim glow from the moon and stars to show her the way up the treacherous hillside.

All she could do was hold tight to Ailin's arm with one hand and try to keep the long heavy skirts up off her feet with the other. The skirts threatened to trip her at every turn, and once she stepped on the end of the long belt and nearly fell on the rocky path.

But Ailin drew her after him like the moon draws the tide in its wake; and in silence, with the tension mounting, they climbed the narrow path up the last part of the hill and finally stood together at the very top.

Christine sighed with relief as the difficult climb ended, too exhausted even to look up and admire the view. She started to smooth her gown and push her disheveled hair out of her eyes, but then stopped suddenly in midgesture.

A crowd of people, silent and still in the glaring torchlight, were already up here. Waiting for Ailin—waiting for her. Behind the people, Christine could just make out the enormous stack of wood that sat waiting for the flames. It was a giant black shadow looming against the stars.

Christine slowly lowered her hand from her hair.

She crept backward until she felt Ailin's body behind her. Pressing against him, she stared at the unmoving crowd as fear began rising in her breast.

Something moved down the back of her hair, as light as the night breeze. She jumped, startled, but then realized that it was Ailin whose touch she felt. He was running his fingers down her hair and lifting the heavy mass from her shoulders.

As he did, there was a soft murmur of approval from the crowd. They were craning their necks to see the torque, which she was wearing and Ailin was displaying for them.

The gold surface and ruby-red jewels of the ancient torque glimmered and flashed in the light from the torches. Several of the people stole glances at each other and nodded before turning back to stare at Christine once more.

"She has come to us," Ailin said, allowing her hair to fall gently back to her shoulders. "She came to me today, when the battle turned and I called upon her. She is Brighid. And she is here."

Christine saw the admiration in the faces of the crowd—admiration that was directed at Ailin. She felt his chest swell with pride as he drew himself up taller.

A thread of indignation began to weave its way through her fear. She was being shown off like a prize won in a contest!

Christine whirled around to look up at him. "Ailin," she said. Instantly he glanced down at her. She gathered all her courage as she stood beneath that piercing gaze, and made herself go on with what she wanted to say.

"I told you—please listen to me. And make them listen to me. I am not Brighid. I am not—I am not. . . ."

Her voice trailed away as she realized that he was not listening to her. His eyes had lifted to the crowd, and they responded to him with a low, whispering chant. The sound rose, growing louder as the moments passed.

Christine listened closely to the voices in the crowd. And with a combination of fascination and dismay, she realized that they were saying her name.

"Brighid," they whispered in a long sighing breath. "Brighid . . ."

She turned away from Ailin and stared at the crowd of chanting people. As their hypnotic sound washed over her she began to feel breathless, dizzy, caught up in something much larger and much more powerful than herself. The carefully prepared argument left her mind and was forgotten.

A million stars wheeled above her head in an endless black sky, and the torches flared in a sudden gust of wind. She was held motionless between the blindly adoring crowd standing in front of her and the powerful, primal warrior whose hands were sliding up her shoulders to caress her windblown hair. At that moment, she could not have moved from the spot if she had tried.

"Brighid . . . Brighid . . ."

She closed her eyes and felt herself carried away by the intense, dreamlike quality of the night. The energy and life force of Ailin and his people and his world surged around her like a living thing, sweeping her away on a tide of emotion and adoration.

Suddenly Ailin's hands tensed on her shoulders. The crowd fell silent. Even the wind seemed to be holding its breath. Christine's heart hammered in her chest—What's happening now? she wanted to cry out—but instead she slowly, slowly opened her eyes, and focused on a small figure standing alone in the shadows at the very edge of the crowd.

He was a man of great age, it seemed, far older than anyone else she had seen here. His hair and beard were long and gray, almost white. He wore a long tunic of heavy cream-colored linen with a cloak of dark green wool pinned over it, and apparently had no jewelry of any kind. He held a long slender staff of gnarled wood with one end resting on the ground.

The man looked plain and simple compared to the rest of the people, who were almost gaudy in their bright plaids and heavy gleaming gold; but Christine could see that this was anything but an ordinary man. All eyes were on him, and the crowd waited in silent expectation for him to make the next move.

Ailin leaned down to whisper in her ear. "That is Ernin," he said softly. His breath burned the skin of her neck. "He is the chief druid at Dun Orga."

Druid!

Panic surged through Christine. It shattered the tide of emotion she had ridden just moments before and threatened to destroy whatever sanctuary she thought she had found with Ailin.

A druid!

All she had ever heard about druids were vague stories of mysterious, terrifying pagan rituals—including human sacrifice. And here she was, standing on top of this mountain in the black of night, surrounded by wild, primitive, torch-bearing strangers who had a huge stack of wood ready for the burning just a few yards away. It was enough to cause the very word *druid* to send wave after wave of fear rushing through her.

Shaking like a leaf in the wind, Christine tried desperately to think. These people would not hurt her, would they? Not if they really thought she was a goddess, or at least sent by a goddess? They had all been so kind—they'd taken such good care of her—or had she been mistaken about that, too?

With horror, it occurred to her that maybe the fine clothes and jewelry and food had just been some kind of preparation for—for—

Her trembling knees threatened to give way. Surely Ailin would not let anyone hurt her! But he only took his hands from her shoulders and stood

103

very still, a wall of strength for her to lean on, as the gray-haired man walked slowly past the crowd and began to approach her.

The druid came to stand just in front of Christine, leaning on his long wooden staff and staring deep into her terrified eyes.

She braced against Ailin until she was sure he must be able to feel the pounding of her heart. But as her body made contact with his, she became aware of the great strength and courage flowing through him—the way he stood unflinching before the druid's gaze, the way he would stand unmoving in a hurricane if one should happen along.

Christine straightened. The sudden appearance of the druid had unnerved her, but she did not want to play the part of the fainting female—not in front of these people, not in front of Ailin—not ever. She had come this far, and she was determined not to falter now.

Courage is where you find it, Christine reminded herself. She closed her eyes and drew some of that strength from the warrior behind her who stood so steadfastly. After a moment she raised her chin and met the druid's eyes.

He stood very still, not saying a word. She saw that though his old gray eyes were bright and sharp, there was kindness in them, too. His lined face softened with the hint of a smile.

Christine found herself beginning to breathe again. The druid glanced up at Ailin, who still stood motionless, and then he turned slightly so that the crowd could hear his words.

His voice was whispery and worn with age. "When men have great need of them," he began, "and call upon them in a pleasing manner, the gods do sometimes choose to answer."

The old man shifted slightly, adjusting the long staff. "The gods and goddesses may appear to us at any time, at any place. It has happened in our past, our ancient, valiant past—and it has happened again today."

Ernin turned back to Christine, gazing at her with soft and shining eyes. "Tonight begins the celebration of Imbolc. It is a time of beginnings, a time of tender spring grass and newborn lambs. It is Brighid's day—and this time, Brighid has chosen to honor us by allowing us to see and feel her presence. Indeed, her presence walks among us all."

He raised a gnarled hand and gently, gently touched the golden torque. Then he turned and walked away, still using the staff at every step, past the crowd and on to the mountain of wood which sat waiting for the flames.

The crowd turned to face him as he walked, leaving Christine and Ailin standing alone behind them.

Chapter Nine

The tension began to ease from her body. Christine drew a deep breath and found that she was proud of herself. She had passed another test. She had faced the fearsome druid and accepted whatever was going to happen.

Her shoulders were still pressed back against Ailin's chest. She could feel his slight movements as he drew breath. Then he shifted, and his heavy iron sword in its leather scabbard came to rest against her leg.

Startled, Christine whirled around to face him. He caught her arms and held her close, steadying her, and as a lock of her hair fell across her eyes he reached up and gently brushed it away.

The smoke from the burning torches drifted over them. Ailin's face was surrounded by stars, and the soft night breeze lifted the edges of his hair. Staring up at him, emboldened by the ordeal she had just come through, Christine could not resist reaching up to touch that hair. It was soft and smooth, bound by the hard gold band around his forehead. Her fingers slid through it once, and then again.

He smiled, and his eyes gleamed like those of a

man granted his fondest wish. "Ernin spoke to you. He called you by your name. You are Brighid, just as I knew you were."

Her fingers stopped. She lowered her hand. "No, Ailin. He said only that—that Brighid had made her presence known. By sending—by allowing me to be here."

He made no answer. He only stared as if he had not heard.

Frustration began to build in her. "I thought that when you followed me—when you chased me on the cliffs—you were trying to help me. I thought you were trying to rescue me. Did you only follow me because you thought I was this goddess of yours, and you were trying to win *points*?"

He shook his head slightly. The gleam never left his eyes. "I followed you because I am your servant and one who loves you, Lady of Fire. I would follow you anywhere—do anything for you."

"Then why don't you listen to me?"

Christine turned away from him. She was sorely tempted to go on shouting, and force him to hear the truth, but fought down her rising temper. She knew that she would not be able to convince him of anything if she got too angry.

"Ernin said that the goddess sent me here—that's all," she said calmly, facing him again. "That's the only explanation for why I'm here. It's the only one that makes any sense in this world, and you'll have to accept it, Ailin. Derval and Slaine have. And in my own way I have, too."

"I accepted you long ago." He stroked her hair with strong, gentle fingers. "I have loved you, worshiped you, waited for you all my life. You are the presence of Brighid walking among us, just as Ernin said. Here for us—here for me."

She wanted to shake him, but it would have been like a sparrow trying to shake an oak tree. As she racked her brain for some way to make him understand, she felt Ailin straighten and pull away from her slightly. Turning to look, she saw the druid standing before the stack of wood with both arms raised and the staff in one hand. The crowd waited, silent.

"When men would speak to the gods, it is with the voice of air and fire," Ernin said, lowering his arms. The only sound came from the snapping, flickering torches. "Now will the young men, the warriors, speak to the goddess. Come forward and ask her if she might choose you in this coming year."

Christine looked up at Ailin. "Choose you?" she whispered. "Choose you for what?"

But he did not seem to have heard. He was looking down at something he had pulled from a leather bag at his belt. Christine leaned close to see what it was.

The object of his attention was a smooth white stone about as large as his fist. He turned it over to show it to her, and it shone softly in the moonlight.

"My name-mark is on this stone," said Ailin with great pride in his voice. His fingers traced the column of short, slanted lines carved down one face of the white stone. "Ernin carved it there for me, as he did for all the young men of Dun Orga." Christine glanced up and saw that a crowd of young warriors stood waiting, serious and proud, near the massive stack of wood. Each one held a gleaming white stone in his hand.

The druid beckoned to them. "Give your names to the goddess! Speak to her now, as you and your fathers and your father's fathers have done, through the voice of the Imbolc fire. If she wills it, she will answer you, and honor you above all men in this coming year. We know that the goddess does, indeed, answer when it pleases her." He looked directly at Christine.

From their scattered places throughout the crowd, the young men surged forward to the waiting mountain of stacked wood. Ailin gripped his white stone and moved forward with the other young warriors.

Christine stayed where she was, suddenly forgotten and out of the spotlight as all eyes focused on the waiting bonfire and the young men crowding around it. The solitude was almost a letdown, but she found that she was relieved not to be the focus of such intense attention—at least for a moment.

She moved quietly to the edge of the gathering, finding a spot in the shadows where she could watch Ailin. No one so much as gave her a glance as she walked over beside a boulder and leaned against it, the stone rough and cold beneath her shoulder even through the fur-lined cloak.

Ernin spoke, and the torches flared. "Give your names to the goddess! Call upon her through air and fire, and if it pleases her, she will honor you with an answer before the next Imbolc!" As the druid's voice fell silent, each of the young men hurled his carved white stone deep into the heart of the tangled mountain of wood.

Christine watched in silence, trying to understand what it was all about. It seemed like a rather quaint custom, tossing a stone with your name on it into the bonfire and then waiting for the goddess to choose you. Choose you for what? she wondered. Ernin had not said. She sighed. Maybe it was just a more exciting version of tossing pennies into a fountain and waiting for your wish to come true.

Derval and Slaine stood at the edge of the crowd with two men who were, no doubt, their husbands. Christine thought briefly about asking them what all this was for, but thought better of it. It would be hard enough to get them to answer without embarrassing them, and she could see that they, too, were caught up in the power of the moment.

It was not a time for interruptions.

"The sun sleeps in winter," intoned the druid. "By the sacred flame of Brighid, it is awakened once more." Suddenly he threw his arms wide, his dark green cloak flaring around him, and cried out, "Now!"

A dozen men with torches pushed forward to the very edge of the stacked wood. "Bring the flames alive! Call the goddess through air and fire! The flames will rise through the wind with your names riding upon them! Cry out to her! Cry out to her now!"

The torches flew through the air as their bearers flung them onto the waiting wood. At first the spots of orange fire only glowed softly, scattered throughout the woodpile. One flickered and nearly died. But then the fire began to take hold, and the scattered spots burned brighter.

The wood snapped as the fire bit into it. The spots of flame spread and climbed with frightening speed. In a moment the top of the great hill was awash in an orange-yellow glare.

The crowd quickly fell back from the snapping, hungry blaze. It roared its furnace breath over them and reached out with lightning-quick tongues of flame to lash anyone who dared stand too close.

Christine, too, stepped back as the mountain of wood erupted into flame, raising her arm to shield her eyes from the intense orange-yellow brilliance. It was painfully bright after the soft darkness and the gentle glow of the moon and stars.

It's like standing beside the sun, Christine thought. It must be visible for miles. She marveled at the beauty of it, at this powerful manifestation of heat and light between the cold stars and the dark, untamed land.

Ailin walked back through the crowd, his eyes now focused directly on Christine with a frightening intensity. The people turned as he passed through their ranks and now stood with their backs to the bonfire.

Everyone stared at Christine. The fire roared and snapped and lashed out behind them.

A brief surge of fear raced through Christine as he

came closer, his face a mask, his eyes boring through her. His red cloak billowed in a cloud of sparks from the fire. The terrifying thoughts of a short time ago—of the druid, these strange people, the huge roaring fire, and this ancient, pagan rite—came rushing back again.

But when Ailin was close enough for her to see the look in his eyes, the fear left her, never to return. There was no danger in those eyes. There was only adoration, only worship, only a love that burned like the fire in its intensity for her.

She stared up at him, hypnotized by his shining gaze, and as he came to stand in front of her he held out his hands and caught hold of her own.

His fingers pulsed as her grip tightened around them. His skin was hot from the nearby flames and from his own intense and tightly controlled excitement. Christine stood breathless, enthralled, caught up in a force much larger and far more powerful than anything she had ever known before.

Behind them the chanting began again; as before, it was just a whisper at first, and then became a sound like the night wind rushing over and through her.

"Brighid . . . Brighid . . ."

Ailin released her fingers and placed his hands on her waist, beneath her cloak. His grip was strong and sure, and the heat of his hands burned her skin even through the heavy fabric of her gowns.

Before she could think, before she even had time to be startled or afraid, Ailin swung her up through the air to the top of the boulder. She crouched there, off balance at first, clutching at Ailin's arm for support. He stood unmoving, his arm as strong as steel; as Christine slowly regained her balance, she stood up, wavering at first, and then standing straight to look out over the heads of the chanting crowd.

Though she stood high above the people, the inferno of the bonfire towered over her, rising ever higher into the darkness of the night. And every person there stared up at her, and spoke her name, and sent her waves and waves of love and adoration.

She released Ailin's arm. His enduring presence remained, standing there just below her. She raised her arms to the black night sky, riding on the prow of the world, soaring through the night on a tower of flame and adoration. She closed her eyes and felt that she might be swept away, never to return.

"Brighid . . . Brighid . . ."

As the fire roared up to the stars, the chanting blended in with the voice of the flames and eventually faded away. The only sounds were the snapping and roaring of the bonfire. The crowd stood in silence for a long moment, and then began filing away down the hillside.

Christine felt the touch of Ailin's hand on hers. Blinking, she looked down at him, and their gazes met and held. Though the ritual had ended and they were alone, the look of worship remained on his face—a look that was both tender in the purity of its love and frightening in the intensity of its passion.

He reached up with both arms and grasped her around the waist, his big hands nearly encircling her. He swung her back down to earth but she barely felt her feet touch the ground.

The hot wind from the fire blew Ailin's cloak around Christine, enveloping the two of them in its heavy red folds. "Goddess," he whispered as the inferno blazed behind them. "Never have I seen any woman so lovely. All things that I do will be done in your name, I will be all that you might desire in a man, and my life shall be lived for you alone."

Christine closed her eyes, hoping that this dream might never end. "All my life I have wanted nothing more than to hear those words," she said. "But how can you be saying such things to me? You don't know me. I only just arrived. How can you say you love me when I am a stranger to you?"

"We are not strangers, Lady of Fire," he murmured. His lips touched her cheek, and his breath burned her skin. "You have always been a part of my life, and always will be. You are she whom I worship and I am your servant . . . we could never be strangers to one another."

Christine felt dizzy and the world went whirling past her. So much had happened, and it threatened to overwhelm her. She stood in this strange and violent land with the flames of a pagan rite roaring their hot breath over her, held fast in the grip of a man who said he loved her, a powerful and magnificently handsome man with strength enough to crush her if he wished. And there was no one here who could stop him.

His hands remained on her waist. She reached up and placed her small hands on his forearms, gripping them tightly for support.

She barely remembered any other life before coming here. It all seemed so empty and dull, so pointless and routine . . . while here she seemed to have come alive for the very first time.

She ought to be terrified of Ailin—but she was not. Perhaps she did belong with him. It was so wonderful to be with him, so frightening and joyous and exciting all at once . . . and at this moment, she could not think of a single reason why she should not go with him, why she should not stay with him as he so clearly wanted her to do. She would stay at his side and find out more about this man who made her heart pound with fear of the unknown and her blood sing with the thrill of his presence.

Perhaps Ailin was right: Perhaps she did belong here with him, had been sent here just for him. And at that moment, as she turned and walked beneath the black night sky with the tall blond warrior whose gold coronet gleamed in the fire's glare, she was prepared to believe that she was, indeed, a goddess, come to walk beside the one man who had the strength to call her to him through the impossible barriers of space and time.

The conversation and laughter inside the feast hall, which had spilled out into the night, fell to a hushed murmur as Christine walked into the hall. Still holding Ailin's arm, she stepped gingerly through the dried grass on the floor as all heads turned to watch her.

The feast hall was long and high ceilinged, with heavy wooden timbers holding up the thatched roof. There was a stone fireplace blazing away at each end of the room and torches flaring brightly from the supporting timbers, leaving a pall of smoke hanging in the heavy air.

Down the center was a table that appeared to be sitting directly on the floor, just big squares of wood laid end to end. It was laden with wooden platters, most of which held meat—huge joints and massive ribs and great roasts of meat. It looked as though an entire cow or sheep had been slaughtered and served. And probably had been, Christine thought.

On either side of the table, sitting on furs and cushions on the fresh layer of dried grass, sat the hundred or so brightly dressed men and women who had been gathered around the bonfire on the hilltop.

A hundred pairs of eyes stared at her with intense scrutiny, yet she found she could endure it. She walked with her head high, unafraid of the strangeness and proud to be walking on the arm of a man like Ailin.

Let them stare all they wished. They wished to see a goddess; well, tonight, for this one time, they would believe they had seen one. Christine had no doubt that this was what it felt like to be a goddess, whether she actually was one or not.

Ailin stopped near the center of the long side of the table, where an empty space had been left. As they stood waiting, the man at their feet rose to greet them.

She knew instantly that this must be Ailin's father. He had the same blue-gray eyes, and the same finely chiseled features were evident beneath a face worn with the cares of kingship and aged with the life of strife and violence he had no doubt led. The light hair was more gray than blond. Yet the same kindness and strength of character that Christine had sensed in Ailin was present in this man, too, and she felt no fear of him.

"This is my father, Donaill, the king," said Ailin. "And my mother, Queen Mor." The blond woman looked up at Christine from her seat on a fur-covered cushion, nodding to her with regal dignity.

King Donaill studied Christine, not quite allowing himself to smile. "You honor us with your presence," he said. "We know what you have done for Ailin— for us all. You were sent to save Ailin's life, and so you did when you dazzled the enemy who would have killed him. You are welcome here, a thousand times welcome, and all that we have is yours."

Christine returned the grave nod, accepting the accolades without protest. The king sat down again beside his queen. Ailin and Christine took their seats beside them on a pile of creamy tan furs.

The conversation picked up once more, though Christine was conscious of the many eyes that remained on her. She blinked in the glare of the torchlight, and with every breath was nearly overwhelmed by the smoke from the torches and the smell of the roasted meats that lined the table. The very strangeness and unreality of it all began to intrude on her again.

She turned to Ailin, and saw him gazing at her with the same love and adoration here in this homey setting that she had seen out there during the ritual on the blazing mountaintop. Suddenly it seemed as though this was the place where she belonged, that her past was only a pale blur, hardly remembered. She looked away and focused only on the here and now, for it was all she had, and she was determined to make the most of it.

Chapter Ten

Christine found that she was hungry, even after the fine meal she had had with Derval and Slaine. Being a goddess must give a girl an appetite. But she was hardly able to find the time to eat, so attentive was everyone to her smallest need, real or imagined.

She sat beside the king himself, and off in a corner someone played beautifully on a small harp—she longed to get a closer look at it—but all attention seemed to be on her. A golden plate sat in front of her, and a matching cup. Servants, bare-legged and wearing plain tunics, moved around the table to cut and serve the meat and bring in new platters as they became empty. But the servants had little chance to approach her. She found that she was being waited on by several of the other men at the feast, the other young warriors like Ailin.

One man, red-haired and powerful, brought her slices of the choicest roast lamb and laid them tenderly on the golden plate. Another strapping warrior offered a round, flat loaf of bread, with pale butter and golden honey. And still another, dressed in blue-and-gold plaid with a thick brown leather belt, approached bearing a polished tray with an assortment of dried fruits and boiled vegetables on it.

Never had she dreamed that she might be the object of such desire. The other young warriors in the hall glared at the three who had served her, seething with frustration, obviously wishing that they could be the privileged ones to gaze into her eyes and speak privately to her. It was intoxicating, and Christine was forced to admit to herself that she was greatly enjoying the attention.

Surely there was nothing wrong with that. She was merely enjoying their hospitality, graciously accepting their kindness, basking in the attentions of a crowd of handsome young men the way any red-blooded young woman—or goddess—would do.

Surely she'd earned it after the kind of day she'd had.

Her plate filled to overflowing, Christine sighed. She would never be able to finish all this food. It seemed a shame to waste it—could she ask for a doggie bag?

Now there was a thought from a far-distant time and place. Raising the golden cup to her lips to hid her smile, she turned to Ailin. "I couldn't possibly finish all this myself. Would you like to share—"

The expression on his face stopped her from saying anything more. Ailin sat very still, staring coldly down the long table, not looking at her. He was glaring and angry, but she could not fathom what he was angry about.

It wasn't her, she was sure of that. His angry stare was aimed across the table at the three young men who had just finished serving her and were sitting back down at their places.

Puzzled, and feeling a slight sting of annoyance, Christine laid her hand on Ailin's arm. His skin was hot and his muscles, rippling as she touched him, were hard as steel. "Ailin," she began, "what is wrong? Why are you angry with those men?" He did not seem to have heard her. "Didn't you tell me this

118

was a family gathering? Aren't all those men your relatives, then?"

His eyes flicked toward her, but his voice was barely a whisper. "Many of us are related in some fashion, Lady of Fire. But none of our family are servants."

"Servants?" Yes, such work would undoubtedly be far beneath a warrior in a culture like this one. "But they weren't acting like servants, Ailin. They were just being kind to me, just making me feel welcome. You don't know how much I appreciate that right now. I don't understand why you should be angry with them."

She glanced down at a sudden motion from Ailin's hand. He had gripped the hilt of his short iron dagger, his knuckles almost white from the tension in his powerful hands.

"May I offer you some wine, lady?"

She looked up. A man stood before her, a tall, dark man thick with muscle. His eyes were dark brown and his hair and soft mustache a shining black. "My name is Tierney."

Christine sat motionless, caught between Ailin and this stranger, but Tierney reached out and lifted her cup without taking his eyes off her. As he poured the wine, he smiled at her—a cold and dangerous smile. Tierney was a deadly handsome man, as dark as Ailin was fair, with an edge of mystery and an air of threat about him that Ailin did not possess.

Yet he was being unfailingly courteous to her, and she returned his smile with the warm generosity that only a goddess could possess. "Thank you, sir. You are very kind to attend me in this manner. I know that you are not a servant."

His eyes still locked on hers, Tierney set down the pitcher. He reached out and slid the tips of his fingers beneath her own, stroking her skin with a maddeningly delicate touch. "You are most welcome, lady," he said in a soft, almost whispering voice. "But you

119

are wrong. I am a servant—your servant." His fingers brushed beneath her hand and began to stroke the delicate skin of her wrist.

Christine drew in her breath, frozen by this stranger's cool touch and piercing, hypnotic gaze. She tried to withdraw her hand but found that she could hardly move.

Slowly, deliberately, Tierney leaned forward until his face was level with hers. He's going to kiss me, Christine thought wildly, realizing that she did not want the game to go this far. Not when she thought of Ailin—his was the only touch she wanted.

She struggled to draw back, to stand up, when suddenly there was a violent crash behind her. Powerful hands grabbed her shoulders, shoving her away from Tierney and sending her sprawling on the soft pile of furs.

Ailin towered over her as she lay at his feet, his fists clenched and his chest rising and falling with each hissing breath. His golden cup lay on its side across the plate where he had slammed it down, a puddle of dark red wine forming on the table beneath it.

Ailin was in a rage fueled by the heat of passion, but Tierney remained cool and calm—and did not back down. "What is wrong, Ailin?" he said softly, almost laughing. "Do you claim the goddess for your own? I don't see how that could be. How can any man own a goddess?"

"No man owns a goddess," said Ailin through clenched teeth.

"Good," said Tierney, glancing down at Christine with piercing brown eyes. "Then why not ask her who she wishes to have pour her wine? Surely you're not afraid of the answer."

"I fear nothing. Least of all a man who treats a goddess like a plaything."

"She is no plaything, Ailin. But as you say, neither is she property. She was enjoying my attentions, as anyone could see. And if a woman enjoys my attentions, no man will interfere."

"She is no ordinary woman—though I would not expect a rutting pig like you to be able to see it. She is a goddess. And you will not place your hands on her again. Not while I live."

Tierney grinned, a slow, malevolent expression that turned Christine's blood to ice. "Then perhaps you will not live, Ailin."

Without another sound, Ailin grabbed his dagger from his belt and threw himself at Tierney. But the dark-haired fighter managed to get his sword out before Ailin landed on him, grunting as the breath was knocked out of his body.

Tierney lay on his back, pinned beneath the enraged Ailin, and with both hands raised his sword across his face just as Ailin slashed viciously downward with his dagger. Metal clanged against metal and the two were locked in a struggle for dominance, Tierney holding the sword up with all his strength while Ailin slowly pressed it down. The tip of the dagger approached the other man's throat.

"He'll kill him!" Christine cried, struggling through the shock and horror to get to her knees. She looked up and down the hall, searching for someone, anyone, who could put a stop to this. "Ailin is going to kill that man, when all he did was flirt with me! Why doesn't somebody do something?"

But the other men in the feast hall made no move to stop the struggling fighters. They were all on their feet, shouting encouragement to Ailin or to Tierney, and some even appeared to be taking bets on the outcome. They had no intention of interfering. This was just entertainment for them!

Fear swept over her again—fear that a man would be murdered because of her, and that she would be only a helpless bystander watching it happen. She had seen a bar-fight once, a brawl between a couple of young men who'd had a few beers too many and taken some insult too seriously. The bouncers had quickly broken it up and the police had arrived a few moments later just to make certain it was nothing too serious. No real harm had been done.

But this was no campus bar, and these were not fraternity boys. This was a different time, a different place; these were powerful warriors trained to kill, and with no inhibitions about killing. If somebody didn't do something a man was going to die before her eyes.

She kicked her heavy skirts out of the way, stumbling once as she got to her feet, and hurried over to Ailin. She grabbed his rock-hard arm and shook it. "No! Please! Stop this!" she cried.

He took no notice of her. She might have been a moth fluttering around his head.

The sword in Tierney's trembling hands was pressed down almost to his chest. "Now, Tierney," Ailin hissed, his face red from rage and effort, "you will have to wait for our next fight in your next life."

"No!" Christine reached out and grabbed the blade of Ailin's dagger with her own hand. She could not force the blade away, but neither did it move any closer to the other man's throat. As though from a great distance she saw, rather than felt, the thin red line that began to form beneath her hand along the dagger's polished edge.

Slowly, his eyes glazed, Ailin turned to look at her. "Brighid, do you wish me to spare him?"

Christine closed her eyes. "Yes. Please. I do. I don't want anyone to be killed for me. No harm was done. Please, Ailin—let him go."

Without a word, Ailin leaned back and dropped the dagger. Christine unclenched her hand, now wet and slippery with blood from the bite of the cold iron, and pressed her other hand hard against her palm as the stinging pain began. Determined to ignore it, she turned once more to Ailin—but he was not there.

Tierney got up from the floor. Without so much as a glance at Christine he went back to his place at the table and sat down again as the conversation returned to normal.

Her knees shaking, Christine looked for the tall blond warrior. There—just disappearing out the door into the night. She gathered up her skirts and ran after him, picking her way through the crowd. Everyone stared, but no one made any move to stop her.

Christine ran out into the cool darkness, grateful for the breath of fresh air after the stifling atmosphere inside the feast hall. She glanced around for Ailin, trying to get her bearings within Dun Orga.

She stood near the center of the circular fort, in front of the long, narrow hall. By the light of the moon she could see the heavy gate, now closed and barred shut. He hadn't gone outside. Here and there a shadowy figure moved across the grounds beneath the flickering torches, but none of them was Ailin.

Where could he have gone?

She turned and crossed the grounds toward the house that belonged to Ailin, the place where she had awakened in this world. The torch in front of it had gone out. The little house was silent and almost dark inside, with only the faint glow from the embers of the cooking fire providing any light. But still she was drawn to it; she was certain he had to be there.

Christine cautiously pushed open the wooden door and took a step inside. "Ailin?"

A hand closed over her shoulder. Startled, she nearly cried out, but only whirled around instead.

Ailin stood towering over her, the streaming white moonlight shining on his hair. His face was still as a mask, his slate-blue eyes serious and somber. For a tense moment his fingers pressed into her shoulder; then suddenly he let go and turned his back to her.

"You search for me, Lady Brighid?"

Catching her breath, and willing her swiftly beating heart to slow down to something like normal, Christine nodded her head—even though he could not see her. "Yes, Ailin. I was looking for you. I—"

"You have found me. In what way may I serve the goddess?"

He still would not look at her. It was frightening being here with him like this, in this dark and shadowy house in the middle of the night. But Ailin was her link to safety and security in this world—somehow, she knew, he was the reason she was here. If he was angry with her, then she had to know why, and try to make things right if she could.

"Well, first you can tell me what's wrong," she said, crossing to the center of the room beside the softly glowing hearth. "Why are you angry with me?"

That got him to turn around. But now the look in his eyes was only one of puzzlement. "How could I ever be angry with you?" he asked, as though she were mad. "I could never be angry with the goddess I serve. No, it is myself I am angry with."

"Okay, well, this is making some progress," Christine murmured under her breath. "I certainly should have realized." Sometimes her sense of the ridiculous broke through at the strangest times; but then again, maybe it was just that sense of humor which was allowing her to cope with all of this in the first place.

She sighed. "All right, Ailin, tell me. Why are you angry with yourself?"

He was a great shadow looming above her within the darkened house. As he bowed his head and looked away, the moonlight glinted briefly off the golden coronet around his head. It made him seem even more like a creature of fantasy, like a ghost or a shadow or a wraith, and at that moment Christine was prepared to believe that he was not really there at all.

But that thought vanished as Ailin took her hand

in one of his, startling her again with the heat and raw power of his simple touch.

"I should have defended you better than I did, Lady Brighid," he said. "Tierney treated you like—like a—in ways that he would not dare to treat even the most ordinary woman of Dun Orga. He played at being a servant so that he could play with the Lady of Fire—when he should have been honored beyond belief just to be under the same roof with her."

"Oh, Ailin, Ailin . . ." She closed her eyes, hardly knowing what to say to him. "You did defend me. You're right—he was going too far, and I wasn't enjoying it. And I'm glad you helped me." Her hand began to sting once more, held tightly in Ailin's own. "But I didn't want you to hurt him. It wasn't that serious. I thought you were—I was afraid you were going to kill him."

His grip tightened. "I was going to kill him. I should have killed him. He threatened to kill me, and I could not simply lie down and let him do it. Is that what you would have had me do?"

"No, of course not." She withdrew her hand, wrapping it in the folds of her skirt and pressing on it to ease the throbbing pain of the long, shallow cut. "But I couldn't let you kill him—him, or anybody else."

"Why not?"

Why not? The absurdity of it all struck her again, and Christine was afraid she was actually going to giggle out loud. Here she was debating the ethics of killing with a man who was essentially a professional warrior—she who could hardly bring herself to set a trap for a mouse that had once moved into her apartment, because it might have hurt the poor thing.

"Because it's wrong, Ailin. Tierney might have been annoying me, but he didn't hurt me. Being an annoyance doesn't carry a death sentence. If it did, there would hardly be anyone left alive in the world."

"I do not believe he would have stopped at being a mere annoyance, Lady Brighid."

"But you couldn't know that for sure. If he had gone too far, and really threatened to hurt me, then other measures could have been taken."

"I was not willing to wait and see. I would not take that chance concerning you."

Christine felt her momentary good humor slipping away. This was deadly serious. "Then why not kill every man who is impolite to a woman? How do you make that decision?"

But he refused to be shaken by her arguments. "I do not make decisions such as this about all men. I only know what happened with you and one particular man. And I acted in the only possible way."

Christine closed her eyes. She had to talk him out of this somehow, or he was liable to go around cutting down every man who looked sideways at her! "Please, Ailin—please, just for me. Promise me that you will harm no man who approaches me—not unless I'm really, truly in some kind of danger. Will you promise me this?"

"Does a goddess ever find herself in danger? Can you not defend yourself from true bodily harm? Why would you need me to defend you from such as that?"

Now she was confused. "But I thought—isn't that why you went after Tierney?"

"It was a matter of honor. Of respect for the goddess and those who honor her."

"But to kill a man for simple rude behavior? You just can't do that! It's not—it's not civilized!"

He stared down at her, and in the darkness she felt rather than saw his blue-gray gaze. "I have not heard this word *civilized* before," he said. "But from what you are saying, I am certain that it is not civilized to allow men like Tierney to abuse the goddess. Nor is it civilized for me to turn my back on her when I should be coming to her defense.

"Of course a goddess can defend herself—but it is up to those who love her to defend her honor."

She saw a flash of moonlight once more on the gold coronet as Ailin bent down to her. Both his hands slid beneath her own, catching them in a gentle grip that carried all the strength of his own powerful life force.

His face bent over hers, and his long blond hair fell feather-soft over the skin of her throat. He murmured something as his lips moved hot and gentle over hers.

"Those who love her . . ."

Christine felt as if she were drowning, so unexpected were Ailin's actions—yet she knew that she had been expecting this all along. Her body knew, even if her mind did not, and she felt like a candle melting in the heat of the sun.

For a long moment she lost herself in the arms of the man who held her as though she weighed nothing at all. Then she realized that he had lifted her up and was carrying her toward the fur-covered shelf where she had awakened that afternoon.

Something of reality came back to her then. *No, I'm not ready for this yet—not now, not yet!*

She struggled against him in the darkness, listening to the pounding of his heart as he crushed her to his chest. "Ailin, no, please—stop. Please. Put me down. I—please. Put me down."

To her surprise, he halted and slowly set her down until she stood in the dried grass on the floor.

Her knees were weak and she felt hot all over. Clutching Ailin for support, hardly knowing what to expect next, she looked up and tried to search out his eyes in the whirling darkness.

"Ailin," she whispered, "I'm sorry. I didn't mean to—I'm just not ready yet. Not now. Not yet."

She waited warily for his reaction. How would a man like him take such a rejection? This was a different time, a different place. And in the past, she knew, a woman often had little to say about such matters.

Both his hands slid around her ribs. Their strength almost took her breath away. She started to cry out as he lifted her up, but stopped suddenly as he set her down on the fur-covered ledge and stepped back, disappearing into the shadows.

She listened for his footsteps, thinking he had turned to go, but then heard his quiet voice. He spoke so softly that she had to strain to catch his words.

"Lady of Fire—forgive me. I am no better than Tierney, no better than the bog-trotters who invaded our home today. You saved me from them. I only hope you can save me from myself. I am truly sorry. I ask your pardon, though I have hardly earned it."

Christine sat very still for a moment, and then smiled to herself in the darkness. She should have realized that a man like Ailin was no rapist, that he would not use force to take a woman he wanted. Indeed, a man like him would hardly need to. *He must have all the women he could ever want*—and at that thought a twinge of jealousy passed through Christine's heart.

"It's all right, really," she said gently, knowing she could trust him. Feeling a little giddy from relief and exhaustion, she added, "You're the nicest man I've met all day. Really."

He drew in his breath as if to answer, but then was silent again. Finally he said, "You must be very tired. Please rest, if you will. I will stay here at your feet. No one will trouble you. I will see to that."

She realized that she was sitting very comfortably on the soft, thick furs of the ledge, and the bone-weariness of the long, strange day finally claimed her. "Yes. Thank you. I am very tired—and these furs are wonderful."

She leaned down to begin unlacing the boots, and then looked up into the darkness once more. "Good night, Ailin—and thank you. For everything."

"I thank you, Lady of Fire. I will be here." And with

that he turned and walked slowly across the room. His footsteps stopped at the ledge on the other side, and she heard the soft rustle of his cloak as he sat down.

In the privacy granted by the darkness, Christine pulled off the boots and set them close by the ledge in the piles of dried grass. She pulled at the heavy leather belt, finally getting it loose, and then carefully gathered up the woolen gown and lifted it off over her head. The room was cold and damp, and the gown's warmth would have been welcome, but she could not bring herself to use such a magnificent piece of work for a nightshirt. Wearing only the linen underdress, she quickly wrapped herself in the heavy furs and long red cloak and waited for their warmth to steal through to her skin.

As she fell into the sleep of utter exhaustion, the events of the incredible day spinning through her mind, she thought of Ailin . . . of the way he had looked at her, the way he had protected and cared for her and set her above all other women . . . and of how he had been within a heartbeat of claiming her for himself once and for all.

Christine sighed deeply, and as she drifted into sleep a last giddy thought passed through her mind. Maybe, as she had always suspected, this was just the kind of thing that happened when a girl went out without her underwear.

Chapter Eleven

The next morning, as the cold sun streamed in through the small window of the house, Christine slowly wakened and opened one weary eye. She was warm and comfortable beneath her thick pile of furs, and wished she could stay there for the rest of the day. She was that unwilling to move.

All the extreme highs and lows of the previous day came flooding back—the terror of awakening here, the unearthly power of the ritual on the mountain-top, and the thrill she felt whenever she was with Ailin.

Ailin. She looked toward the other sleeping ledge, but there was no sign of him.

Her heart began to sink as she remembered what else had happened last night. Ailin had lifted her up in his arms and carried her to this very ledge, but she had refused him. He had not seemed angry last night, but how would he feel this morning?

She rubbed her fingers beneath the heavy torque and adjusted the new golden bracelet where it stuck tightly to her arm. He was her only link with this world. Should she have accepted him last night, just to make certain he would not reject her? Had she made a terrible mistake?

Her lips tightened. No. She would not trade her body for protection, not even in the most desperate of circumstances. If he was angry with her, she would just have to face that and try to make him understand as best she could.

Groaning, she started to sit up, but found she could barely lift her head. It was like being hungover, after the intoxicating experiences of the day and night before.

Last night she had been caught up in strange, wild events far beyond her control, swept along in a fantastic, otherworldly experience. She had been daring and bold, strengthened by Ailin's presence and the unearthly ritual at the bonfire, doing her best to meet her strange situation head-on.

Now, in the cold light of day, Christine was simply a woman lost and alone. Everything she had ever known was gone and she had no idea of how to find it again. There was only this rough little house and the frightening strangers who surrounded it.

Being a goddess seemed easy compared to the idea of actually living day-to-day in this primitive, unknown world.

But she would have to face that challenge, too, just as she had faced the wild rituals of the night before— though it made her tremble just to think about it. She forced herself to get out of her warm nest and sit up on the edge of the sleeping ledge to pull on her boots.

She was just not willing to tiptoe barefoot through the deep rushes—yes, rushes, she remembered now, the grasses on the floor were actually dried rushes, cut from along a pond or a river or a lake and used to cover a bare earthen floor. She must have read that sometime during her many history classes, and had just been too distracted to think of it yesterday. After lacing the boots, she went to tend to her needs using the basin of fresh water and the earthenware chamber pot that had been left for her.

She felt better, but what she really wanted was a bath. Her hair smelled of smoke from the bonfire, and her skin felt clammy and sticky from sweat and dampness.

As she dried her face on the sleeve of the linen gown, there was a small knock at the door. It opened slightly, and Christine was very glad to see the familiar faces of Derval and Slaine peering into the house.

"Good morning," she said to them. "Oh—did you bring all this for me?"

In one hand Derval balanced a wooden tray laden with flat bread and butter and honey, and in the other held a golden cup of clear water. "That we did, lady," she answered, placing the tray and cup on the edge of the hearth. "And what else may we do for you today?"

"Oh . . ." She hesitated, not wanting to cause them any more extra work than she already had, but the feel of the damp linen gown sticking to her skin convinced her to go ahead. "There's just one thing that I would really, really like. A bath."

"A bath." Derval and Slaine looked at each other. "Of course. That can easily be arranged. Give us a few moments and we will have it ready for you."

Christine sat up on the ledge to eat her bread and honey, and wondered just how one went about taking a bath here. She knew they didn't exactly have a bathroom with hot running water just outside the door. As she watched, Slaine took several large, smooth rocks from a neat pile next to the hearth, placed them on the smoldering fire, and used a long, slender iron shovel to cover them with the hot ash. Next she brought down a large, flat bronze basin from its place against the rear wall and set it down on the rushes.

The two women left and came back a few minutes later with two heavy wooden buckets of clear water and a stack of clean white linen fabrics. Slaine set the buckets in the far corner next to the basin, and then used the iron shovel to carry the hot rocks from the hearth. She dropped three into each of the buckets, and hissing steam rose into the room.

Derval brought the fabrics over to Christine. There was a smooth tan lump of something on top, looking like a large pebble. "Here is a small cloth for washing, lady, and a large one for drying off after. And, of course, a bit of soap."

Soap! Of course. "Thank you again for all your help," Christine said, truly grateful. "As soon as I'm clean I promise you I'll start pitching in to help. I don't want to just sit around here being waited on hand and foot, being useless. I'm sure there's plenty of work here to go around."

Slaine just smiled at her. "We would care for you the rest of our lives, lady, and be happy for the privilege," she said. "You have already done more for us than we could ever hope to repay." And with that, the two of them gathered up the breakfast dishes and left Christine to her bath.

The large and small cloths were of coarse linen, and underneath she found a woolen dress in red-and-gold plaid—with, wonder of wonders, her own soft white cotton nightgown, clean and dry! It was all that remained of her old life and she hugged it close, reveling in its plain softness after the beautiful, but scratchy, linen and wool.

She set the nightgown aside. Picking up the linen and the soap, she went to investigate her bath. It would seem that one took what was basically a sponge bath, while standing in the basin. The water in the two buckets was deliciously hot.

She stepped out of the boots, pulled the linen gown over her head, and tossed it aside. Soaking the small cloth in one of the buckets, she worked up lather with the raw, strong-smelling lump of soap—lye soap, she guessed.

Well, it was hardly luxurious, but it was certainly

better than nothing. She washed out of one bucket and then dipped the cloth into the other one, rinsing off the soap as quickly as possible. She wasn't sure what the strong stuff would do to her skin.

She shook out the larger piece of linen and dried off as best she could with the thin fabric, and then wound it around her like a bath towel. Only one more thing to do. Getting down on her knees in the basin, she shut her eyes tightly and then dunked her hair into the soapy bucket.

The cut on her hand burned like fire from the soap as she worked the thin lather through her hair, but she gritted her teeth and forced herself to keep scrubbing. It seemed to be a clean cut, but Christine was terrified at the thought of infection setting in. These people were obviously quite knowledgeable about some things, but she hoped she would never have to test their knowledge of medicine. There were no antibiotics or anesthetics here. There were definitely some things they just would not be able to do for her—or for anyone.

Then again, she told herself, hastily wiping her stinging eyes, there couldn't possibly be a germ anywhere that could survive this soap.

As she scrubbed away at her tangled hair, trying to get her fingers through it down to her scalp, she was certain that the ladies who cut her hair at the beauty salon would throw their hands up in horror at the idea of washing her hair with lye soap. But she had little choice—it was this or go around with greasy, stringy hair. And for Christine that was no choice at all.

When her hair was as clean as she could make it, she rinsed it in the bucket of clear water and then wrung it mostly dry. She just hoped she'd be able to get a comb through it.

A few moments later she was back on the ledge in her boots and white nightgown, patiently untangling her hair with the wooden comb. Derval came in bearing more things.

"Here, lady, we thought you might want these," she said. "They are for you. Please keep them." And on the ledge she set down a small bronze pot and what looked like a long-handled mirror.

Picking up the mirror, she saw that the back of it was bronze with a lovely curving design on it. Turning it over, she was startled to see that there was no reflecting glass—she'd subconsciously been expecting that, although she realized that would have been even more startling! No, there was merely a highly polished bronze surface.

It was a little difficult to see herself, but with some experimentation she found that it actually worked pretty well. "At least I'll be able to check my appearance from time to time," she said, chuckling. "I suppose a lady being treated like a goddess could have the courtesy to look the part, after all!" Derval gave her a hesitant smile, but offered no reply.

Christine lifted the lid on the small bronze pot and found that it was filled with some type of heavy, waxy cream. Puzzled, she looked up at Derval.

"We use it to smooth our skin," she explained. "It is made from beeswax and the oil from the wool of the sheep."

"Oh—lanolin," Christine said. Then, on seeing Derval's confused expression, she added, "Back where I come from, that's what we call it."

She remembered the stuff because Eliza had to avoid it like the plague—she was allergic to it and was always scrutinizing labels. Christine had once had to return an expensive imported face cream she'd bought for Eliza's birthday because it had had lanolin in it.

The thought of Eliza brought a sinking feeling deep inside her. She was forced to think of the life, and the people, that she had left behind, and a wave of sadness swept over her.

135

Never to see her home again—her apartment, the university, the peaceful, congenial town filled with family and coworkers and friends, dear friends.

I want to go home. I will never really belong here. I will always want to go home.

Never to see Eliza again—her lively, generous friend whom she had practically grown up with, who had always been there for her, and whom Christine had believed would always be there.

Eliza, too, must be wondering what had become of her friend.

I won't forget you, Eliza. I don't know if I'll ever find a way to see you again, but I promise you I won't forget you.

The bronze lid grew heavy in her hand. Christine drew a deep breath and briefly closed her eyes, pushing the sadness away before it could overwhelm her. She touched her finger to the cream in the pot and rubbed a little of it between her fingers. It did feel nice—quite a relief after the lye soap. "Thank you, Derval. It's just what I needed."

"You are most welcome, lady."

Christine worked small dots of the cream into the skin of her arms and legs, being careful to avoid the cut on her hand. "Oh," said Derval, coming closer to look at her hand. She frowned in concern. "I did not know. . . ."

"It's not that bad, really," Christine said. "But is there anything I can wrap it in? Just to keep it clean during the day, while I'm working?"

Derval thought for a moment, and then reached for the damp linen cloth that Christine had just used as a towel. "I could tear off a strip of this and wrap your hand—it is clean."

Christine thought about it. Clean, yes, but certainly not sterile. The thought of what would happen if the cut got infected stirred her to action.

"Derval, let me tell you what we can do. Take strips of this clean linen, put them in a large cooking pot—

like that one on the hearth—and cover them with clean water. Then build up the fire and let the water boil until—"

Until when? She'd been about to say "thirty minutes," but who here had a clock? "Ah, until the water is half gone," she said, thinking fast. That should certainly be long enough! "Then let the strips dry on a clean rack in the sun, and quickly fold them and put them away. Use them for anyone who's been injured. It will help them get well and help keep them—or anyone else—from getting any sicker. I promise!"

Derval had listened to the instructions wide-eyed, hanging on her every word. "I will do it, lady," she said, already moving to tear the linen cloth into long strips. "The wrappings will be ready for you in a very short time. We thank you."

Christine smiled, thought she regretted causing yet more work for Derval. She sighed and went back to the slow work of combing out her stiff, tangled hair.

The task seemed nearly hopeless until she thought of working just a little of the cream from the pot into the ends of her hair. It did help—a small amount made the comb slide right through.

She stood up and pulled on the red-and-yellow plain wool gown. It was not as fancy as the one she had worn last night, but she was almost grateful for that—she had been so afraid that something might happen to the priceless embroidery. She fastened on the belt, laced up her boots, and was ready to face another day.

"All right then, Derval," she said, putting away the pot and comb and mirror in the chest at the foot of the sleeping ledge, "now I'm ready to help you. And it's about time. What can I begin doing around here to earn my keep?"

Derval looked a bit confused at first, but then seemed to understand. "Why, lady, I will be pleased to show you the daily tasks done by the women of Dun Orga, and you are most welcome to join us if you will," she answered. "But right now, I am to tell you that someone awaits your presence outside."

"Outside?" Her curiosity rising, Christine grabbed the fur-lined cloak from the ledge and hurried out into the morning.

In the clear, cold brightness of the late winter morning, with the sun gleaming on the white buildings and sparkling on the last of the dew on the bright green grass, Christine was greeted by the most extraordinary sight she had ever seen.

Patiently waiting for her to make her appearance, and standing as tall and still as though he were prepared to wait forever, Ailin stood in his chariot holding the reins of a snorting, pawing team of horses.

His red cloak flowed over his golden yellow tunic, and the gold of his coronet and brooch flashed in the light of the sun. Before him were two small, shaggy horses, each a bright red chestnut color with a long, thick, golden mane and tail.

The horses tossed their heads. One of them suddenly neighed long and loud. Christine walked cautiously to the back of the chariot, and Ailin extended his arm to her.

"Come with me, if you will, Lady of Fire, and I will show you this Eire-land that you have chosen to visit."

Christine grasped his leather-wrapped wrist, and he lifted her into the woven-wicker chariot with a single motion of his arm. "Thank you, Ailin. I can think of nothing I'd like better. Please show me Eire-land."

He said nothing, but his blue-gray eyes shone as he spoke a single word to the team. Christine clutched tightly to his arm as the horses jerked the swaying chariot around and headed toward the wide-open gate, galloping into the morning and this wild new land.

She kept a firm grip on Ailin's arm with one hand and grabbed the side of the heavy wicker chariot with the other. The conveyance was open in the front; it consisted only of the floor and the two sides, and Christine was sure she'd never get used to riding this way. But her nervousness only added to the thrill of the day, and after a moment she stood up straight and looked around her at this new world she had come to.

The horses cantered along the same path that Christine and Ailin had followed to the bonfire the night before. Now, in the bright day, she could get a clear look at Dun Orga.

It was a circle a few hundred yards across, completely enclosed by two high earthen walls, one inside the other. Both walls were grown over with short green grass, and the deep ditch in between was partly filled with rainwater. The high, heavy gate was the only way in.

Inside was a scattering of small white houses like Ailin's. Two long white buildings sat haphazardly across the center. One of the buildings had a couple of wooden fences connecting it to the earthen walls, forming a paddock for the horses.

"It looks like a fortress," Christine said.

Ailin glanced down at her and followed her gaze. "It is a fortress, lady," he said, turning his attention back to the horses. "Strong and well guarded. You can feel safe there."

He stood tall in the swaying chariot, his feet braced wide apart, holding the reins in one hand and clutching Christine's waist with the other. She was pressed up close to him, his thick leather belt hard against her side, and she felt as though she were one with the strength of his powerful body. She looked up at his noble face, his eyes narrowed against the bright morning sun, and realized that she would feel safe and secure wherever she was so long as she was with him.

The horses followed his slightest wish. She could hardly see the reins move, and he gave them no vocal commands, yet they turned off the path and eased to a steady trot as if they had read his mind.

It seemed natural to Christine that a man who seemed to be one with the forces of nature would so easily control the half-wild horses, the way a modern man would control a high-powered sports car with a touch of his finger and never give it a thought. Yet the idea of cars and pavement seemed dull and ordinary compared with the glorious sights that surrounded Christine now.

The team started down a wide, gentle slope into a broad valley. The sky stretched over her, blue and fresh washed with high white clouds, and the cold breeze was sweet as wine with the scent of new grass crushed beneath the chariot's wheels and the horses' hooves.

"Hie!" Ailin cried out to the red-and-gold horses and gave them their heads. They charged into a full gallop, jerking the chariot after them, and as her heart rose into her throat Christine grabbed the heavy wicker side and held on for dear life.

Into the wide green valley they flew, the horses racing madly to keep the bouncing, rattling chariot from running over their heels. The breeze became a wind whipping Christine's hair about her head, and she clung to Ailin's arm, grateful for his tight hold around her waist.

Finally they swept onto the broad valley floor, like a great flying machine coming in for a graceful landing. As they leveled off Ailin steadied the team to a trot over the thick, lush grass, and Christine found that she could breathe again. She eased her grip on the rough wicker side and eagerly looked around her.

The valley was lined with trees high on either side and was wide open down the center. As they trotted along, the valley made a gentle curve; rounding it, they came in sight of a pair of small circular fortresses. These were like Dun Orga, only smaller, with just two or three small buildings inside.

"Who lives there, Ailin?"

He glanced over. The sunlight on his gold coronet danced in her eyes. "Some of the farmers live there," he answered. "They are under my family's protection, in return for looking after the sheep and cattle. And there is the herd—do you see it?"

Christine squinted against the bright, pale sun, trying to see what Ailin was pointing at. All she saw was a wide dark place in the fresh green, like a huge brown carpet. It's just dead grass, she thought, wondering why he would be showing her something like that.

Then the sound reached her—a plaintive bleating sound. As Ailin brought the team closer she suddenly realized that the carpet was moving.

"Oh! There! Are those—are those sheep?"

The dark covering wasn't dead grass at all—it was a flock of sheep. All dark brown sheep, with not a white one among them.

She laughed. "I thought sheep were white, Ailin!"

"White sheep, lady? Never have I seen a white sheep."

"Well, I've never seen sheep like these—of course, the only ones I have seen up close were at the state fair. They were short and fat, with smooth white wool. Not at all like this!"

No, these animals were tall, long-legged beasts with long rough coats of ragged, dark brown wool. No wonder she hadn't recognized them as sheep.

"In a few weeks' time, after the danger of frost is past and the grass is well grown, the herders will take them to the high pastures," Ailin explained. "For now, the sheep stay safely in the *rath* while the lambs are born, and are taken out in the valley to graze for a time each day."

Christine fingered the heavy wool of her gown and

touched the dark red crimson of Ailin's cloak. She remembered the endless platters of meat at the feast tables the night before and the little bronze pot of softening cream Derval had given her that morning. Yes, sheep would be worth a great deal here.

"Do the sheep all belong to you, Ailin? To your family?" she asked. "Do you sell the wool and the meat?" Maybe that was where the wealth of Ailin's family came from. It was obvious to Christine from the fine clothes and ornaments and abundant food that Ailin's was a well-to-do family for these times.

He stopped the chariot and turned to her, looking somewhat puzzled. "The sheep do not belong to me or to my family alone, lady," he answered, looking back at the rough brown flock as the horses tossed their heads. "They belong to all of us at Dun Orga, and all share in the meat and milk and wool. Like the land they graze on, the sheep belong to us all."

"I see," Christine said, nodding her head. "It does make sense, living out her like this."

These people would certainly have a much better chance of surviving, even prospering, in this harsh way of life if they all helped each other instead of competing. One person couldn't possibly do everything for himself here—they were all dependent on each other for their very lives. No, riches here would be measured in the animals, and the grass, and the lush fertile fields.

She gazed up at the surrounding hills, feeling a deep sense of peace and security out here in this isolated valley. How nice it was, after being the center of attention from the moment she had arrived, simply to rest her head against Ailin's shoulder and relax, safe and alone and away from prying eyes.

Chapter Twelve

Deep within the shadows of the trees, a shaggy black-haired man cautiously lifted his head to look at the man and woman in the chariot below. A twig cracked, and his brother quickly slapped him back down.

"Quiet, Garvan!" he hissed. "They'll see ye."

"Yeh, yeh," Garvan said, crouching low once more. "I'm down. But those two got eyes only for each other, not for me or you, Becan."

Becan tossed his shaggy hair out of his eyes and peered closely at the couple. "Just what do ye make of her? Do ye think she's really the one they say she is?"

"Huh. She's the one who got Dur killed, that's who she is. If she hadn't run out of that house—made the poor lad look away when he did—it'd be Ailin lying dead now, instead of our brother."

"But they say she was sent by Brighid. That—that maybe she's Brighid herself."

"Brighid! That?" Garvan snorted in disgust. "Brighid wouldn't bother coming here to follow some man about like a brainless bitch in heat." He dismissed the pair with a wave of his hand. "That's

143

no goddess. Just a murdering, troublemaking woman."

"But where'd she come from, then? From nowhere? No one here ever seen her before. She just appeared out of that house wearing that torque—the same torque Ailin says the goddess took from him right before the battle." Becan's eyes were wide, and his voice quavered. "What else could she be?"

"Huh! Do ye believe everything ye hear? Ye're falling for their story, which wouldn't frighten a sheep if it thought about it. No, she's a woman, all right. Just a woman. There are plenty of women who haven't lived their whole lives at Dun Orga and she's one of 'em. And that's all."

But Becan was not convinced. "We've got to know for sure. I've got to know. And I'm not convinced."

Garvan shifted and scowled. "All right. We'll watch and wait for a time, just to show ye—and anyone else that might be a sheep like ye are. If she is the goddess"—he snorted again—"then we'll leave them be. But if she isn't, then she and Ailin both will pay for the life of our brother."

Becan gave him a quick nod. And with that they crept back into the undergrowth, heading back to their poor campsite at the edge of the dismal bog.

It was a day like no other Christine had ever experienced, or ever hoped to again. They left the farmer's ringed fortresses behind and toured the wild green land in Ailin's chariot. The two horses trotted and cantered along the worn trails through the valley, beneath the high grazing lands where the sheep and cattle would be turned out in late spring, and past several more small ringed forts with homes and sheltered animals tucked safely inside. The winter sun shone brightly all the while, and the fresh cold wind blew in sweet from the sea.

Finally, in the late afternoon, Ailin slowed the horses to a walk and drove them to the edge of a sparkling brook so they could drink. Christine stepped out of the chariot onto the soft, thick grass, feeling as though she had sea legs after standing and bracing herself for so long in the swaying vehicle.

She watched as Ailin led the team to a stout oak tree, tied a cord around their necks, and tossed it over the branches of the oak. He walked back to the chariot and took out a large leather pouch.

"I hope that's got lunch in it," she called. "I'm starved!"

"Food for us both, lady," he answered. "I will spread my cloak on the grass for you near the edge of the brook."

And so he did. Christine sat down with a sigh on the thick red wool and stretched her legs. "Ah—sitting feels wonderful!"

Ailin sat down beside her, and from the pouch took out flat bread, slices of cold roast meat wrapped in a square of linen, a handful of dried apples, and a single golden cup.

Before today, Christine would hardly have considered eating such a meal, but now things were quite different. "That's what I call a feast," she said, grinning up at Ailin.

But he only stared at her, serious and solemn, and offered her the food without a word. "Thanks," she whispered, and turned away to gaze down into the valley across the brook.

Every time she looked at Ailin, she felt stirrings of this handsome and powerful man that she had felt for no other. It hurt her to realize that he was not looking at her in the same way. It was even a little insulting, considering what he'd been about to do last night.

"Ailin," she said, turning back to look up at him, "you don't have to treat me like I was made of glass, you know. I won't break. I need a friend here in this place that is so strange to me, and I want very much to think of you as a friend as well as a— I mean, I need to know that I have someone I can trust, some-one I can count on."

Instantly he was up on one knee. "You can always trust me, lady," he intoned. "I will always be here for you, she whom I worship—"

"No, no! That's not what I meant at all!" Exasperated, Christine tossed aside the remains of her lunch. "Look—let me show you."

She pulled off her boots, scrambled to her feet, and with a little squeal splashed into the icy waters of the brook.

"Oh, it's cold—but it feels wonderful!" Gathering her skirts, she stepped quickly through the brook to the grassy bank on the other side and then waded in again, delighting in the silvery spray of the crystal-clear water. "Look how beautiful it is!"

Ailin got to his feet, watching her with an uncertain expression. "I just—I did not know that a goddess would . . . play," he said, clearly confused but absolutely having to say the words.

She grinned back from where she stood with her skirts lifted up to her knees, precariously balanced on a half-submerged stone, and made as if to kick water toward him. She nearly lost her balance and with another squeal and a cascade of giggles skittered through the water and up onto the soft lush grass. "Everyone needs to play, Ailin," she said, catching her breath. "Even me. Especially me."

"I just did not expect—"

"I know what you expected. But I'm sorry—you didn't get it." She sat down again in the grass, tucking her cold feet up into the wool skirts. "Maybe the connections got scrambled, and someone else who was expecting an ordinary redheaded lady is now trying to cope with a goddess. I really don't know. But you didn't get your goddess, Ailin—you just got me. And I'm sorry to disappoint you."

Slowly he sat down beside her. "I am not disappointed, lady. But I am afraid you are."

"Me?" She glanced up at him, curious. "I'm confused, yes, and more than a little scared, I don't mind admitting. But what makes you think I'm disappointed?"

"You keep saying that you are not the goddess—that you are not the one I asked for." His face was closed to her, his eyes cast down. Suddenly she longed to see that shining blue-gray gaze, and placed her hand on his powerful forearm. But he did not move or respond.

"Is it because I do not worship you properly, Lady Brighid? You took the gift I offered, yet now you say you are not the one I called. What more can I do to please you?"

Christine closed her eyes, her fingers still resting on his arm. Oh, there were so many things he could do to please her—and her mind was beginning to run away with the possibilities. But she could not forget her precarious situation, and she made herself say the words she had wanted to say since awakening here.

"What I really want more than anything is just to go home." But even as she spoke, her hand closed around his wrist.

At that gentle pressure, he finally raised his head to look at her. His eyes were still expressionless. "Home," he repeated. "Where is home? Where is it that you wish to go?"

Her heart beat faster. She did not know how to explain it to him, now that she finally had his full attention focused on the question, but she knew she had to try.

"It's like I said to you last night. I'm from a place very far away, one that would seem very strange to you. It's even beginning to seem strange to me and I've only been here a day. It's a land very different from this one, but it's my home and I must go back. I have no choice."

Yet her heart turned over with the certain knowledge that if she did somehow get home, she would never see Ailin again. She would never see such strength and gentleness and sheer masculine presence all in one man. With each passing moment, it became more difficult to think of leaving him forever.

"But I would miss you, Ailin. I would miss your kindness, and your strength, and your—your . . ."

He turned and raised himself up over her. Startled, she leaned back from him. "Then why would you leave me?" he whispered. "Why did you come to me, if only to say you are not the one? I do not understand. If you are not she whom I called, then who are you?"

His burning eyes and steady gaze held her spellbound. She almost forgot about any other life, about anything other than Ailin. Finally she looked away and closed her eyes to block out the sight of him, just so she could think.

"I am a woman, Ailin. Not a goddess. Just a woman who is lost and alone and trying to find her way home.

"We all have to go where we know we belong. That's what home is. And though this land is beautiful, and the people very kind, and you . . . you . . ." She nearly forgot what she was saying, as she looked at Ailin and the force of his presence surged over and through her like a tide. But she made herself finish.

"It's not home. I cannot stay here, Ailin. Somehow, sometime, I've got to go back."

Ailin reached for her hands. He got to his feet, raising her up with him. "And I will always want you here."

Christine stood facing him, her fingers lost in his strong hands. Her heart warmed at his words and at the way he looked at her—adoring, devoted—but then he spoke again.

"Here with me, the goddess at my side . . . come for me . . . only for me."

She froze. "No, Ailin. You haven't heard me at all. I said—" And then she stopped, pulling her hands away from him.

Shock and pain welled up inside her as sudden realization dawned. "I'm not good enough for you the way I am, am I? You only want me if I'm a goddess! You don't want a woman at all—just some supernatural being that you can't even touch!" She whirled around, lifted the hems of her skirts, and stalked off toward the brook.

"Where are you going?" Ailin called.

"Nowhere! Absolutely nowhere!" Her temper was rising but she told herself firmly that if she was going to lose it, it had better not be in front of Ailin or anyone else. No telling what they might think—or do—if the "goddess" started shouting and demanding! She had to keep her wits about her if she was to survive here and somehow, someday, find her way home.

It hurt that he did not want her for what she was—that he only wanted some glorious goddess come for his pleasure alone. Why hadn't she been able to see that before? She'd been so blinded by Ailin's powerful good looks and magnetism that she only saw what she wanted to see, heard what she wanted to hear.

At last, many yards away from Ailin and the chariot, she threw herself to the grassy bank to cool her feet in the cold, clear water. She just wanted a few minutes alone, she told herself, a chance to be herself without being onstage and stared at and worshiped and wondered about.

She kicked at the heavy, scratchy skirts, wishing mightily that she could just pull on a pair of comfortable jeans and a T-shirt and relax in an overstuffed chair in front of a TV. As she tossed her head in frustration, the torque shifted uncomfortably on her collarbone.

She rubbed at her slightly chafed skin, realizing

that she hadn't had the torque off since first putting it on. She pulled the metal ends slightly apart and yanked the heavy thing off, rubbing her aching neck in relief.

The sunlight became filtered and dim, as if it had gone behind a cloud—but there were no clouds this day. The air wavered, as though it had turned to silver and begun to shimmer.

Christine froze. She still held the torque tightly in her hand. She thought she heard Ailin calling to her—she could see him looking at her from where he stood farther upstream—but he seemed to be speaking nonsense. His words were in a strange language that she'd never heard before, and it frightened her that though she could plainly hear his voice she could not understand what he was saying.

The blood pounded in her ears. Shaking, she looked down at the gleaming torque. Here was the answer. She wasn't crazy, and she hadn't fallen or hit her head or lost her memory. This strange object was the key.

The torque had brought her here when she put it on. Would it let her go home again if she took it off?

She gripped the golden piece in trembling hands and tried to think as her panic rose. The world was fading into darkness once more and she had no way of knowing where that darkness led. Was it home? Or was it some other strange place, even more frightening and forbidding than this one—and one that did not have Ailin in it?

Perhaps it was merely death.

A shiver ran through her at that thought. As before, when she had stood on the edge of the towering cliff, she had no wish to use death as an escape. Yes, this life was fearsome and strange, but it was the only life she knew she had.

Then, as though from a great distance, she could see Ailin approaching her. He seemed to move in slow motion through the wavering, shimmering air.

If she dropped the torque and let the darkness take her, she might go home—or somewhere else—or simply die—but one thing she was sure of. She would never see Ailin again.

Already this strange, wild man, whom she had known for such a short time, had become a part of her. She could not bear the thought of leaving him forever. It would be almost like death, never to see Ailin again. . . .

Quickly she slid the torque back on her neck and pressed the ends close together to hold it securely in place.

The sun came out, bright and golden, and the world was real and solid once more. "May I offer you water, lady?" Ailin was saying.

"Oh . . . yes . . . thank you." She rose and took the dripping cup from his hands, drinking deeply of the cold fresh water. And as his eyes met hers, she knew that he—more than any fear of the unknown—had made her replace the torque. A life with Ailin, strange though it might be, was far preferable to any life without him.

As they drove back over the crest of the hill that led to Dun Orga, Ailin surprised Christine by turning the horses away from the fortress and trotting them in the other direction.

"Where are we going?" she asked. "Is something wrong?"

"Nothing is wrong, lady," he answered. Following his gaze, she saw that he was looking toward the top of the highest hill, where the bonfire had been held the night before. "It is time to search the Imbolc fire."

"Search the fire? Why?"

Ailin's eyes flicked toward her. "We must see for ourselves if anyone has been chosen by the goddess."

"Chosen? For what?"

"For . . ." He paused, and the only sounds were the horses' hooves on the path and the creaking of the

151

heavy wicker chariot. "For herself."

Christine almost laughed. "What does a goddess need with one of you?"

But then she covered her mouth with her hand. Oh, now I've done it, she thought. It might have been a good joke any other time—but how would Ailin react to this kind of flippancy?

He merely stared straight ahead, apparently lost in thought. "A goddess does not take what she needs. She takes what she wants."

He continued to drive the horses at a steady trot toward the hill. "I will tell you what I know, lady. If a warrior cannot find the stone he cast into the flames, it means that the goddess has chosen him for herself. She will call him to his next life before the next Imbolc."

His next life . . .

Christine knew what that meant. She remembered all too clearly Ailin's snarling words to Tierney when the two of them had struggled on the floor of the feast hall. *Now, Tierney,* Ailin had said, *you will have to wait for our next fight in your next life.*

The next life was death.

A cold tremor of fear ran through her. "What are you talking about?" she demanded, pulling his rock-hard arm and making him look at her. "Are you saying—do you mean you'll be killed if you don't find your stone?" Her voice shook. "That—that you'll be sacrificed?"

His eyes narrowed, and he was clearly baffled by her response. "We do not sacrifice the innocent," he said, as though explaining things to a frightened child. "We have never believed that the gods are pleased by cold murder. And they hardly need our help to take those they really want."

He reached out and gently stroked her hair. "You have no need of explanations, Lady of Fire, but if it pleases you I will tell you what I have always been told," he said. "If the goddess chooses a man in this way—if the stone he offered her cannot be found in the remnants of the fire—it means that she will see to it that he leaves this life for the next one before the next Imbolc. He might die in battle, or the sea might take his boat, or his chariot horses might drag him—but die he will, by whatever means she has decided."

"Have you—has this ever happened before?" Christine whispered.

"It has," he answered. "The last was my cousin Cormac, last year. He did not find his stone, and by midsummer he was dead—a wheel came off his chariot as his horses galloped full speed. His head struck a rock."

Christine continued to hold tight to Ailin's arm as she struggled for control. "But surely you don't really believe such a thing," she said, her voice catching only a little. "Just because Cormac couldn't find his stone in that huge fire had nothing to do with why a wheel came off his chariot four or five months later. I just—I can't go along with that kind of superstition. And that's all it is," she insisted, hoping that if she said it firmly enough she would believe it. "Just superstition!"

Ailin halted the chariot. They had reached a grove of trees at the foot of the hill and he stepped out, helping Christine down to the soft grass.

He tied the horses to a tree. The red-gold team stood quietly, tired after their long day, with their heads together and their long tails blowing in the cold evening breeze from the sea.

Ailin offered Christine his arm and together they began the climb to the top of the great hill. This time she paused to look out at the huge orange-gold sun setting into the calm gray sea. Her real home was somewhere far across that sea, but she didn't know if she could ever reach it. Not only was there an ocean of water separating her from her home, but an ocean of time as well. She reached up to touch

153

the torque around her neck and then walked with Ailin the rest of the way up the hill.

At the very top the remains of the bonfire smoldered, a gray and ghostly blot of ash with the skeletons of burned-out timbers scattered through it. Walking carefully through the ashes, cautious of the thin curls of smoke that still drifted upward here and there, were a dozen or so young men—the other young warriors like Ailin. They searched carefully through the site, using long sticks to poke through the ashes and turn aside the charred wood and blackened stones.

Suddenly one young man, after rubbing away the grime from one stone and carefully examining the surface, turned and bolted from the site. He went flying down the hill as fast as his feet would carry him, the stone held high over his head.

"He has not been chosen. It is not his time," Ailin said. And with that he caught up a long stick and walked into the ashes to begin his own search.

The minutes passed. One by one the other young warriors found their stones and fled, running like the wind, until at last only Ailin was left. He had searched every inch of the site and there was nowhere else to look. Finally he had to look up at Christine.

"I cannot find it," he said.

Christine felt a coldness steal through her at his words. Surely she didn't believe this little game. She refused to be caught up in some ancient superstition that said if you couldn't find your stone, you would die before the next Imbolc.

It was just the thought of being here without Ailin—no, she corrected herself as he walked toward her, his face serious and calm, his bearing one of nobility and courage—it was the thought of being anywhere without Ailin that sent a terrible sense of loss and loneliness throughout her heart and mind.

And there was one small and frightening thought

tugging at the corner of her mind, one that she could not banish. If it was true that he might not live to see another year—if she might only have a short time with him—how could she leave him now?

It was a long ride home in the early twilight, a long quiet ride during which Christine said little and Ailin even less. It was enough for her to be in Ailin's company, to stand at his side and feel his great strength as his wide red cloak blew protectively around her shoulders.

What he was thinking she could not tell; he was very quiet, but seemed proud and pleased. Perhaps it was because he rode with her, whom he thought to be a goddess favoring him with her presence—and who now, perhaps, had "chosen" him through the bonfire. Perhaps it was just his male vanity, showing her off to his friends and family.

But at this moment she did not care who he thought she was. It was still Christine that he rode beside, Christine who rested her hand lightly on his leather-banded wrist, Christine whom he looked at with such adoration and protectiveness.

She knew that she would always long to go back to her old life, her real life, in the comfortable modern world. But she also knew that she had a decision to make.

Pulling off the torque had shown her, with frightening clarity, that without it she would be lost to this world—just as she was now lost to the modern world. Pulling off the torque had led only to darkness and fear, not to her old life.

She must accept the fact that there would never be a way for her to return to that life. And if she did not accept it, if she were to spend every day and every hour and every moment longing for something that could never be, then she would be wasting whatever life was left to her here in Eire-land.

Her only other choice was to make a new life for herself. And she was determined that that life would begin with Ailin, her best source of strength in this strange new world. She drew a deep breath and faced her future as she faced the beautifully setting sun over the sea—with courage, and with awe, and with hope.

Chapter Thirteen

On a cool spring morning, with sunlight streaming in through the windows of the little white house, Christine opened the carved wooden chest at the foot of her sleeping ledge. Rummaging through the piles of gold jewelry and stacks of clean folded linen, she found her small knife and her calendar stick and lifted them out.

The stick was a slender piece of oak, with a large letter *M* carved awkwardly near the top. Carefully working her knife, she marked a single notch beneath the *M*.

March first.

Each morning she had faithfully marked the passage of the days, using pieces of oak from the lightning-struck tree. She'd decided that the day she arrived must have been the same day here that it had been in her world—January 31—and so she had started her own version of a calendar that very week.

The door opened and a short, round young woman with a cheerful face came bustling in. "Good morning, lady!" she said, closing the door and setting her basket on the hearth. "I have your favorite again this morning—bread and honey, with new milk. The cows are calving at last, and I walked up to the pasture this morning myself to get the milk for you."

Christine sighed. "Una, I've told you—you don't have to do all this for me. I appreciate it, but it's not—"

"Why, of course I do!" Una said indignantly. She lifted the polished wooden tray, laden with food, from the basket and set it on Christine's sleeping ledge. "My family allowed me to leave our *rath* and come to Dun Orga to serve you—and I don't want Derval and Slaine to have to come back and replace me! They have their own families to care for, and I am determined to do the best I can for you. Besides," she said with a grin, "I rather miss the cows and calves. And it is such a lovely morning."

Christine grinned back. "All right then. But in that case you'll have to share the milk with me."

Una opened her mouth as if to protest, but quickly closed it again. Pouring some of the milk from Christine's golden cup into her own wooden vessel, she drank it down in one long draft.

Christine carried her knife and stick back to the chest, closing them safely away before sitting down on the ledge to start on her breakfast. Una cocked her head at the sight, unaware that the milk had left a thin white line above her lip.

"I've never asked you this before, lady," she began, "but why do you do that? Why do you carve the lines on the stick each morning?"

"Ah . . . well," she began, thinking carefully. She did not want to confuse Una, or chance offending anyone. There was still a great deal she did not know about this place and she could never be sure whether something might be considered superstition or even heresy.

"You see, I was taught to measure time in a way that is different from you. You have thirteen months in a year—"

"One for each cycle of the moon," Una said, nodding.

"—and you count nights instead of days."

"Of course," Una said, chuckling. "The moon is the keeper of time for us, and she shows her face best at night. How else would anyone do it?"

Christine smiled. "It does make sense, I have to admit. The lines on my stick just help me to feel a little less . . . disoriented."

Una set down the empty cup. "I know of something else that would make sense, lady," she began.

Christine gave her a wary glance. "What's that?"

"You see . . ." She looked down, but then peered up at Christine from beneath her thick black brows. "I don't have to stay here at night. I can sleep in the hall with the other servants, and then—"

"But Una," Christine broke in, "you know I'm very glad to have you stay here with me. I'm grateful for all the work you do, truly I am. And I'm sure it's more comfortable here than in a crowded corner of the hall."

"Oh, no, lady, that's not what I meant at all!" Una said, her eyes round. "I love staying here with you, in this fine house. But . . ." She sighed, but then went on quickly, obviously determined to finish. "He's sleeping outside your door at night."

"I know he is. He's moved into his brother's house."

"But he watches over you each night. He stays right outside your door. Wouldn't you rather have him inside with you?"

Una looked so serious that Christine almost laughed. "Well, Una, it's not that I don't *want* him with me—I just—I'm not . . ." She sighed. "It's a little hard to explain."

There was a knock at the door. Una gave her a knowing glance and then hurried over to pull open the door.

Christine slid down from the ledge and stood wait-

159

ing. She felt hot and cold all over, all at the same time, as Ailin walked into the house and stopped just inside the doorway. "Good morning, lady."

He looked golden and tan, dressed in smooth leather breeches and a light linen tunic. "You must be going hunting today," Christine said. "I don't see any sword or shield."

Ailin smiled, and she thought that perhaps she would forget about her own tasks that awaited her today . . . she would just . . . she would just . . .

"You are right, lady. My brothers and I hunt together. We will be gone at least until sunset, and so I wanted to bring you this."

He held out an exquisite circular golden brooch, the kind used to fasten the heavy woolen cloaks. She accepted the priceless object—"Thank you, Ailin"—and opened the wooden chest to tuck it safely away with her growing hoard of bracelets, brooches, necklaces, earrings, and armbands that he had made for her.

"I don't know where you find the time to make all these things, but they are so beautiful. I do love them all." She closed the lid, wondering how long it would be before she'd need a new chest to store her treasures.

"I do not leave for the hunt until later in the morning," Ailin said. "The king has matters to attend to, and the rest of us await him. I wonder if I might—if I would be permitted to sit at your feet while you are sewing this morning?"

Christine hesitated. She started to speak but then glanced at Una, who took the hint, picked up her basket, and hurried out the door.

"Ailin." She walked over to him, standing in his warm golden shadow, and once again tried to find the right words. "You don't have to ask my permission for something like that. Of course I would love to have your company, at any place, at any time. Any woman would love that—and I am a woman just like any other."

"Not like any other, lady. You—"

"Oh, yes, I know. I am your goddess and you worship the ground I walk on." Turning away from him, she picked up her wicker basket and began collecting the things she would need for her work that day—a bundle of red-and-gold plaid fabric, the wooden spindle half-filled with new red yarn, her two favorite iron needles.

All these weeks she had been hoping she could gradually break down the barriers between them. She had tried to make him see that she really was just an ordinary woman who did ordinary things—eating, sleeping, cooking, cleaning, and sewing.

But it had had little, if any, effect.

"You swear you love me, and you give me gifts whose value I can only imagine, but you treat me like I was made of glass! I can't even talk to you—and oh, how I would like to—I would like to—"

She stared up at him from across the room, lips parted, her heart racing. But he made no move at all. As always, he awaited her words, her actions, her pleasure—and she knew he would wait until the end of time, if necessary.

She closed her eyes and turned away. She wanted to be angry with him, but found that she could not. He was so kind, and so thoughtful, and so gentle with her, and so protective that Christine had no doubt he would lay down his life for her in an instant.

It was impossible to be angry.

She turned back to him and smiled in spite of herself. Even after all these weeks, the mere sight of his tall strong body and fine noble face was enough to make her catch her breath and set her heart to pounding.

"Ailin," she said gently, "do you have any idea how happy I would be if you simply kissed me, or even held my hand?"

He waited for barely a moment. And then he was right there in front of her, close enough to touch, so near that she could smell the warmth of the sun in his smooth fair skin and golden hair.

He lifted her hand between his own, pressing it gently. His fingers were as strong as steel. And then, as Christine gazed up at him, unable to look away, he leaned over her, his long hair falling on the skin of her throat.

His lips were soft, and hot as the sun . . . and Christine tasted the life force of a primal warrior as Ailin kissed her.

She floated in warm darkness, unable to open her eyes, hardly knowing where she was or what she was doing. She was only aware of Ailin's powerful body leaning over hers, of his lips so near her own. She reached out to him, wanting to clasp him to her and hold him there forever; she would never let him go—

But he had moved away from her. Opening her eyes, blinking against the dizziness that swept over her, she saw him standing calmly and waiting, as always, for her next move.

"I hope I have made you happy, lady," he said somberly.

Christine almost laughed—the laughter of despair and frustration. "Oh, Ailin, you have no idea."

He seemed to take her words as affirmation, for he smiled and moved toward the door. "I will walk with you when you are ready."

Though her heart still pounded and her body still ran hot from Ailin's touch, she knew that he had not closed the gap between them. He had done what she had asked—oh, how he had done it! But he had only been following orders.

The whole thing was frustrating. It was maddening. But at the moment she had no idea what to do about it. She picked up her basket, took a last drink of milk from the golden cup, and set out for the hall.

* * *

While Ailin spent his days hunting, or training with his sword and shield, or making gifts of jewelry for Christine, or learning the craft of kingship from his father, Christine spent her days among the women of Dun Orga.

She'd quickly learned that she wasn't much more of a cook in these ancient times than she'd been in the twentieth century, but also discovered that she did not mind helping with the spinning, weaving, and sewing that were vitally necessary to the clan. She especially enjoyed learning to do the magnificent embroidery, which Derval was teaching her.

Each day a group of the women gathered in the feast hall for these tasks and Christine always joined them. The work kept her busy, provided her with company, and allowed her to feel that she was earning her keep and finding a place in this society.

Inside the long hall, in place of the wooden squares on the floor that were used for the feasts and gatherings, two weaving looms had been set up. Una sat at one, and another serving maid worked the other. A dozen or so women sat on benches or on cushions on the rush-covered floor, occupied with spinning thread, sewing gowns and tunics, or doing embroidery. Small children played underfoot, giggling and squealing and racing up and down the hall as their mothers talked and laughed.

Christine sat down on a wooden bench placed against the wall and shook out the pieces of her new gown. She had spun the wool, dyed it, and woven the cloth herself, so that she could learn each step of the process. Never again would she take clothes for granted!

True to his word, Ailin sat down in the rushes at her feet. A hush fell over the hall as everyone turned to stare at them. What was a warrior like Ailin doing in the women's hall in the middle of the morning?

Into the awkward silence, Christine suddenly

tossed a question. "Ah, would anyone like to hear a story?"

Instantly the air was buzzing in response, and there was a rustling of rushes and a dragging of benches as the women gathered close around Christine. They all loved her stories, since the tales were all brand-new in this place and time. Who here had ever heard of Shakespeare or Danielle Steele? Christine's stories were always the highlight of the day, though no one had ever quite gotten up the nerve to ask her for one directly.

She thought quickly, once again thankful for her education. Who said a liberal arts degree was of no use? She knew plenty of wonderful stories; the only difficulty was in choosing one.

She glanced down at Ailin, silent and strong at her feet, and made her choice.

"Once, long ago," Christine began, carefully threading her curved iron needle, "there was a king who needed a queen. But he had never found any woman who could live up to his idea of the perfect mate—all of them fell short of his dream, his ideal.

"He decided to create a woman for himself. The king was also a fine sculptor and so he made a beautiful statue out of stone, carving the cold and silent marble into the image of the woman he wanted—or thought he wanted.

"He named his creation Galatea, and the statue was indeed so beautiful, so perfect, so exquisite, that the king fell in love with it. Here, surely, was perfection itself, a mate worthy of a king! He would be the envy of the world!"

"But Galatea could not return his love, or even know of it; she was only a stone carving, after all. Finally the king began to realize that an unfeeling statue, no matter how perfect it appeared or how he worshiped at its feet, was no match for a warm and lively queen—even if she was human and had a few human flaws."

She gazed down at Ailin, and there was a tremor in her voice. "He—he asked the goddess Aphrodite to transform his cold and lovely stone into a living woman, for he was no longer content merely to worship her from afar. When she was brought to life Galatea only seemed more beautiful to the king, and . . . and so they were married."

Christine bent her head and quickly looked away from Ailin, concentrating on stitching the bright red-and-gold gown. No one said a word.

"Of course, she would have been a very young mate for him," said Slaine, trying to be helpful by breaking the silence. "Though she looked like a woman, she was really like a newborn babe—wasn't she?"

Christine smiled. "That's a good point. I really hadn't thought of it that way before. Maybe—"

"After all, I wasn't married until I was all of sixteen years, and that was over a year ago," Slaine continued.

Christine stared at her. "You're only seventeen?" she asked in amazement.

"She is, lady," said Derval. "She is like a little sister to me. I was five years old when she was born, and we have grown up together."

"And you're twenty-two," Christine said slowly. These people were younger than she had realized. The harsh lives they led would no doubt age them faster.

Then another thought struck her.

Her eyes shifted to Ailin. As though knowing right away what she wanted to ask, he saved her the trouble.

"I am twenty years old, Lady of Fire."

Christine nearly dropped her needle. "Twenty?" she managed to gasp after a moment. "You're twenty?"

He nodded, getting to his feet. "Last winter."

"But I—I'm—"

Her fragile sense of security had just been dealt another blow. On top of everything else, she was ten years older than the man of her dreams!

Sensing her distress, the other women took their benches and cushions and went off to busy themselves in other parts of the hall. Only Ailin was left with Christine, and all she could do was stare at him in shock.

"Lady, what is it?" he asked. He reached up to clasp her hand, his arm resting on her knee.

"You're twenty years old," she repeated, holding tight to his hand. "You're twenty, and I'm—"

"You are ageless," he said, and she found herself looking directly into his slate-blue eyes. "A goddess has no age, and so it cannot matter how many years I have lived—for you have lived forever."

She turned away from him, pulling her hands back into her lap. "You don't understand," she said, her voice shaking. "I will never belong here. I will never fit in. I'm from another place, another time, and I'm as out of place here as a—a housecat in the middle of the ocean. Realizing how much older I am than all of you just brought it home to me, that's all."

Christine closed her eyes. "Sometimes it seems that my past is the dream, and this is the only reality. But if that's true, why do I still long for the things I used to know? Books, and the university, and even a long, hot shower . . . why can't I forget them, if my past is just a dream?"

She folded the pieces of the plaid gown, pressing them down into a tight ball in her lap. "And if this is real, how could I have fallen—how could I be so attracted to a man ten years younger than I am?"

"I do not know, lady. I can tell you only that it makes me happy to hear you say you are attracted to me." His eyes shone, and he looked like a man at peace with the entire world. "A goddess has no age. She chooses who she wants, and cares nothing for the years he might have—or not have."

There was a sound of hoofbeats and the rattle of chariots outside. "Ailin!" came a distant call.

He stood up. "The hunt is leaving, but we will be back before sunset," he said. "I promise you, when I return I will have something for you that will make you feel happy again."

Near the top of the barren hillside, shrouded in fog and grayness, Becan and Garvan walked past a half-dozen or so ragged makeshift tents and sat down on a fallen boulder to eat their share of the day's bread and hard cheese. They kept their voices down so none of the others would hear them.

"He didn't find it," Becan said, mumbling around a mouthful of bread.

"Find what?"

"His stone. In the Imbolc fire. Ailin didn't find his stone."

Garvan snorted. "So? Maybe the goddess will take him away from here herself and save us the trouble. I still aim to make him pay for Dur's life."

"But don't ye think that's why she's here? To take Ailin away?"

Garvan looked up at his brother, scowling. "Ye still think that red-haired piece is the goddess herself, don't ye? Well, like I told ye before, I don't think so. If she wants a man, she just takes him. She wouldn't have to move in at Dun Orga and carry him off on her back."

"But if . . ." Becan paused to wipe away the dampness that dripped from his matted black hair into his eyes. "She might have come for him. She could do that, if she wanted. She would come for him, and he wouldn't find his stone, and he'd never see another Imbolc."

"All right!" Garvan turned away and spat in frustration. "We'll keep watching. And we'll find out once and for all what that woman is. If Ailin is dead before Imbolc, and that flame-haired woman disappears,

167

then maybe . . ." He spat again. "But if she's just a woman like any other, then we carry out our revenge ourselves. And soon. All right?"

They pulled their ragged cloaks a little closer, and huddled together on the cold rock as the rain began to pour.

Chapter Fourteen

Somehow Christine managed to make the rest of the morning pass. She worked feverishly, listening to the merry gossip and bawdy stories of the other women and watching the children play and laugh. She tried to drive her despairing, anxious thoughts away, but they remained churning just beneath the surface.

Her head bent in concentration, she hardly noticed as Derval came to sit beside her, followed a moment later by Slaine. They sat with her in silence for a time, and finally Derval rested her hand gently on Christine's arm.

"What is it, lady?"

Christine forced herself to think of something, anything, besides Ailin. The pain of her loneliness and of their strange, precarious relationship was simply too great; it would have to wait for a time, until she felt she could endure it.

She closed her eyes tight. She could barely see the needle and fabric anyway, with the tears burning her eyes. "Books," she whispered. "Books."

"B-bucks?" said Derval. "I don't understand, lady."

Christine glanced at her and smiled a little. "Books," she said again. "Things that don't exist in this world. And I miss them—oh, how I miss them."

"Can we get them for you, lady? Can we find them, or make them?"

Christine stared at Derval, who gazed back with a wholehearted desire to help. "Make them," she repeated. "You know, maybe we could!"

"What is a 'buck,' lady?" asked Slaine.

"A *book*," Christine said, grinning now, "is a story on paper. Instead of being spoken, the words are written down. We use symbols, called letters, for the different sounds, and we combine them to make words, and sentences, and paragraphs, and chapters, and books!"

"I think I understand," said Derval. "Like the ogham lines that the druids use to represent words."

"The what?" Now it was Christine's turn to be confused. "Did you say 'ogham' lines?"

"Yes, lady. Like the lines carved on the stones the young men hurled into the Imbolc fire."

"Ah. Yes. I remember." Christine thought fast. "Maybe I could learn them, and then find some way to write down stories, and histories, and information!"

Her mind raced. "I could do it—learning a new alphabet would be a challenge; it would keep me busy! It would almost be like being back at the university!"

She stood up, brushing aside the plaid gown. Slaine caught it before it could fall into the rushes. "How can I learn ogham writing? Could you teach me, Derval?"

Derval's eyes widened slightly. "Lady, I cannot. I am sorry, I have not the skill. Only the druids possess knowledge of ogham."

The druids. "Ernin," Christine said. She had become used to seeing him at Dun Orga. He was a quiet, faintly mysterious presence, usually with the king and the warriors. "Would he teach me? Could I ask him?"

Derval and Slaine looked at each other. "You are one who could ask him, lady. If you wish, we will walk with you to his house."

"Let's go!"

The three women walked across the Dun beneath the warm noonday sun. Christine's spirits rose with every step they took.

How she would love to read and write again! She could think back on all the stories she had ever learned and write them down, either in English or in the strange alphabet of lines that Derval had called *ogham*. Surely Ernin would agree to teach it to her!

They found the druid alone inside his small house. He stepped outside with them and stood quietly, gazing at Christine, waiting with infinite patience for her to speak.

"Writing," she said at last. "I-I want to learn your way of writing. The ogham alphabet."

He cocked his head slightly, his old gray eyes bright with curiosity. "And what would you do with this writing?" he asked in his whispery voice.

"Oh, so much!" she said eagerly. "I could write down the stories that I know—and the ways of doing things—and teach the others to read and write. It would be wonderful!"

"Ogham lines are for carving in stone, or in wood, Lady of Fire. How will you write down a story in stone? Will you carve the whole of Eire-land for your stories?"

She stared at him. "But surely you have something else to write on! Not paper, I know—but what about vellum?"

He merely stared back at her.

"You know, calfskin! Fine calfskin. It's very good for writing on. Many ancient cultures used it before they learned to make paper. I know there must be plenty of it around here. And maybe later I could figure out how to make some kind of paper to write

171

on—or even use linen! Yes, linen, that's it! And dyes instead of ink—there's lots of linen and good dye around here, too!"

The druid never moved. He did not say a word. He simply gazed at her. Derval and Slaine, too, were silent.

"What is it?" Christine finally asked. "Don't you understand me? What is wrong?"

Ernin's steady gaze never wavered. "Lady," he said, "would you have our people become passive and weak?"

Christine blinked. "What are you talking about? Of course not. What on earth does that have to do with learning to read and write? Those things only make a person stronger!"

"You do not understand," the old man said gently. "If the words are written down, the bards would have no reason to memorize them—to make the words, and the knowledge and power contained in the words, truly a part of themselves."

He shifted, leaning on his long, gnarled staff. "They would need only stare at the writing, passive and at ease, to find the things that should be stored forever in their hearts. They could pick up the words at their careless leisure whenever they felt the need to find facts—facts that should be inscribed in the deepest parts of their being."

Christine could feel her heart sinking. She was treading on forbidden ground here. She should have thought of that before rushing off to ask Ernin to teach her to read their alphabet.

He had talked about books the way people in her world talked about television!

It was just that she had been so excited at the prospect of writing, of reading, she had not thought. . . .

She had not thought.

"I am sorry," she whispered. "I did not understand. I am sorry."

"There is nothing to be sorry for, Lady of Fire. We

are the ones who must apologize to you—apologize for the weaknesses that make it so necessary for us to learn with our voices and our hearts, instead of simply using our eyes and mere words preserved in writing."

Christine sat alone in the hall, lost in the dusty dimness of the late afternoon. The curved needle in her fingers moved quickly, mechanically, up and back down through the heavy red-and-gold plaid wool, up and back down. She kept her eyes on her work and listened for the sounds of Ailin's return.

At last, when it was nearly too dark to work any longer, she heard the familiar rattling of the wicker chariots and felt the pounding of the horses' hooves. Tossing the newly sewn gown aside, she got up from the bench and hurried out into the sunset.

She was always happy at the sight of Ailin, but this time her happiness was accompanied by a sense of relief. Only he could take her away from her thoughts of books and writing and the modern world she would never see again.

"Ailin!" she called. She dashed out to meet him, her heart yearning for the comfort of his strong embrace. This time she would run straight into his arms, she didn't care what he—or anyone else!— might think.

Then she stopped in her tracks.

At the sight of her, Ailin had stepped out of his chariot and dropped to one knee. "Lady," he said, his eyes shining, "I have brought you a special gift, just as I promised. Here, these are for you." Proudly, certain that the things he had brought would make her happy, he waved his arm toward the chariot.

Christine approached him, dimly aware that a crowd of people had gathered in the yard and were watching her closely. Resting one hand on the rough wicker of the chariot, she leaned over and peered inside.

On the floorboards lay four baby rabbits, their eyes glassy in death. Blood spattered their creamy tan fur.

With horror, Christine realized that this was the fine luxurious fur she had so admired in the boots and cloaks she had been given. She could only imagine how the little creatures had died. Rabbits screamed when they were frightened or in pain. She could hear their screams, their pitiful baby screams of fear and agony as Ailin killed them—

"These will make a fine new pair of boots for you, lady," he said. "I know how you liked the fur that lined the other pair, and these four are even younger than the hares I trapped to make the others. Their fur will be finer still."

She made herself look up at him, and at the faces of all the other people of the Dun. Every one of them was completely dependent on the animals for shelter and food. In this place, *harvest* did not mean just harvesting crops that grew in the ground. It also meant harvesting the living animals of the forest and the field and the sky.

Ailin's words were innocently stated, she knew. He was not a cruel man, and he had not killed the baby rabbits for sport. Here in this beautiful, savage place, everything carried its price. Beneath a lovely exterior often lay suffering and death.

The evening wind ruffled the soft tan coats of the little creatures, exposing the creamy white fur underneath. Tears sprang to Christine's eyes but she was determined not to let anyone see. She would maintain her dignity—at least, her dignity as a woman, even if not as a goddess.

"Thank you, Ailin," she whispered. "They are—Thank you." She turned away and retreated across the Dun, not caring where she went. She wanted only to get away from the staring crowd and the small dead rabbits, and be alone with her thoughts.

Near the front gate of Dun Orga, a rough wooden fence stretched from the dun's earthen wall to a long, low shed. She leaned against the fence and reached out her hand.

"Sunshine," she called.

She was rewarded by a soft nicker. A small golden mare walked out from the shed to the fence, and pushed her velvet-soft nose against Christine's outstretched hand.

The horses had become some of her first friends at Dun Orga. Christine had always liked horses, having fond memories of riding at scout camp years ago, and Sunshine had quickly become a special favorite.

"I'm sorry, sweetheart, I didn't bring you anything," Christine said. "Not bread, or dried apples, or sugar." She ruffled the little mare's creamy gold mane and smooth coat, blinking back the tears that refused to go away. "In my world horses love sugar. But there is no sugar here, and there won't be for more years than I can even imagine."

There was a footstep beside her. She felt, rather than saw, Ailin's presence. Though she wanted nothing more than to turn to him and lose herself in his powerful embrace, she simply stood unmoving, gazing at the small golden mare.

"I am sorry that you did not like my gift, lady."

Christine smiled through her tears. "It's all right, Ailin. You give me far too many gifts as it is. I know you were only trying to be kind."

His red cloak brushed against her side. She closed her eyes, wanting so much to reach out to him, to hold him, to touch his smooth, warm skin—and willing herself not to.

"Would you prefer this mare?"

"What?"

He looked down at her and smiled gently, as though she were a silly child. "This mare. The one you call Sunshine. Would you like to have her as a gift?"

"Oh . . . Oh!"

She looked at the lovely golden horse, so gentle and friendly, and renewed hope surged through her. "I used to love to ride when I was young," she said, "but I haven't done it in years." She thought quickly. "If I cannot use books and writing as an outlet—something to learn—maybe I can use riding instead!"

"I will speak to my father about it, but trust me, it is done already," said Ailin. He smiled down at her, completely happy with her response. "I am so glad you are pleased with my gift, Lady of Fire."

She gave him a quick glance. "I thank you," she said, her voice low, "but you must understand I cannot be bought. I don't want things from you, Ailin, I want . . . I want . . ."

He stared down at her, waiting for her next words, and Christine knew he would say nothing until she finished her statement. But how could she tell him what she really wanted? Why did she not just say to him how she longed for a simple embrace, the caress of his powerful hands, the touch of his lips? Her knees grew weak at the mere memory of the one kiss he had given her.

And yet she knew exactly why she did not—could not—tell him what she wanted. Because he would give it to her.

He would give her all that she asked for, all she had ever dreamed of and more, and it would be wonderful. And it would be false. False because it would not be for her, Christine, the woman from another time and place who had somehow come to his world. It would only be for his imaginary goddess, for whom she had become an unwilling stand-in.

Christine stared hard into his eyes. "I want to make the most of my life here," she said. "I must live as though all the rest of my life will be spent in this place."

"I hope that it will be, lady," Ailin said fervently. He turned to go, and offered her his arm. "Please, it

176

is growing late. Let me walk with you back to your house."

She placed her hand on his smooth, hard arm, thinking. It was no longer enough for her simply to accept her fate and be willing to live quietly in this place. It was time to turn her mind to more practical things.

Each day she sat with the women as they worked, watching their children play and seeing their men come for them each evening. She knew that she would not be willing to live alone much longer, guarded and honored, lonely and untouched.

That night, Christine sat alone in the little white house, struggling to mend the torn hem of her favorite blue gown with only the fluttering light of a single candle to see by. Finally she threw the heavy wool aside in exasperation and swore under her breath as the sudden breeze it created put the candle out.

She had tried to lose herself in endless tasks but it simply wasn't working—not tonight. Sewing held no interest for her, nor did cleaning or cooking or anything else that usually took up her time.

It was dark now. And silent. She caught herself listening for the slow tick of the wall clock, as if she were back home in her own wonderfully modern but equally silent apartment.

Ailin waited right outside the door. He guarded her every night, and Christine did not have to look to know that he was there.

All she had to do was open the door and go to him . . . give him a word, a sign, a glance . . . and he would be with her in an instant, her loneliness banished, the dark and silent house filled with his passion for her and the brightness of their love for one another. . . .

Christine closed her eyes.

Her thoughts of the afternoon came rushing back

like cold water on flame. She had tried everything to convince him that she was just a natural, ordinary woman, but nothing had worked. Even when he had kissed her—and her heart beat faster at the mere thought of that single kiss—he had simply been doing the goddess's bidding.

Her fingers tightened on the furs covering the sleeping ledge. If she went to him and invited him to come inside the house, would he accept because he truly wanted her or because he still believed he was worshiping a goddess?

The silence closed in and suddenly she could not endure it a moment longer. She slid down off the ledge and stood ankle-deep in rushes, alone in the darkness and the silence.

The time had come. She had waited long enough, held back long enough, been alone in a strange land long enough. Maybe there was one way she could convince Ailin once and for all that she was no supernatural being, but a woman of flesh and blood like any other.

If he would not come to her, then she would go to him, and this time there would be no misunderstanding. He might embrace her as the worshiper of a goddess, but he would leave knowing her for the woman that she truly was!

Chapter Fifteen

Christine opened the door.

Soft clouds chased the crescent moon, parting here and there to show a few bright stars against the blackness. She stepped outside the house and there he was, sitting against the white wall, his sword across his knees.

Instantly Ailin was on his feet and the sword was back in its black leather scabbard. "Lady—does something trouble you so late? What is it?"

Christine went to him, silent, unwilling to put into words what she wanted. She stood before him and rested her hand on his arm. Looking up into that shadowed, noble face, she could see the soft gleam in his eyes. In silence she turned her face up to him, pulled herself up against his chest, and kissed him.

He stood very still, and his mouth was hot and soft, but there was a sudden tension in his body—a flare of strength controlled only by the force of his will.

"Come with me," she whispered against his mouth. "Come inside with me. . . ."

She held still, half-expecting him to lift her up and carry her to the sleeping ledge as he had on her first night in this place. But he only stepped away from

179

her and held the door open, following her inside and closing the wooden door securely after them.

Night filled the house. Yet the distant light of the stars and moon stole in through the small window and gave a gleam to Ailin's gold coronet, a soft shine to his long blond hair. He waited still and silent before the door, but Christine could hear his quickened breathing and feel the ever-rising tension that he held at bay only through sheer determination.

It was for her to take his hand and lead him to the fur-covered ledge. As she sat down, she heard the sliding of leather and the soft clicking of metal as Ailin removed his sword belt and unfastened the brooch that held his cloak. There was a heavy rustling as he let them fall to the rushes, and then silence again. He was waiting for her.

Her heart racing, knowing she must reach him now if ever she was going to, Christine quickly unfastened her long leather belt. She pulled her linen underdress and woolen gown off over her head as if they were a single garment and tossed them to the rushes with Ailin's cloak and sword-belt.

Squaring her shoulders, she sat up tall and proud on the ledge. The faint moonlight would reflect just enough off her skin to show Ailin that she wore nothing more than the beautiful golden torque he had made for her.

She had no care for who else might see her this way, naked and alone with her chosen lover. Who would think it wrong or obscene, here in this young and pagan land bursting with life?

Still, Ailin did not reach for her. He made no move at all. But Christine found that she did not care. It was right that she should lead him through this first encounter. He would have no chance to seize her blindly and ride away on some frenzied tide of passion, telling himself he made love to a goddess.

No, on this night she would make him see her and feel her during each and every moment. He would know who and what he held. He would have no choice but to see her for what she really was.

Gazing at him, another thought crossed her mind. If she were to come away from this with a child, it would present no problem here in Dun Orga, in ancient Eire-land. She would welcome Ailin's child . . . a son or daughter as strong and handsome and kind as he was . . . and if he did not want to marry her she would live alone and care for herself, living among the servant women in the hall if need be until she could build her own house.

She reached out to him. With the lightest touch she ran her fingertips over the linen of his tunic, feeling the heat rising through the fabric. Quickly Ailin pulled the tunic off over his head and dropped it to the floor. The gold coronet on his brow was undisturbed, and glinted softly in the moonlight.

His body was hers to command, hers to cherish. She could not keep from touching him, from caressing the fair skin of his neck, his shoulders, his powerful arms.

With a cry she grasped him and pulled him close, her head thrown back, aching for the feel of her breasts pressed against his hard chest. For a long time she clung to him, lost in the heat of his strong embrace and the scent of the sun in his hair.

Finally she leaned forward and rested her head against his. "So long," she whispered against his cheek. Her eyes were wet. "So long I have waited for this . . . wanted this. . . ."

He held her gently, stroking her hair with one hand. His strong heart pounded against her chest until it seemed it was her own heart she was feeling.

Christine took a deep breath and sat back from him, and then reached for his black leather breeches. Again, at her touch, he followed her unspoken wish. He stepped down into the rushes and Christine heard the rustling and creaking of leather. In a moment he sat before her on the ledge.

Once more she reached out to hold him, this time pressing him gently down until he lay on his back on the thick furs on the ledge. The light of the moon and stars showed her the clear outline of his fair-skinned body, with its warrior's grace and power. For a time she simply looked at him, drinking in the sight, and ran her fingers over the hard muscles of his long legs and slim hips.

Though she could feel his fever heat, he made no move or sound, even when she closed her fingers around his hot, smooth masculinity. His skin was velvet-smooth, hot and pulsing with life and power. Never in her life had she imagined a man like this one. Finally she released him and moved to claim him, all in one swift motion.

He raised his arms almost involuntarily to hold her as she slid one leg across him to straddle his hips. She reached beneath his neck and pulled him close even as she moved to slide down over him, to bring him inside the deepest part of herself, to welcome him into her body and into her soul and into her heart.

He caught his breath and tightened his embrace. She held him fast and offered him a kiss; he returned it, long and soft. With a little moan of happiness she pressed her cheek against him and began to move, rocking against him, making love to the most magnificent man she had ever known, holding him closer, closer, moving with him. He was a part of her, they were as one creature, never again to be apart. . . .

Suddenly he gripped her tightly and his breathing quickened. Christine's own waves of pleasure began as he filled her with an offering of life. Finally, passion spent, she leaned down to him once more and they held each other close.

He had not spoken a word since she brought him inside the house.

* * *

The moon rose high in the sky, moving on past the window and leaving the little house in shadow. The lovers within rested together on soft thick furs and neither one made any move to go.

Christine felt as though she could stay where she was for the rest of her days. It was not possible that she would ever be more content than she was at this moment. She and Ailin had come together as woman and man, and it had been everything she had ever dreamed of. There could be no question now that he accepted her as a real, live, and very earthly woman.

She almost giggled to herself, burrowing deeper into the heavy furs. Surely no ethereal goddess had ever felt the way she had just a short time ago!

Ailin turned to look at her, raising himself up on one elbow. He smiled back as he saw her joyous expression and, to Christine's surprise, bent down to kiss her softly.

"I know that being kissed pleases you," he said, his face still very close to hers. "I remember well that you once asked me to kiss you. I would do anything to please you, anything you might desire."

A faint shadow began to creep across Christine's bright, moonlit happiness. His words were wonderful, all that any woman might long to hear—but what was behind them?

"What I desire most, at this moment," she said, their lips almost touching, "is to hear you tell me that—that now you know I am not a goddess. That after this, you have no doubt I am a woman like any other. That is what would please me more than anything."

He stopped just before his mouth touched hers. "You are like no other woman, Lady Brighid. If I was not certain of that before, I am now." He sat back slightly and Christine could feel his gaze, even in the darkness.

Even as her heart began to sink.

"Never have I known love with any woman of the

earth as I have known it here with you. On the first night that you came to Dun Orga, I carried you to this very place but you bid me stop—and stop I did. I believed that you would come for me when the time was right, and so you did."

He found her hand and raised it to his lips. "I would have waited for you until the end of this life, and the next, and the next, if need be. A love such as I feel for you, a night of loving such as this—those could not be of this earth, but only of the Other-world, where the goddess dwells.

"I do not know how long you will choose to stay with me in this world, but I will show you all the love I have, all the adoration I can give you, in the hope that you will stay with me for all of my days."

Slowly Christine withdrew her hand. The combination of the heights of ecstasy with the shock of Ailin's words simply left her numb.

"Ailin, what can I do to make you understand?" she whispered, her voice beginning to break with sorrow and frustration. "You cannot love me if you do not accept me for what I really am! You would only be in love with a fantasy!"

But he only kissed her gently on the forehead before rolling away from her. She heard him stand up in the rushes, heard the creak of his leather breeches as he pulled them on and the heavy rustling of his cloak as he picked it up.

"I will guard you well, Lady of Fire," he said. The wooden door opened and closed. Christine did not need the moonlight to show her that he was gone.

The next three days passed for Christine in an unsettling mix of happiness, uncertainty, and frustration. Each morning when she emerged from the house Ailin was there, and she knew he had remained all night. Each morning he waited for her with a cup of new milk or a piece of golden honeycomb for her breakfast, or a length of the finest new wool fabric, or yet another gift of gold jewelry.

Her instincts told her to wait and see what would happen after the night they had spent together, to see how his feelings had changed, to let him make the next move. She had certainly made it clear to him where she stood, hadn't she?

Of her love for this noble, powerful man she had no doubt, but it would mean nothing if he did not feel the same way about her.

Yet as the days went by, she found to her dismay that even though she had gone to him as a lover—as a woman desiring the man she wished to spend her life with—nothing had changed. He made no move to claim her, gave no hint that he would ever think of coming to her bed simply because he desired her for himself and wished to show her the physical side of his love for her.

Oh, she knew that he would come to her again in an instant if she asked—if he was certain he was following the express wish of she whom he worshiped, just as he had the first time. But that was not what Christine wanted!

Her gentle seduction of Ailin had only caused him to become more devoted to her than ever. She was still a goddess, and he was still her servant.

The day was wild and beautiful, the cold wind blowing with the violence of early spring. Every few moments the sky changed from a high canopy of brilliant clear blue to an ominous lowering cover, heavy with rolling black clouds and silvery curtains of rain. Then the wind blew the clouds inland and opened up the sky once more to the shining sun.

Christine stood with the men and women of Dun Orga in a circle of three towering oak trees, high atop a hill overlooking the crashing sea. She wore a white linen gown with a blue overdress and a soft green woolen mantle, and smiled to herself. *Glorious. I match the day!*

185

The tops of the massive oaks merged together to form an interlaced ceiling of tender new branches and delicate pale green leaves, and gave the assembly some shelter from the winds. Christine faced the wind and breathed deeply. Could anyone ever get enough of the fresh sweet scent of spring rain and new leaves? It was so beautiful up here that, at least for the moment, it took her mind off the apprehension she felt at waiting for yet another mysterious ceremony to begin.

At least there was daylight this time, and no sign of a bonfire.

No one seemed to know why they had been asked to gather in this place. King Donaill, with Ernin at his side, had led all the men and women of the Dun to this circle of oaks high in the hills. The children and servants remained behind. No one had asked a single question of their king or his druid adviser.

Ailin stood at her side, but like the others he said not a word. Christine resigned herself to waiting patiently and telling herself that she would know soon enough what was to happen here today.

Finally, at a word from the king, all the men moved to the front of the grove. Ailin went with them and spared only a brief glance for Christine. The women stayed where they were and seemed content to watch and listen and whisper among themselves.

Christine found herself standing near the back with Derval and Slaine beside her. "What's going on?" she asked.

"We are wondering what they are voting on," Derval answered, wrapping her bright green-and-gold plaid mantle a little closer.

"It could be a new law," Slaine added. "Or maybe they're going to choose the tanist."

"About time," Derval said.

But Christine was startled. "Voting?" she asked. "You vote on things? On laws?"

Now it was her two friends' turn to look startled.

"Of course," Slaine said with a little laugh. "It has always been that way. We vote on laws because—because the law says we must!"

Christine shook her head. "I guess I must have been asleep in class that day. I thought that ancient bar— that ancient people decided everything through inheritance or through battle, not through elections!"

Derval hesitated, appearing to be both shocked and amused, and trying very hard not to show it. "It is true, lady, that the tanist must be selected from among the men of the king's family. But the manner of his choosing is extremely important to us. How could the Dun accomplish anything if all were not in agreement? The king knows that his fighters will serve him without question, because they were the ones who chose him."

"It does make sense," Christine said with a grin. "But didn't you say 'we'? It looks like the men are the only ones doing any voting today. Aren't the women included, too?"

"Only the free men of the tribe have a voice, lady," said Slaine.

Christine sighed. "I should have known," she said. Then she shrugged her shoulders. "I guess half a democracy is better than none—but I can tell you, one day women will feel very different about this sort of thing."

"Men of Dun Orga!"

The crowd fell silent at the king's voice. The men gathered closer around him in the dappled shade of the oaks, and Christine had no trouble spotting Ailin's broad-shouldered, red-clad figure in their midst. "Today is the day that you will choose your tanist."

"Tanist," Christine repeated, and then lowered her voice when a few of the others glanced at her. "Slaine, you mentioned that word before. What does it mean?"

"The next king," her friend whispered.

187

Next king! "I guess I just thought that Cronan would step in when his father died." Cronan was Ailin's oldest brother, and the husband of Derval. "I never heard of a king being elected! Doesn't the king have to be the firstborn, and all of that?"

"Not here in Eire-land, lady," Derval said. "That is not our way. The tanist may be any man of the king's family—a son, a brother, a cousin, an uncle."

Instantly Christine began to wonder: if the people had some say in the matter of their king, rather than just hoping that an accident of birth would provide them with a worthy leader, what better choice could they possibly have than Ailin?

This could be very, very interesting.

"Consider the man you wish to follow as your king." Donaill, tall and blond, so like Ailin, paced the wind-whipped grass with his hand on the hilt of his sword. "He is the man you will trust with your laws, the man you will follow into battle; that he must be trustworthy, fearless, and strong hardly bears mentioning.

"Yet consider also that a king is more than a leader. He is a symbol to his people, a manifestation of their strength and honor and courage that all may see and touch and hear.

"It is he who becomes the husband of the land— and because the land will accept no less, a king must be free of disfigurement and perfect in form."

Christine almost giggled out loud. Quickly she raised her hand to her face. If the king had to be "perfect in form," Ailin was certainly qualified in that department! No other man could even come close to his physical perfection—no other man had his towering height, his broad chest and shoulders, his arms banded with muscles strong as steel. . . .

She noticed Slaine looking at her with curiosity in her eyes. These people always became so concerned, so unnerved, whenever Christine did anything even slightly out of the ordinary—like stifling a laugh at a public gathering.

"Ah, a king must be perfect in form?" Christine asked, keeping her voice low. "What does that mean? How are we—I mean, how are the men going to vote on that?"

Slaine smiled. "Oh, lady," she whispered, " 'perfect' simply means that a king must not have any part of his body crippled or missing. He must not walk with a limp, or have a finger or hand that is missing, or any other such thing."

"It is very important," Derval added. "It is as though the land itself, or the people themselves, were weakened and incomplete, if the king be marred in such a way."

Christine shook her head. "In the place where I am from, we used to think that 'damaged' people were simply to be pitied and were of no use. But we have learned that all people, even those who are less than perfect in some way, are still to be valued."

"All are valued here, too, lady," Derval said quickly. "We know well that all have something to offer. But a king—a king is very different."

Christine was not sure she entirely understood, or condoned, such thinking, but before she could respond King Donaill raised his voice to the assembly.

"Here in this gathering are all the men of my family. Choose from among them the man you would have as your king! Stand with him now as evidence that you will stand with him always! He who gains the most followers shall be the tanist!"

One by one, each man came forward to stand beside his choice. Christine saw Ailin start to move toward Cronan—but before he could stand with his brother, a half-dozen men surrounded Ailin.

On and on they came, until each had made his choice. And when the choosing was finished, two men stood with Cronan beneath the wild spring sky;

two more with his next-youngest brother, Finn, the husband of Slaine; and all forty-five of the rest stood with Ailin.

Ailin, now tanist, the next king.

Chapter Sixteen

At that moment Christine's heart went out to Donaill, whose son had just been chosen as the next king of the people of Dun Orga. The older man said nothing. He simply stood aside in the bright spring sun and watched as Ailin accepted the cheers and good wishes of the men who had named him tanist.

Donaill's face was serious and still, and there was a strange gleam in his eyes. Christine wondered at the sight.

This powerful, battle-hardened warrior . . . the leader of these strange and primitive people . . . moved to tears at seeing his son become heir to his crown.

Finally, as the wind swayed the towering oaks high above the rippling grass of the grove, the king began to approach Ailin.

The crowd of men moved back to let him through. But to Christine's astonishment, Ailin turned away from his father and walked straight toward her.

In a moment the fresh green world and high-flying white clouds seemed to fade away. She was conscious only of Ailin standing over her, tall and proud, handsome and fair, his red cloak moving to enfold her as he stopped and reached for her hand.

"Lady," he whispered. "Stand with me now. Honor me with your presence, as my men have honored me with their choice."

So many thoughts flew through her mind as she looked up into his shining slate-blue eyes. Happiness that he had thought first of her, even at this moment of great triumph. Frustration at the nagging thought that he still insisted she was a goddess. Despair that she might never be able to convince him to see her for herself, that she might never have the joy of knowing he loved her for the person she truly was.

His fingers closed over her own. At that gentle pressure, her heart made the decision for her.

Ailin was the finest man she had ever known, in this world or any other. Now he stood before her as a prince, as the tanist, the chosen king of his people, asking her to share with him what was surely one of the finest hours of his life.

He had become a part of her that she could no longer imagine living without. His unwavering love for her, out of the ordinary though it was, gave Christine the strength to face whatever obstacles his worship of her might place in their path.

In that moment, she could not have refused him anything.

Together they walked across the sweet rippling grass until they reached the front of the crowd. The men and women all stood together now, watching Ailin and Christine and waiting for their king to speak to them.

Donaill approached them, walking slowly, his left hand resting on the hilt of his sword. Ernin remained a pace behind him. The two of them stood in silence and stared hard at Ailin. And suddenly Christine realized that something was very wrong.

A moment before, the king had been filled with pride and deeply moved by his son's accomplishment. But now he stood rigid and cold, as if all his pride had swiftly changed to anger.

Ailin, too, had pulled himself up tall, but still he held Christine's hand in his own. He braced himself against the king's stony glare, meeting his father's eyes and returning that glare with equal hardness.

Christine could feel the tension in the air between them. There was no question that the two men were violently angry with one another. But why? What had happened to so suddenly overturn the feelings of joy and triumph that had filled this beautiful windswept grove?

A chill passed through her as realization dawned. King Donaill was angry at Ailin for bringing her to stand with him at the front of the gathering. But why?

"Here is your tanist!" The king's voice had a trembling edge to it, but that trembling came now from rage—not from pride. He looked away from Ailin and spoke only to his people.

"And I tell you that your tanist will soon be married." A shock ran through Christine at those words, but before she could react Ailin's grip tightened so suddenly on her hand that she almost cried out in pain. "His bride will be brought to him at Lughnasa! At Lughnasa the wedding will take place!"

And with that the king turned his back on Ailin and Christine and pushed his way through the crowd, which quickly broke apart to let him through. Murmuring in surprise, his people hurried to follow him down the hill. Only a few spared a glance back at their new tanist.

Christine looked up at Ailin. He kept his gaze fixed firmly on the departing group, but seemed to relax ever so slightly. He took his hand from his sword hilt and then looked down at her. There was a small smile on his face, as though he had just won a small but significant triumph.

"What has happened?" she demanded. "I mean, I know that you're going to be the next king—and I think it's wonderful! Your own people chose you, and I could see how proud your father was. But what happened after that? Why did your father become so angry when you brought me up to stand with you?"

"It is of no importance, lady," he answered gently. "I decide who stands with me. That choice is mine to make. What matters is my love for you."

She closed her eyes for a moment, and her heart began to pound. Even at a time like this, having just been named a king, Ailin thought only of her—yet she could not let him distract her from the question she had to ask, from the answer she dreaded she would hear.

"Your father talked about a wedding," she said, forcing her voice to stay steady. "He said that your bride would be brought to you at—at some place I've never heard of. Please, I have to know. If you're going to be married, I have to know."

"Of course you must know, lady." He bent to kiss her. His breath warmed her face, like the warmth of the gentle spring sun on a newly opened flower. "It is just as my father said. We will be married at Lughnasa, if you will have me."

If you will have me . . .

After escorting Christine back to the house and leaving her in the care of Una, Ailin walked straight to the hall. He knew his father would be there and Ailin had no wish to wait for a summons. This was one battle that had waited long enough.

They fell silent as he walked in, Ernin and the king and a few of his warriors; and then all but the king looked at each other and quietly slipped away. Only the old druid spared a glance for Ailin.

The hall was quiet now, and dim, save for thin shafts of sunlight that speared the heavily thatched roof and lit the spiraling dust. He walked straight to the carved wooden bench where his father sat alone. Glaring his defiance at the king, Ailin stood with his feet apart and his hands on his belt.

"I will not marry her," he said.

Donaill did not move. He met his son's gaze without any show of emotion. "Then you will be the one to explain to Mealla—and to Dun Fada—and to your own people why you will not marry her, Ailin the tanist."

Ailin's temper flared. "There is nothing to explain! My wish to marry this powerful, magical lady, Lady Brighid, and make her queen, requires no explanation to anyone! She is the one I love, and I tell you— and all of Eire-land—that I will have no other!"

"I! I! I!" roared Donaill. In an instant he was on his feet. "All you speak of is what *you* want—as though you were the only one affected! Do you recall the crowd of people who stood around you today, Ailin? They made you their next king! If it is not too inconvenient, it might be a good idea for you to think of them, too!"

"I have thought of them." Ailin set his teeth. "I have thought of what it would be like for the people of Dun Orga to have a pale infant for their queen, when they could have such a one as the Lady of Fire."

Donaill looked away in disgust. "Can you for one moment turn your mind from that woman's rump and think of your people! I am speaking of the alliance! We need Dun Fada's numbers to help us hunt down the *gadai* and clean them out once and for all! Have you forgotten what happened over last Imbolc? We need Dun Fada—and though it would pain them greatly to say so, they need us."

"I do not understand your reasoning!" Ailin shouted. At his father's cold stare he lowered his voice, but only slightly. "Why do we go begging for warriors to aid our poor weak men? Why must we barter to get fighters for little Dun Orga, using children like Mealla as the goods? If we need more fighters, we should get them the honorable way—by conquering Dun Fada and making them our own!

195

Why do we wait? I will organize a war party right now!"

He turned to go but his father grabbed his arm. "Stop your raving and listen, tanist." Ailin heard the anger in his voice and made no further move. "Have you heard nothing that I've said? Our numbers are too few! In a battle to conquer Dun Fada we would almost certainly lose as many of ours as we would gain of theirs. Do you consider that a wise thing? Is this how you will lead your people when I am gone?"

Ailin shook off his father's grip. "I will lead them with strength, not with begging and compromise! I will never find myself at the mercy of another tribe, needing them to defend my own!"

"You consider compromise to be weakness?"

"I consider letting others do our fighting for us to be worse than weakness!"

Ailin braced himself for his father's answer, but the king only closed his eyes. "We have already lost too many of our warriors in fights over nothing. I do not want to lose you and your brothers, too."

Such weakness! Ailin nearly spoke the words aloud, but stopped at the last moment. He was shocked at the turn his father's thoughts were taking—but then remembered that he himself had heard a similar sentiment not so long ago, and had been glad enough to listen to it.

To kill a man for simple rude behavior, she had said. *You just can't do that! . . . It's not civilized.*

He ground his teeth, but said nothing. Father and son glared at each other in the dusty dimness of the hall.

"No one can force you to marry Mealla," the king said at last. "But you are the tanist now. If that is not sufficient reason for you to put your own tribe first, then I fear for the future of Dun Orga."

Instantly Ailin's fury returned. "Do you believe that I am not strong enough, as a fighter or a king, to marry the woman I want and still defend my own?

That I must go crawling to the scum of Dun Fada for help for my own poor men?" His anger built to rage. His face grew hot and his hands tightened into fists. "You say you are afraid for Dun Orga if I become king! Think on this, Father: what kind of king would I make if I could be pushed into marriage with a weak-willed child whom I do not want, because I am afraid of a battle? What kind of king would I be if I told my own warriors that I could not depend on them to defend their own Dun?

"No, Father, I will be no such king, and I will have no such queen! I will trust my own men. I will fight my own battles. And most of all, I will marry she whom I love, and make her my queen!"

Christine peered out the window of the little house but saw only darkness and a starless black sky. She had dozed fitfully, not really sleeping. Ailin's words would not let her sleep.

If you will have me . . .

She had to talk to him. The man had asked her to marry him, and now he was nowhere to be found!

After the ceremony he had walked with her as far as the house but then left quickly, insisting that there was someone he must speak to, some arrangements that must be made. It had certainly seemed understandable at the time, in light of what had just happened out in the grove, and she had given it little thought.

She had been left alone to think of what it might mean to be Ailin's wife—and had not seen him since.

Another dawn came, but it did not bring the bright sun and clear skies of the previous day. Instead the morning was cool and misty, the sky a featureless gray, the air sweet with the promise of gentle spring rain.

"You know, I thought I didn't like rainy weather, but this really isn't bad," Christine said as she walked with Una and a dozen or so women and children through the gates of the Dun. "It's kind of refreshing."

"A soft day, we call it," Una said. The younger woman, broad and strong, carried both Christine's large empty basket and her own. "A good day to go out, even if it's just for kindling."

Christine smiled in agreement. She found that her woolen clothes protected her from any dampness or chill. Her hair had been twisted into a knot, fastened with a slender wooden pin, and then covered with a light woolen mantle. Her boots kept out the water quite well and she was dry and comfortable, even as the light rain began to fall.

They walked toward the mountain where the bonfire had burned, and turned off the path into a patch of woods to begin gathering the fallen twigs used to feed the fires.

She was glad for the simple task, glad to be out here beneath the trees and soft gray sky and away from the confines of the Dun. If she looked away from the other women, seeing only the oaks and willows and hearing only the calls of the songbirds, she could for a moment believe she was back in her own world . . . just spending a pleasant weekend camping in a quiet, misty forest, away from traffic and television and the bustle of modern life. . . .

She was startled by a sudden touch on her shoulder. Whirling around, she saw Ailin standing before her with mist playing about his feet. He looked as though he had simply appeared out of the air.

"Ailin," she said softly, catching her breath. "I wanted so much to speak to you last night. You were not outside my door—at least, not the last time I looked outside, hours after darkness had fallen. Where did you go?"

He smiled gently. "Into the forest, lady. I am sorry I was not there for you. I will not disappoint you again, I promise."

As if you ever could! "It's all right. You must have a lot to think about. It's not every day a man is told he's going to be king."

The sight of him never failed to send a thrill straight through her. He wore his heaviest brown leather breeches and boots, and was bare-chested in the soft rain. Thick brown leather covered his forearms from elbow to wrist. "Sword practice today, I see."

"There is, lady."

"Then why are you here? Your men will be waiting for you. I doubt if gathering kindling would count as a substitute for swordfighting."

"It would not. But the practice can wait. I am here for you."

Her heart leaped, and she caught her breath. The heavy wicker basket dropped to the damp forest floor. Was it happening at last? Had he come to claim his bride here in the forest, in this soft and quiet place, to truly make her his own?

Christine fought down the impulse to reach for him—or to let him reach for her. Even though the rush of excitement threatened to overwhelm her, she had the presence of mind to realize there were things they must talk about first.

"Yesterday you asked me to marry you, Ailin," she said. "If I would have you, you said. But I must ask you the same question. Will you have me?"

He took a step closer, his face serious and still. "Of course I will have you, lady. How could you ever think I would not? There is nothing I want from this world except to have you."

Boldly she looked up into his eyes, her heart pounding, and said the words she could not hold back. "Is that why you've come here now? To make me your own? To tell me that I am the woman you love, the woman you wish to marry?"

She looked away from him, fighting down the

hope that he would reach for her, and make her look at him, and . . . and . . .

But he only reached into a small leather pouch at his belt. "You are she whom I love. Never doubt it. But I am here now because I have brought you a gift."

A gift!

Christine shut her eyes tight. She didn't even want to see what it was. And at that moment she came to an ironclad decision.

She turned to face him, fists clenched at her sides. "I will accept no more gifts, Ailin! You've already given me far too many things. I don't want things from you. I want . . . I want . . ."

Her voice faltered as she looked up into his eyes. How could she ever make him understand?

Instantly he was down on one knee in front of her. "What do you want? You have only to tell me, and it is yours."

His face was nearly level with hers. Gazing down at his damp hair, she longed to reach out and touch it—to lift aside the gold coronet and run her fingers through that shining softness, down to the hot, smooth skin of his powerful neck and shoulders.

Her fingers twitched. She willed her arms to hold still.

"I want you to come to me because you want *me*— not because you're worshiping your goddess. I wish you would . . . I wish . . ."

He reached for her hands with both of his own. She was forcefully reminded of the strength and sheer masculine power of the man who knelt at her feet as he gently covered her small white hand with his iron-hard fingers.

"I did come to you once, lady." His voice was low and calm, but held just a note of trembling—of urgency. "I lifted you in my arms and carried you to your sleeping ledge. But you told me you did not wish it. I did not touch you after that until I was

200

certain that it was your true desire, and yours alone."

Yes, I know! she wanted to scream. Her hand tightened and she slid her fingers around his, reveling in this simple touch—the feel of his smooth, warm skin and sure, gentle grip.

"I do want you, Ailin. Surely you must know that now." *Oh, how I want you! How I wish you would lift me in your arms and carry me into the forest, right here, right now, in this soft day! Make me yours forever!*

But she could not say the words. He would only give her what she asked for, just as he had the last time, and nothing would have changed. And she knew that even with the dizzying effect Ailin had on her, simply sharing her body with him was not all that she wanted.

His hands shifted. Catching her breath, she made herself go on.

"If we are to be married, we must be married as equals." At his puzzled look, she smiled a little and reached out to cover his strong hands with her free one.

"I mean we have to be on the same level. You can hardly know me—much less love me—if you've got me up on some kind of pedestal. That only separates us. It means that you're down here and I'm way up there somewhere. And I don't want to be way up there. I want to be with you. I want to be where you are."

He never moved. He seemed to be staring at something far off in the distance.

Christine sighed. "I'm not a goddess and I don't want to be treated like one. Frankly it's been pretty boring so far." Yet it occurred to her, even as she said the words, that countless women spent their lives trying to achieve the exact opposite.

Just as she had, back in her own world.

Finally Ailin smiled up at her, but his eyes remained serious. "I understand your wish for us to be married as equals, lady. I know I could not ask you until I had been named tanist—until I knew that I might be worthy of a goddess."

Worthy?

Caught off guard, she stared at him, but his expression never changed. "Ah . . . what did you say?"

"If being married is what you wish—and if having the goddess who walks the earth for my queen, for Dun Orga's queen, is what I fervently wish—does that not make us equals? Does that not give each of us what we want most?"

"No!" Christine jerked her hands away from him. His eyes widened.

Her cheeks flamed with a wild combination of anger and embarrassment. "Yes, I want to be married. I won't deny it, and I'm not ashamed of it. A husband and a family would go a long way toward making me feel as though I truly had a place here. But not like this—not like this! I will not marry you until the day you accept me as a real, mortal woman, because that's what I am! No more and no less!"

Pain tore at her heart, along with a terrible dread that she might be destroying their relationship forever, but her mind was made up and there was no turning back now.

"I am not a goddess, Ailin, and until it is me that you love—and not her—I will not marry you."

He looked stricken, lost, but she merely turned around, picked up her basket, and stalked off to join the other women at their work. "And don't you dare bring me any more gifts, either!"

She had won this time, but knew in her heart that she would not learn the price of her victory until much later.

Chapter Seventeen

It was a glorious summer day of sun and shadow and racing clouds, the middle of May, by Christine's reckoning, and she found it all but impossible to concentrate on spinning her share of the wool into yarn. She could not stay indoors a moment longer! The instant her work was done, she was out the door of the hall and hurrying to the shed to get Sunshine's bridle.

The little golden mare stood waiting at the gate of the pen. "Hello, gorgeous!" Christine said, pushing open the gate. "I'll bet you don't want to stay cooped up in here any more than I do." Sunshine nudged her arm with her soft nose.

"Let's be daring today. Let's go outside, instead of just riding around in here." Christine slipped the bridle onto the mare's head and led her out to the grass-covered yard of the Dun.

"Do you ride today, lady?"

She turned around to see Ailin standing in the warm sun. He stood watching her with an uncertain expression, holding what looked like a thick bundle of rolled-up padding beneath one arm.

The sight of him was enough to make the sweet

summer day complete, but she forced herself to keep her feelings masked. Nothing had changed since that day in the mist when she had stood up to him, insisting she would not marry him unless he accepted her as a real woman. She would not go back on her word now—though she knew the warmth spreading through her was not entirely from the heat of the summer day.

"Yes, Sunshine and I are going for a ride. It's far too beautiful to stay in." Christine glanced at the bundle he carried, her curiosity growing. "What is that?" She frowned. "It's not another gift, is it?" He had not offered her any more presents since that day, that soft day out in the forest.

"It is not for you, lady. It is for the horse."

"Oh. Well. That's different."

"Here, let me show you." He unrolled the bundle and placed it on Sunshine's back. It was a thick wool pad covered with soft fur, with leather straps firmly stitched to it. Ailin fastened the straps around the mare, and Christine grinned up at him, truly pleased.

"Now, back home at Girl Scout camp," she murmured, watching as Ailin carefully checked the fit of the pad, "we would have called that a bareback pad. A bareback pad and a gentle horse are all anyone needs to go trail riding, whether it's the fifth century or the twentieth century." The little mare bobbed her head as if in agreement.

Grasping Sunshine's mane, Christine swung herself up to sit on the mare. It hadn't taken her more than a few tries to get the hang of it; the mare's back was only as high as Christine's waist, and vaulting aboard wasn't difficult at all. Christine's skirts were wide and full enough to allow her to straddle the small horse without difficulty, only hiking it up to the top of her boots.

"Are you certain you want to ride alone, lady? I will take you anywhere you wish to go on the chariot—wait, I will harness the team."

Her pride was quick to return. "Chariot? No, thank you! Riding is my freedom. I don't want to be just a passenger, completely dependent on someone else to take me everywhere! I want to get out for a little while, and that's exactly where I'm going. Out!"

She turned Sunshine toward the gate, tapping the little mare's round sides with her heels. Ailin hurried to walk with her. "Please, lady, do not go out of sight of Dun Orga. It looks as though storms are rising, and you have never ridden out alone before—"

But Christine cut him off. "What do I have to fear from storms or unfamiliar terrain, Ailin? Only a mortal woman—a real person—would need to be concerned about such ordinary things. But I am a goddess, remember? I need not give any thought to such things!"

And with that she grabbed Sunshine's mane, kicked her sides, and took off at a gallop through the gates of Dun Orga.

A short time later, after slowing Sunshine to a walk, Christine rode through the sun-warmed afternoon and thought back, as she so often did, to the things she had said to Ailin on that day in the mist.

She still felt sure that she had done the right thing. She had vowed to herself that she would do nothing for Ailin, or around him, that she wouldn't ordinarily do. She would continue simply to be herself, and no one else, and not permit him to worship her ever again! He would just have to see for himself that she was only human and accept her accordingly.

Christine followed the path over the rise and began descending into the lush green valley, along the same trail that Ailin had taken with her in his chariot on that long-ago day. She kept Sunshine to a leisurely walk, breathing in the intoxicating scents of the sea and the sun and the fresh green grass, and listening to the sweet sounds of the birds singing.

Suddenly she was startled by a distant flash of

lightning. The low rumble of thunder followed several seconds later. Twisting around to look over her shoulder, she saw a wall of black clouds approaching.

It was one of the sudden rainstorms that were so common here. One moment the sky would be clear and sunny, and then before you knew it the black clouds would fly in from the sea with their silvery rain and flickering lightning. She hadn't been paying attention to the changing sky until now, lost in her thoughts of Ailin and the beautiful day.

Another flash made her realize that she'd better head for home. Such storms were nothing to toy with, especially out here in the open.

The mare snorted and began to fidget and dance. She was unwilling to go any farther, and Christine finally allowed her to turn around.

But just as Sunshine swung for home, there was a blinding flash and an air-splitting crack. The mare leaped forward and Christine grabbed wildly for her mane.

She was too late; the little mare shot into a panicked run and Christine tumbled off into the soft grass, rolling over and over down the steep hill.

She looked up just in time to see Sunshine galloping for home, her tail flagged high over her back. The horse raced up the hill and disappeared over the rise.

Christine started to get to her feet, but as she did the world began to waver and fade. Her mind reeled and she sat back down in the grass, bracing her arms behind her.

Had she hit her head when she fell? Was that why she felt so dizzy? The blood roared and pounded in her ears, and darkness faded in—the storm clouds must be black indeed, to make the world so dark in midafternoon.

Suddenly, horrified, she reached up to her neck. The torque was gone.

She must find it or else this world—and Ailin with

it—would be lost to her forever. Frantically, in the thundering noise and dizzying light of the storm, in the frightening darkness of her faded world, she dropped to her hands and knees and searched through the thick grass. She said a silent prayer to whomever might be listening, hoping beyond hope to see a glint of bright gold before it was too late.

The skies opened and the rain began to pour. The dizziness overwhelmed her and she fell to the ground, searching blindly with her hands. Dragging herself forward a last few inches, she stretched her hand out one last time—and closed it around cool, twisted metal.

She had it. The world still wavered in darkness, and it moved in slow motion, but it did not fade any more than it already had. She tried to lift the torque to place it around her neck but found that she could not move her arms. She could not move at all.

The lightning flashed and the cold rain poured as Christine gripped the golden torque with the last of her strength. As the thunder crashed over her, she closed her eyes and whispered a single word.

"Ailin . . ."

There was a faint rumbling in the earth. Christine opened her eyes, blinking against the spattering raindrops. After a moment she was certain that the sound was not thunder. It was hoofbeats. Slowly, fighting for strength, she raised her head.

Through the murky, wavering air, she saw Ailin leap down from a horse's back. He started toward her, then hesitated. His eyes were wide with awe, and something else.

Fear.

Ailin was afraid of her, and she had never thought to see him afraid of anything in this world.

But no, wait—she was no longer lying in the rain-soaked grass in a valley in long-ago Eire-land. She could see the outlines of her bedroom in her own apartment—the dresser, the nightstand, the walls,

Janeen O'Kerry

the door. She was certain she felt the smoothness of a quilt beneath her, the familiar softness of her own bed.

Then the outlines faded and she could see the valley once more, see Ailin and his horse and feel the cold wet grass. Now they merged together, one above the other, like a double-exposed photograph.

Christine shut her eyes against the sight. From Ailin's expression, she knew that he must be seeing her fading in and out the same way that she was seeing him, that he could see the outlines of her former life crossing into this one.

She hung suspended between the worlds, between two times.

"Please," she whispered, looking up at Ailin. "Help me get the torque back on my neck."

Slowly he came toward her, and Christine knew it took more courage for him to approach her now than it ever had for him to face the fiercest enemy. His own hand closed around the shining torque and covered hers. Lifting her up with his other arm, supporting her shoulders, he helped her raise her arm up to her neck.

Together they slid the torque back into place.

In a moment, stillness returned to the world. The air cleared, and she could hear the birds calling.

Christine sat up. She was sitting on wet grass on the steep slope of an Irish valley, feeling the sea breeze on her face as the last of the storm clouds fled inland. The sun came out again, warm and pleasant on her face after the cold rain.

She looked up at Ailin, grateful that he had arrived so quickly to help her. But she was stopped by the look in his eyes. The fear had left them, but the awe and amazement remained.

With a sinking heart, she heard his one whispered word. "Goddess," was all that he would say.

Slowly, and in silence, Ailin lifted Christine in his arms and placed her on his horse's back. He walked

208

along beside her, leading the fiery chariot horse, until they reached Dun Orga and stood before the door of his house. He helped her down and left her at the door, giving her only a gentle touch on her cheek before leading the horse away.

Safe within the familiar little house, Christine quickly stripped off her wet clothes and wrapped up in the furs to get warm. She wanted to rest, to sleep, to put the awful experience out of her mind, but it was impossible.

Why hadn't she just let go of the torque and gone back to her life? She had known what was happening out there in the valley. She had begun to make the leap between this place and her own time, and that meant she could go home again. She could leave this strange and primitive place and go home to a world of books and electricity and long hot showers.

A very lonely world.

Christine closed her eyes. If she went back, never again would she know the thrill of Ailin's presence, the strength of his arms, or the magic of his touch. Never again would she see the sheer masculine beauty of his chiseled face and perfect body and long flowing hair. This kind and noble man, this prince who had been friend and companion and protector and lover, would be forever lost to her.

She could not leave him. She had had the chance to do so, and found it impossible. No, she would do all she could to make the best of things with him here, and build a life for the two of them in whatever way she could.

If he loved her, as he swore he did, then surely he would come to accept her for herself and forget this nonsense of trying to worship her as a goddess. He had just been a little shocked and caught off guard by the way she had arrived—well, hadn't they all? And hadn't she understood when Derval and Slaine mistook her for a goddess at first, too? But they'd seemed to have gotten past that notion quickly enough—and so, she told herself, would Ailin.

After all, when was the last time she'd worked any magic for anybody, or performed any miracles? She never had—and wasn't likely to, either!

This day's experience out in the valley had been frightening and strange, she would certainly admit. But it had been no stranger than the way she'd arrived here in the first place.

Sooner or later the time would come when Ailin would accept her for herself. She was certain of it. And perhaps, she thought, sitting up straight on the hard ledge, she would see to it that time came sooner rather than later!

Her cloak wrapped tightly around her, Christine walked into the misty gray-black twilight and made her way across the yard toward the gate. The wet grass was fresh and cold under her bare feet and her hair rippled in the dampness from the mist and the sea.

The moment her saw her, Ailin got to his feet and followed closely, as she had known he would.

Outside the torchlit confines of the Dun, Christine stepped into fog and darkness and felt them swallow her. Close behind she could hear Ailin's footsteps and soft breathing, and could almost feel the rippling of his heavy wool cloak as he moved. In the all-encompassing blackness she could scarcely see her own hand in front of her face, but she did not hesitate; she only drew a deep breath and pressed on into the soft, wet night.

Before long the grass began to thin and there was smooth ground beneath her feet. Here was the familiar worn path leading away from Dun Orga. She followed the path for a few moments, and then turned away toward the black and silent woods that lined it.

Slowly, carefully, Christine felt her way along the rough, wet trees. She kept one arm raised to shield her face from low-hanging branches, until finally her searching hands found only empty darkness.

This was the clearing where she had gathered kindling with the other women so many weeks ago—the same clearing where she had told Ailin she would not marry him until he accepted her as a live, mortal woman.

All was darkness here in this place of nature, here in this small, secluded piece of the night that was like a hidden room all their own.

Facing Ailin in the blackness, knowing he was there and feeling his breath and heartbeat even though she could not see him, Christine unfastened her fur-lined cloak and let it fall to the damp forest floor. She opened her arms wide and reveled in the cool softness of the mist as it swirled over her skin.

Hearing the cloak fall, Ailin reached for Christine. His breathing quickened as he ran his hands down her shoulders and over her waist and hips.

She wore nothing at all save mist and darkness.

He withdrew his hands, and there was a rustling sound. In a moment she reached out to him and found that he, too, wore nothing but the night.

Now they faced each other as any man and woman might, in any time, in any place. There was no sight or sound to remind Christine of where they stood. She saw only the darkness, heard only the soft wind in the trees.

These night-shrouded woods might simply have been part of the rural countryside back home in her own time, instead of the wild forest of ancient Eireland. And the tall, broad-shouldered man she drew into her arms could have been a man from her own time and place.

But this man was not like any other she had ever known, in her own time or in this one. Here in this timeless night with her stood Ailin, who seemed to possess all the power of a god of the sun—such was the power that ran through him and into her as she touched him.

It was so good to hold him again, so good to press her body full against his and feel his heart beat against her chest until it seemed that their two hearts were truly one. Her lips parted and she raised her face to him, searching for his tender mouth and sighing with pleasure as he returned her gentle kiss.

She had chosen this place with a purpose, for here in seclusion and darkness she could go to him as any woman might go to any man she loved. He would have to admit that in scent and sound and touch she was no different from any earthly woman—*all cats are gray in the dark!* Christine almost giggled out loud as the old saying popped into her mind, but instead she found Ailin's face again and began covering it with a rain of kisses.

Christine was amazed at her own boldness, now that she was completely covered by the dark. She was any woman, she was all women, and as she drew Ailin down with her to the cloak on the soft forest floor she was determined that he would find firmly in his grasp the earthiest female he'd ever imagined!

Placing her hand on his broad chest, she pressed him back until he lay flat on the cloak. Just as she, at this moment, felt herself to be the essence of womanhood, Ailin was surely the essence of manhood, and he lay stretched out beneath her in the darkness like a banquet on which she could feast.

Kneeling down, she kissed his face. How smooth the skin of it was, how soft and delicate his eyebrows . . . but she did not linger there. She began moving her kisses to his neck, and shoulder, and chest. Christine had every intention of making him experience the kind of very earthly pleasure that— she was quite certain—no imaginary goddess could possibly provide him!

Never before had she made love to a man in this fashion . . . never before had she felt the freedom, the bold desire, to express her love in such a daring way. Her hair fell across his chest and slid slowly along his body as she moved her kisses from his chest to his slim waist and straight hips.

He caught the ends of her hair lightly in his fingers, and suddenly his grip tightened as she found the heavy shaft which lay hot and pulsing against the velvet skin of his thigh.

She wanted it all, the scent of him, the taste, the incredible softness of his skin against her face, and she did not hesitate to take all of these things for herself as she knelt beside him. Lying across him, she felt him writhe with pleasure beneath her daring touch, and heard his deep, groaning sigh even as his pulse throbbed against her bare skin.

But this time he wasn't content to lie passively any longer. Sitting up with a low growl, Ailin caught her around her waist, and then lifted her astride him as though she weighed nothing at all. She slid her leg across his body and leaned down to kiss him, even as she moved to bring them together into a single creature joined by the pleasure of love.

"Ailin," she whispered softly against his face as he began to move within her, "I love you. Please tell me . . . I want so much to hear the words . . ."

She could say no more, for she was drowning in darkness and the heat of pleasure, and could only hold him tightly as their passion reached its peak and swept over them both like a wind-driven flame.

Chapter Eighteen

Slowly Christine opened her eyes. She saw only darkness but knew right away where she was. Ailin still lay beneath her, and the two of them were entwined together so closely that she could hardly tell where her body ended and his began.

It was so comforting, so reassuring, to lie with the man she loved, in the simple and very human tie of lovemaking. After the frightening, otherworldly experience of the afternoon, when she had lost the torque and been caught helplessly between her world and this one, she had instinctively sought out the primal bond which would anchor her to this time and place—and to Ailin.

The two of them were damp from sweat and from the misty night air, and the wet breeze began to feel uncomfortably cool on Christine's bare skin. Slowly she slid down from Ailin to lie close beside him on the fur-lined cloak.

In the cool darkness he was as warm as the sun on a summer's day. She stretched out her body full-length and pressed close against him, reveling in his warmth and great strength and letting that strength fill her heart and soul.

"I am so happy to be here with you," she whispered. "I was so frightened today . . . out on the hillside . . . and this is what I needed to feel all right again. I-I need you, Ailin, I'm not ashamed to tell you, I am so happy when I am with you. I only hope that you can tell me you feel the same about me."

He rose up in the darkness, holding her close. His heart beat against hers and she could swear he was smiling, though she could see nothing but the night.

"Indeed I can tell you, Lady Brighid. I am happy only when I am with you—pleasing you, serving you, living only for you. I will make no move, perform no task, unless it is by your express wish—just as I have done tonight."

A chill ran through Christine that had nothing to do with the damp night air.

"Why did you come out here with me tonight?" Her voice began to shake. "Did you come with me because you wanted me, wanted the two of us to be together like any other two people in love would want to be together? Or did you—did you—"

"I am here for you, Lady of Fire, because I believed it was what you wanted." He shook his head. "I truly do not understand. Did you not want me to be here for you? To serve as the instrument of your pleasure? I thought that you were pleased, indeed I have never heard such sounds come from any mortal woman that I have ever—"

"No!" She could not bear it a moment longer. "I don't want to hear anything more!"

Weeks ago she had asked herself why she did not just come out and tell Ailin what she wanted from him—just tell him that she wanted so much for him to love her, and make love to her, and allow her to love him in return.

She had not said the words because she had been afraid of the result—afraid that he would give her all that she asked for, and more. And she had been right. She had been right. He was doing what she asked,

215

but it was purely out of worship for his goddess Brighid, not out of love for the woman Christine.

Grabbing at the cloak, she got to her feet and practically pulled it out from under him. "Never again!" she cried, her voice shaking with anger and humiliation. "I will never come to you again—not so long as you are only doing this as a way to worship your goddess! *You* must come to *me*—you must come to me as a man coming to claim the woman he loves."

Throwing the heavy damp cloak over her shoulders, Christine turned away from him and walked into the blackness. "Find someone else to play the role of goddess for you, Ailin, because I will never do it again!"

Three days went by, and almost to her relief Christine saw nothing of Ailin. He was nowhere to be found in the Dun, and she finally got it out of Derval that he had taken his chariot and gone away. Derval had reassured her that he was safe and would return when the time was right.

Christine had the feeling that that time would not come for a while. And she was so torn between her longing to see him and her pain at his continued rejection of her humanity, that by now she was almost numb.

Most likely she would not see him today. There was no need to dwell on the night they had spent in the misty forest, no reason to worry about what she must say to him this morning or this evening. Christine decided there was no use tormenting herself with it any further and sternly told herself to think only of ordinary, practical things.

Right now she needed time to think. She needed time alone to consider where she and Ailin were headed, to decide whether they even had a future together at all. Losing herself in simple, pleasant tasks was the best way she knew to think about such things calmly and at length.

She put on a new blue gown of heavy linen with a lightweight, cream-colored gown beneath it. After making another notch in her calendar stick, she stepped outside to face the new day.

Today she would start another gown, she decided. Perhaps she would dye all of the yarn for this one a shade of deep green; she found that she preferred solid colors to the gaudy plaids that were so popular here.

This blue gown had turned out surprisingly well; it would be nice to have something else in this color, too, perhaps a woolen mantle to keep out the dampness. The gown was decorated with some simple embroidery at the neckline and cuffs, just a band of creamy white outlined in green against the bright blue of the gown. . . .

Lost in thought, Christine rounded the side of the hall. Suddenly she stopped short—frozen in her tracks. All thoughts of clothes and embroidery—and her future with Ailin—vanished from her mind.

Gathered in the yard between the hall and the gate, standing in silence beneath the cloudy summer sky, was the entire fighting force of Dun Orga. A dozen chariots with their snorting, pawing teams of horses were surrounded by the warriors of the tribe. All of the men carried swords and spears, and wore leather breeches and linen tunics with heavy leather belts around them.

In the chariot nearest her she saw King Donaill with his team of coal-black horses. On the ground beside the king's chariot stood the druid, Ernin, and in the background seemed to be every woman and child who lived in Dun Orga.

In the eerie silence, one of the chariots moved forward with a rattling of wheels and a jingling of harness. Its team was red-gold with thick golden manes and tails. In the chariot, tall and fierce and proud, stood Ailin, spear in one hand, reins in the other.

His sword was belted in black leather around his

hip. He was bare-chested, wearing only black leather breeches and soft black boots, and he had wide black leather bands wrapped around his forearms.

"We go to attack the *gadai* where they live, Lady of Fire," he said. "My father the king has given me leave to lead the attack in your honor. I have been to Dun Fada these past three days, and their men have agreed to go with us."

Christine stood motionless. She could not move. Instead she tried to think. The *gadai*? Who were the *gadai*? Oh, yes, the tribe who had attacked Dun Orga on the day she had arrived. The rough-looking men—Ailin had killed two of them before her eyes.

"We have waited until the time was right for this attack," Ailin continued. He stood rigid and proud, but as she stared at him she saw a slight flicker of uncertainty in his eyes. "Waited until the *gadai* had wandered out of their miserable bog and onto the high pastures—we have done this to please you, of course, to—to honor the goddess by defending our home and families."

His voice faltered ever so slightly. She was probably the only one who noticed. But she had seen that there was a small chink in Ailin's determination, just the smallest trace of uncertainty. Surely he knew how she would feel about such a thing, whether he could admit it in front of his warriors or not!

She had to move quickly, before it was too late.

The assembled warriors were a horrific sight as they stood waiting beneath the leaden gray skies, waiting for her words, but Christine faced down her initial terror and tried to think as calmly as she could.

If she could not convince them to call off this attack, she had no doubt that many people would die. She knew that the *gadai* were thieves, even killers, but she could not condone the wholesale slaughter of their tribe—some of whom must be innocent, some of whom must be women and children. And she had no doubt that wholesale slaughter was exactly what Ailin and the men of Dun Orga intended.

Taking a deep breath, and looking directly at Ailin, she said, "Men of Dun Orga—I am certain that it is not the will of the goddess that you slaughter the *gadai*."

Her words fell into silence. No one moved or spoke, but she could feel their confusion.

Not the will of the goddess? But we are warriors! We want our revenge!

"Do you think the goddess wants to see powerful warriors such as you wasting your strength on a band of rabble? In a sneak attack? Are the warriors of Dun Orga no braver, no stronger, than this?"

She had their attention now. Flicking her glance across the fearsome warriors, she saw that while their faces remained expressionless they were at least listening to her.

Keep trying, girl!

"Could you not easily defend this fortress against such as the *gadai*, even if the thieves should have the nerve to come sneaking back again? Surely the goddess wants to see you fight only worthy opponents—those against whom it is truly necessary that you fight with all your strength. I cannot believe she has any wish to see this mighty army march against beggars and thieves!"

She stopped, her heart pounding. Would it be enough? Would they be persuaded? Or would they turn and dash through the gate, bringing unspeakable horror to the people of the bog?

The warriors remained unmoving. Then, one by one, they turned to Ailin, the tanist, their chosen prince. It was clear that his would be the example they would follow.

Ailin lay down his spear and got out of his chariot. Looking away from Christine, refusing to meet her beseeching gaze, he said only, "We shall heed your wish and do your bidding, Lady of Fire." Then he turned, caught his team by the reins, and led them away.

The other warriors also turned to go. The charioteers led their horses back to the shed, and the rest of the men and women made their way back to their houses.

In just a few moments the yard was empty.

Christine leaned back against the side of the hall, still trembling at the thought of what might have come to pass in her name. Being a goddess was the last thing she wanted—she would fight the idea with her dying breath—but apparently it did, at times, have its uses.

For the rest of the day, Christine passed the hours by spinning wool thread for her new gown and trying not to dwell on what had happened that morning.

Una crept over, a stack of folded woolen cloth in her hands. She sat down on a cushion in the rushes at Christine's feet and quietly threaded her needle.

"Lady," she began, concentrating on her threading, "may I ask a question?"

"Of course, Una," Christine said. For the thousandth time she wished these brave people did not feel the need to be so shy and tentative with her. "What is it?"

"Are you distressed? The warriors did as you asked. They called off the attack. Are you not pleased with them?"

Christine pulled another bit of fluffy wool from her basket and began twisting it between her thumb and forefinger, the beginning of yet another spool of heavy woolen thread. "I *am* pleased. I'm relieved and happy that a bloody battle was avoided. It's just that—"

She stopped, surprised at her own thoughts. Una sat waiting, gazing up at her, wide-eyed with expectation.

"I just hope that Ailin will understand," she whispered.

"Why would he not?"

"He is a warrior. His whole life is dedicated to fighting, to protecting his home and family."

"And you asked him not to do that very thing." Una's voice was gentle, nonjudgmental.

"That's right." Christine set down her spinning. "But he had to know that I could never let a massacre happen if I had the power to stop it! What else did he expect me to do, when I have told him over and over that I am not this goddess of his?"

Una made no reply. Christine gave her a tight smile. "Maybe this will go a little way toward convincing him of that, once and for all."

Becan raced up the side of the barren, rocky hill to the campsite, scattering the few scrawny cows as he stumbled and hurried over the rough ground. "They're coming! They're coming!" he shouted, gasping for breath.

"Who's coming?" an old man said, squinting at him from beneath his ragged hood.

"Dun Orga! Dun Fada! All of them! They want revenge!"

The man threw up his hands and howled, and then ran as fast as he could to the little crowd of makeshift tents on the side of the hill. "They're coming! They're coming!"

"No! Wait!" A booming voice grabbed their attention. Becan turned to see his brother Garvan coming toward them, out of breath after his long run but still able to cut through the panic with his gravelly voice. "No one's coming!" he roared. "Now pitch those tents and get back to work!"

Becan grabbed his brother's arm. "What're ye talking about? We both saw them! We both heard!"

"We did, but I was the one with the wit to stay and see what happened while ye ran from home like a panicked dog," Garvan growled.

"What do ye mean? We saw the fighters! Every last man of them! The chariots, the weapons—where else would they come but here?"

"Where else, fool, if ye'd stayed to hear it, is nowhere." Garvan shook off his brother's grip and began walking down toward the woods.

"What do ye mean, nowhere? Did they go after someone else?"

"They didn't go after anyone." Garvan kicked a clod of earth at the skittish cattle, driving them back up the hillside to find what grazing they could. "After ye ran away, they put up their weapons, unharnessed their horses, and went back to their homes."

Becan stopped and stared at him, dumbfounded. "Why?"

"Why? Because of that woman. That flame-haired woman who makes calf's eyes at Ailin."

Becan's jaw dropped. "The goddess?"

Garvan glared at his brother. "She came out and spoke to them, and the battle was called off." He walked after the wandering cows, and Becan hurried to catch up.

"Why would she do that? Just to save Ailin? Or did she—did she have some other reason? Something only a goddess would know?" His voice shook, and Garvan scowled at him.

"I don't know about that. But I do know that all I need is one thing—one piece of proof—that tells the world she's mortal, like I think she is. And when we have our proof, we'll be free to carry out our revenge on Ailin ourselves. We won't wait for no battle to come to us. They got warriors and weapons, and a whole lot o' both. No, our fight is with Ailin and that woman. We'll meet them at a time and a place of our own choosing. We'll meet them on our own terms."

Unable to sit and work a moment longer, Christine walked out into the summer evening and breathed deep of the sweet, warm air. Her spirits rose when she looked toward the gate; it had not yet been closed for the night and still stood wide open.

Hurrying out of the Dun, she climbed the grassy rise and looked out into the twilight—first toward the sea and then to the distant hill where the Imbolc bonfire had blazed.

Something moved a short distance away, on the path that led from the hill. Straining to see, she could just make out a tall figure in a red cloak.

Ailin walked in silence down the path, his head held high.

In a moment he was within a few yards of her. He had to see her, but gave absolutely no indication that she even existed. Then, as if it had been his plan all along, he walked to the side of the path and sat down with his back against a tree. He gazed up at the deep blue twilight and newly emerging stars.

Christine walked over to him, emboldened by her daylong irritation at his ignoring her simply because she had done the right thing. She sat down on the grass not three feet from him. He'd have to look at her now.

She studied his face in the soft light, transfixed as always by being in his presence. But her resolve quickly returned. Refusing to face a difficult situation never solved anything. Whether he wanted to talk about it or not, she was determined that he would hear her side of the story!

"Ailin," she said. "Look at me. Please."

Slowly he raised his head. His face was serious and grim, closed to her. His eyes looked her way but he did not see her.

He refused to see her.

Christine swallowed. "I wasn't going to let you slaughter those people. Not if I had anything to say about it. And evidently I did."

His eyes flicked to her. "You asked me once not to attack anyone who threatens you—not unless you

223

are in imminent danger," he said quietly. "And I have honored your request."

She caught her breath at the memory. "So you have, Ailin. So you have. And I'm very glad you did."

But she could feel his anger rising. "How could you not want us to attack the *gadai* after what they did?" he said bitterly. "They would have killed us all. Would you rather we had all died?"

"Of course not. And you didn't all die. I've heard over and over that they're nothing but a poor lot of beggars and thieves. You and your men would have slaughtered them all—right down to the last woman and child."

His brow furrowed slightly. "There are no women or children among them, lady. They are all outcast, criminal men."

"They're still human beings. And not all of them tried to attack Dun Orga." She shifted on the damp grass. "I absolutely am not a goddess, but I will fight to stop such slaughter with whatever power I do have."

That got his attention. "Not a goddess," he whispered between clenched teeth. "I saw you when you fell from the mare, drifting between the worlds. How can you expect me to believe you are not a goddess after I witnessed such a thing with my own eyes?"

"You know I can't answer that. I don't know how I got here any more than you do. But I do know that it's just not civilized to go around murdering the neighbors."

"And you also know that this word of yours, this 'civilized,' has no meaning for me."

Christine cocked her head, as something new occurred to her, and stared him down. "Why is it so important to you that I am a goddess? If you love me, as you say you do, then why must I be a supernatural creature? Isn't it enough for you that I am a woman, and that I am here?"

He got to his feet and started to walk away—then

224

stopped. His back was turned to her, but she could hear his voice as the sky turned to deep blue-black and the stars began to come out.

"I have asked myself that question a thousand times," Ailin said quietly. "What right have I to be the consort of the goddess? I love her and worship her like no other man, but should I not be content with an ordinary woman—or women—like other men are? Why should I spend my life existing on the edge of hope, holding on to the dream that someday the goddess might come for me?"

He turned and looked toward the deep blue twilight, and Christine gazed at his profile while he spoke. His hair moved slightly in the soft evening breeze.

"All my life I have been told how special I am . . . the son of a king, the best at everything . . . the favorite, the chosen, no doubt, of the goddess. In return for her favor, I dedicated myself to learning all that I could . . . metalwork and swordplay, horsemanship and kingcraft . . . so that I could be all that a man might be, and more.

"It was not done for myself. It was done out of love for she who had given me so much. And as I grew and became a man, I began to hope that someday she might come to me herself—if I was good enough. There are many stories of such things happening to heroes of the past. What man would not become all that he could if it meant reaching such a woman?"

Ailin turned his head and gazed directly into her eyes. "And when I called upon her, did she not answer? Did I not look up to see a woman who possessed such beauty and spirit and knowledge that she could not possibly be of this world?"

Her heart breaking, Christine searched for words, but could find none. Then, before she could move, or think, Ailin stepped forward and drew her close.

Her arms slid around him, across his broad back, and in relief and joy she leaned her head against his chest and listened to the beating of his heart.

How good it felt to stand within that powerful embrace, safe and protected and loved . . . oh, yes, loved, surely this was what love felt like. . . .

His breath was warm and sweet on her neck. His body pressed against her, and her knees grew hot and weak. She felt like a candle in the hot sunlight, softening and melting in the heat and the tides of the all-powerful sun.

But her sworn vow came back to her. It nagged at the back of her mind even as her body yielded to his. "Ailin," she whispered into his ear, breathing in the warm scent of his neck and falling hair, "please tell me . . . tell me that you know I am a woman. Tell me that you love me . . . that you love *me*."

"I do love you," he murmured without hesitation. He leaned down and began to kiss her neck, and Christine felt as though she were drowning in waves of heat and passion. "I have loved the goddess all my life . . . you are my life. . . ."

. . . loved the goddess all my life . . .

A bitter shock of frustration and disappointment passed through Christine. Her body stiffened. Only her anger allowed her to pull back from Ailin and look into his eyes.

"There is nothing more I want in life than to love you," she said evenly, as he stared at her in bewilderment and disbelief. "Nothing more—except to hear you say that you love me for myself."

And with that she pulled away from him and walked into the night alone, back to Dun Orga; for she knew that if she stayed a moment longer she would never be able to leave.

She listened for Ailin's footsteps, but heard nothing. Though it tore at her heart to leave him—and her body still demanded his embrace—she knew that she would never be able to love him, truly love him, if he did not accept her for herself. Her future with him depended on it, and she was determined to hold out at all costs.

And then with a little laugh, the kind of laugh that was at least better than crying, she told herself that maybe she was making progress with Ailin after all. Not once tonight had he called her Lady of Fire.

Chapter Nineteen

The weeks flew by on the wings of the Irish summer. Christine lost herself in the beauty of the land, the sweetness of the air, and the ever-changing visage of the sky—the sky that seemed to change as wildly as her moods.

The delicate promise of the sunrise might lead to a clear morning and warm, gentle breezes, or be quickly and violently shaken by thundering black clouds and lashing cold winds and rain. Just as easily could follow a soft gray afternoon, a glorious golden sunset over the sea, a beautiful moonlit night, or yet another menacing storm.

Her own emotions followed a similar pattern. Each morning, with the other women, she would start anew and throw herself into the hard physical work that was a fact of life in the Dun—yet always the emotional storms were waiting to shake her fragile sense of security and belonging.

When Una lugged in wooden pails brimming with warm new milk, rich and creamy from cows grazing on the lush summer pasture, Christine volunteered for the backbreaking task of churning the milk into thick golden butter. When the farmers brought in wicker baskets of long, rough, burr-filled wool from the coats of the half-wild sheep, Christine combed out the burrs and dirt and brushed the dark wool until it was clean enough for spinning. And when game was brought in, wild hare or goose or the occasional deer, she steeled herself and helped with the butchering so that all of them might eat.

But always nearby was Ailin. It seemed that each time she looked up she would catch sight of him out of the corner of her eye, out in the Dun with the other men training with sword and shield, or coming over the hill in his chariot pulled by the racing red-gold horses.

The sight of him always made her heart leap and joy surge through her—until she remembered the promise she had made to him and to herself.

"Why do you stay so?" Una would ask her. "Why, if you can't accept him, or he you, do you keep yourself apart from all other men? Even one sent by the goddess can desire a man, as any woman might, and you could have any man of Dun Orga. Why wait and wait for the one who causes you such pain?"

And Christine would wonder, yet again, how she could explain. She only knew that she found solace in her work and in the strength of her convictions—in her unmovable stance that she would not share her love with Ailin, or marry him, until he accepted her as a woman. As much as she loved him, her determination that he accept her for herself—that he come to her on her own terms—was stronger still.

Sustaining her through the hours and days was the belief, the faith, deep down, that Ailin truly did love her as much as she loved him. She felt certain that, given enough time to accept her humanity and know her well enough, he would want to spend his life with her just as she wanted to spend hers with him.

All of this gave her the strength to go on with her work day after day; it gave her the courage to remain, and not pull off the torque; it gave her patience; and most of all it gave her hope, hope for a future with the man she loved with all her heart and soul.

"I am willing to wait," she would say to Una, "if waiting means that I will have Ailin."

On an evening in late summer, by the last light of the sun, Ailin stood in the sweltering heat of the forge house and wiped the sweat from his eyes. With a pair of heavy tongs he reached into the glowing coals to grasp a large and shapeless piece of red-hot iron, ignoring its hissing protests at being pulled out of the flames and into the air. Resting it on the forge, he raised his massive hammer and began beating the angry iron into shape.

He struck it again and again, and each ringing blow of the hammer caused the glowing iron to leap and quiver and hiss and spark. At last, slowly, still resisting each strike of the hammer, the iron began to yield to Ailin's strength. A flat three-sided shape gradually emerged from the mass. It had an ever-sharpening point at one end.

"Niall!" Ailin shouted.

After a moment Niall came struggling in with a heavy wooden bucket full of water. "Where—"

"Right here!" Ailin said before Niall could say anything more. "Get back!" And he seized the hot and seething iron with the tongs and plunged it into the cool, clear water.

Niall jumped back at the hissing cloud of steam that shot out from the bucket. The water boiled and spat and leaped onto the dirt floor of the forge house. For long moments Ailin held the iron down beneath the surface, until finally the water grew quiet and was content to merely bubble and steam.

"A spear head," Niall whispered as the steam faded away. "And the biggest one I think I've ever seen." He frowned. "It's nothing like the things you usually make—elegant weapons, beautiful things for your lady. What will you do with this?"

Ailin seemed not to have heard him. With the tongs he pulled the giant spear head from the water and raised it up to look at it. It was now black and heavy, dangerous and sharp, and Ailin set it down on the stone ledge of the forge. It rested there, dark and brooding and enormous. A thin line of water ran from beneath it to the dirt floor below.

"What do you plan to hunt with that?" Niall asked again. "Anything you struck with it would be split in half and save you the trouble."

"I will hunt what needs hunting," Ailin replied, his jaw tight. "I will hunt what hunts me."

Niall glanced at the menacing thing on the forge, and edged toward the door. "Come outside and cool off, Ailin," he urged. "I've brought you some water." He stepped outside, blinking in the deep golden light of the setting sun, and sat down on the rough wooden bench which leaned against the white clay walls of the forge house.

After a moment Ailin came out to sit beside him on the bench and accepted the golden cup of spring-water Niall had brought. He took a long drink from it, splashed the rest over his own hot neck and shoulders, and then leaned back against the wall and closed his eyes.

All was quiet in the Dun. Most of the people were inside their houses for the evening meal. From the bake house beside the forge came the aroma of hot new bread, and from the more distant hall drifted the mouthwatering smell of roasting meat. "Are you hungry? I've hardly eaten since dawn," Niall said, leaning forward as if he were about to stand up, but Ailin said nothing. He only sat unmoving, morose and silent, as if he were alone.

Niall sighed. "I can see that something is wrong," he said. "What has happened? Is there some way I can help you, something I can do?"

Ailin stared at nothing. "No one can help me. And I do not expect them to."

Niall paused. "It's been some time since we've talked about Mealla," he said quietly. "Have you thought about what you will do?"

"I have thought about little else."

"You will not have time to think much longer."

Ailin closed his eyes and leaned his forehead against clasped hands. "Perhaps you were right. Perhaps my father was right. There will be a war if I refuse her. Some might follow me and some might follow my father. Fighting Dun Fada is one thing, but I cannot fight Dun Orga, too. I cannot risk dividing the people I am sworn to lead. If I marry Mealla, the Dun will be at peace and everyone will be happy."

Niall snorted. "Yes, everyone will be happy. Everyone except you and Mealla . . . and . . ."

"And who?" Ailin turned and glared sharply at him. "The Lady Brighid? She does not want me, Niall. She has refused me."

"Re— What? Refused to marry you? I don't believe it!"

"Believe it. She insists that I stop my worship of her and treat her as I would any other woman. She may as well ask me not to love her—ask me to forget who she is—ask me never to desire her, never to dream of her—"

He stopped, for the pain was clear in his voice. He set his teeth. "So long as I am tanist, I will do what is right for the Dun—but I will never stop my love and worship of the Lady of Fire. Though I may never understand her, I will never cease to love her."

"Don't underestimate the people of Dun Orga," Niall said. He met Ailin's gaze without wavering. "They don't expect you to follow them. They expect to follow you."

"That is true. So I must be mindful of where I lead them."

Niall frowned, making no secret of his confusion. "But surely you have not changed your mind about Mealla! Are you saying that you will go ahead and marry her just to placate everyone, and abandon the lady?"

"I am saying that I will do what is right for the Dun," Ailin repeated. "The lady will not have me—and even if she would, do I dare risk all the people of Dun Orga simply for what I want?"

Niall smiled. "Now you sound like your father, Ailin the tanist."

Ailin glanced sidelong at him. "So I do—but do not confuse the two of us. He has long years of kingship behind him. He also married the lady of his choice, one who loved him in return and still does to this day—yet he expects me to walk away from the one I love without a backward glance. Would he have been so willing to do the same, all those years ago?"

As Ailin and Niall watched the twilight sky deepen into blackness, King Donaill, flanked by two of his warriors, strode across the grounds of the Dun and kicked open the door of the feast hall.

Inside, the servants froze in place. They stared up at him from the tasks they had been performing—stirring the cauldron of boiling vegetables, turning a newly slaughtered calf on a spit, buttering fresh-baked loaves of bread, and laying out stacks of both plain wooden cups and plates for their own suppers and fine golden vessels with which they would serve the family of the king.

"Tomorrow is the day," Donaill said coldly, "and I am told that nothing is ready. You have all known of this for months. Why has nothing been prepared?"

No one moved. No one offered the king an answer. Finally Una gathered her courage and took a single step forward. "Neither Ailin nor the lady said anything to us, *Ri* Donaill. We thought it meant—we hoped—"

"It meant nothing," the king roared, "because nothing has changed! Tomorrow is the day, just as it has always been! And all had best be ready by nightfall tomorrow, or I will have done with the lot of you!"

He turned and strode out of the hall, his warriors by his side. The wooden door slammed shut behind them.

As the summer sun rose into a cloudy gray sky, Christine selected another stick of wood—the seventh one yet—from the pieces she had gathered of the lightning-struck oak. Using a gold-hilted knife blade, one of Ailin's many gifts and sharp as a razor, she carved a neat *A* at one end of the stick.

She jumped as the door suddenly crashed open. "Oh, lady!" Slaine said, rushing inside. The morning was warm and humid, and her face was flushed and damp. "I am sorry to disturb you—may I please borrow your cauldron? Thank you!" And before Christine could say a word, Slaine had lifted the huge bronze cauldron off the stone hearth and wrestled it outside. The wooden door slammed shut behind her.

"Of course you can borrow it," Christine said aloud to the empty room, and laughed. Maybe this was a good sign! Slaine hadn't even bothered to wait for permission to take the cauldron—she'd just grabbed it and gone, like any trusted friend might do.

Christine's spirits rose. She set her knife to the calendar stick once more and carved a perfect letter *U.*

The door slammed open. She nearly dropped the knife and stick.

"Lady!" It was Una this time. She hurried over to the sleeping ledge and began grabbing the furs, piling them up in her arms. "We must have your furs— the hall—I will bring them all back myself, I promise. I know which ones are yours!" Nearly hidden behind the heavy stack of beautiful soft furs, Una bustled out the door and gave it a kick to close it.

Christine sighed and gathered up her knife and stick. What had gotten into everyone today? She'd better get outside and find out—only one more thing to carve, a single straight line—

The door banged open.

"Lady, please excuse me." Derval hurried in, breathless. She began searching through the carved wooden chest at the foot of the sleeping ledge. "I must have—Oh, here they are! Thank you!" And with that, Derval caught up Christine's best golden goblets and flew out the door—this time not even bothering to close it.

What on earth was going on here? Even Derval had dispensed with the formalities! Christine grabbed her basket of new wool and tossed her calendar stick and knife onto the now-bare sleeping ledge.

The stick rolled back against the wall. *AU 1*, it said. August first.

The morning air was heavy and still, but the lawn was a picture of noisy confusion. Servants and nobles alike rushed and hurried everywhere and in every direction, carrying food, hauling water, bringing goblets and dishes and hangings and furs.

Baffled, and more than a little worried, Christine made her way across the lawn and tried to stop one or the other of the servants. "What is happening here?" she cried, trying to catch hold of an elbow or a sleeve. "Please! Tell me! What is going on?"

But for once, they virtually ignored her. After months of worship and respect, of nothing short of star treatment, this sudden loss of center stage—no matter how welcome—was the most confusing part of all. "Oh, excuse me, lady! Pardon me, lady!" was all the answer she got from anyone.

Finally she stopped, as the whirlwind of activity went on around her. She could see that it was centered on the hall—most of the food and furs and fine gold dishes were being taken in there—and so she lifted the hems of her skirts and went directly to the hall.

She pushed her way through the crowd at the door

and moved down the center of the long room, staring in amazement at the frantic activity of both servants and nobles. Even Derval and Slaine were right in the midst of it.

The weaving looms were being dragged out for storage elsewhere. The old rushes were being gathered and removed and replaced with fresh ones. The flat square boards were being carried in and placed down the center of the floor.

As before, no one paid the slightest attention to her.

Finally Una came in through the knot of people at the door, bearing the heavy pile of furs she had taken from Christine a short time before. "Ah, there now, all freshly shaken out on the west wind," Una said briskly, and began laying them out on the rushes alongside the floor tables. "The guests will surely—" Then she looked up and saw Christine. She stopped in midsentence.

At Una's silence, another of the rushing workers stopped and looked up. Then another. Then a few more. And then the entire hall was filled with silent, staring people who seemed somehow guilty.

"What is going on here?" Christine asked, looking about the hall at the suddenly halted chaos. No one moved. "It's another feast, I can tell that much—another holiday—but why is everyone rushing around like this? I've never seen you prepare for a feast at the last minute before! Now what's *really* going on?"

Finally Derval spoke up. "I am sorry we took your things," she said. "There will be many visitors, many more than usual."

Christine frowned. "Why? What's so different about this feast—this holiday?" When no one responded she took a step toward them. "Please—I can't look it up in a book! There's no one I can call on the phone! If you don't tell me, there's no way for me to know!"

"Lughnasa, lady," Derval said quietly. "Tonight is the start of Lughnasa."

Christine frowned. "I've heard that word before." There was something very important connected with that word. . . . "Oh! I remember now! The king—the king said that the tanist was to be married at Lughnasa—"

Suddenly she stopped, white with shock. "Married at Lughnasa," she whispered. "Lughnasa isn't a *place*—it's a *time*! It's *now*!"

She turned and raced out of the hall, and this time everyone quickly backed out of her way. The words she had heard at the tanist-making ceremony all those months before flew through her mind.

His bride will be brought to him at Lughnasa. . . .

At Lughnasa the wedding will take place. . . .

All this time, she had simply assumed that Lughnasa was a place—probably a ceremonial hill or rock or valley where important ceremonies like marriage were conducted. It had never occurred to her that Lughnasa was not a place but a time, another of the great festivals—one that had been rapidly approaching with each passing day of the dreamlike summer.

She ran through the Dun, through the heavy gray morning, searching for Ailin. She was determined to find him, determined to make him explain!

A bright gold coronet on shining blond hair caught her eye. There he was, standing quietly with his brothers a short distance from the frantic preparations going on in the rest of the Dun. They seemed to be doing nothing at all—except waiting. *Waiting for what?*

"Ailin!"

Slowly, like someone in a dream, he turned and looked in her direction. It was a long moment before he actually seemed to focus on her, to recognize her. Then he simply stood and waited for her to approach.

He was dressed in a beautiful new linen tunic and

soft brown leather breeches. The gold-capped hilt of his sword, and the ornate circular brooch that closed the neck of the tunic, both gleamed in the dull gray light of the morning.

Now she was completely baffled. Wearing such fine clothes, it was clear that he was not going hunting or to sword practice with the other men today. "Why are you dressed like this? Is the feast beginning now? Why was I told nothing about it?"

He spoke softly, gently, but she could hear the pain in his voice—pain that she had never thought to hear from him, and it tore at her heart even as her growing fear tore at her very soul. "There is to be a marriage ceremony, lady."

She closed her eyes. "Please, I must know," she whispered. "Is it you who is going to be married?" Her voice trembled as she made herself say the next words. "I remember what the king said all those months ago. If you are to be married at Lughnasa, and Lughnasa begins tonight—why have you said nothing to me about it?"

Ailin gripped her shoulders and looked into her eyes. "You told me you did not wish to marry me, Lady of Fire," he said. "You told me that you would never marry me unless I considered you to be an ordinary woman like any other. And that is the one thing I cannot do for you, for you are no ordinary woman and you are like no other. You are the Queen of War, the Lady of Fire, she whom I love and worship—and never shall you be anything else."

Christine felt cold with shock. "Then who—then who—"

There was a thundering noise outside the walls of the Dun. As Ailin and his brothers turned to look, chariot after chariot swept through the gate. The hooves of the teams pounded the earth. When a dozen vehicles stood crowded together on the grass, the last one to enter pulled away from the others and advanced on Ailin.

This chariot was driven by a huge red-bearded man in a worn black cloak and stained gray tunic. Beside him stood a small figure shrouded in an over-size red cloak.

The big man elbowed his diminutive passenger, who looked up at Ailin with huge, frightened eyes.

"She is here," Ailin whispered.

In a trance, in a dream, Christine stood alone beneath the still gray clouds and watched Ailin approach the chariot that held his bride.

She felt cold, strangely numb, as though she were simply an observer of events that were occurring very far away and to someone else entirely. This was something that simply could not be happening. There had been no warning, she had had no idea—how could this be happening?

She reached up to her neck. The torque was still there, just as it had always been. She was still safely in this world, in Ailin's world. Then how . . . ?

There were people standing close to her. They placed gentle hands on her shoulders. Christine turned to look, dispassionately, first on one side, then the other.

Derval.

Slaine.

"We are so sorry, lady," Slaine whispered.

"We did not think—we hoped it would not come to this," Derval said softly.

Christine was amazed to hear the slight break in the always-composed Derval's voice. She turned to look closely at the woman she had come to trust so much over all these months.

"Then this is really happening?" Christine said. "You knew about this?"

Derval made as if to reply, drawing a deep breath, but her face was pale, and Christine could see the pain and confusion in her eyes. Finally her glance flicked back to the wicker chariot, and Christine quickly followed her gaze.

The visitors hardly looked as though they were escorting the future queen of Dun Orga. The bridal chariot, worn and broken-down, was pulled by small, coarse, mismatched horses—one brown, the other dull black. Its driver, the huge angry-looking man with the red beard and stained clothes, only glared at Ailin as he came to stand at the back of the vehicle. The rest of the men, whose garb and chariots and tired horses looked no better, merely stood sullen and watching.

Ailin held out his hand to the woman in the chariot. The scowling driver gave her a push on the shoulder to turn her around, and slowly she reached out to Ailin.

Christine still could not see the bride's face. The woman was covered from head to foot by the long red cloak, even in the humid warmth of the summer morning. But the moment this stranger touched Ailin's hand, Christine felt a surge of shock and jealousy like nothing she had ever thought to experience.

Now she knew what betrayal was. Now she knew what that word truly meant. It caught in her throat and sent pain throughout her entire being, like a dagger plunged straight into her heart.

She could not look as the two of them walked toward her—but neither could she look away. Searching out the face of the bride, Christine looked closely beneath the shadow of the red cloak—and there, just for an instant, she saw peering back at her the eyes of a frightened child.

Chapter Twenty

Briefly, Ailin and his bride waited in front of King Donaill and Queen Mor. Christine could not hear what they were saying. But after a moment the king nodded to someone behind him, and to Christine's astonishment Una hurried around to stand beside the bride.

The little party bowed to the king and queen and then started off across the Dun. Other servants came out to lead the horses and chariots away and to escort the men to the hall where they would wait for the ceremony to begin. Derval and Slaine, with a quick pat on Christine's arm, hurried away to finish their last-minute preparations for the wedding feast.

She stood alone on the grass in the center of the Dun.

For a long moment, all she could do was stand and stare at the nobles and servants and horses and chariots as they disappeared into the buildings and barns. She tried to catch her breath, but her chest was so tight that it hurt to breathe the damp summer air. Her head pounded and she tried her best to think, to make herself decide what she should do, before the shock and betrayal overwhelmed her. She must find some course of action or else she would run straight from Dun Orga to the cliffs and throw the torque into the sea.

She looked across the grass toward her house—Ailin's house. Three figures stood before the door. One was short and round, one was hidden in a long red cloak, and the other was tall and powerful and gleaming with touches of gold.

As she watched, the door of the house opened and the three of them went inside. In a heartbeat Christine lifted the hems of her skirts and raced across the Dun, all thoughts of the sea forgotten.

She dashed inside the house and almost crashed into Ailin. He caught her arms to steady her and she looked up into his eyes, wanting to shout at him, to demand some kind of answer—but the words caught in her throat and she could say nothing.

All she could do was look at the pain and grief in his eyes, and listen to the agony in his quiet voice. "I must go, lady. I must go now." Gently he moved her aside and then walked out the door, never looking back.

A cold wind seemed to blow through Christine's soul. Never had she felt so empty, so alone. It was as though Ailin had taken her heart and soul with him when he left the little house.

Trembling, she turned to look inside the dimly lit room. Two figures stood close together on one side of the stone hearth. Una was one, but the other—the other—small and bowed and hidden beneath a heavy red cloak . . .

Una lifted off the cloak, and Christine caught her breath. She saw not a woman but a girl, really not much more than a child—a pale, frightened child in a worn gray dress.

Christine took a step forward, as curiosity and puzzlement began to push aside her pain and anger—at least for now.

The girl stood barely as tall as Christine's shoulder, and wore no jewelry at all except for a battered bronze coronet around her long, straight brown hair. She stood close beside Una as though looking for comfort.

How could this simple little creature be Ailin's intended bride? Ailin was the tanist of Dun Orga, he was a prince, the most powerful, dauntless warrior in all of Eire-land. A match between those two would be like a match between a roaring lion and a shaky little kitten!

"What's your name?" Christine said, almost whispering.

The girl quickly glanced up. Her eyes were large and glittering with fear, her face pale. Her hands were hidden within the folds of the faded gray woolen dress, but Christine had no doubt that they were shaking. She looked at Christine, and her eyes flicked.

Christine became aware of how she, a stranger, must look to this girl—this plain, simple, terrified little girl. Here she stood, rich and glittering, in a fine wool gown of soft red-and-gold plaid; a pure white linen undergown; and a shining gold torque and gleaming gold bracelets and earrings, all of which Ailin had made for her.

Add to that her bright red-gold hair, which was no doubt flying wild in the humid summer air, and her fair skin flushed with shock and pain. And her manner—bold and questioning, not deferential like the others. She must look wild and frightening and otherworldly, like a princess or a queen or—or—

"Mealla," the creature said, and quickly looked away.

"Mealla." Christine took another step toward her through the rushes. "Please, Mealla, tell me. How old are you?"

The child seemed about to answer, but only took a deep breath or two before turning to hide her face in Una's shoulder. "She has just begun her fourteenth year, lady," Una said, gently stroking Mealla's hair.

"Fourteen!" Christine almost laughed. "Una, you're telling me that Ailin wants to marry a girl who would barely be in high school yet, back where I come from?"

She walked over to Una and Mealla, shaking her head in very real confusion. "I'm supposed to believe that the most powerful man I've ever seen in this world or any other—a man who could have anything and everything he could ever possibly want—a man who has literally been worshiping the ground I walk on for the past six months—you're telling me that this man has suddenly tossed me over for a scared little girl who's obviously being pushed into this without a word to say about it?"

She could only stare at Mealla in complete bafflement. Another *woman*, now that would have been different. If that chariot had held some beautiful, tender twenty-year-old who had alighted in obvious delight at the prospect of wedding Ailin, things would have been different. Perhaps she would have stood up to such a woman, insisting that Ailin belonged to her, or demanded of Ailin right then and there to know why he had so suddenly and coldly abandoned her for another.

But for now she only wanted to know why in the world Ailin intended to marry this unwilling child, for whom she had nothing in her heart but pity.

Neither Una nor Mealla made any move to answer her. Finally Una looked up at Christine with a pleading expression, and that sent her into action.

There were going to be some explanations made, starting right now! "Una, please. Get her some food, make her comfortable. I'll be back!"

She found him in the darkness of the barn, pulling a wooden comb through the thick golden mane of one of his chariot horses. There was no reason for him to be grooming the horse himself, she knew; such work belonged to Niall, his charioteer. Clearly Ailin had come here to hide, to be alone.

"Ailin."

He looked up, startled. The red-gold horse snorted and flicked his ears in her direction. "Did you think I would not find you here?" she said, carefully walking around the horse until she stood looking across the animal's neck at Ailin. "Did you think I wouldn't walk every last inch of Eire-land to find you and make you tell me what on earth is going on here?"

He said nothing, but she could see the frown on his face and the tight set of his jaw. He went right on combing the horse's mane as though she were not there at all.

She reached out and clamped her hand over the wooden comb. The horse bobbed its head and took a quick step backward. Ailin stood unmoving, waiting for her to make the next move, still looking off into some corner of the barn.

"Why, Ailin?" she whispered, withdrawing her hand. "Who is she?"

He never moved, but she could hear his soft intake of breath. "She is the daughter of the chief of Dun Fada. My father wants an alliance with them, and they want one with us." His voice was low and expressionless. "My marriage to Mealla will seal that alliance."

The knife in her heart twisted at those last words, but she pulled herself together and pressed on. "But how is it that this is happening so suddenly? Why did I know nothing at all about it? Why didn't you tell me?"

He sighed, and again pulled the comb partway through the horse's golden mane. "I told my father months ago, even before you came to Dun Orga, that I would not marry Mealla. I could not stop Dun Fada from bringing her today. That would have been up to my father, and he would do no such thing."

"You're saying that the king—that your parents want you to marry her, too?"

"It is the only way to make the alliance. The two Duns have never really been at peace—we are too different—but we need each other. We are both small and isolated. Dun Orga needs an ally, and so does Dun Fada. It is a matter of need, not want."

She shook her head, feeling ever more dazed as shock after shock continued to hit her. "But surely your mother and father know how you and I feel about each other. They must know that we—"

"They know what I know, lady. They know that you have refused me, that you will not marry me, that you do not want me."

Anger suddenly broke through her confusion and pain. "That's not true!" The horse jumped and snorted. "You know that's not true! I've explained it to you a thousand times! And if your father doesn't know, then I'll go straight to him right now and explain it to him!"

She picked up her skirts and whirled around to go, but Ailin reached across the small horse's back and grabbed her arm. "It is too late," he said, as the horse danced between them. "No one can stop the wedding without starting a war."

She withdrew her arm and walked around behind the skittish horse until she stood facing Ailin. "Then you're going to marry her? There is nothing I can do, nothing I can say?"

He gazed at her for a long, long moment. "I cannot marry you if you will not have me. And you well know that I will never renounce you, that I will never believe you are not a goddess."

"So you would marry that—that little girl," Christine whispered. "But surely you won't—you wouldn't—"

"I will never touch her, lady. It would be a marriage in name only."

She relaxed slightly, but still the knife remained in her heart. "But for how long, Ailin?"

His piercing gaze met hers for an instant, and then he looked away. She turned to go, and looked up at him once again. "I will be in the house with Mealla. She's frightened to death and needs someone to look after her."

He gazed back at her in astonishment. "You would do that? You would care for her, instead of despising her?"

"What's to despise? She doesn't want this any more than you do. Probably less." She pressed on. "So you are going to make a marriage that neither of you wants—just to please everybody else?"

"You do not understand," he said, looking down at the horse. "I am tanist now. In time I will be king. If I refuse to marry her there will be a battle. Do I have the right to risk the lives of my men in this way? Would that be . . . civilized?" His eyes shifted and he looked closely at her, studying her.

Christine stared up at him in shock, the knife twisting again as she heard her own words used against her. She shook her head, unable to comprehend any more. "I don't know, Ailin. This is your world, not mine. I only know that I will never believe you can marry another until I see it with my own eyes."

Somehow she made her way back across the Dun, her head spinning with confusion and pain. A rising anger began to build in her—anger at Ailin for his betrayal and at all the rest of them for not telling her about it—but then a terrible thought occurred to her, one that she could not push away.

Was Ailin right? She *had* refused him. She had plainly told him that she would not marry him, much less make love to him, until he accepted her on her own terms and admitted that she was no goddess. And he had told her, just as plainly, that that was the one thing he would never do.

Why shouldn't he marry Mealla, or anyone else he chose? What reason did he now have to wait for Christine Connolly? A terrible despair settled over her as she realized that all her patience might well have been for nothing.

Finally she reached the house, and paused in the doorway before going inside. At one of the sleeping ledges Una worked busily, trying her best to polish Mealla's dull bronze coronet. The girl's gray wool gown was laid out beside it on the ledge, and Christine could plainly see how worn and faded and old the gown was. Close to the hearth Mealla sat on a little bench, eating quickly from a wooden bowl, her heavy red cloak draped over her shoulders. She dipped up the rich brown gravy with chunk after chunk of fresh bread as though she hadn't eaten in days.

Christine frowned. She would have thought the child would refuse to eat at all, as nervous as she was—but clearly it had been some time since Mealla had had a decent meal for herself. Or a decent dress. Now, if ever the folk of Dun Fada would want her to look presentable, wouldn't it be on the day of her wedding to the tanist of Dun Orga?

"Una," Christine began, moving toward her, "what is going on—"

There was a clatter as Mealla dropped her wooden bowl and jumped to her feet, wide-eyed and frightened as though she had suddenly been caught stealing. "I should not be sitting—"

But Christine caught her before she could scuttle away, and gently led her back to the small wooden bench. "It's all right, Mealla," she said. "You've got to eat. Here." She took another bowl from beside the hearth and ladled out more of the steaming venison stew from the cauldron. "Finish this. Please. Una . . ."

With Mealla safely seated, food in hand, Christine

walked through the rushes to the sleeping ledge where Una worked. The gray gown looked even more tattered on close inspection. "What's going on here?" Christine whispered. "She looks like she's been living on scraps and wearing rags! Isn't she a princess or something?"

Una shook her head, still briskly rubbing the battered coronet. "She is the daughter of a chief, yes, but old Flann is the chief of a very poor Dun. They have little to give her and she's of no use to them except as a means of gaining this alliance—now that her brothers are old enough that she need not mother them."

"So they send her to her own wedding looking like a starving orphan." Christine glanced at Mealla, still working on her bread and gravy at the hearth, and then at the wooden chest sitting at the end of the sleeping ledge—a wooden chest overflowing with fine wool gowns and gleaming gold ornaments. She placed her hand on Una's, stopping her from any further polishing. "Never mind that. I've got a better idea!"

Somewhere behind the heavy gray clouds, the sun struggled toward its height. Christine, too, her face damp with sweat, struggled up the hill toward the cliffs by the sea, slipping on grass still wet from the frequent summer showers.

She followed some distance behind Ailin and the king and queen, who were in turn surrounded by all the people of Dun Orga. They made their way past the dead and crumbling hulk of the old oak tree until they stood just beside it, where Ailin stopped.

Christine looked up. The king seemed to want to go on, but Ailin stood tall and immobile, legs braced and fists on his hips, making it plain that he would go no farther.

The moments passed slowly for Christine, who still felt the shock of the morning's revelations. A warm, heavy breeze moved lazily over her, stirring the long folds of her gown only slightly before giving up the effort. Her mind raced as she stood looking down at the Dun from the side of the hill, watching for Ailin's bride to be brought to him, watching and waiting.

There was a gentle touch on her arm. "Lady, I am so sorry," Derval whispered.

Christine managed a small smile. "It's not your fault," she said quietly. "But why did no one tell me? Didn't the rest of you know?"

"We thought it was for Ailin to tell you, if indeed you did not already know," Derval answered. "We were never told to prepare for wedding guests from another Dun—we thought it would only be our own Dun celebrating the feast of Lughnasa at the full moon, when it is always held, and that the tanist would be married at that time—married to the lady of his choice," she finished, her voice trailing away.

"It's all right," Christine said. "It's no one's fault but mine."

"Your fault? Lady, how could that be?"

Christine smiled again, a tight and bitter smile. "Because I just wouldn't give in to him. I could have given in—oh, it would have been so easy. All he wanted to do was worship me, and if I had let him I would have lived happily ever after—*very* happily.

"But it would have been a lie. Worship is not the same as love. Love is what I want, the real thing, or nothing at all."

"Oh, lady, will you watch him marry another?"

Christine closed her eyes, and for the first time tears welled up in them. "If I must—but I won't believe it until I see it. Not until I stand here and see it for myself."

She glanced up at Ailin where he stood motionless beside the ruins of the lightning-struck oak. For a long moment their gazes locked, and then Christine looked away.

* * *

Slowly, painstakingly, the bridal party began to make its way up the hill. It was led by the same grim, silent crowd of warriors that had come to Dun Orga that morning, but now they were all on foot. The lone chariot held the huge scowling man, whose name was Chief Flann, and his daughter Mealla. Flann slapped the reins on the backs of the tired brown-and-black team. Their heads dropped even lower as they labored to pull the vehicle up the steep hill.

The chariot stopped a short distance from Ailin. His eyes widened and his brow furrowed ever so slightly as he stared at Mealla.

She was quite a different sight from what she had been that morning. Gone were the worn gray gown and dull bronze coronet. Though Mealla still clutched the side of the chariot in obvious terror and kept her eyes fixed firmly on the floorboards, she now wore one of Christine's fine woolen gowns—bright red it was, over a spotless white linen undergown. Her brown hair, freshly combed, hung down past her waist. Bright gold objects straight from Christine's overflowing wooden chest adorned her from head to foot—a belt of gleaming gold links, shining earrings, beautiful brooches, and a priceless coronet.

Ailin glanced at Christine. Her mouth twisted and she lifted her chin as she met his eyes. If he really wanted to marry someone else, he would have to do it while being blatantly and brazenly reminded of Christine every time he looked at his chosen bride!

Flann stepped out of the chariot and made a great show of helping Mealla down to the wet grass. He walked with her to the lightning-struck oak, where Ailin stood braced and unmoving, and then held Mealla's hand outstretched toward her intended bridegroom.

At that moment, Christine's momentary resistance began to fade away. She closed her eyes as sorrow and pain and loss began to wash over her, drowning

251

her hopes the way a cold rain drowns a brightly burning flame.

Her pride and her spirit and her sense of the ridiculous could not help her now. She would have to stand here and watch Ailin marry another, marry a girl who stood glittering with the golden gifts he had made for Christine with his own hands . . . a girl who would not be a girl much longer, who would soon outgrow her childish aversion to Ailin and desire him as a husband, even as Christine did. . . .

She heard Ailin's voice and willed herself not to listen. She did not want to hear him say the words.

"I cannot marry her, Flann. I have brought you gold to pay the honor-price for breaking the contract—more than pay it, pay it three times over. I am sorry. But I cannot marry her."

Christine's eyes snapped open. For a moment the world swayed, and then steadied. This was nearly as much of a shock as hearing this morning that he was going to marry someone else. What on earth could possibly happen next?

Flann stood locked in place for a long moment. His stern frown slowly turned into a glare, and then into a look of pure hatred. He threw off Mealla's hand and she shrank away as he began to rage.

"Cannot marry her! Are you telling me that the women of Dun Fada are not good enough for you? That my own daughter is inferior?"

He grabbed the hilt of his sword. "What's the matter, Ailin? Doesn't she meet with your approval? Not fine enough for you? She's certainly been gilded up for you by someone! Isn't she good enough for you as she is? How much more gold should we pile on her to make her acceptable?"

Christine took a step back, as did all the rest of the crowd in the wake of Flann's boiling outrage—all except Ailin. He stood immobile and unaffected as Flann's venom spread over them all in a malevolent wave.

"For all of my life, I have loved another," Ailin said quietly. "I gave my bride-gift to her, in this very tree which burned with the flames she herself had struck. She took my gift and gave me my answer—when she returned that gift to me resting on the shoulders of the only one I have ever loved or will ever love.

"I would rather die than betray the goddess by marrying another."

Chapter Twenty-one

Derval leaned close and whispered to Christine, "There is your answer, lady. That is why he never told you he was marrying another. He never intended to marry another."

Christine's heart began to lift. Did she dare believe it? She had been pulled back and forth so much this day, did she dare?

Flann looked to be close to bursting a blood vessel. His face turned deep red and his thick hands clenched into fists. "And the alliance, *tanist*?" he hissed through grinding teeth. "Will you throw that away, too? Is this how you will lead your people?"

"I have a great care for where I will lead my people," Ailin answered. "I would not expect them to follow a man who would turn his back on the woman he loved, simply because he lacked the courage to fight for her. If I cannot keep both my people and my chosen queen, what kind of king could I ever hope to make?"

Ailin reached down and picked up a heavy wooden box. He remained quiet and cold, holding out the box to Flann. "As I have said, I've brought you gold enough to—"

With a roar of rage, Flann struck the box with his enormous fist and sent it flying out of Ailin's hand. Shining nuggets of gold ore and a set of beautifully wrought gold bracelets scattered across the lush green grass. The finely made wooden box cracked and splintered from the force of the blow and crashed in a heap alongside the glittering gold.

"That is what I think of your alliance! That is what I think of Dun Orga! That is what I think of you!"

Flann's warriors stirred and moved closer to him. King Donaill took a step forward, his hand on the hilt of his sword. Ailin stood his ground and spared not a glance for the gold at his feet.

"We will be in the valley, Ailin! Your valley! And we will be there waiting for you until you come to meet us, either alone or with whatever lying, dishonest, oath-breaking rabble you can pay to come and fight for you!"

With a final kick at the splintered box, Flann turned on his heel, grabbed Mealla by the arm, and dragged her away. Christine could hear the girl's muffled sobs as Flann wrenched her, stumbling, back into the wicker chariot. She wondered what was worse for Mealla—having to leave home, such as it was, and marry a stranger, or hearing herself rejected and left to face her raging, insulted, humiliated father.

Christine turned to Ailin, where he stood beside the king. She started to go to him, but then he turned and looked at his father.

King Donaill said nothing. He only gazed coldly at his son for a long, long moment. Finally the king looked away and started straight down the hill to Dun Orga. The others quickly followed—all except Ailin.

Christine ran to him. "I knew you would never do it," she said, taking hold of his arm.

Her heart soared as she finally allowed herself to believe that he was not going to marry someone else.

She felt that she had never loved him so much as she did at this moment. No matter what else happened, she would never love any man the way she loved Ailin.

She leaned her face against his powerful arm and held it close, but his arm remained rock-hard beneath her cheek. "It is not over yet, lady," he said, and his voice trembled—with anger, or pain, or something else, she could not tell.

He started down the hill toward the Dun, pulling her after him. All she could do was hold on tight and stay with him as best she could, the way a would-be rider might hang on to a wild stallion as it raced away.

Ailin left her at the house and strode away without a word. He did not seem angry at her, just entirely preoccupied. Once again confused and exasperated, Christine turned on her heel and went back inside the house.

Una and Derval were there working busily, almost frantically. Una filled a collection of earthenware jugs and leather skins with water. Derval stood at the hearth with a stack of old linen and hastily ripped the pieces into long strips, then rolled them up. Christine stared at them, making no connection between what they were doing and what had just happened out on the hillside. She was still just thankful that Ailin had indeed rejected his child-bride.

"What will happen to Mealla?" Christine, walking to the hearth. "What will they do with her?"

"I do not know, lady." Derval ripped another long strip of cloth and quickly rolled it up. "But it will not go well for her—a rejected bride, a shattered alliance—no doubt Flann will place the blame squarely on her. I can only imagine what—"

Christine held up her hand. "So can I. Well, we can't let her go back to Dun Fada! I'll speak to Ailin about it."

She turned to leave, but Derval gently stopped her. "Ailin has concerns of his own right now, lady," she said, "and so do we."

Christine finally shifted her attention to what the other two women were doing. "What is happening now?" she demanded, waving her hand at the jugs and the linen strips. "What is all this for?"

They paused and looked at her, and Christine felt herself growing cold. "There can be only one outcome when a bride is rejected and the honor-price refused," Derval said. "There will be a battle."

"A battle." Christine could only whisper the words. With a shock the scene became clear to her. Una and Derval were preparing water for the exhausted fighters and linen strips to bandage their wounds. For a moment she saw only visions of horror, of slaughter and death. Men would die . . . Ailin . . .

But then she steeled herself. "I stopped a battle once before. Maybe I can do it again." The two women only looked at her with pity in their eyes. "I have to try," Christine told them firmly. "I have to try!"

She turned away from them and began searching through the wooden chest for her linen undergowns, even as doubt and fear surged through her. Could she stop the fighters once again? This time it would not be just the men of Dun Orga, Ailin's own family. At this moment the cruel strangers of Dun Fada waited for them in the valley.

"Una, take those linen strips from Derval and start boiling them in the cauldron," she directed, pulling out a stack of linen gowns. "I'll have these ready for you in just a moment." Christine took her best white gown from the stack and began to tear it into long, wide strips.

After some ten minutes of frantic preparation, she began to hear it.

Coming from somewhere far away was a deep, repetitive pounding. It seemed almost like distant, rolling thunder, but this was thunder that did not stop. It kept on, coming in regular waves, over and over.

Christine stopped her work and looked up, glancing at Una and Derval. They too had stopped what they were doing and looked up.

It sounded like a slow, faraway drumming. And it was growing louder.

Christine threw down the strips of linen and raced outside the house, across the empty yard to the open gate of the Dun. She held tight to the massive gatepost as she tried to think, tried to make sense of yet another unknown terror on this shocking, terrifying day. But all she could do was listen to that sound.

From the valley it came, a pounding, booming sound, like some monstrous beast with a thousand legs hammering its way up the hill toward Dun Orga. Over and over the sound struck Christine. The monotonous, insistent pounding of this unseen, unknown terror sent fear rising through her as nothing here ever had before.

This was nothing anyone could stop, nothing anyone could control.

She stood with one hand on the huge wooden post of the gate, trying to keep her fear from turning into panic. She was about to turn and race back into the house when Dun Orga's chariots began to sweep past her and out the gate.

Each chariot held a driver and two or three warriors, all but the last two. Of those, one was drawn by a pair of shining black horses and carried King Donaill; the other was pulled by the familiar red-gold team and bore the tanist.

They all swept past her without a word, without a glance. Even Ailin did not seem to see her. The sound from the valley kept on, pounding, hammering, again and again.

Hurrying after the chariots were the most of the women of the Dun. All of them carried baskets and jugs and waterskins. Christine saw no children with them, so presumably some of the women would remain to care for them. But where were the rest going?

In a moment she was surrounded by Derval and Slaine and Una, all three of them carrying their own baskets of bandages and jugs of water. "Come on, lady," they urged, catching hold of her arms and pulling her along with them. "Please. You will be needed. Please come now!"

The very earth seemed to shake from the force of that relentless, repetitive pounding. Christine held tight to Derval's and Slaine's arms, and together they left the Dun and followed the path that led to the valley.

The men of Dun Fada waited in the valley, lined up side by side, beating their wooden shields with the flat side of their iron swords and sending up that terrifying, overwhelming sound. Now they added some kind of roaring chant along with it. The hair stood up on the back of Christine's neck when she realized what they were saying.

"Ailin! Ailin!" The warriors slammed their shields with their swords, working themselves up into an ever greater rage. "Ailin! Ailin!"

"What's going to happen?" Christine said, stopping at the top of the hill. She felt petrified, unable to go any farther, and reluctantly Derval and Slaine halted with her.

"A battle, lady," Slaine said, raising her voice over the noise.

So it was true—just as Derval had told her. "Because of—because Ailin refused to marry Mealla? For that they would all start a war?" She had been too concerned with Mealla's fate, too relieved that Ailin had decided not to go through with the marriage, to think of the consequences of his actions. She was not sure what she had expected after hearing Ailin refuse to go through with the ceremony, but she hadn't expected a war!

"Ailin paid the—the honor-price, and he apologized—surely they can't expect anything more than that! Are you going to tell me that people here are forced to marry, whether they want to or not?"

"It is no longer about the marriage, or the honor-price," said Derval. "Flann was insulted, humiliated, in front of his own men. He has long been very—ah, sensitive about how he has been treated by Dun Orga. He believes that we look down upon him, that we think his people are poor and unworthy, barely a step above the *gadai*."

"And lazy," said Slaine.

"Greedy," added Una.

"Dishonest—"

"Dirty—"

Derval silenced the two of them with a look. "When Ailin rejected Mealla, Flann took it as a personal insult. Ailin's reasons no longer have anything to do with this. It is now a matter of resolving the injury done to Flann and to Dun Fada—and that can only be resolved on the battlefield."

They continued down the side of the hill, the very same hill where, months before, she had fallen from Sunshine's back and lain helpless between the worlds. The women of Dun Orga gathered halfway down the hill and stood watching the armies far below, like spectators in a stadium assembled for a pleasant afternoon of baseball.

But this was no game. "People are going to die here, aren't they?" Christine said.

Derval glanced at her and then quickly looked away to the assembled armies. "It will be a battle, lady," was all that she would say.

Abruptly the pounding stopped and the warriors of Dun Fada began shouting in rage. Christine turned and saw Ailin far below in his chariot, with

Niall, his charioteer, driving the red-gold horses onto the battlefield.

Ailin stood tall and braced in the swaying vehicle, his sword strapped to his hip, with the biggest, most vicious-looking spear Christine had ever imagined standing up beside him. The massive black spearhead looked as dark and dull and malevolent as a threatening storm cloud—as though it would strike and slash without warning at anything it could reach, with no care for whom it might harm.

Christine shuddered at the sight of it.

"Do you mean we're all just going to stand here and watch them kill each other?" she asked, her voice shaking. "Isn't there anything anybody can do?"

Derval and Slaine looked at each other, and Una looked at the two of them. "Ernin, lady," Una said. "Ernin could stop it if he wanted to—he's the only one who could. Only a druid can stop them!"

"Ernin," Christine said to herself. And before any of the women could stop her, she began running down the hill toward the armies, where the white-robed druid stood waiting behind the lines.

"No, lady. I am sorry. I can do nothing."

Ernin stood calmly before her, leaning on his staff as always, his voice soft and whispery even in the midst of these screaming, battle-crazed warriors.

"But Una told me that you—that a druid—"

He made a small motion with his free hand, stopping her. "If a battle is unjust and goes against the law, I can tell them so, and they will stop. But this battle is not unjust."

Christine fought off her rising sense of despair. "Surely a battle is never just! There is never any reason to go around killing anyone, unless it's self-defense—and this is not!"

He studied her, his old gray eyes shifting slightly. "A battle does not always mean death, lady. A battle

261

is for settling a matter of honor as often as it is for killing. And this is one matter that must be settled, or it will only fester and grow."

"Please—I don't understand! If they're not going to kill each other, then what are all these weapons for?"

He seemed not to have heard. "Both sides have done wrong," he said, gazing out at the shouting, raving fighters. "Ailin should have made his wishes known to Chief Flann regarding his marriage to the daughter of the chief of Dun Fada. Chief Flann should have at least considered the honor-price instead of destroying it."

"But is there no other way? I know you have laws here! It's not just rule by the strongest! Is there nothing—"

"Also in question is Ailin's fitness to rule," Ernin continued. "The last time his men prepared for battle, he was persuaded to turn away."

Christine gasped. He was talking about that day when she had rounded the corner to find the army of Dun Orga preparing to attack the *gadai*. She had convinced him to call it off that day, and thought she had done the right thing.

"A tanist is chosen, to be sure, but he must prove himself still," the old druid said. "And Ailin must prove himself today. Only the rigors and rituals of battle will set things right today—all things."

Christine set her jaw and clenched her fists. "I'm not through yet," she said to Ernin. She turned away from the impassive white-robed figure and set out for the battlefield.

Far below in the shadowed valley, lined up and facing each other, the armies of Dun Orga and Dun Fada pounded their shields with their swords and shouted their rage across the wide empty strip of the valley floor.

"The grass will be slick with your blood! Your

horses will fall to their knees in it; your chariots will be useless!"

"All your heads will hang from the doorposts of Dun Orga!"

"No man's voice will be heard again in Dun Fada— only the wailing sounds of the women and the children!"

Christine shook as she walked down onto the battlefield. With each step she moved deeper into the horrors of the battle to come. The bellowed threats, the pounding swords, the snorting, stomping chariot horses, the raving men—the terrifying scene closed over her in a dark cloud of terror. Yet she pressed on, running now, racing to Ailin's chariot, determined to put a stop to it before it could begin.

"Ailin!"

She grabbed the heavy wicker side of his chariot and leaped in, grasping his arm. It was rock-hard beneath the wide gold band that encircled it.

Astonished, he turned to look at her. Niall quickly steadied the horses as they jumped, causing the chariot to rock. He, too, looked over his shoulder at her in amazement.

Ailin leaned down close to her, catching tight hold of her arm. "Lady Brighid! Why do you come here? You cannot ride with us into battle! Please wait with the women—you must go quickly."

"I'm not going anywhere!" she cried, waving her arm toward Dun Fada's shouting army. "They don't want Dun Orga. They want you! They'll all come straight for you, and they'll kill anyone who gets in the way!" His face paled, and he could only stand and stare at her.

She took a deep breath and tried to speak as calmly as she could. "I want you to call it off, Ailin. Please. People are going to die here. You could die here. I want you to call it off."

Christine could see his jaw set and his teeth grind. "Lady, you do not realize what you ask."

She became aware that silence had descended upon the valley. Everyone was standing and staring at them. Christine knew that she must seize the moment while she could.

"You can't send your men to their deaths over something like this! You've got to stop it! I'm asking you to stop it!"

He grabbed her wrist, and for a moment she was shocked by the look on his face—anguish, despair, and ever-rising rage. "I will do as you ask. But you are right. There is only one way to stop this." He released her wrist, gave the evil black spear to Niall, and leaped out of the back of the chariot.

Ailin strode onto the battlefield alone, and immediately the roaring and the shield-pounding began again. He walked straight up to Flann's chariot and shouted to him.

"This is my fight, Flann! And I demand a champion's battle! I demand it now! Send out your champion to face me, or live forever in the stench of your own cowardice!"

Flann leaned forward in the big wicker chariot, elbowing the cowering Mealla out of his way. "He is coming, tanist," Flann said, a sneer in his voice. "But this time you will wait for us. Wait and you will face him." He turned and lumbered out the back of the chariot, disappearing into his mob of fighters.

Christine grabbed the side of the chariot, her mouth open in shock. "No!" she said frantically. "That's not what I meant! I wanted him to stop it!"

"He has stopped it, lady," Niall said quietly. "But no one can stop what is to come."

"We'll see about that!" She'd been able to stop things like this before—it was almost becoming routine, though the fear that rose up through her would never become routine. But she had to try. A terrible battle was about to begin, a battle between Ailin and only God knew what else. She could not stand on the sidelines and watch him die!

She jumped to the grass and started after Ailin—when a firm hand stopped her.

"Have you no wish to watch the battle, lady?" Dizzy, light-headed from fear and draining terror, she looked up toward the voice. It was King Donaill.

Relief flowed over her at being in the king's presence. Yet her great fear for Ailin and her determination to stop the fight if she could remained unabated. "I have no wish to see Ailin murdered," she answered, her voice shaking. "I don't want to see anyone killed—not anyone!"

The king released her and stood motionless as she gazed up at him. It was so strange to stand here with him, for he was so like Ailin: powerful and tall, blond, and fair, with an immovable strength of both body and spirit. Yet the weight of his kingship rested heavily about him. She could feel it, almost a tangible thing that held him fast in its grip and allowed him very few choices.

"Death is not the only thing to be concerned with here, lady," the king said. He looked closely at her. "Do you not know what will happen if Ailin wins this battle, yet is wounded?"

She closed her eyes. "I don't want to see anyone wounded any more than I want to see them killed. I don't want any of this to be happening! I only want to put a stop to it!"

"Would you have Ailin lose everything, even if he should win this fight?"

She looked up at him, into the steely slate-blue eyes of Ailin's father. "Lose everything? What are you talking about?"

The king sighed, and glanced at his son where he stood waiting for Flann's champion. "Ailin was chosen tanist, and yet he once called off a battle simply because you asked it of him. His men had begun to talk of this when he could not hear them. Some even wondered if he was still fit to be king."

Christine's indignation flared. "They could find no

better king than Ailin—and I am sure you would say
that yourself! Surely you're not telling me that a man
who can stop a bloody battle and save his own men's
lives is looked down upon—that you'd rather have a
king who would massacre another tribe at the drop
of a hat, instead of a man who would try to find
peace!"

He stared at her for a long moment, and then to
Christine's astonishment he turned away and looked
down at the grass. "I feel as you do, lady," he said
softly, almost whispering. "But for a king, peace, too,
has its price."

"Is this to be a fight to the death?" Christine asked
in despair. "Is that what you're telling me?"

The king turned his gaze on her again. His heavy
gold coronet shone even in the dull gray light of the
summer afternoon. "Ailin will have to kill—or at
least cut him down so that he can fight no more. But
the champion . . ." He paused, and Christine was
amazed to hear the slight catch in his throat. "He
need only wound Ailin enough so that he is no longer
whole. A man whose body is not sound and whole
can never serve as king."

Christine paled as the words of Derval came back
to her. *It is as though the land itself, or the people
themselves, were weakened and incomplete, if the king
be marred in such a way.*

There was only one thing left that she could try.
One card left for her to play. And although she hated
what she was about to do, she did not see any alter-
native—except for watching Ailin die.

Christine faced the king and forced herself to say
the words. "King Donaill—you and your people believe that I am a goddess, the goddess Brighid. Very
well, then. I am telling you, as a goddess, that I do
not want this battle to take place."

She held her breath, but refused to back down.
Surely he would listen to this appeal—surely the
voice of a goddess would be heard, even by a king,

even above the madness of the fighters and the cold logic of druidic law.

His eyes narrowed. "Lady . . ." he began, and then took a step toward her. "You are a part of Dun Orga, a part of all our lives, and you will always be welcome here. We believe that the goddess Brighid chose to honor Ailin by sending you to be with him for a time—but you do not speak with Brighid's voice."

"Then tell that to Ailin!" she cried. "I've been telling him that since I got here!"

"Ailin believes what he will, and none can sway him from that," the king said, and for a moment he almost smiled. Then his face once more turned grim. "All believe what you always have said. You are a gift from the goddess, but not the goddess herself."

Christine felt cold, empty. "For so long I have tried to convince Ailin of just that very thing," she whispered, "but at this moment I wish I were a goddess, so that I could stop this battle."

She backed away from the king, slowly shaking her head. "Whatever I am, I cannot allow this," she said, as a kind of numbness began to set in. "I cannot allow him do this." And then she turned and started across the battlefield toward Dun Fada's dark, ragged, and bloodthirsty army, where Ailin stood waiting.

Chapter Twenty-two

Christine stepped boldly in front of Ailin, turning her back on the hideous fighters. "Please," she began, "don't do this. I cannot watch you do this! You cannot expect me to—"

But suddenly a deafening roaring and pounding rose up from both armies. Ailin grabbed her arms and pulled her around alongside him, so that once again she faced the army of Dun Fada.

Now a man stood there before her, a muscular, black-haired man who seemed very familiar. Then he grinned—a slow, malevolent grin—and with sudden horror she remembered who he was.

"Tierney!"

"Yes, lady. I am so pleased that you remember me." He bared his teeth once more in that evil smile, and Christine's blood ran cold at the sight.

She leaned in close to Ailin. "I thought he was a part of your clan—a kinsman."

"I *was* a kinsman," Tierney said, stepping closer. He was all thick black leather armor and rusted iron fastenings, creaking as he walked. "I am part of Dun Fada now. I gave justice where justice was due for one of my former clan. And for that—"

"You mean you murdered one of your own cousins in cold blood," Ailin snarled. "It wasn't a battle, or even a fair fight. You killed him while he slept."

But Tierney only laughed. "It will be a battle today, Ailin. Drop your red-haired baggage and come out to face me."

Ailin ground his teeth. He attempted to push Christine behind him, but she stepped away and boldly stood her ground between him and his intended adversary—as if she could keep them apart. "She asks me not to fight you, Tierney. Perhaps there is another way to settle this."

Tierney grinned. "Another way?" Then in an instant, before Christine could move, he seized her by the hair and dragged her close to him.

"Here is another way, Ailin!" cried Tierney, pulling her backward toward Dun Fada's lines. "Of course she does not want me to fight you—she wants me to take her for myself, and so I will!"

With a shout of rage, his fury unleashed at last, Ailin drew his sword and swung it straight at Tierney's head. Tierney ducked and let go of Christine, shoving her aside.

She picked herself up off the ground and scuttled out of the way. She caught sight of the king, and then of Derval and Slaine and Una behind him, and hurried, breathless, to stand with them.

There was nothing more that she could do. The battle had begun and she could only stand by and watch it—watch it and pray that Ailin's great heart and strength would win.

Ailin and Tierney circled each other like a pair of enraged lions. Both were eager for blood and death. "I was always a good killer, Ailin!" Tierney shouted, with a grin of pure malice. "I'm a better one now!"

Ailin said not a word, but his eyes were glazed and his face was a mask of hatred. The sword in his hand trembled with his eagerness to use it.

Christine could hardly bear to look at them. She

closed her eyes and clutched Derval's arm. For an awful moment she grew dizzy and actually thought she might faint.

"Stay here for him, lady," Derval said, leaning down to her and holding tight to her waist. "He will need you now as he never has before. You must help him."

"Help him? How?" Christine whispered "What can I do now?"

"He knows you are here. He will see you, feel you, hear you, even as the fight goes on. You are what he is fighting for, truly! You are the strength of his heart, of his spirit—he cannot do this without you. You must stay here for him!"

For him . . . For Ailin. Ailin needed her. She must help him.

She opened her eyes and forced herself to look at the heart-stopping scene in front of her, in the deep shadow of the floor of the valley.

Ailin's rage had exploded at last. He slashed viciously at Tierney, again and again, his iron sword striking his opponent's shield and sword but never touching Tierney himself. Christine could have sworn she heard Tierney laughing even as Ailin roared and lunged and swung at him over and over again.

She shivered. Though no man was a match for Ailin in a fair fight, she could feel his loss of control as his fury overwhelmed him. Instead of dealing measured and powerful blows from his long iron sword, he slashed wildly, hitting the air as often as he struck Tierney's shield. He saw only his bloodred rage, not his target.

It was clear even to her unpracticed eye that Ailin could lose this fight.

"Help him, lady," whispered Derval.

She almost took a step toward the battlefield, but then stopped herself and tried to think. With all her heart and mind she focused on Ailin, on her love and trust of him, hoping that somehow he would feel her presence and know that she was with him even as she stood on the sidelines. By sheer force of will she reached out to him, determined to break through his seething fury and make him regain his control.

It was his only chance of emerging from this terrible struggle alive.

The battle raged on as Christine waited and watched. Then, just as she began to fear that the horrific scene would never end, Ailin's eyes met hers.

Here was her chance!

Think! I am with you! Use your mind! You must regain control!

Their gazes locked—and in that moment, a change came over him. With all his strength he shoved Tierney away and then raised his sword with a smooth, practiced move. The raging desperation of a moment before was gone, and he stood coolly as Tierney charged again.

Though he still swung as fiercely as before, Ailin began to wait for the openings he needed. He watched his opponent and sought to control him rather than just slashing wildly. Slowly, methodically, he began to drive Tierney back.

Christine let herself breathe again. The battle had turned. For whatever reason, the battle had turned.

But the worst was not over. A chill of horror crept over her as, now, Ailin's iron sword began to find its mark. Tierney's black leather armor showed rips and slashes in its weather-beaten surface. Lines and streams of blood appeared on his arms and hands and even his face.

He slowed and staggered but would not yield, would not go down. Now he was the one kept in the fight by rage alone, like some monstrous bull gravely wounded by the matador but refusing to the last to surrender.

Christine tried to find some solace in the fact that Ailin did not appear to be hurt. She told herself that

Janeen O'Kerry

soon, soon, this would all be over—but though Tierney was now covered in his own blood, the terrible fight went on and on.

Finally, as his maddened opponent rushed him yet again, Ailin shouted "Niall!" Christine heard the familiar rattling behind her and turned to see Niall driving the chariot and red-gold team to the battleground.

He halted beside the fighters. With a superhuman effort Ailin pushed Tierney to the grass and caught the long black spear as Niall tossed it to him.

Christine gasped. She could have sworn that he had actually caught the ugly weapon by its razorsharp edge, as if the vile thing had turned on him and bitten his hand—but no, he showed no sign of pain. He braced his legs and stood over Tierney with the huge black point of the spear aimed at the fallen man's throat.

"Yield or die, cousin," Ailin said, hefting the awkward, heavy weapon in his sweat-slick hands. But though his eyes were glazed and his blood pooled in the grass, Tierney got to his feet and charged at Ailin like some unstoppable demon.

Ailin raised the spear high and hurled it with all his strength. Christine looked away just as it struck Tierney's chest.

"Lady, it is over," Derval said softly.

Christine closed her eyes. She could not watch another moment of this blood-covered struggle to the death. Did she dare to hope that it was truly finished?

After a long moment she looked up at the battleground. Just disappearing into the lines of Dun Fada's army was a group of men carrying the body of Tierney. She quickly looked away to see Ailin walking slowly toward her, the huge black spear dripping red with every step he took. He stopped before her and extended his right arm.

The sight of him held her motionless. His breathing was still ragged from the exertion of the fight. His gold coronet was gone and his hair fell in wet tangles over his slate-blue eyes, eyes that still had the look of some wild and predatory animal.

Her eyes flicked to his outstretched arm. The brown leather armor protecting his right forearm hung loose and ripped. The arm beneath it was red and soaked from elbow to fingertips.

She steeled herself, aware of the silent, staring crowds surrounding them, aware that they were waiting for her to make the next move. But most of all she was aware of Ailin, the man who had just fought a battle to the death for his people—and for her.

Gingerly she rested her fingers on his leather-covered wrist and walked with him back to his chariot. Just as she was about to step up into the vehicle, a small movement caught her eye. She looked up and saw Mealla.

The girl stood shivering in Flann's chariot. She tried to pull her heavy cloak closer around her but her hands shook so badly that she kept dropping the folds.

Christine paused as sudden questions flew through her mind. What would happen to Mealla now? How would Flann treat her once they were back in Dun Fada? What kind of future could this hapless child possibly look forward to?

She made her decision. Now it was time for her to prove her courage, in her own way, just as Ailin had proved his.

Leaving Ailin standing alone beside his red-gold team, Christine set out once more across the battle-ground. Boldly, not looking left or right, she walked straight through the lines of Dun Fada's warriors to the back of Flann's chariot.

She reached up and took hold of one of Mealla's trembling hands. The girl shrank back in terror as she looked up and saw who it was, but Christine only smiled gently at her. "Come with us," she said. "Come."

After a moment of frozen indecision, Mealla began to move toward her. "Come," Christine said again, with a small nod of encouragement.

Flann turned around and stared at them, aghast. Then, as it dawned on him what Christine was doing, he gave a shout of anger and frustration. "Take her!" he roared. "Take her, then!" And he gave Mealla a tremendous shove that sent her sprawling on the grass below, the breath knocked out of her.

Slowly, and with all dignity, Christine helped Mealla to her feet and straightened her cloak. She took the girl by the hand and led her calmly through Dun Fada's lines toward Ailin's chariot.

Behind them, sounding almost hysterical now, Flann kept up his shouting. "Take her! I don't want her! Get her out of my sight!" But neither Christine nor Mealla looked back. Ailin helped them both into his chariot without a word.

Niall spoke a word to the team and started them on their way back to Dun Orga. Though Mealla still trembled, she was quiet, as though somehow resigned to her fate. Perhaps she had decided that life in Dun Orga, no matter what it might bring, would be far better than any kind of life she might have in Dun Fada.

Ailin leaned close to Niall and whispered something to him, though Christine could not hear what he said. He stood in silence at the front of the chariot and seemed to have withdrawn inside himself, completely closed to her.

They rode through the heavy gray day for a time. Christine breathed a sigh of relief when she saw the gates of Dun Orga, but to her amazement Niall sent the horses trotting on past the gate and headed them toward the cliffs overhanging the sea. She could not imagine where they were going now, but said nothing and resolved that she would simply wait to find out.

On this day she was long past being surprised.

They drove to the very top of the cliff, where Niall finally halted the horses. Ailin slid past Christine and Mealla and stepped down to the windblown grass. Without a word he reached up to Niall with his left arm and took the massive black spear.

Ailin walked near the edge of the cliff. For a long moment he stood motionless beneath the dark windy clouds, looking out over the heavy gray sea. Finally, awkwardly, using his left hand, he raised the evil-looking spear and hurled it with all his strength high into the air. It seemed to Christine that the blade gleamed red in the dark afternoon before it plunged out of sight and fell down to the sea far below.

Slowly, quietly, his head bowed, Ailin walked back to the chariot. With the final act of hurling the spear off the cliff, something seemed to have gone out of him. The fire and the rage and the adrenaline rush of battle were over. Christine was shocked to see that he cradled his right arm as he walked.

With great effort he climbed back into the chariot. Niall turned the team and began to jog them slowly home. Her apprehension growing, Christine placed a firm hand on Ailin's shoulder and made him turn around to face her.

She gasped. Even Mealla made a little sound. Ailin's cradled right arm was slashed open from palm to elbow and blood still streamed from the wound. As Christine stared at him in horror, she saw that he was growing pale and beginning to shiver.

She had to help him—but how? No one could dial 911 in this time and place!

Terrifying scenes began to race through her mind. He would fall unconscious from loss of blood. They would never get him back to the Dun in the small chariot. He would die before anyone could help him—she would have to stand helplessly by and watch it happen—

Then she looked at his half-closed eyes, and steeled herself. No. It would not happen. He needed her, even as he had needed her out on the battleground this day, and she would find a way to save his life.

Her own courage now fully engaged by Ailin's need, Christine gripped his arms tightly. She pushed herself against his body to steady him, to lend him her strength as he had so often lent her his.

Niall glanced back at them and his eyes widened. "Hurry," she cried, her voice urgent. "Get him home, get him home now!"

Without hesitation Niall shouted to the horses. They leaped into a gallop and were soon sweeping through the gates of Dun Orga.

Together, Christine and Mealla helped Ailin into the little house. He lay back on Christine's ledge with a soft sigh, closing his eyes as if in sleep—and then his right arm slid down from the ledge and hung out over it.

A stream of blood ran down into the rushes.

Christine thought her heart would stop—but instantly she went into action. She seized Ailin's arm and raised it straight up, pressing her hand hard against the long, long slash that kept welling and welling with blood.

"Mealla! Help me with him!" She feared that the already terrified child would simply curl up and hide in a corner, but Mealla hurried to her side and stood waiting for her next words.

"Unfasten his cloak. He's got to breathe. That's it, get the brooch."

Mealla's trembling fingers turned Ailin's heavy gold brooch, unpinned it, and pulled it out of the thick red wool of his cloak. With his throat bare now, Christine could just see his pulse, fast and faint beneath his pale damp skin. His eyes stayed closed and his chest barely moved, so light and rapid was his breathing.

"Mealla," she said, continuing to press her hand against Ailin's wrist, "go and find someone—Una, or Derval, or Slaine, anybody! They don't know he's hurt. We've got to have bandages! Hurry!"

Wide-eyed, Mealla nodded slightly and then left without a word. Christine laid Ailin's arm down over his chest and kept pressure on the slash with one hand, while with the other she reached down and began working her carved leather belt loose from its knot. After a few moments of frantic pulling she got it free. The heavy gold ring at one end dropped into the rushes.

She wrapped the belt around Ailin's arm just beneath his elbow and pulled the leather tight. Christine raised his arm up high again, pressing her hand hard against the stream of blood and praying that the frightening red river would stop before his very life ran out between her fingers.

After what seemed like hours, but was surely only a few minutes, the door of the house burst open. Derval, Slaine, and Una rushed in, with Mealla close on their heels.

Each of them carried an armload of supplies—baskets of rolled linen bandages, jugs of water, mysterious small bundles wrapped in squares of linen. Derval started to pour water from a jug onto a linen rag, intending to clean Ailin's wound, but Christine stopped her.

"No! The water must be boiled first—and the linen," she said, still holding Ailin's arm up high. "Hurry, fill the cauldron with water—"

"The linen has been boiled and placed in the sun, lady, just as you directed months ago," Derval said calmly. "And we boiled this water today, before the battle."

Christine breathed a sigh of relief. "Good." She

didn't know how much longer she could have kept Ailin's arm tied off and raised without danger to him from loss of circulation. She eased the arm back down to the ledge and loosened the thick belt. "Let's get it wrapped up. Hurry!"

She and Derval washed the terrible wound and then covered it with thick rolls of linen. Christine began wrapping strip after strip snugly around his arm to hold the rolls in place, and glanced over her shoulder as she worked. "Una, put another cauldron of water on to boil. No telling how much we're going to need. Help her, Mealla. Slaine, please . . ." She frowned. "What is that?"

Slaine stood at the hearth, unwrapping the small linen bundles. Carefully she laid them out for Christine to see. "Herbs, lady," she said. "They will help him. I will add them to the boiling water and the drink will be ready when he wakes up."

Christine hesitated. She could not help but be concerned; she had no way of knowing just what those herbs were or what they might do to Ailin, especially in his weakened condition. "A healing draft," Derval said. "It will ease his pain and help to mend the wound." She smiled. "We give it to all the new mothers as soon as the baby is born."

Well, there was no arguing with that. She would have to trust them on this issue. "All right, then," Christine said. "Let's get it ready for him."

The moments turned into hours. Twilight began to fall. Christine felt another touch of panic when a deep red stain began to creep through the heavy linen bandage, but it stopped before soaking through. Ailin's breathing seemed to steady and he did not grow any paler. They placed warm furs across his body against the evening chill and waited for him to awaken.

After a time he stirred slightly, and his eyes opened just enough for them to know he was awake. Slaine quickly gave him the hot herbal drink, which he took without complaint, and then he fell into sleep again.

Christine settled beside him in the darkness, as did the other four women. The vigil had begun.

The hours turned into days. Christine and Derval changed the bandages once each day, and Slaine continued to give him the herbal drink whenever Ailin seemed restless or in pain. But on the third day he refused it and asked for food instead. Una brought him bread and milk, and Christine was overjoyed to see him eat.

Almost hourly she looked closely at his arm, examining it minutely for any signs of redness or swelling—any indication that infection might be setting in. But none appeared, and after a week it became clear that the wound was indeed healing normally. Ailin would have a fearsome scar, but he would not lose the use of his hand.

Finally the day came when Ailin stood in the hall before his father the king and his mother the queen. Behind them were Ernin, and Ailin's two brothers, and a group of the king's most trusted fighters.

At Ailin's side was Christine, her fingers held lightly in his right hand, and her heart soared with happiness and relief that this day had finally come. With the help of Derval and Slaine, Una and Mealla, his life had been saved and he would recover completely. Yes, he was still very quiet and withdrawn and hardly spoke to her at all, but she took that to be the aftermath of his devastating injury and long period of healing—to say nothing of the strange medicine he'd been dosed with. She had no doubt that soon he would be back to his old self.

Donaill stepped forward. "I say to you all this day that Ailin is well and whole and recovered from his injury. He has won the champion's battle and thus ended the matter of his marriage to the daughter of

Dun Fada. Ailin, what is your wish in regards to the girl known as Mealla?"

Ailin glanced over his shoulder, where Mealla stood proudly beside Una. In the few short weeks since the battle, the young woman had attached herself to Una and spent every waking moment out on the green hillsides—she milked cows, tended calves, and threw herself willingly into whatever task might be at hand. She had lost much of her shyness and fear and seemed to be truly happy, probably for the first time in her life.

"She wishes to stay in Dun Orga," Ailin answered quietly. "She has offered to work alongside the serving women and will remain in the care of the one called Una."

"Is this your wish, Mealla?" the king asked.

The girl nodded to him. "Yes, it is my wish," she said in a whisper, and though her voice did shake a little, she met the king's gaze directly.

Donaill paced across the front of the room and then turned back to address the assembly. "Now, Ailin has stood alone to face and vanquish an enemy—an enemy of his people. He did this to save his people from a battle without honor, and to win the lady of his choice. He has behaved as a tanist should.

"Also I say to you that the lady he has chosen is worthy of a tanist and of Dun Orga. She has shown courage of her own in trying to stop a dishonorable fight and in her skill at healing Ailin after a wound that might have claimed his life.

"Finally I say to you there can be no doubt of Ailin's fitness to serve as tanist and king. If any disagree, I will hear him speak now."

He waited, motionless. No one made a sound.

Christine turned to Ailin and smiled up at him, unable to contain her happiness at the king's words and the thought of their future together. But though he kept hold of her fingers, he did not look at her, and after a moment Christine turned away.

Chapter Twenty-three

As Ailin recovered and once again took his place in the life of Dun Orga, Christine had great hopes for their future together.

Surely his long convalescence, and all that the two of them had been through, would only bring them closer! But instead of tearing down the walls, she found that the whole episode had only built those walls higher.

Though Christine had healed Ailin's body, it seemed that she had not been able to heal his heart. She had been delighted when King Donaill had acknowledged her as a worthy consort for the tanist, and truly believed that now Ailin would accept her for herself just as his father had.

But much to her despair and frustration, Ailin barely spoke to her, barely looked at her. He went through the days in bitter silence, still locked away behind a wall of guilt and anger and pain at Christine's refusal to marry him and allow him to make her his queen.

But worst of all, he had redoubled his efforts to worship her as a goddess.

Each night he rekindled the fire outside her house

and kept vigil there until dawn. Each morning he
brought her another beautiful piece of jewelry that
he had made himself. And every time she turned
around he was there, guarding her.

She wondered when he slept.

More than once she had gripped the golden torque
tightly in her fingers, knowing that all she had to do
was pull it off and this would all be over.

At last, one afternoon, standing inside the little
house, she raised the lid on the carved wooden chest
to get her knife blade and wondered, for the thousandth time, what she could do to convince him of
her humanity. There had to be something she could
do to force his attention away from worship and
onto womanhood—something she could do that a
goddess never would. But what?

The gleaming gold ornaments, heaped in the
wooden chest like the most fabulous treasure any
pirate could imagine, caught her eye. Suddenly she
jumped up and ran to the door.

"Una! Come here! I need your help!"

A few hours later, evening came over the Dun. This
was the evening before the autumn equinox, when
the day and night were of equal length. The druids
knew when that time occurred, though Christine
was not sure just how they knew, and they offered
no explanation.

But at any rate, the first night of autumn was an
occasion to hold another feast, and as Christine sat
beside Ailin in the crowded hall she had no thoughts
for the mysteries of the druids. She could think only
of how uncomfortable she was.

Frustrated and angry, determined to break
through Ailin's stubborn worship of her and make
him see how wrong it was, she had—with Una's
help—put on virtually every piece of jewelry he had
ever given her. She hoped it would make him see that
spending so much time and effort on mere objects

was not what she wanted. It almost seemed as though he were trying to buy her affections by giving her so much.

Maybe goddesses could be bought with gold and jewels, but Christine Connolly could not!

The heavy coronets, and the huge earrings looped with slender cords over her ears, were giving her a terrible headache. The massive rows of bracelets and armlets reached from below her wrists to above her elbows, and were so stiff and heavy that she could hardly raise her arm to drink from her goblet. She wore so many rings that it hurt to bend her fingers.

The front of her newly finished blue-and-green plaid gown was covered with enormous pins and brooches, which were tearing holes in the fine wool fabric. Thick belts made of shining gold links hung from her waist.

She hoped she'd be able to get to her feet when this was over.

Christine was acutely aware that all the other people of Dun Orga were confused and rather embarrassed by her display. These people loved gaudy jewelry and brightly colored clothes, and no one would ever accuse them of being restrained when it came to fashion; but it was clear that piling on every piece of jewelry one owned was a little much even for them.

Worst of all, though, was Ailin. He sat beside her on a cushion, his face burning with anger and humiliation. He would not look at her, but she could hear his low whisper.

"You ridicule me, lady." It sounded as though his teeth were clenched. "You do not do this out of love or gratitude. My gifts—"

"Your gifts were meant for a goddess," Christine broke in. She lifted her cup and stared hard at him, her rising anger making her bold. "Would a goddess behave this way? Would a goddess wear enough jewelry for twenty people and embarrass herself like this?"

He made no answer. All she could hear was his low, heavy breathing.

"No, she wouldn't." She took a sip of cool water from the cup. "But a woman—now, a real woman would do whatever it took to break down the walls between herself and—and the man she loves."

His breath caught for an instant, but still he would not look at her. Christine set the cup down hard. Ailin flinched.

"She would force him to see her as a flawed, but real, human being. And if that made him angry, well, then he would just have to get angry!"

When the feast was finally over, Christine struggled to her feet. Ailin stood by and watched her, but did not offer to help. Good, she thought as she slowly straightened up. I wouldn't take his arm if it meant I had to stay sitting here for the rest of my life!

She lumbered outside into the darkness, holding her head high and refusing to show how difficult it was to walk. *This must be what it's like to wear armor!*

At any other time the whole situation would have been funny, but as she struggled against the weight of Ailin's gifts she realized that his worship of her was much the same. It was an encumbering, confining, paralyzing trap that had nothing to do with the freeing, life-affirming relationship of real love.

She turned. Of course, Ailin was right there, just a step or two behind her as he always was. "Well, Ailin?" she said, her voice trembling with frustration and pain. "Are you satisfied? Have I become the goddess for you now?"

"It is clear to me that you are not satisfied, lady." He looked at something far in the distance. She could hear the tension in his voice—he was angry, and keeping it tightly leashed. But Christine's despair and long frustration rose up within her and let her say what she wanted to say.

284

"Look at me, Ailin! Please!" He raised his eyes at her command, but his noble face was grim. "I want you to look at me, not at some goddess-being that I am not and will not ever be. Why can't you do that? Don't you see how silly it is to make a goddess out of me?"

"You make a fool of me, lady," he said, his voice low and hard edged. "I do not know why. I have done all I know how to do."

"But you haven't! You haven't! You have never looked at me and seen Christine—only your precious Brighid! Never again, Ailin. Never again!"

Her heart pounded, and she was filled with anguish and pain. She wanted desperately not to lose Ailin—but how could she lose him if she had never had him to begin with, if he could not accept her for who she really was?

"Never again!"

With that she turned her back on him and started toward the house. As she walked she began tearing off the jewelry. She stripped the rings from her bruised fingers, grabbed the coronets off her aching head, unhooked the heavy belts and earrings, tore the bracelets from her sore arms, and pulled the pins and brooches from her ruined gown.

By the time she reached her doorway, a trail of priceless objects lay behind her on the damp ground. The only piece of gold she still wore was the gleaming torque.

Ailin had followed her. His face was still a mask, but she could see the shock in his eyes.

"I'm going to bed now, Ailin," she announced loudly, knowing that everyone else in Dun Orga was listening. "I'm going to bed because *women* need their sleep—unlike goddesses, who need none! And you had better not bother me again if you're coming to see the goddess Brighid—only if you want to see the real woman, Bridget Christine Connolly! Good night!" And with that she went in the house and slammed the door.

She stood in the darkness and then leaned back against the door, trembling with anger and pain and loss.

It must be tonight, she told herself. He must come to her tonight—come to her bed to love her and claim her for his own.

Tonight or never. She would wait no longer.

Christine woke suddenly, dreaming of books. Shelves and shelves of books in wonderful, glorious libraries. But after a moment, she groaned and rubbed her head in disappointment. It was only the same old dream again.

But quickly crowding out her dreams of books were thoughts of a man, a tall and beautiful man whom she loved. He had not come to her. She was alone, and would remain that way.

He was a man like no other, but he did not want her for herself. He only wanted his vision of what he thought a woman should be.

He wasn't going to change. She'd tried everything to make him change his mind, to see her as she really was, but he refused. Or else—or else . . .

Maybe he did see her as she was, and was disappointed in the reality. She was not good enough for him as herself, only as some imagined goddess.

A coldness stole through to her heart. It was a chill that had nothing to do with the damp night air. Either way, goddess or no, Ailin did not want her. Did not want *her*.

He would never want her.

There was no chance of getting back to sleep now. And no reason to sleep, either. She got up from the ledge, slipped on her boots, and fastened her fur-lined cloak over the linen gown. Opening the creaking wooden door, she walked outside.

Ailin was not there. She looked up into the autumn

night, and it was a beautiful, breathtaking sight. The sky was clear as crystal, shining with stars and glowing blue-white from the light of the enormous full moon high overhead.

She reached up to touch the torque. There was no reason to stay here any longer. All she had to do was pull off the torque and toss it away. She would be back home in moments, never to return.

All this could be dismissed as some bizarre dream, and she could live out her life in a comfortable world of books and central heating and men who did not expect her to be a goddess.

Her fingers tightened on the spiraling metal. But her gaze returned to the beautiful skies, and to the lovely hills glowing beneath the pure white luminous moon.

She could not leave without saying farewell to this world. She would never see it again, would never see any place like it in her life.

Neither did she want to risk pulling off the torque here in the Dun and having someone see her disappear. And she did not want to leave this world cowering inside the dark little house—the house she had hoped to share with Ailin as his beloved, as his wife.

Then, far away in the still, silent night, she heard the distant voice of the sea.

Yes, that was the answer. She would go up to the cliffs, say good-bye to this strange and beautiful world, and pull off the golden torque and send it flying to the sea far below.

There would be no trace left of either herself or the torque.

The moon lit her way, and she walked without fear. Christine climbed up the hillside, past the blackened ruin of the lightning-struck oak tree, until she reached the summit and could see the ocean far below.

It lay calm and glistening beneath the shining

moon, so quiet, so peaceful. Once again she reached for the torque, tracing the cool metal spirals one last time and running her fingers over the red jewel stones and the delicate, noble faces of the women at each end.

But then another glint of gold caught her eye. Whirling around, she saw a slight movement beneath the old oak tree near the cliff's edge.

The figure stood up. Its dark cloak rippled in the breeze from the sea. The moonlight shone on the bright gold coronet and gleamed on shining blond hair.

It was Ailin.

She turned away, but he approached until he was near enough to touch her if he wished.

"Why do you come to the cliffs, lady?"

"What does that matter, Ailin?" she asked, gazing calmly out to sea. "I am a goddess, remember? I can do what I like, without explaining to anyone."

He hesitated, searching for words, but before he could speak she turned to face him. "On that first day that I was here, why did you follow me and stop me from leaping off these cliffs? Would a goddess need saving?"

He bowed his head, and she could hear the despair in his voice. "I . . . I did not know for certain. Perhaps it was a test of my own courage . . . a test by a goddess in human form. Or—or maybe—"

She seized the opportunity. "Yes, maybe! Maybe I wasn't a goddess at all, but just a real, live, human woman, frightened and lost and in need of help."

"Maybe! Perhaps!" He towered over her in the darkness, but she held her ground. "I do not know! How can I know what you are? How can I know what you want?"

"I have told you what I want. And since you cannot give it to me, I have no reason to stay in this world any longer. I have come here to throw the torque into the sea."

He grabbed her shoulders, a stricken look on his face. He knew what would happen if she took off the torque.

He had seen it.

"It was this beautiful golden piece that brought us together, Ailin—this piece you made yourself, with your own strength and skill and love for your goddess. Maybe love does have the power to cross the centuries. If I did come here from another time and place, it was your love that brought me, and not any powers I have from being a goddess.

"But if that love cannot bridge the gulf between us now—if you cannot love me for what I truly am, instead of waiting forever for something that does not exist . . ."

She turned away from him to face the moonlit sea and reached up for the torque.

But Ailin grabbed her wrists. He pulled her to him, his grip hard and strong. Unafraid, she threw back her head and looked straight into his eyes as the night wind lifted her hair.

"You will not leave me," he whispered, his voice low and urgent. "I will not lose you now—I cannot let you go. I swear it—goddess or no, this time I shall make you mine forever."

He lifted her up in his arms and carried her beneath the sheltering trees. She was crushed against him in the darkness, carried away by strength she had only imagined until now. The sounds of the sea were drowned out by his hammering heart and ragged breath.

At last he had come to claim her. There would be no stopping him now. And Christine found that she had no intention of stopping him, that her passion matched his own, and that she intended to claim him just as he would claim her.

He set her down on the grass. He reached up to rip away his cloak, but she caught his wrist and drew him down to her. His soft hair fell across her breast and throat as he leaned down close to her, and she ran her fingers through its shining blond softness.

She kissed the smooth skin of his neck and held him tight, unable to get enough of him. But at the touch of her lips his body grew hard as steel, and he was no longer her plaything.

He raised her up in his powerful arms and fastened his mouth upon hers. The world swam in hot darkness, and Christine was conscious of nothing but Ailin's pounding heart and his body stretched out against hers, pressing her into the soft earth, locking her into an embrace from which there could be no escape.

He tore at her gown and ripped at his leather breeches, and suddenly there was nothing at all between them. His skin burned her own with the heat of the sun, and his arms held her to him with all the force of life itself.

And then, there on the moonlit edge of the world, just as his body claimed hers, she heard his voice again and knew that her joy would be complete.

"I love you, Bridget Christine. In this way you become the goddess, for you are the woman I love."

The moonlight gleamed on heaps of gold. A trail of priceless jewelry lay on the wet grass of Dun Orga. Ailin and Christine walked up to it together, their arms wrapped around each other, the soft wind out of the darkness blowing their cloaks wide.

Ailin knelt down and began gathering up the shining pieces. When he had as much as he could hold in his hands, he turned to Christine and offered it to her without a word.

A warmth spread through her at his action, a warmth that came straight from her heart. She was both touched and impressed by his willingness to offer her, again, this treasure she had so lately rejected.

She smiled down at him and carefully lifted a single golden bracelet from his hands. Slipping it on, she said, "Thank you, Ailin. I will keep these beautiful gifts you have made for me—but from now on I will wear just one at a time. I promise."

"That is as befits a lady of the earth," he said, getting to his feet. "Although I think that even a goddess would not need so many pieces as you wore today."

Christine grinned. Then she laughed. And then Ailin, too, smiled and laughed, and they fell into each other's arms, laughing together.

"I don't think we've ever laughed together!" Christine said, gasping for breath. "It's about time!"

"It is time," Ailin agreed. Then his face became serious, and he looked deep into her eyes.

"I am sorry for the pain I must have caused you. I—"

"Oh, Ailin—"

"Please. I must finish. I thought—I felt—that you were a woman, not a goddess, the first time I saw you out on the cliffs. But I could not be sure. How could I be sure?

"I have known many women, Bridget Christine. I was fond of them, but I did not love them. Can you understand that I wanted my love, and the life I would spend with her, to be perfect? As it could only be with a goddess?"

Her lips parted, but Ailin touched them with a gentle finger. "I know now that the joy of loving a real woman far outweighs the loneliness of worshiping a goddess. And even so, I was not wrong about you. The goddess lives in every woman—but none so much as you."

She smiled at him. "I am a goddess because you love me, Ailin, as every woman is when a man truly loves her."

"I do not care where you came from, or how you are here," he whispered. "I only care that we are together. Marry me, and be my wife, and let me love you as your husband."

She held tight to his arms and pressed hard

against him, the strength of her passion matching his own.

"Yes, Ailin. Oh, yes, I will marry you, and I will love you."

He lifted her up, and holding her close he carried her into the small white house. Their house. Their home.

Chapter Twenty-four

The next evening, as the high clouds faded among the stars, King Donaill gathered everyone together in front of his house. Standing between Ailin and Christine, he began to speak.

"Last Imbolc Eve, there came to Dun Orga she whom we know as the Lady. We did not know where she had come from, or why; we only knew that she saved Ailin's life when she appeared; and stayed to become a part of our family here in Dun Orga.

"Yet now we have learned that the Lady is, indeed, a woman—sent by the goddess without doubt, but a mortal woman meant for Ailin alone. And so there will be a marriage ceremony on the next Imbolc Eve. Wish them well, for I do, as does the queen."

There was silence for a moment. Then all the woman crowded around Christine, laughing and congratulating her, and began walking with her toward her house.

"There are so many things you will need to keep your own household as a married woman!" Derval said. "New gowns and linens and—"

"We'll have everything ready!" said Una. "I'll see to it!"

"So will I!" added Mealla.

"A white dress? But surely you will wear red!" Slaine exclaimed.

Christine looked over her shoulder as the women took her away, and saw that the men of the Dun were leading Ailin away and congratulating him, too. It was a wonderful, exciting time, as happy as Christine had ever hoped the announcement of her engagement might be.

Outside the high walls of Dun Orga, hidden from sight, a tribesman crouched down low against the grass-covered wall and listened to every word of the king's statement.

The Lady is, indeed, a woman. . . .

A mortal woman meant for Ailin alone . . .

. . . A marriage ceremony . . . next Imbolc Eve . . .

On the day of her wedding, Christine awoke in the cold darkness before dawn, and a shiver of sweet anticipation ran through her. She'd thought so many times that this day would never come. And now, at last, it was here.

There was a soft knock at the door. "Come in," she called. The door opened just enough to reveal three faces looking in, one above the other above the other—Una, Slaine, and Derval. "It is your wedding day!" they said, laughing merrily as they crowded into the little house. "Your wedding day!"

Una carried her basket to the hearth just as Christine sat up on the edge of the ledge. "Now, lady," she began briskly, "I've brought you bread and butter and honey and—"

But Christine held up her hand. "I don't think I could possibly eat anything," she said. "I'm much too excited! But I'll tell you what I do want—a bath."

"Of course!" said Slaine. "We knew you would insist on a bath. We've brought everything you'll need."

Christine hurried through the bath, grateful for

the steaming hot water—the air seemed unusually cold this morning. She dried off quickly, wrapped up in the long linen cloth that served as a towel, and got back to the ledge to begin dressing for her wedding.

The first thing she put on was her own cotton nightgown, the one she'd been wearing when she came to this place so long ago. It was wonderfully soft and smooth against her skin, after all the linen and wool.

"This is very special to you, isn't it, lady?" Derval asked, gently running her finger down the sleeve of the white gown.

"It certainly is," Christine said. "It's my only link with—with the place I came from. Sometimes I think that if I didn't have it, I'd never believe that other place existed at all."

That other place . . . The thought of her old home brought with it a wave of sadness, for it also made her think of someone that she missed very much right now.

Eliza.

She had always hoped that Eliza would serve as matron of honor at her wedding, but that was not to be. Yet, as Christine had promised, she had not forgotten her old friend.

You'll be right here with me today, Eliza. Right here with me and with Ailin.

Then she glanced up at Derval and smiled. "And speaking of that faraway place, one of the wedding traditions there says that brides are supposed to wear 'something old and something new.' I guess this nightgown is either very old or very new, depending on how you look at it!"

"What is next, lady?" asked Slaine.

"Oh, the new wool underdress," Christine said. It was a long, heavy gown of creamy white wool; she had woven and sewn it herself especially for this day. "I'm going to be walking and standing outside today for who knows how long, and I want to be warm. I'll no doubt be shaking enough from nervousness, and I don't need to be shivering with cold on top of that!"

Together she and Slaine pulled the heavy mass of wool over her head, and as Christine pushed her arms through the sleeves the rest of the long gown slid perfectly into place. Instantly its solid warmth began to steal through her.

"Are you ready for this now, lady?"

She turned to see Derval and Una holding up her wedding dress. "We are so glad you chose to wear more than just white," Una said.

No, she was not wearing only white this day. For her wedding gown she had spun fine wool into yarn and then dyed it a deep and beautiful red, the color of life, the traditional color for brides in the ancient land of Eire. She'd woven the yarn into cloth and then cut and sewn the gown entirely with her own hands.

Derval gazed at the interlocking bands of cream and gold embroidery that covered the neckline and sleeves and hem of the red gown. "I remember the many evenings we spent by the fire to complete this," she said.

Christine reached out to the gown, happiness filling her heart. "It's beautiful," she whispered as they lifted it over her head. "It's my wedding dress."

From the same creamy white wool that she'd used for her underdress, Christine had fashioned a sash and a soft, flowing cloak. One of Ailin's gold brooches fastened the cloak. It was the only jewelry she would wear, aside from a slender coronet and her ever-present gold torque. After tying up her new fur-lined boots, there was just one more thing.

Slaine walked over with a comb and a long wooden pin. "Here, lady, I will fix your hair for you and then help you with the—the 'vell.'"

"That's 'veil,'" Christine said with a grin, as Slaine twisted her shining red-gold hair into a knot at the back of her head. "And for me, it's as important a part of getting married as a red dress."

From the carved wooden chest at the foot of her sleeping ledge, Christine lifted out a carefully folded piece of fine, bleached white linen. When she shook it out, it formed a circular shape that was taller than she was.

"Now that's what I call a veil!"

Her face was not covered, but the wide circle of linen, held on the back of her head with the gold coronet, floated down past her shoulders and nearly to her knees.

She was finally ready. The little group stepped outside, and as they did Christine caught her breath.

The dawn of Imbolc Eve was cold, and crystal-clear, and completely covered with white frost. The grass crunched beneath Christine's boots, and she blinked in the brilliance of the new morning.

The pale sky was nearly white in the thin light of the winter dawn, and the entire landscape as far as the eye could see was covered with a blanket of frost. It was pristine and perfect, white and gleaming, as if the world had been transformed into a cathedral for the occasion of her wedding.

"What is it, lady?"

Christine thought she would break into tears. "All my life I dreamed of having a white wedding," she whispered. "And now, it seems, I will have one."

They walked across the sparkling, frost-covered grounds of the Dun, headed toward the massive gate. There a group of eight men, all warriors dressed in their finest wool garb and adorned with gleaming gold, stood waiting for them.

Christine recognized Cronan and Finn, the husbands of Derval and Slaine, but was uncertain about the others. "Who are they?" she asked.

Derval gently touched her arm. "Since you have no family—ah, no blood relatives—here in Eire, Slaine and I asked the men of our own families to escort you to your wedding."

Slaine took her other arm, and Christine smiled her heartfelt thanks at these two women who had become dearer than sisters during her long, strange year in the land of Eire.

Together they walked to the gate where the men awaited them. The wedding party left Dun Orga, walking through the gleaming, silent white world. They started up the path to the oak grove atop the hill, the site of the Imbolc bonfire.

The frost-covered mountain of wood stood waiting once again, ready for the torches that would flare it into life. Christine's wedding was only a part of the Imbolc celebration this time. The same ritual that she had seen last year would be held again tonight, just as it had been for more years than anyone knew.

Waiting for them at the top of the hill, within the oak grove, were King Donaill, Queen Mor, the druid Ernin, and the entire population of Dun Orga, as well as many of the neighboring relatives. And then, as Christine and her party approached, Ailin stepped out from behind the nearest oak.

He was truly a prince from head to foot, dressed in his black leather breeches, the shining white linen tunic which Christine had cut and sewn for him, and a new red wool cloak. He gleamed with touches of gold—in the ring of his black leather belt, in the brooch that held his cloak, on the hilt of his sword, and on the coronet that held his shining blond hair.

He walked out to Christine and took her arm. Together they went to stand before Ernin, who leaned on his staff beneath the largest and oldest of the oak trees.

The ceremony was a simple one. Ernin read the marriage contract so that Christine and Ailin and all assembled might hear it—just a legal document, really, just an agreement that the two of them would live together and share all that they had between them.

But when Ernin's reading was concluded, he held out one hand. Opening it, there was another glimmer of gold against the frosty white world. In his palm rested two rings, bands of twisted gold that Ailin had made at Christine's request. From memory, the druid recited the simple vow that Christine had asked be a part of her wedding.

"Will you, Bridget Christine Connolly and Ailin, son of Donaill, tanist of Dun Orga, accept and love each other as you are today?"

"I am the woman who loves this man," Christine answered.

"And I am the man who loves this woman," Ailin said.

They reached out and took the rings from Ernin's hand, and placed them on each other's fingers. "Then you are now married, in your hearts and by our laws and in the sight of this company," Ernin said.

Christine looked up at the face of the man who was now her husband. His blue-gray eyes gleamed against his fair skin, and his feather-soft hair fell gently across her cheeks as he bent to kiss her.

His lips were hot and soft, and they carried the promise of a lifetime lived in love, and in passion, and in joy. She closed her eyes and knew that, whatever else might happen to her in the future, nothing could take away the perfect joy she felt right now. She had just married the man of her dreams, the man she loved, the man who loved her in return.

The wedding party retired to the feast hall, where the celebration lasted nearly all the rest of the day. There was even a cake of sorts, a special wedding cake, which Christine had had her heart set on. It was baked with the finest wheat flour and dried apples and sweetened with honey. And of course there was a lavish feast with endless quantities of the very best winter food—roasted beef and mutton, fresh bread, boiled vegetables, and dried fruits.

Finally, late in the afternoon, just an hour or so before dusk, the people began to file out of the hall. "Why is everyone leaving?" Christine said to Ailin. "I'm having such a wonderful time, I never want this to end!"

"To prepare for the Imbolc ceremony, my lady wife," Ailin answered. "Did you forget that you asked for your wedding to be held on Imbolc Eve? You will have to share that ceremony with your wedding feast."

"I'd nearly forgotten," Christine admitted. "But I'm sure no one will mind coming back afterward and continuing the party. I've never seen anyone here need any excuse to eat and drink and talk and have a good time!"

"You are right about that," Ailin answered. Then, pulling her close, he murmured, "But perhaps we will not return after the ceremony."

Her heart jumped as she leaned against him, the black leather of his sword belt creaking slightly as she wrapped her arms around him. She was convinced that she would never have enough of him— of his smooth and powerful body close against hers, of the force of his passion, of the power of his embrace and the hot softness of his lips.

"Let me congratulate you on your wedding, Ailin. And you, too, Bridget Christine."

Christine blinked. She drew back slightly from Ailin so that she could think clearly. Whose voice was that? Oh—it was Ernin, come to wish them well.

"Thank you, Ernin." Ailin looked up as something caught his eye. "I see that my father is calling me. Wait here for me, please, my lady. I will be back in a moment."

"Of course." She smiled at Ernin as Ailin disappeared into the crowd. Her fear of the druid was long gone now; she knew that he was a wise and gentle man, held in esteem as a priest or professor of her own time might be.

"It is nearly time for another Imbolc," he said. He studied her closely with his faded gray eyes. "Are you prepared for it, Bridget Christine?"

"Another Imbolc," she said. Suddenly her thoughts went back to what had happened at the last one. "Ailin didn't find his stone last year," she said, looking at Ernin. "In the bonfire. But here we are, at another Imbolc, and all is well. In fact, things couldn't be better for Ailin and me."

Ernin shook his head sadly. "But I must remind you—this year's Imbolc is not here yet. It does not even begin until sunset."

An icy chill went straight to Christine's heart as the druid turned and walked away, leaning on his gnarled oaken staff.

A year ago Ailin had said that any man who did not find his stone in the bonfire would die, by accident or in battle, before the next Imbolc. He believed that, even if she did not—or could not.

Now the beginning of this next Imbolc was only an hour away. What could happen in an hour? She began trembling as she thought wildly of all manner of things that could, indeed, happen. . . .

But as she caught sight of Ailin across the room, talking to his father the king, she steeled herself and forced her thoughts away from superstitious nonsense. Today nothing would destroy her happiness. She had just married Ailin, the man she loved more than life itself, and she would make the most of every second they had together.

The hour passed slowly for Ailin and Christine, sheltered within their small white house and finding joy in each other beneath the soft, warm furs. When at last they began to dress and prepare for the ceremony, afternoon had become evening. The assembled families were leaving to go up to the hillside to light the bonfire and watch the casting of the stones.

They had again put on their wedding finery, and

301

just before they stepped outside Christine looked up at Ailin, her husband, and kissed him one last time.

"I just want you to know how happy you have made me," she said. "Happier than I ever knew it was possible to be."

"You have done the same for me, my lady wife." He returned her kiss, gently as always, but the strength and passion that always left her breathless remained just beneath the surface—a promise of things to come.

They walked out into the winter evening, the last of the people to leave Dun Orga. As they started across the grass, Ailin suddenly gave a startled cry and fell hard to the ground.

Christine whirled to look at him. She froze in horror as fear surged through her like a tide.

A mob of rough and surly men had Ailin pinned down, holding him by his arms and throwing themselves across his chest. "We've been waiting a long time for you," one of them said, struggling to hold Ailin's arm. "Watching and waiting to catch you alone—it's you we want, to pay for the life of our brother."

It was them! The rough men! The ones she had seen one year ago—they had attacked Ailin then—now they were back!

The Dun was empty, the warriors gone. What should she do? No one could hear a cry for help. It would take too long to go and get the others.

No. She would not leave Ailin. She would not leave her husband!

Christine raced inside the house and grabbed the long iron shovel off the hearth. Before she could get back out, Ailin roared his rage and fought his attackers with superhuman strength. With all the force he possessed, he stood up and threw off two of the ragged men even as the rest of them shoved him back into the house.

"Bridget Christine!" he shouted, stumbling across

the threshold. "Go to another house! Bar the door! Hurry!"

Screaming, she leaped up out of their way and stood on the sleeping ledge as they staggered inside and fell to the rush-covered floor. Ailin and the six men continued to struggle just inside the doorway, blocking it.

But Christine had no intention of running away. She raised the heavy shovel and swung viciously at the nearest man. "Get out of here!" she raged. "Get out of my house! Get away from my husband!"

The shovel struck one of the black-haired men on the back of his head. He threw up his hands and opened his mouth as if to scream, but then fell unmoving to the floor.

She stared at him in amazement. Had she knocked him out? Or was he dead?

But there was no time to worry about him. The other five invaders had managed to push Ailin back to the far wall of the house—but as they did, he had taken the time to get his sword out of its scabbard.

Instantly he slashed down one of the men. Now there were four, dancing back out of reach. They were unable to get close enough to reach him with their short swords; Ailin's iron sword, long and flashing, kept them at bay.

Another man fell screaming to the floor. Another turned and fled, tearing out the door before Christine could reach him with her shovel.

As she raised the heavy iron implement, she heard a roaring, cracking sound overhead. Looking up, she cried out in horror and leaped back just in time.

Flames devoured the thatched straw roof, racing in ever-widening lines directly over Christine's head. She covered her face with her arm and turned away just as the burning straw and timbers collapsed with a roar and a towering column of sparks.

"Ailin! Ailin!" she cried when she could look again. He was still there in the corner, shielding his eyes from the glare of the flames that surrounded him. His last two attackers, realizing they were trapped in a burning house, had forgotten all about Ailin and were screaming and clawing at the walls.

Ailin looked at Christine across the wall of fire. "Get out!" he cried. "Save yourself! Go!"

But in that instant she knew that there was only one thing she could do. Standing tall, she cried out to her husband across the roar of the flames.

"Come with me, Ailin! Come with me, wherever I am going! Come with me!"

And she ripped the torque from her neck and sent it flying through the flames, into Ailin's outstretched hand.

The last thing she saw as the world faded away was Ailin looking at her across the flames, holding her golden torque in his hand. Once more she saw her surroundings waver and fade, shimmering like the air in the heat from the fire.

As the world grew dimmer and thinner, Christine felt herself rising, rising, upward on the drafts of the fire as they blew her white cloak wide, following the arcing path of the torque; and then falling, falling, headlong into the roaring, leaping flames.

Chapter Twenty-five

Christine woke with a start. She lay alone on her bed, resting comfortably in the darkness of her room. The curtains were partly open and she could see snow falling in the glare of the streetlight. Somewhere in the distance a car roared past.

Everything was here: bed and dresser, walls and door, curtains and lamp. Real and substantial and ordinary, just as they had always been. She still wore her familiar long white nightgown.

Then she raised her hand to her neck. The torque was gone.

She heard a hammering sound, faint at first and then growing louder. She knew that sound. It was knocking. Someone was knocking at her door.

Slowly she sat up and swung her feet down to the floor. It was cold and bare. She walked down the hallway, listening to a curious ticking sound. Oh, yes. The wall clock. Of course. It was right above her bookshelf.

Her bookshelf.

Reaching the door, she unlocked it and pulled it open.

"Hey, lady! Aren't you dressed yet? It's already after seven, and we're supposed to meet your profs at seven-thirty. We've got to get going!"

Eliza bustled in, setting her oversize handbag on the floor. She was dressed in tight black jeans and a new white sweatshirt with a brightly painted clown on the front, edged in gold glitter. She looked up at Christine through the large frames of her glasses and grinned.

"Like it? Jim gave it to me today. He knows I've started collecting clowns."

Christine stared. "Ah, yes," she said finally. "Yes, I like it."

Eliza frowned. "Did you just wake up or something?"

"That's right. I did. I—I just woke up."

"Well, go ahead and get dressed. You know I'll make myself right at home." She clicked on the TV set and sat down on the couch.

Christine gazed, blinking, at the pictures on the screen. She saw cars, and guns, and men with short hair wearing suits and ties and eyeglasses. All things she had not seen for a very long time.

Or had she? How long had it been?

Moving slowly back down the hall to her bedroom, still feeling as if she were dreaming, she tried to remember what had happened. A few moments ago she had awakened from a nap, late for her night out with Eliza. And before that—before that . . .

Her mind was filled with the sights and sounds of another place, another time, of a strange wild land of beauty and terror. A place that held a man she had loved and who had loved her fiercely in return.

He had been tall and strong, with slate-blue eyes and long blond hair. He was a man she had cherished, a man she had married.

Such a dream she had had . . . such a dream . . .

Moving slowly, as though she were walking in her sleep, she pulled open a dresser drawer and found a pair of pants. Jeans, black jeans, like Eliza was wearing. Another drawer held sweaters, one thick and soft, made of wool. White wool.

She got herself dressed, amazed at the tight fit of the jeans and how they so clearly outlined her body. The sweater was soft and loose, comfortable. A pair of high black boots stood in a corner of her closet, their soft suede tops sagging against the wall. She lifted them out and sat down on the edge of the bed to pull them on.

She went to look in the mirror, startled at the clarity of her reflection, and reached for the brush to smooth her red-gold hair. But instead she raised her hand to her throat and touched the bare skin, and was filled with a terrible sense of loneliness and loss.

"It's awfully late," Eliza said, shaking her head as she started the car. "It's past eight now, you took so long getting ready! Do you think they'll wait for you?"

"I don't know," Christine whispered. "I don't know."

"Well, even if they don't, we can still have dinner— a very nice non–birthday dinner, that is. This place has the best lasagna—and the best salad, and the best breadsticks. . . ."

As Eliza drove through the dark winter night, Christine was struck by how drab and plain and colorless everything seemed. The air reeked with the smell of gasoline and fumes and exhaust, and the streets and buildings made a monotonous display of dull gray and black and dirty white.

When Eliza finally parked the car at the rear of the Village Green, the first thing Christine did upon stepping out was look up at the sky.

The night was clear, for she could see the bright full moon high above, and elsewhere small red points of light moved slowly across the darkness. Airplanes, of course. But there were scarcely any stars. Squinting in the glare of the streetlights and headlights and floodlights, she could not see the stars. This world, it seemed, did not have them.

They walked inside the restaurant. "Do you see your friends?" asked Eliza. Christine blinked and scanned the roomful of diners. They were a blur of bright hard colors, painted faces, and perfectly sculpted hair. She could only shake her head at Eliza's question and wonder at the strangeness of this place.

There were no drafts in here, and no heavy smell of smoke. The air was fresh and clean. It was softly lit, with candles on the tables, and warm, so very warm.

Yes, she thought, as she followed Eliza to their table, in this world she need never be cold. She could, if she wished, go home and take a long, hot shower, and then curl up beneath smooth, clean sheets and quilts in a warm room with a book. As many books as she ever cared to read.

But as she sat down and stared at the slick plastic menu the waiter handed her, she realized that, pleasant though they were, material comforts didn't matter now. All that mattered was Ailin.

Ailin. The man she loved more than life. But he was gone forever, far beyond any means she had of ever finding him again, and it was her fault. She gazed into the flame of the candle as painful memory surged through her mind.

If she had not stopped the battle that day—if she hadn't convinced Ailin and his warriors not to attack the *gadai,* then perhaps those outlaw men would not have been around to attack him on the day of their wedding. The first day of their life together would not have been their last, with Ailin hopelessly trapped in the flames of their house as it burned down around him.

But if he had ridden out with his warriors that day, he might have been fatally wounded during that battle—and she would not have been on the battlefield to throw him the torque and save his life.

But had she saved his life? She could not ever know what had happened in the burning house. Had he put on the torque? Had it transported him as it had transported her? And if it had, where had he gone?

Finally she made herself stop. There was nothing to be gained by tormenting herself with it now. She would never know what the right answer was—or should have been. But why was she thinking of all this now? It was only a dream. What else could it have been?

"Christine, haven't you decided yet?"

She looked up to see both Eliza and the patient young man with the order pad staring at her, waiting for her to make up her mind. "Ah . . . I'm really not sure. . . ."

Eliza sighed, and then snatched the menu out of Christine's fingers. "That's all right. I'll order for both of us. Really, I don't think anybody's thirtieth birthday ought to be this serious—not that it's even your birthday until tomorrow!"

Christine tried to remember why it was so important for them to go to this particular restaurant tonight. Professor Vaughn had someone who wanted to talk to her—someone who was leaving? Yes, the visiting historian, the handsome blond man who was leaving the country tonight.

She almost smiled. Her memory of the Irish visitor had him looking just like Ailin, tall and blond and powerful and, oh, so kind and attentive to her.

Would she never be able to forget?

The man had wanted to see her tonight about her torque, because he believed it was real. But the torque wasn't real. It was gone. And she would never see it again, just as she would never see Ailin again.

She would have to accept that or she would surely go mad. She would start to see him around every corner, convinced that every tall blond haired man might be him.

Just as she had caught herself staring at a man who had walked in a moment ago. He stood now with his back to her, asking one of the managers about something.

The man was tall and long-legged, slender and no doubt strong. Even hidden as he was beneath his long overcoat of dark red wool, she could sense his strong and dynamic personality. His hair, long by modern standards but neatly trimmed, was shining blond. He was no ordinary man, she was sure of it, no doubt he was—

She stopped herself. Already it had started. She was obsessed with a man who was nothing but a dream, had never been anything but a dream, who simply did not exist.

As the blond man stood with the manager, one of the waitresses hurried up to them and held out a cream-colored wool scarf. The man accepted it gratefully. *There, you see, he's just an ordinary man who forgot his scarf and had to come back to get it.*

Then the man turned to leave, and Christine saw his face.

Time stopped for Christine, though she no longer had a golden torque to perform such magic for her. The sight of those slate-blue eyes, those fine noble features, had been enough.

The man walked out into the night. He had not seen her.

In a single motion Christine was out of her chair and racing for the door. She heard Eliza's startled cry of "Christine!" but never looked back.

She raced outside to the parking lot, lost beneath a cold black sky. Her breath came in cold clouds as she looked frantically up and down the rows of cars. Where had he gone?

No, not again! I cannot lose you again!

There! Two men, walking down the last row of the

lot. One short and gray-haired, the other tall and strong in a coat of dark red wool.

"Ailin," she whispered. Then, as they reached their car, she cried out, "Ailin!"

The tall blond man looked up. And in that moment he saw her.

Saw *her*.

He stood motionless beside the waiting car. She was the one who went to him, slowly at first and then faster, her red-gold hair flying, the tears streaming unheeded down her cheeks, to fling herself into his waiting arms.

He held her with the strong embrace she knew so well, and had thought she would never know again. Leaning her head against his broad chest, she could hear his swiftly beating heart and feel the trembling that ran through his body. She clung to him with all her strength, afraid to open her eyes, fearful that she would awaken and all this truly would be only a dream.

"How is this possible?" she whispered against his coat. "How can you be here?"

He placed a gentle finger beneath her chin and drew her gaze upward. Opening her eyes, she saw the face of the man she had believed lost to her forever.

"Do you not know how I am here?" he said. His was a gentle Irish voice, one that went straight to her heart. She could only shake her head slightly, unable to speak.

He reached beneath his coat and took out the golden torque.

Christine reached for it, and their hands closed around it together. The gold surface brightened and glimmered briefly, as though reflecting the light of a fire. Then its light faded and it was simply an ornament, a lovely antique, just an old curiosity.

"Yes, this was the key, this was always the key,"

Janeen O'Kerry

she whispered, running her finger over the twisted gold. "I found it at a little sale . . . I bought it from a nice old woman, out in front of her house . . . but when I walked past the place again later in the day there was no trace that she had ever been there."

"The goddess wears many faces," he answered. "She can be young and new, or womanly and strong, or ancient and wise. She gave you the torque with her own hands, and brought us together as gifts to each other."

"So she did." Christine closed her eyes, knowing now that it hadn't been a dream, it really had happened, and all those people were real . . . Derval and Slaine and Niall and Mealla and Una . . . King Donaill and Queen Mor. . . .

Quickly she looked up at him. "But what happened to them? It was so long ago, so very long—"

"My brother Cronan was the next choice to be named tanist. I have no doubt that that was what he became. So that means—"

He stopped as Christine broke into a delighted smile. "Derval became the next queen! Oh, no one would make a finer queen than Derval. She was so wise and good, so gentle and kind!"

Her joy quickly faded. "But they all must have thought . . . thought that you and I were lost in the fire." She felt terrible to think that such a horror had been inflicted upon her friends—no, more than friends now, her family.

"Do not distress yourself," he said. "They would have mourned our loss, but would also believe that we had gone to the Otherworld together—where we would spend all of time with each other, in happiness and in love." He smiled down at her. "And they would have been right, would they not?"

"Oh, yes, yes," she whispered fervently, and leaned her head against his chest for a long, long moment as he stroked her red-gold hair.

Finally she looked up at him. "Why didn't you tell

me?" she asked. "The first time I saw you . . . in Professor Vaughn's office . . . why didn't you tell me who you were?"

He folded her hands over the torque and let go of the golden piece, taking Christine in his arms once again. "I could say nothing about who I was or how I came to be here. Think of it. If I had tried to explain, would you have believed me?"

"Oh," she breathed, "I would have loved you anyway—I would not have cared how you got here. I—"

He stilled her words with the touch of a gentle finger on her lips. "You had a journey to make," he answered. "A journey back through time."

He leaned his cheek against the top of her head, and his hair brushed softly against her face. "It could only happen on its own. The choice to wear the torque or no, to save my life or no, to love me or no, could only be yours."

There was a small cough behind them. "Ah, I see you remember Mr. Donalson," said Professor Vaughn.

Christine looked up into the familiar slate-blue eyes, puzzled. "Mr. Donalson?"

He smiled, and his eyes shone even brighter. "I am Allen Donalson now, my lady. And Allen Donalson I have been for some fifteen years."

Now she truly was confused. "Fifteen years? How could that be?"

He looked away, into the blackness of the night, and began to speak.

"In that burning house, so long ago, I caught the torque and watched you vanish. The flames closed in and I knew there was no choice. I looked at this golden torque, the gift I had offered to the goddess— a gift she had returned to me for reasons known only to her. I placed it around my neck, and the world turned to darkness.

"When I awakened, it seemed as though a very long time had passed; it was as though I had awakened from a dream I could barely remember. Yet I remembered you, and I felt so strongly that you were near. I set out at once to find you—but I could not."

"Fifteen years ago," Christine murmured in amazement. "Of course—it was fifteen years ago that I was first in Ireland. I was visiting my great-grandparents—"

"And the torque brought me to that time and place, because that is where you were.

"I spoke no English then, only Gaelic, and in my wanderings I was fortunate to find an old couple living in a cottage near the sea. They understood my words and did not fear me. I lived with them for a time, and cared for them, while they taught me something of the ways of this world. When they died, I buried them, and made my way into this strange, miraculous place called the twentieth century.

"All the while I searched for only one thing—for the woman I loved. I knew that I had come to your world the way you had come to mine, and I swore that I would never rest until I found you."

He pulled her close, gently stroking her hair. "Until I found you, Christine."

"No—not Christine," she said smiling up at him in pure joy. "It's Bridget, Allen. I am the woman you love, and for you, my name is Bridget."

Don't miss these passionate time-travel romances, in which modern-day heroines fulfill their hearts' desires with men from different eras.

*Frankly, My Dear...*by Sandra Hill. When a voodoo spell sends Selene back to the days of Scarlet O'Hara, she can't get her fill of gumbo, crayfish, beignets—or an alarmingly handsome planter. Dark and brooding, James Baptiste does not share Rhett Butler's cavalier spirit, and his bayou plantation is no Tara. But fiddle-dee-dee, Selene doesn't need her mammy to tell her the virile Creole is the only lover she ever gave a damn about. And with God as her witness, she vows never to go hungry or without the man she desires again.

_4042-5   **$5.50 US/$6.50 CAN**

There Never Was a Time by Gail Link. Drawn by inexplicable forces, Rebecca journeys to the once resplendent Southern plantation where her forebearer had loved and lost a Union soldier. And there, on a jasmine-scented New Orleans night, she discovers that passion unfulfilled in one lifetime can defy fate and logic and be reborn so much sweeter in another.

_52025-7   **$4.99 US/$5.99 CAN**

Dorchester Publishing Co., Inc.
65 Commerce Road
Stamford, CT 06902

Please add $1.75 for shipping and handling for the first book and $.50 for each book thereafter. NY, NYC, PA and CT residents, please add appropriate sales tax. No cash, stamps, or C.O.D.s. All orders shipped within 6 weeks via postal service book rate. Canadian orders require $2.00 extra postage and must be paid in U.S. dollars through a U.S. banking facility.

Name _____
Address _____
City _____ State_____ Zip_____
I have enclosed $_____in payment for the checked book(s).
Payment <u>must</u> accompany all orders.□ Please send a free catalog.

DON'T MISS THESE TIMELESS ROMANCES BY

LINDA O JOHNSTON

The Glass Slipper. Paige Conner does not consider herself a princess by any stretch of the imagination. She is far more interested in pursuing her research than attending gala balls or dressing in frilly gowns. Then the feisty beauty's bumbling fairy godmother arranges for her to take a job that lands her in a small kingdom—and in the arms of a prince with more than dancing on his mind. Enchanted from the first, Paige longs to lose herself in her royal suitor's loving embrace, yet she fears that his desire is a result of a seductive spell and not her own considerable charms. And Paige won't agree to live passionately ever after until she has claimed the prince's heart with a magic all her own.

_52111-3 $4.99 US/$5.99 CAN

A Glimpse of Forever. Her wagon train stranded on the Spanish Trail, pioneer Abby Wynne searches the heavens for rain. Gifted with visionary powers, Abby senses a man in another time gazing at the same night sky. But even she cannot foresee her journey to the future and into the arms of her soul mate.

Widower Mike Danziger escapes the lights of L.A. for the Painted Desert, but nothing prepares him for a beauty as radiant as the doe-eyed woman he finds. His intellect can't accept her incredible story, but her warm kisses ease the longing in his heart.

Caught between two eras bridged only by their love, Mike and Abby fight to stay together, even as the past beckons Abby back to save those trapped on the trail. Is their passion a destiny written in the stars, or only a fleeting glimpse of paradise?

_52070-2 $4.99 US/$6.99 CAN

Dorchester Publishing Co., Inc.
65 Commerce Road
Stamford, CT 06902

Please add $1.75 for shipping and handling for the first book and $.50 for each book thereafter. NY, NYC, PA and CT residents, please add appropriate sales tax. No cash, stamps, or C.O.D.s. All orders shipped within 6 weeks via postal service book rate. Canadian orders require $2.00 extra postage and must be paid in U.S. dollars through a U.S. banking facility.

Name _____

Address _____

City _____ State _____ Zip _____

I have enclosed $_____in payment for the checked book(s). Payment <u>must</u> accompany all orders.☐ Please send a free catalog.

THE OUTLAW VIKING

TIMESWEPT

SANDRA HILL

Winner Of The Georgia
Romance Writers Maggie Award

As tall and striking as the Valkyries of legend, Dr. Rain
Jordan is proud of her Norse ancestors despite their warlike
ways. But she can't believe her eyes when a blow to the head
transports her to a nightmarish battlefield and she has to save
the barbarian of her dreams.

He is a wild-eyed berserker whose deadly sword can slay
a dozen Saxons with a single swing, yet Selik can't control
the saucy wench from the future. And if Selik isn't careful,
the stunning siren is sure to capture his heart and make a
warrior of love out of the outlaw viking.

_52000-1 $4.99 US/$5.99 CAN

Dorchester Publishing Co., Inc.
65 Commerce Road
Stamford, CT 06902

Please add $1.75 for shipping and handling for the first book and
$.50 for each book thereafter. NY, NYC, PA and CT residents,
please add appropriate sales tax. No cash, stamps, or C.O.D.s. All
orders shipped within 6 weeks via postal service book rate.
Canadian orders require $2.00 extra postage and must be paid in
U.S. dollars through a U.S. banking facility.

Name _____
Address _____
City _____ State _____ Zip _____
I have enclosed $_____in payment for the checked book(s).
Payment <u>must</u> accompany all orders.☐ Please send a free catalog.

TIMESWEPT
PASSION...
TIMELESS
LOVE

SANDRA HILL

"Picture yourself floating out of your body—floating...floating...floating..." The hypnotic voice on the self-motivation tape is supposed to help Ruby Jordan solve her problems, not create new ones. Instead, she is lulled from a life full of a demanding business, a neglected home, and a failing marriage—to an era of hard-bodied warriors and fair maidens, fierce fighting and fiercer wooing. But the world ten centuries in the past doesn't prove to be all mead and mirth. Even as Ruby tries to update medieval times, she has to deal with a Norseman whose view of women is stuck in the Dark Ages. And what is worse, brawny Thork has her husband's face, habits, and desire to avoid Ruby. Determined not to lose the same man twice, Ruby plans a bold seduction that will conquer the reluctant Viking—and make him an eager captive of her love.

_51983-6 $4.99 US/$5.99 CAN

Dorchester Publishing Co., Inc.
65 Commerce Road
Stamford, CT 06902

Please add $1.75 for shipping and handling for the first book and $.50 for each book thereafter. NY, NYC, PA and CT residents, please add appropriate sales tax. No cash, stamps, or C.O.D.s. All orders shipped within 6 weeks via postal service book rate. Canadian orders require $2.00 extra postage and must be paid in U.S. dollars through a U.S. banking facility.

Name_____

Address_____

City _____ State_____Zip_____

I have enclosed $_____in payment for the checked book(s).
Payment <u>must</u> accompany all orders.☐ Please send a free catalog.

A Double-Edged Blade

JULIE MOFFETT

Bestselling Author Of *A Touch Of Fire*

Lovely British agent Faith Worthington is sent on a mission to expose a ruthless IRA terrorist. But a bullet to the thigh knocks her back to seventeenth-century Ireland...and into the arms of rebel leader Miles O'Bruaidar.

Known as the Irish Lion, Miles immediately suspects the modern-day beauty of being a spy. He takes Faith as his hostage, only to discover her feminine wiles are incredibly alluring.

But desperate to return to the future, Faith has no time for love—at least not from a mutton-feasting, ale-quaffing brute like Miles. Yet with each passing day—and each fiery kiss—Faith's defenses weaken. Torn between returning to her own time and staying with the charming rogue, Faith knows her heart has been pierced to the quick, but she wonders if their love will always be a double-edged blade.

_52096-6 $4.99 US/$5.99 CAN

Dorchester Publishing Co., Inc.
65 Commerce Road
Stamford, CT 06902

Please add $1.75 for shipping and handling for the first book and $.50 for each book thereafter. NY, NYC, PA and CT residents, please add appropriate sales tax. No cash, stamps, or C.O.D.s. All orders shipped within 6 weeks via postal service book rate. Canadian orders require $2.00 extra postage and must be paid in U.S. dollars through a U.S. banking facility.

Name _____
Address _____
City _____ State _____ Zip _____
I have enclosed $_____ in payment for the checked book(s).
Payment <u>must</u> accompany all orders.☐ Please send a free catalog.

ATTENTION PREFERRED CUSTOMERS!

SPECIAL TOLL-FREE NUMBER
1-800-481-9191

Call Monday through Friday
12 noon to 10 p.m.
Eastern Time
*Get a free catalogue
and order books using your
Visa, MasterCard,
or Discover®*

*Leisure
Books*

LOVE SPELL